THE
GATHERING
★ STORM ★

Captain Keenan Carlisle: He fought alongside a vicious Japanese commander in Manchuria. But after a bitter battle he was on the other side—fighting for his life with Mao Tse-tung's revolutionary army . . .

Major Chad Belvale: In the bloody tragedy that ended at Dunkirk, he faced Hitler's awesome war machine. Ready for war, experienced in battle, his next lesson would be in love—with a woman he could never have . . .

Major General Charles "Crusty" Carlisle: The combative old soldier told the U.S. Senate that America must prepare to fight. But the politicians wouldn't listen—until it was too late . . .

Lieutenant General Preston Belvale: In the family war room at Kill Devil Hill, Virginia, the retired cavalryman dreamed of the glory of the old days—as a new kind of war already claimed its first Carlisle-Belvale dead . . .

Nancy Carlisle: Clinging to an unhappy marriage and the hope that her husband, Keenan, was still alive, she returned to the Carlisle home in Virginia—where she met a Georgia politician who wanted her for reasons of his own . . .

Books by Con Sellers

Brothers in Battle

The MEN AT ARMS series

Book 1: The Gathering Storm

Published by POCKET BOOKS

Book 2: The Flames of War
Book 3: A World Ablaze
Book 4: Allied in Victory

Coming soon from POCKET BOOKS

MEN ★ AT ★ ARMS

BOOK 1

THE GATHERING STORM

CON SELLERS

POCKET BOOKS

New York   London   Toronto   Sydney   Tokyo   Singapore

This book is a work of fiction. Names, characters, places and incidents are either the products of the author's imagination or are used fictitiously. Any resemblance to actual events or locales or persons, living or dead, is entirely coincidental.

An *Original* Publication of POCKET BOOKS

POCKET BOOKS, a division of Simon & Schuster Inc.
1230 Avenue of the Americas, New York, NY 10020

Copyright © 1991 by Con Sellers

ISBN: 0-671-66765-3

First Pocket Books printing September 1991

10 9 8 7 6 5 4 3 2 1

Printed in the U.S.A.

For my stepmother, "Miss Elsie" Sellers,
who sweated me through this and another war

THE GATHERING STORM

CHAPTER 1

AGENCE FRANCE PRESSE—Saigon, French Indochina, August 22, 1939: Reports filtering out of the remote West Manchurian border area of China disputed by Japan and Russia say a bloody clash is underway in the Nomonhan region. Both sides claim victory, but no casualty figures are available.

It was good he'd been with them long enough to beat himself into some kind of shape. He'd never match these incredibly tough little bastards, but who could? You had to be half-samurai and the rest animal for that, and screw that mix, even without the blind fanaticism thrown in. But Keenan Carlisle, captain, Infantry, United States Army, wasn't about to give the officers of Dai Nippon another excuse to sneer. He'd stay with the column in this boiling dust, at this killing dogtrot, if it cost him his front seat in hell.

The strutting little turds didn't need excuses to be arrogant and for sure, they were as good as they thought they were. Last time out the Chinese army bloodied them at Shanghai, but they corrected faults and came back sharper and stronger. Strong? Keenan rolled a tiny stone around in his dry mouth to make the saliva flow and trotted beside Major Watanabe. Ahead, the reserve regiment's bandy-legged soldiers never wobbled under their immense loads.

Hell—they didn't dare fall out. A severe beating was the least they could expect, but some officer might whip out the long sword and take the head off the fallen man. It was an effective demonstration, and Keenan thought the one he'd seen had been partly for his benefit. He wouldn't forget the scene or the calculated savagery behind it. So much blood, a spurting fountain of arterial red that was gulped by roadside dust while the passing column pretended not to notice the body. It would be stripped by men of the rear supply wagon, then rolled aside and left to the vultures that wheeled high above this party of marching troops.

Christ, who had he pissed off at the War Department to draw this observer duty with the Japs? Probably nobody; this was the kind of brainstorm that old son of a bitch in Virginia was noted for. Okay, Maj. Gen. Preston Belvale, Cavalry, (Ret) had a reasonably good idea—get a line on an army he figured the U.S. would be fighting before much longer. But nobody back in Washington would believe the reports Keenan was sending back. The Old Guard "knew" the Japs were too small; that their slant eyes prevented them from shooting worth a damn, and that Tokyo would not dare to start anything with the United States. That would be a far bigger mistake than getting smart-ass with Admiral Perry's black ships a hundred years back. War with the Japs was ridiculous. Where would they sell all those paper fans and other cheap crap?

Rolling the pebble over his tongue and sucking for dampness, he leaned into the yellow dust stirred by fifteen thousand pairs of enlisted hobnail shoes and by officer boots. The dust stank of human shit used to enrich this worn and flinty land over countless centuries. The choking air carried wisps of armpits dripping fish oil, the easier odors of gun grease and the clean, sharp sweat of pack artillery mules.

Keenan concentrated upon pumping his legs, tilting more uphill now in this miserable land of hate and hunger, up and down, one damned mountain after another. Now he could hear the far rattle of small arms fire as the lead regiment engaged. He didn't know who they were going against, Chinese or Russians, for Major Watanabe hadn't considered telling him, this long-nosed foreign soldier, this *gaijin* forced upon him by orders from Tokyo. Only after the battle would he lecture Keenan upon the Imperial Army's superiority in all things military and spiritual. He spoke the

2

easy colloquial English of UCLA, but overlaid with the tough-guy gutterals all male Japanese worked at; to make up for their size, Keenan thought.

The major admitted that some Americans might grasp a few battle tactics, but they would need five thousand years of building upon inner strength to come near to understanding *Bushido,* the sacred code of the warrior. They would never understand the national spirit of Divine Nippon and the God Emperor.

"I have studied in America," he had said. "Your country is so young, but already decadent. You depend upon machines rather than upon the warrior soul, and your undisciplined soldiers will certainly be afraid of death, and therefore not soldiers worthy of the name."

Small arms fire thickened ahead and signals passed down the column to halt. Keenan cocked his head, picking up deeper explosions that had to be heavy enemy artillery. He knew the sound of the Jap pack howitzers, and this wasn't it. He didn't think Jap recon and intelligence expected the big stuff and that might change things. Machine guns fired and stopped, short professional bursts, and he thought he could make out the noise of motors, many motors. The enemy had to be Russian then; Japanese rolling stock was in short supply.

Major Watanabe offered his water bottle, a half smile twisting road-grimed lips below the standard droop of the samurai mustache. The little shit knew Keenan had sucked too much water today and that the bigger U.S. issue canteen was riding near empty upon his hip.

Tucking the pebble carefully behind his teeth, Keenan smiled back, wider. "No, thank you, Major—*iea, arrigato gozaimas.*" He thought he caught a flicker of something in the hard eyes, but it was quickly gone. Score a point for the decadent and undisciplined. Keenan was learning to play these games of face gained or lost, but with caution. It was the Jap game and they changed rules as they pleased.

Keenan lost his face point when the first enemy shell whistled overhead, a low and throaty whir that dropped him swiftly to one knee. He flinched when it exploded far behind. A World War relic 75, French, he thought, and glared

3

at Watanabe standing braced with boots wide apart and flicking a horsehair fly whisk at one muscled thigh.

"Where are we," Keenan asked, "besides somewhere in Manchuria?"

"Not Manchuria, but Manchukuo," Watanabe said, lifting field glasses to his eyes. "Manchukuo is part of the resettlement program. At this moment, we are about to teach the Russian dogs another lesson, this time exactly where our border lies."

Sighing, Keenan thought of Chinese soil trampled by two invaders, of simple Chinese crushed if they got in the way and ignored like so many lowly bugs if they tried to stay and scratch out a miserable existence on their own tiny patches of scrubland. Even then, the Japs would more often than not steal any unhidden handful of rice and line up to rape any unhidden female under sixty.

Slam-slam!

"Left flank," Watanabe announced, and shouted something in Japanese to his aides. One company wheeled and trotted out toward the unseen gun that had dropped two high explosive rounds into this rear unit. Staring at the major, Keenan saw the frown creasing the man's forehead. Up ahead, Colonel Nobusho's lead regiments had walked into something totally unexpected, and with flanking fire already coming in, Keenan smelled a trap.

He was certain when a pair of heavy guns fired on them from the opposite side, the right flank—*wham-wham!* This time three tattered Japs and a hand-drawn Nambu machine-gun cart pinwheeled into the air and hot shell fragments cut down a sublieutenant standing close by. This time, Major Watanabe hit the ground on his belly, right beside Keenan. The samurai sword bounced over and slapped the man's back. Useful weapon, Keenan thought.

Spitting dirt, his ears ringing, he said, "No flankers out, Major? Those guns should have been easy to find."

Watanabe's glare was poisonous. "Colonel Nobusho did not order flank guards and at dawn those guns were not in place. Motorized; the Russian dogs are heavily motorized; the messenger said we face at least five mechanized brigades and three infantry divisions."

The major rolled on his right side and yelled orders. Obediently, two more companies wheeled and spread out as skirmishers as they jogged forward behind their overlong bayonets.

Up ahead the battle roared louder, confused, pocketed by clanking sounds that only meant one thing to Keenan. He'd heard them enough at Fort Benning when Georgie Patton was running his small armored outfit over anything he could mash and not have to pay for. "More than motorized," he shouted to Watanabe over the noise, "those are tanks."

"Impossible! Colonel Nobusho said no armor exists in this area."

There it was, the first major tactical flaw the Japs had shown, this blind obedience to higher authority. Keenan had seen it all down the line in the way discipline was handled, superior private slapping private and being in turn slapped by a corporal. But he had assumed that field grade officers would change and adapt to the combat situation as it unfolded. Evidently not; Major Watanabe was as fearful of bending an order as any wrap-leggings guy in the ranks.

Crawling, Keenan found a shallow gully twisted downhill by old rain from the mountains. He tucked into its cover only moments before a sheet of bullets raked the road, slightly plunging fire from both flanks, bullets that scythed bloody through Watanabe's advancing troops and ricocheted from rocks and the beaten soil of the road.

Keenan peeped from his hole and saw Watanabe standing right out in the open and waving that damned sword while he yelled commands. No soldier turned and came back to find protection, to hole up and fight from some kind of cover. So the crazy bastard was screaming at his men to continue the attack.

Outflanked, caught in a box, no matter the losses, the regiments would carry out Colonel Nobusho's orders. Watanabe lacked the initiative and imagination to supplement them. Attack, attack! Imperial Japan's soldiers must always attack, never retreat. That was a great way to bring on a shortage of Jap soldiers, at least temporarily and at least right here and now. Another note home to General Belvale:

the Japanese stick to prebattle plans, no matter how changed the situation becomes.

And sometimes the stoic animalism of the soldiers broke; a gut-shot man screamed across the road, and between bursts of deadly accurate fire, others moaned. Worse was the diminishing shriek of a gut-shot mule. But somehow the pack artillery was unlimbered and started firing.

Flinching when Watanabe touched his shoulder, Keenan accepted the pistol handed down, and nodded when the major shouted that withdrawal had been commanded by Colonel Nobusho, but a slow and honorable withdrawal, fighting all the way.

Keenan hefted the pistol, a Shiki Kenju Type 94. "I'm not arguing about arming a neutral observer, because I don't think those Russians can tell one uniform from another, or give a damn."

He climbed out of the ditch and hunkered low as machine-gun bullets whipped and whined overhead. At Watanabe's side, he said, "Why are you suddenly interested in my welfare?"

Leading the way through a battery of howitzers firing steadily and deafeningly uphill where Keenan assumed the tank attack was underway, Watanabe waited until they reached a makeshift aid station. Then he turned glittering eyes on Keenan. "Only because you are my responsibility, my duty. If you are killed too quickly, I will be thought careless. I do not doubt that you will be killed, but I prefer it to happen later, and out of my jurisdiction."

Deep breathing for control, Keenan squatted and watched too few corpsmen trying to patch too many wounded soldiers. From first glance, he could see that most of the casualties would never make it farther down the road. The clatter of tank treads rang louder and closer, and a shot from a long Russian gun exploded upon the outer edge of the aid station. Pieces of bodies, some previously and uselessly bandaged, leaped and mingled with the geysers of bloody dirt. Lead tank, Keenan thought, stopped on a little rise while its turret swung slowly back and forth, the gun bird-dogging for the best targets. The Jap howitzers tried for it, but the first round missed and the Russian knocked out two guns with its first fire. The next round erased this rear regiment's artillery support.

So damned arrogant, sitting there like an uncrushable beetle; the tank commander so certain of his invincibility that Keenan figured the leading Jap regiments had been chopped to bits and now it was only mop-up time. More, it was already well past get the hell out time for Dai Nippon's survivors.

Major Watanabe screamed something, and a pair of soldiers, look-alikes, dumpy and undistinguished in mustard-colored uniforms, snatched up heavy canvas carriers and ran directly toward the tank. The Russian machine gun cut one down before he made twenty yards, but the other man, zigzagging frantically at top speed, closed in. All around Keenan, Japanese fired small arms at the tank, trying for the driver and gunner slits, spanging bullets off steel in every direction.

The runner made it in under the depression limit of the machine gun. Then as the treads began to clank forward, he rolled beneath one and blew himself, the tank track and one side plate to hell.

Grenades; the poor bastard had carried a sackful of grenades. Now other Japs rushed at the crippled tank and fired into the ripped metal opening. Nobody even glanced down at what was left of the man who had given them the kill. Another grenade flipped into the tank and men scattered as its gas and ammunition blew with a thunderous roar and flare that spat smoke high enough to warn and slow the rest of the armored column. Enemy guns on the flanks fell silent, and Keenan made out Japanese soldiers, still dogtrotting, although some staggered or limped, drifting back along both sides of the road. The attack regiments had taken a terrible beating, for the lines were thin, but they were coming to the rear and wiping out Russian artillery positions on the way. Keenan's palm sweated around the oddly curved butt of the Kenju pistol. There could be no tougher soldiers in any army, and if old General Belvale was right, if the United States would soon fight them, then the U.S. had catching up to do, maybe too much.

Wide-eyed, he stared at wounded soldiers dragging

themselves—and more grenade sacks—up the road, ready to sacrifice themselves to stop any other tanks. In the fields, the retreat went on, but not a rout. Major Watanabe said, "Colonel Nobusho committed *seppuku;* his aide reported that he died as a samurai, without even a grimace of pain. Captain Koto stood by to deliver the neck stroke, but he said it was only a formality."

"Jesus Christ!" Keenan said. "*Seppuku*—suicide? Why—for Christ's sake?" Watanabe shouted orders and his soldiers moved out, leaving the badly wounded behind. "Not for the sake of your weak and forgiving Christ. The colonel led this division into defeat. He paid for it in the honorable tradition of *Bushido*." He pointed at the wounded men that could not be carried with the column. "As will those men. See how they have taken off one shoe so they can toe the triggers of their Arisakas as they hold the muzzles in their mouths. At the proper moment, they will demonstrate their indomitable spirits to the Russian dogs."

The Jap pistol was solid in Keenan's hand, something real. He knew the 8mm was a bastardized composite of handguns of several countries, set for mass production without problems caused by hurrying the standard Nambu. He also knew that the damned thing was probably the world's worst pistol, wildly inaccurate and more dangerous to the user than any enemy. But it felt solid in his hand, metal and springs and wood that made some kind of sense. All else going on around him wasn't logical—mysticism and ritual suicide and a culture that not only accepted death, but worshipped it.

Unaware that he was speaking aloud, Keenan said, "Oh, my god."

Major Watanabe said, "No; *my* gods."

CHAPTER 2

REUTERS NEWS AGENCY—The Crown Colony of Hong Kong, August 23, 1939: Although all news from Manchuria has been officially blacked out, responsible sources report that Japanese forces are suffering a major defeat there.

It slapped him hard along his left cheek and whirled him half around. Keenan pressed his hand to the bloody gash and didn't think that the bone was split. On his belly again, he twisted a lopsided bandage from his bandana and knotted it into place. So this was how it felt to be shot, even though this hit was only a deep crease. As a kid, he had marveled at the sleeve wound stripes from the Big War when the family gathered in formal uniform, wondered and worried that a bullet might hurt so much he might not wear the gold V and a Purple Heart as proudly. Back then he had even wondered if he might be cowardly and run. As he grew older, he realized that any family member who did had to keep running to the end of the world. And still he would never get away from himself, much less face Crusty Carlisle, which was worth a tour in purgatory.

The first hammering burst of fire from what was supposed to be the trains, the Japanese rear, was close in and murderous. It cut down startled soldiers and pack mules; it butchered rearing wagon horses whose screams knifed through Keenan like bayonets. Back in New York State, he had grown up without horses, but on Virginia visits, he had interwoven his life with bouncy colts and fillies. He had become part of them on through the time when the thoroughbreds broke from their first track gate and sometimes broke their champion hearts. That part he hated, as he now hated that these poor animals were forced to suffer for men's sport or men's wars.

"Cut off," he said to Major Watanabe. "While we were sweating out their tanks, they swung the trucks in behind us."

Watanabe did not answer. His uniform was ripped and dirty, but he held the naked samurai blade tightly in his right hand. Ancestral symbol of pride and some sort of glory, like the horn bow and buffalo hide shield of the Comanche, all useless against modern killing weapons. General Belvale would support the sword, for was not the Kill Devil blade still venerated at the Hill? But Crusty Carlisle would say *bullshit*.

Sliding to the side of the road, Keenan took the Arisaka rifle from the dead hand of a Jap, a newer Meiji Model 1905. He drew the cartridge belt from around the bloody waist of a kid who should have been helping his parents plant rice. Keenan still had the lousy Jap pistol tucked into his web belt, and this was no time for playing neutrality by the book. The Russians meant to slaughter everyone caught in their box, and there was only one possible way out, head-on through the thinnest part of the surrounding loop, to the rear. No tanks or big guns were there yet, but troops blocked the road and were strung out along both sides. There was a chance because the Russians had no time to dig in.

Watanabe leaped to his feet, hot sun gleaming from the lifted long sword, yelling *banzai! banzai!* at his stunned men. They got up to follow him, and damned if the little son of a bitch didn't have some powerful warrior ancestor looking after him, because although Keenan saw the man's jacket jerk and breeches flap from bullets plucking at them, Watanabe kept going, his troops gathering beside him and picking up the cry of ten thousand years—*banzai!*

On one knee, Keenan took aim at a dusty, off-blue uniform and centered it as the rifle bucked against his shoulder. The almost straight-back bolt handle was clumsy, but a shade quicker to work than the Model 1903 Springfield Keenan was used to. As the screaming Japs charged into the roadblock, Russians fanned out along the flanks, and Keenan fired twice more, dropping one man and missing the next. Emptying the rifle with his next two shots, he thought he rolled one Russian over and made another leap for safety.

Keenan reloaded, thumbing the five round clip of 6.5mm solidly into the integral box. A shorter barrel would have suited him better, and if he found time, he'd throw away the damned bayonet. It dragged on the muzzle and pulled his aim off. Ah—but the bayonet was an extension of the sword, or a glorified can opener, depending upon the viewpoint.

The Japs ran right over their own dead and wounded, shrieking and firing, thrusting and hacking with their long bayonets. And the Russians broke; the Japs closed with them and the Russians gave way, slowly at first and then in a wild panic. Japs slashed at them, and even the emperor's wounded stumbled after the foe in a frenzy of maniacal blood lust. Keenan saw Watanabe's samurai sword chop down and split a running man from neck to hip, opening him like a side of beef.

Flowing through the gap, the major's decimated unit hurried to the next knoll, and as Keenan came panting after, turned in a tight, disciplined semicircle. Gone to ground on knees or bellies, they fired to cover fellow soldiers beating their way out of the box. Keenan joined the covering fire, picking his targets carefully and exulting when he nailed down a three-man squad trying to set up an iron wheeled Maxim machine gun. It was one of the old water-cooled jobs acquired from the Kaiser's Germans, but it wouldn't open fire now.

Then, rumbling and clanking, their cannon fire searching blindly ahead, the Russian tanks nosed carefully along the road again. Their shape was unmistakable: the turret too far forward, the 45mm gun and two machine guns. Watanabe ordered his men out, and they took off at that ground-eating trot, a rear guard dropping out every hundred yards or so. These roadblocks laid down a harassing fire for a few minutes, then pulled out; down the line, another group would pick a good defensive spot. By the book perfect, Keenan thought. These soldiers didn't panic. He found a rock to sit beside where Watanabe rested, the gory blade of his sword across his knees.

"Fine troops, Major, no hint of panic."

The major had a bloody shoulder and a purple bruise on his forehead; his hat was gone and dirt crusted his cropped hair. He only nodded at Keenan's remark and, still watching back down the road, offered his water bottle. When Keenan hesitated, he said, "You have earned this drink, *gaijin,* and I wish it could be ceremonial *sake.* You fought with us when you did not have to. Do all your officers shoot as well?"

So few men straggling back, less than a quarter of the fifteen thousand who had gone forth to teach the Russians where the Manchurian border lay. Good lord, Keenan thought—that meant about eleven thousand casualties, which meant dead men. All the conscious wounded waiting with rifle muzzles in their mouths; all the unconscious wounded slaughtered by furious Russians.

Keenan said, "Some of them do." He took the water bottle and swallowed once, just once, before handing it back. "*Arrigato.* I am sorry for your heavy losses, Major."

Climbing up, Watanabe signalled his men on down the mountain. A rattle of rifle fire from over the hillcrest reminded Keenan that roadblocks were still in action, enough to keep the tanks cautious. He thought the Russian battle order had been given wrong; It was more like three armored brigades and two motorized infantry.

"The only sorrow lies in defeat," the major said. "To a Japanese, death is light as a feather, while duty is heavy as a mountain. All soldiers who die for the honor of the emperor will wake again in ten days in what you foreigners would call paradise."

Maybe there was a magnolia Eden for the fallen of the South; the Keep in Pennsylvania didn't look like the promised land.

The tanks had stopped rolling; Keenan could hear no clank of metal tracks, but now the Russians were wising up;

the armored column fired the 45mm guns like rolling artillery, walking a barrage along both sides and up the center
of the road. Stopping at intervals, the tank commanders
gave their machine gunners opportunities to clean up any
knots of resistance.

"New equipment, all new," Watanabe muttered, "even
the tactics. Like us, they still pull artillery with horses and
their trucks are few. Every tank they possess must be on
this road, and every truck. Of course they knew we were
coming—the filthy Chinese warned them."

Keenan had seen no higher ranking officer come back
from the lead regiments that had taken the brunt of the
ambush; Major Watanabe must be in total command. Keenan
said, "You saved all that could be saved."

Staring back along the road, Watanabe didn't wince when
a tank round exploded too close, stinging Keenan with rock
fragments and shrouding them both with dirty smoke for a
long moment.

On his feet then, the major shouted orders to move out,
to hurry—*haiyaku! haiyaku!* Then to Keenan he said, "Aircraft; we needed air reconnaissance at least, if not direct air
support, but—" he cut off his complaint and Keenan figured it was before he said too much, before higher command was openly blamed, even if blame was deserved.

"Now," Watanabe said, "we must flee in disgrace."

"Not in disgrace," Keenan said, tightening the bloody
bandana around his cheek wound, "but to return another
day."

Watanabe wiped the gory blade of his sword along his
thigh and sheathed it. "Any retreat is shameful, but yes—we
will come back and avenge; Russians, Chinese—they cannot stand up to us. No army can."

First Manchuria, Keenan thought, then city by bombed
and besieged city, the Japanese would occupy all the great
sprawl of China, and then Russia? Nippon was taking bites
far too big to chew and swallow. Not Russia then; Japan
was too deeply committed in China to back out, especially
since Roosevelt had insisted they give up the invasion and
threatened to cut off all sales of oil. The Japs wouldn't pull
out now and lose face before a watching world. Keenan had

learned that much about their rigid pride and the code of the warrior.

Another 45mm shell landed behind them, so far back that Keenan couldn't hear the rip of metal fragments. The Russians, being overly careful, had let this group survive. And as the major said, they would some day return to collect a blood debt, but Keenan would just as soon not be with them. He had gone through his baptism of fire and come out all right, but for the gash in his cheek. He'd been too busy to know fear, and even if combat got more rough, he thought he could handle it. That was the code of the pure at heart, the true believer, even the profane denier.

Some wounded were being helped along, and Keenan swung one small man piggyback, carrying him right behind the marching column. The guy had been shot through both legs and the wounds plugged with torn uniform strips. He clung to Keenan and the only sound he made was the deep rasp of his breathing. It was a long way to any kind of cover where Major Watanabe would allow his tired, hurt troops to regroup and rest.

Heat and dust and the weight of the man on his back; Keenan's mouth dried, then his throat, and the rims of his eyes burned, but doggedly, he kept going. Think of something else, concentrate upon anything else, that was the trick. The Hill, its church services so bayonet clean and inarguable. If the services didn't fortify, they left an unavoidable duty. I think of Sandhurst Keep and its hard, cold promise.

With the Japs spread thin through China and without the manpower to take on a full-scale war with Russia, where would they reach next? For oil, of course: the Dutch East Indies, other rich little spots throughout the South Pacific. The Philippines, French IndoChina, Singapore?

General Preston Belvale was right, as usual, divinely so or not. Sooner or later, there would be a facedown between the Japs and the United States, and it would be a bitch when it came. If the general could make Washington understand and get the ball rolling, build up and decently arm the regular army. He'd need the help of the Yankee branch of the family for that—General Charles "Crusty" Carlisle, the irascible boss of Sandhurst Keep. Silly damned name, great legend.

He blinked and creaked his neck around when somebody bumped his shoulder. Feet spread wide for balance, he looked into Major Watanabe's face. The man said, "Sentimentality does not become an officer. One show of softness, two—and the men begin to expect special treatment. Next they will question authority."

Keenan's throat was so dry that it was difficult for him to speak, and what struggled out was a croak. "I save one of your soldiers and you—you—" He cut it off before he said what should be said.

"You saved nothing. The man is dead."

Stiffly, Keenan turned to slide his burden to the ground. "No, it's only his legs." Then he saw the gaping wound between the man's shoulders. "Damn it! Why didn't he—he never moaned or complained. Damn it."

Head swinging loosely upon his aching neck, Keenan saw men sprawled along a long, narrow gulley. Partway down, some soldiers were refilling their water bottles from a spring. A few twisted trees offered dabs of shade. It was a good place to rest.

Watanabe said, "He said nothing because you are an officer and it was not his place to deny, or even speak. Until you know this about the Japanese soldier, you will never understand our national spirit."

"I'm trying to understand," Keenan said. "I'll keep trying."

He already knew more than he could emotionally handle, but he needed to know it all, every devious twist and contorted thought. If the U.S. had to fight these people, somebody sure as hell had better understand how their minds worked.

He glanced down at the dead man he had carried so far, for so long. Keenan wanted to throw up.

CHAPTER 3

AGENCE FRANCE PRESSE—Danzig, Poland, September 1, 1939: The first shots of what foreign officials believe will become World War II, were fired here today by the old German battleship *Schleswig-Holstein*. The ship's 11-inch guns hurled shells into the Fortress Westerplatte, which guards Danzig's harbor on the Baltic Sea. Squeezed between Germany and East Prussia, this narrow Polish corridor cannot hold out long, according to neutral observers. Already other reports say that above the village of Lidzbark, 90 miles south of the East Prussian border, the sky is black with Nazi high-level bombers heading for Warsaw.

Walton Belvale's breath caught in his throat. It was so beautiful—the sun gleaming off highly polished brass, the magnificent Arabian horses, white or dapple gray, with full flowing manes and tails flagging in the wind. Guidons aflutter and riders leaning over their horses' necks, the Polish cavalry charged at the gallop behind lowered, glittering lances. White-gloved officers flashed sabers in the sun as bugles sounded.

It was so damned stupid, cruelly and incredibly stupid.

The Pomorska Cavalry Brigade, elite of the Polish army, was attacking German tanks, throwing horseflesh and man blood head-on against tracked steel, 47mm cannon and unforgiving machine guns. The horses—the poor goddamned horses! They shrieked as only a disemboweled horse can, in that moment of great sorrow and agony and betrayal keening through blood frothed mouths. The betrayal was worse, Walt thought. From the time they were foaled, they had been given food and grooming and protection.

A special closeness ever grew through the training of man and his horse, then came this ultimate treachery that hurled the horse to a gory death. The man usually had some kind of choice; the horse, never.

Clamping his eyes tight shut, Walt wished he also could stop his ears. Thousands of miles away, the thoroughbreds of Kill Devil Hill must feel the echoes of these cosmic screams in their heart of hearts. The mares would snort and kick their stalls; the stallions would whistle and strike, quivering in every satiny muscle. War-horses, yes—the hot-blood steeds that strained tendon and bone in a futile attempt to outlast the tougher, sturdier Morgans of Vermont.

Walt gripped the worn stock of the bolt action rifle he'd picked up on September 1, when the German assault shattered thin defense lines that should have been pulled back from most of the borders and into a tight defensive perimeter. He could almost hear his uncle, the chaplain with too much rank and damned little compassion: "Pride goeth before a fall."

Stiff-necked Polish pride, their mulish determination not to give up a yard of sacred soil so hard won only a few years ago, would defeat them. Even those 150 years of alien dominance weren't enough to balance against another, more complete, defeat. They would lose, and quickly. Walt was sure of that; it was a classic military blunder often pointed out by tactics instructors at VMI.

Rip-rip-rip! RIP-RIP! And then a long burst from that unbelievably quick-firing German machine pistol. Another horse bellowed in shock and pain. Goddamn! Lifting his head carefully, Walt lay the Polish-made Mauser—granted by German patent—across the stone wall and looked for a target for the 6.5 bullets. He had yet to shoot a man; as a neutral observer, he wasn't supposed to fight. But he desperately wanted to punish those jack-booted bastards in gray-green, the grinning infantrymen who flitted behind the light panzers, the bastards who climbed over dying horses.

Smite, the general would say—smite hip and thigh. Crusty would say shoot them in the balls.

What day was it? Walt wasn't sure. He couldn't remember napping more than an hour or so at a time, but he knew he would never forget this slaughter, nor ever forgive either side for it. Eyes steady along his sight alignment, he thought this must be the third or fourth of September. Back home it might be Labor Day, and after that, schools beginning another year in the gorgeous Shenandoah Valley, the hazy Blue Ridge Mountains. He missed those places; he missed Kill Devil Hill and pretty Penny Colvin. He should have married Penny right after graduation, despite Great-aunt Minerva urging them to wait until he gained more rank. Minerva was more sound than fury, but traditional Old-Virginia sound that could be overwhelming.

He intended to marry her earlier, although he realized what Minerva really meant was for him to wait until she could set him up a good military match, or if not that, find the right senator's daughter. It was easier to defy her from far away, to avoid unpleasant conflict for the sake of the general, but after battle and the things he had seen, nobody would again dominate him. He was a man and could do as he pleased, especially about pretty Penny Colvin.

God, she was lovely—slim, leggy and sleek, midnight hair and a rich mouth that had a cute uptilt at its corners, as if she were ready to laugh. And her deep brown eyes were always direct, even when she joked, which was often.

But she had been serious at the ceremony in Vegas.

A riderless horse clattered through a break in the stone wall just ahead of a ball of smoke and flame, eyes rolling. "Go—keep going!" Walt yelled, and, as the acrid smoke rolled by, peered through a break in the choking stuff.

A lancer was down on his back, and as Walt watched, the man sat up to retrieve first his tall, blocky-topped hat, and then the ridiculous sword he had dropped. Moving deliberately, the man stood and brushed off his uniform, settled his cape about his shoulders. He didn't even see the German rifleman bearing down upon him at a dead run, reaching with a long bayonet.

Drawing a deep breath, Walt exhaled according to the

book as his finger tightened upon the trigger, taking up slack just as the breath ran out. The Mauser butt plate kicked his shoulder and the Kraut trooper tilted over to jam his bayonet in the earth. The rifle whipped back and forth as the man ran a few more steps to fall on his face. His helmet rolled off and up to the tips of the Pole's shiny boots. Casually, the lancer toed it away and looked over one shoulder, sword blade slanted up over the other.

"Over here!" Walt yelled. "Come on, you idiot!"

The cocky son of a bitch strolled to the wall and looked down. His English was thick but the words understandable. "Thank you. But what are you? English—Yankee? Ah, yes, a Yankee. Shall I join you?"

"You'd better!" Walt squinted through the rifle sights at a wide-bodied German sergeant and two privates, one Schmeisser and two rifles. As moving background, a small panzer clanked up the road, tipping to one side or the other as it ground over the bodies of horses and men, some dead and some not.

The sergeant was heart-shot and went over backward. One private stood openmouthed, a metal tooth gleaming wetly before the Mauser slug caught him in the throat and blood sprayed. The other man got his rifle to his shoulder. Working his bolt swiftly and deftly in a smooth pattern learned on the range at VMI, Walt shot this one in the belly, then in the ribs as he spun. It was easy, after all. It was easier than putting down a horse with broken legs; nothing emotional here, unless it was a pure satisfaction. Taking a long angle, he fired the last shot from his rifle at a five-gallon can on the rear deck of the German tank.

Fluid spattered turret high and ran down upon the motor breathers as the panzer kept moving. Even though the armor looked flimsy and the tank itself almost toylike, its kind had raised hell with the Poles.

A sudden explosion rocked the tank just as it began to clear a curve in the road. Flames shot high and flared wide for a brief moment. Then the thing blew up. Inside, machine-gun ammunition exploded like a string of deadly firecrackers, and only a heartbeat later, the 47mm shells tore themselves and the turret apart.

"Wonderful," the Polish lancer said, standing erect with gloved hands fisted upon his slim hips. "A fortunate hit into extra fuel strapped upon the cantle—ah, the back part of the panzer."

Thumbing a strip clip of five rounds into the magazine of the rifle, Walt slid the bolt forward. "Get down, you damned fool."

Shrugging, flipping one end of his gold-edged cape over one broad shoulder, the man sat tidily upon an upended stone. The only weapon he carried was that silly sword. Light winked from his silver and red collar flashes, but Walt couldn't quite see the man's rank.

"Hold this," Walt said. "I suppose you know how to use a rifle? I'm going for that machine pistol."

Up and over the fence, running low, he drove forward to the spread of bodies puddling blood. Crouched, he heard the rumble of other panzers, and Germans shouting back and forth. Grabbing the Schmeisser and ripping off the belt with ammo pouches, he spun and raced back toward the wall. A bullet kicked dirt between his flying feet and others snapped viciously around his head—that hot, terrifying *snap-pop!* of death short inches away.

Throwing himself over the wall, he hit hard upon one shoulder and rolled to one knee, trying to whirl in time to get the Schmeisser into action. More bullets snatched at him, one nicking his flat helmet with a hell of a clang; the Krauts had him cold. Every muscle drawn taut in anticipation of the slugs that would tear out his life, Walt threw up the Schmeisser muzzle for a good-bye burst.

Unbelieving, he stared as five Germans went down almost in a clump, as the Pole kneeled and turned the Mauser rifle into a semiautomatic weapon, working the bolt faster than Walt could imagine. Each shot was perfectly zeroed; scything the enemy infantry before they knew what hit them. If the shots had been fired from that kneeling position on the range, they would all have been pinwheels.

"A fair weapon." The Pole smiled and his waxed blond mustache lifted around a smile. "May one request more ammunition?"

Looping the machine pistol belt and pouches over his

shoulder, Walt dug into his gas mask carrier and thrust a handful of stripper clips at the man. The guy might look like a comic opera soldier, but he was certainly an expert rifleman.

"Let's get out of here," Walt said. "We're attracting attention."

Keeping a shattered barn between them and the enemy, Walt moved quickly to reach a stretch of thick woods and a winding country lane. Sweating, alternating between a trot and a fast walk, he navigated the tidy forest and thought how old it was, how cared for. So many European countries had practically stripped themselves of timber over heedless centuries, and now every dry branch was precious. This forest was birches and pines, with the cones of mushrooms peeping from leaf falls, a harvest of mushrooms.

Sounds of battle faded, then vanished, leaving only the faint echoes of advancing armor, always the panzers. Tiring a bit, he slowed when the lane brought them to worked fields and more stone walls; beyond sat a small barn attached to a farmhouse. Going to ground behind a thin bush, Walt flinched when the Pole tapped his shoulder. He had almost forgotten the man. A sign of panic or exhaustion?

"We travel southeast, yes? To Lidzbark and Mlawa, one presumes. You have been there before?"

Walt continued to watch the house. His Polish mentor had been killed from just such a quiet house. Shot low in the belly, Captain Juralski had taken a long, painful time to die. Walt had stayed with him, holding his hand until the end. Unable to fire back at a hidden sniper, Walt had considered circling the house and nailing the bastard. A column of German tanks changed his mind.

"No," Walt said, "but I figure your people will fall back on Warsaw for a last ditch fight. My compass reading says we have to go past this house. What does it look like to you?"

"As a home does when it is abandoned. See—no cart in the yard, no horses and no cook-fire smoke."

Walt shook his head and adjusted the clumsy, flat helmet. "My liaison officer was killed by one shot from a house like this. We'll wait a little longer."

Upon his haunches close by, the Polish lancer said, "Lieutenant, isn't it? It is good to have an ally from America, but one must accept the responsibilities of rank, yes? May I introduce myself? Col. Jerzy Prasniewski, Third Lancers, Pormorska, Calvary Brigade."

Blinking, Walt said his own name and waited. Somehow, in that instant he felt lighter. General Belvale always said the weight of command could break a soldier's back if he didn't learn to carry it properly. Walt didn't want that kind of weight unless it came to duty. A full goddamn colonel who could shoot like that; a bird colonel who would throw his horse at armored vehicles. Then Walt wondered what he would do if the old general gave him such an order. Charge, what else? The general didn't question destiny, and nobody questioned the general.

"Thank you," Prasniewski said. "You have done well, Lieutenant, but I know my own country a bit better, I think. If you will remain to guard me—"

On his feet quickly, the colonel strode directly at the house, sword in its scabbard, rifle swinging casually at his side. Coming to one knee, Walt rested the Schmeisser barrel on a green branch. The man was as fearless as a crawdad caught on a railroad track, rearing back and waving its claws at the oncoming freight engine. But Walt had never heard of a crawdad winning.

Prasniewski walked right up to the door and knocked. He must have said something, too, for the door swung open. Walt stood up, weapon still at the ready. There was a movement beyond the colonel, but he turned and waved Walt down to the house. Walt made it in a hurry, for off past the forest they'd threaded, the deep growl of panzers lifted again; the Krauts weren't slowing up. At this rate survivors of the Danzig corridor might not even make it to Warsaw for a last stand.

The small house was neat and spotless. One woman stood at the white tiled kitchen stove, a straight-backed woman with streaks of gray in her dark hair. She placed kindling in the firebox and lighted it, glancing over one shoulder. How old, Walt wondered—forty-five, a little more? Her shabby black dress was loose, hiding any curvings of her body.

"The house is occupied, after all," Walt said.

Prasniewski's smile, brilliant and approving, wasn't directed at Walt, but at the woman. "Ah—but by the proper party, yes." He swept off his cape with a flourish and removed his hat, running one hand over his hair. When the woman's eyes widened at the sound of a foreign language, the colonel bowed and made introductions. "Madame Kurtzba, Lieutenant Belvale, Amerikanska."

The woman murmured Amerikanska as if it truly meant something to her, gave back a smile to the colonel and turned to the stove to boil tea. Then Prasniewski seated himself in a straight chair and thrust out his boots, the spurs clinking. "A brave and stubborn woman, the Kurtzba. Her sons are in the army, and two daughters departed to Moscow after marriage. She loaned her neighbor the horses and kept only her goat. She has refused to run before the Germans. I have advised that she make herself much older and much uglier before the Nazis arrive. A woman of such attraction . . ."

Walt looked again. The woman was still old to him and mother to how many—four grown children? Was the colonel that old, too? The guy was making a pass, in the middle of the war with the panzers coming, and Prasniewski was about to make this widow lady.

Lifting a pale eyebrow, the colonel said, "We must have food, water and wodka for your canteen. Madame will prepare bread, kielbasa and cheese for our bellies. As food for the heart—"

"Good God," Walt said. "Okay, I'll eat outside—so long as you hurry."

"I suppose one must; hardly proper, but did not one of your generals say that war is hell?"

Seated on a bench outside, munching spiced sausage and goat cheese set between thick slices of gray rye bread, Walt listened hard but heard no near approach of armor. Luckily, they were off the main line of advance here, but follow-up troops would be sure to fan out behind the spearheads to secure the rear areas and cut short any partisan activity before it got started. So long as they stuck to the back roads and took cover in deep woods, they should make it to Warsaw before an unbreakable ring closed around the city.

Then what? The colonel had said he expected the French to throw a million troops against the Germans, but Walt figured they'd better hurry, or there would be no Poland left to save. The British—what about the British? Maj. Chad Belvale was with them as an observer. It would be fun to meet Uncle Chad on the job. Before outside radio communications were cut, word came that France and England had declared war on Germany. But Walt thought that the Brits would never get across the Channel before the collapse.

Swallowing the last of his huge sandwich, he took a sip of fiery vodka and chased it with cold well water. Tactics instructors at VMI never thought of a situation like this, of a single lightning strike by one army heavy with armor and aircraft simply rolling up the defenses of the opponent in days, at the most a few weeks. But if all Polish officers were like the one inside taking care of the widow Kurtzba, if even half of them were that kind of expert rifleman and smiled at danger, the Krauts were in for a rough time yet.

An attractive widow, Prasniewski said, and Walt had a hunch the man was expert with women, too. Walt admitted that he had a lot to learn there, but he'd as soon his education stopped with pretty Penny Colvin. Everyone called her that, all the guys, anyhow; most girls made faces after she passed or pretended they hadn't seen her. He was so damned lucky, meeting her as soon as he stopped being a Brother Rat and became an upper classman at Virginia Military Institute. As a freshman, he was too busy studying and being harassed to even get into the city of Lexington, and Penny had come out from Richmond to visit kinfolks just at the right time for him. When she said "I do," he had never been happier.

A flight of three Stukas roared overhead, the JU-87 so terrifying in direct ground support, so accurate with its two thousand-pound bomb load and machine guns. The Stukas, their fixed-spats undercarriage so like the talons of a killer bird, the nerve-wracking shriek of their motors and sirens—it all tied in to paralyze and pin down troops while the ground forces came on at a rush.

Flinching when the door opened, Walt stood up and slung the Schmeisser as the colonel came out, only to turn and bow over the woman's hand. Stepping back, he clicked heels and bowed again, then wheeled about and gave Walt two sacks of food and another bottle of potato whiskey.

"Okay," Walt said, "*R-H-I-P.*"

Walking ahead, the absurd sword swinging at his hip, Prasniewski said, "Pardon?" His spurs jingled at each step, and Walt wondered if he'd taken off his boots when he bedded the widow.

Walt translated: "Rank Hath Its Privileges. I'll carry the chow."

Again they traveled into a forest; again, the dive-bombers swept low ahead of German armored cars and light panzers while the high-level bombers with their offbeat throbbing of motors came forth from airfields in the West to savage Warsaw, then sail back untouched for more bomb loads.

Hours later, when dusk came probing through the tree trunks, the colonel was agreeable to a break. Walt broke out more of the widow's food while Prasniewski rolled up mattings of interlocked pine straw.

"You don't mean to build a fire, Colonel?" Goddamn; Walt hoped not, but this Errol Flynn type might not fret over getting their asses shot off.

"Our forests give us much," the colonel answered. "Tonight it will also warm us with these *pierzyna*—natural quilts."

Better, Walt thought; much better, and breathed deeply of pine scent, of the freshness of a night he hadn't been sure he would see. General, he thought, I have had no problem here. It all works pretty much as you said; stay busy and there's no time for panic. Only a fool isn't afraid, but controlled fear is healthy; it helps keep a soldier alive, more so than a promise of Eden.

The vodka was warming, the kielbasa and bread filling; they would wake to goat cheese and rye bread tomorrow—if a Kraut patrol didn't come upon them during the night. The colonel's tall hat served as a cigarette shield as they passed one smoke between them, a dry mouth Sonder-Mischung.

Prasniewski said, "Even the weather is against Poland. The rains did not come in time to slow the panzers, to perhaps hold them in muddy roads until a good defense could be brought about. Low clouds would have helped us against the airplanes, yes? We will continue to fight, but Poland is finished. Its sons will return; we will be back to sweep the Teutonski from our land and reclaim it."

Rolled gently into the dry pine straw blanket, Walt focused upon a single star gleaming through high interwoven branches. There was no point in taking turns playing sentry, tucked low into the trees as they were. If German scouts came probing through the forest, Walt would hear as quickly as the colonel, and they were perfectly camouflaged. He thought of pretty Penny until he fell into a shallow sleep.

And woke at dawn to the roar of planes, to swift, dark shadows against the lightening sky. Walt came out of his warm cocoon to see Prasniewski scraping his face with a little folding razor. Then the man used vodka to stiffen his mustache.

"Colonel," Walt said, "I suggest we eat on the move, and move fast. Will we run out of forest before we're near Warsaw?"

Accepting slabs of goat cheese and bread, Prasniewski nodded. "If the Germans have ringed the city, entry may be found. There are *kanaly tubes;* how do you say—sewer pipes?"

Oh goody, Walt thought. They hadn't stepped in enough shit; now they would have to crawl through it. Crawl—not swim, please.

CHAPTER 4

THE MANCHESTER GUARDIAN, special to the *New York Times*—London, September 3, 1939: The British passenger ship SS *Athenia*, 13,500 tons, has been torpedoed and sunk by a German submarine for a loss of 112 lives; 28 American citizens were aboard. The *Athenia* was en route to Canada.

ASSOCIATED PRESS—Washington, D.C., September 3, 1939: The man in the street here is furious. A crowd has gathered before the White House and another one before the Congress, demanding some action be taken for the sinking of the *Athenia* and the murder of 28 Americans. So far, no announcement has come from the President's office, and no move against Germany has been forthcoming.

A strong wave of anti-German feeling is sweeping the country, causing German-American Bund offices and meeting places to shut down. The shrill voices that call for an isolated America to stay out of Europe's wars are for the moment silent.

VOLKISCHER BEOBACHTER—Berlin, September 3, 1939: High-ranking Party members here declare that the sinking of the SS *Athenia* was arranged by Winston Churchill to create an incident between Germany and the United States.

The convoy halted on the German side of the border and, by the feel of things, would not join the main force until day light. Unless, of course, an enemy counterattack brought them from the reserves. An armored spearhead and mechanized strike troops already roared well into Poland.

Feldwebel Arno Hindemit had his platoon climb down from the line of trucks and spread out on both sides of the muddy secondary road. The landsers muttered in the dark and stumbled over each other. Arno heard his name cursed. Better that they damn him than be packed dry but helpless in the trucks when an enemy plane came bombing and strafing.

A thin shadow angled close; the new platoon leader, Unterleutnant Franz Witzieli. Arno grinned; it must have been difficult for the schoolmaster-turned-officer to find his way in this blackness. He constantly adjusted his thick glasses and seemed to be looking around for a blackboard.

"Sergeant?"

"Sir?"

"Do you think an attack by aircraft might be imminent? During the night, that is? I do not suppose their pilots can see in the dark."

"No more than ours, sir. But most planes carry parachute flares; they can turn night into the sun at high noon."

Or if a pilot lined up his propeller on the road, he would not need to actually see his target, just fire down the road where the convoy was parked, a road that would show a lighter color against the black. Polish fliers would think of the road, and although their army was not up to date, even primitive, they were fighting hard.

The *leutnant* cleared his throat. "Reichsmarschall Goering said the Poles have only a few outmoded planes which the Luftwaffe will destroy on sight."

"The Polish Air Force may not have heard that, sir."

Arno drew a breath. He did not want to irritate this officer, but neither did he intend to allow his own authority to be weakened. The men would sense that and become troublesome, attempting to play one rank against the other.

"Sir, the men must realize that the army promises them only the chance to serve their country. No soft beds, no dry bivouacs, no beer or sausage or women. Duty comes first and last."

Gott, Arno; did that pap come out of you? Perhaps Herr Goebbels can use it in his propaganda speeches. Arno's father would have choked on it. He could hear his father now: It is enough that a man dedicates his life to becoming a soldier. He is not a politician or the weaver of pretty words, even if there be any truth to them. This he learned from his father, also, and he was right. The stiff-necked Prussians strut and shout commands, but the sergeant sees that those orders are carried out. If the orders are stupid, the sergeant outflanks them and makes the Prussians believe he is carrying out the orders to the letter.

Oberfeldwebel Gustav Hindemit went to his grave believing in God and army, believing that honor was not taken lightly, and that civilians had no business meddling with the Wehrmacht in any form.

Gustav Hindemit's jaw would set and he would lean forward in his wheelchair: Such excuses for losing the Kaiser's war. Stabbed in the back by traitors at home, betrayed by cowardly allies? *Nein* and again *nein:* the Prussians got their holy asses kicked and the ass-kissing ministers of Berlin were only a part of the defeat.

When Arno was old enough, there was an army to join. Part of what killed his father was being out of uniform during the riotous aftermath of the Great War, of having no direction to his life. Gassed at Verdun, his father aged visibly day by day. Breath ratcheting in his thin, corded throat, he choked out that the army would not long remain a tool for that bastard Austrian corporal.

But it was Hitler himself who ordered the shameful Versailles Treaty bypassed. It had been a gamble that France, Belgium and England would not march in to enforce the treaty. With most of the troop strength still on paper, Germany could not have stopped the invasion. Hitler's gamble paid off, and rebuilding the skeleton Wehrmacht roared ahead. Now it was of a size and strength to defend Germany's borders.

If not for his father—no, damn it, he could not lay all blame on his father, except when Arno was very young and dazzled by the uniforms, especially the grand spiked helmets and supper-table talk of wars, of honor and glory. Now he had been a soldier long enough to become hardened to the career he had chosen, if not cynical.

This war would prove to himself who and what Arno Hindemit was; that was the important thing. His father said that goose-stepping and road marches and disciplined life in the *casernes* was just the outer skin of a soldier. Only in combat could a man come face to face with his raw self. If a touch of pride and fleeting fame grew from that, all right.

But with the baptism of fire about to explode at any minute, Arno sensed a change in the air, a sullen tension in the platoon, as the braggarts turned quiet and contemplative; the playful young men ran out of jokes. Arno understood the mood, for no soldier knew how he would react when the bullets first flew.

"Very well, *Feldwebel;* I leave the men to you. Heil Hitler."

"Sir," Arno said aloud, and to himself: *heil, scheissen.* If another friendly army was handy, Arno would join it. On the surface, the Wehrmacht appeared bright and hard, a vast, well-oiled machine. But it operated in constant strain, pushed and pulled a dozen ways by high and powerful men seeking yet more power—the Sturm Abteilungen: the SA, the Schutz Staffeln, the SS, probably the fucking Gestapo, and of course, the fuehrer himself.

When the schoolmaster was gone a reasonable amount of time, Arno cupped his hands to his mouth: "All right, you miserable bastards! Complaining about a little mud? Bring out the entrenching tools and dig in. If any of you conveniently forgot a tool, you will dig with your bayonet and shovel with your helmet. . . . *Dig in!*"

(Oberkommando der Wehrmacht/OKW) year dated only
(1939) via Berlin police file F-11340 and Gestapo dossier
AA-2328 [Secret] signed out by the order of Gruppensturm-
fuehrer Reinhard Heydrich.
   Subject of investigation report: COLONEL GENERAL WERNER
FREIHERR VON FRITSCH

General Wilhelm Witter von Thoma did not mind sitting
against the wall, shadowed, faceless and blameless in the
background. Two clerks sat nearby, their heads bent over
note paper, pens poised to take down every word.

Just being in the same room with the fuehrer should be
enough thanks for a true soldier. And other powerful men
would remember that Von Thoma had helped a bit, especially Reichsfuehrer Himmler. The SS commander had waited
a long time for the opportunity to rid the army of a crotch-
ety old man—one whose rank and time in grade made him
the choice for the ultimate promotion to Commander-in-
Chief of the army—and probably be named Minister of
War. Fritsch was an irritation to the fuehrer. He did not
recognize Hitler's military genius, and headed up the army's
general-staff clique of traditionalists, the hidebound generals who insisted that the Wehrmacht remain free of politics—
which would continue Prussian control and independence
of the strongest entity in Germany.

Reinhard Heydrich, with the tacit approval of, if not the
instigation of, the fuehrer, was about to terminate Fritsch's
career. Thoma smiled as the old man stood at rigid attention, veins bulging in his face, the prized Heidelberg Academy dueling scars red across locked jaws. The Knight's
Cross with swords gleamed at his throat, but that was from
another time and place—another, lesser, war.

Von Thoma wore scars also, but his had been surgically
and carefully placed. No clash of sabers for him, no wild
blades that might take out an eye or cut his throat. There
were better ways to prove his manhood than dueling with
live swords while shunning protective masks.

Peripherally, claiming the privileged "von" was, or some time ago had been, legitimate. Any records of another claim no longer existed. So he became the first Prussian general to publicly cross the line and stand behind the Reichsmarschalls in this room, to put himself fully at the fuehrer's command.

So now he was privileged to partake of history being made in this sanctum sanctorum, to watch Hermann Goering and Reinhard Heydrich destroy Fritsch. The fuehrer sat very still behind his walnut desk table and said nothing as yet. The fact that he had not asked Fritsch to be seated said enough. Goering bulked heavy upon his chair; Heydrich sat on the other side of the room, shuffling papers with quick, jerky movements. Behind them slouched a slim young man in civilian clothes.

"General, this is your dossier, furnished by the Berlin police." Heydrich said. "Do you deny that you are a homosexual?"

In a strangled voice, Fritsch said, "I do not lower myself to answer such a charge—either to corrupt police or to imitation officers of the SS. I will not speak to a man cashiered from the Naval Officer Corps for scandalous conduct."

Von Thoma leaned forward. "Interesting; but which one?"

Heydrich went red. "I am not on trial here."

The fuehrer sat impassive, his silent presence threatening.

Goering lifted a fat, pale hand and the young man swayed forward, not daring to look at Hitler.

"Your name?" Goering asked.

The answer was soft and tremulous, seeming to slither across the room: "Hans Schmidt."

"Where do you work?"

"I—I sometimes help the police."

As an informer, Von Thoma thought. Having seen the paperwork, he knew that Schmidt's income was based upon blackmail of well-to-do homosexuals.

"Have you seen this man before? Do you know him?"

"He has given me money to keep quiet about his sleeping with boys."

Fritsch lifted his chin, jowls trembling. He did a military aboutface and marched from the room, his shoulders squared.

Heydrich leaped up. "General Fritsch—"

Now the fuehrer spoke. "Let him go. He will shoot himself or resign his commission. Either way, I am done with him."

CHAPTER 5

REUTERS NEWS AGENCY—London, September 3, 1939: Neville Chamberlain, England's 75-year-old Prime Minister, believed Hitler's assurances that after annexing the Sudetenland, Germany had no further territorial ambitions. Today, so soon after his "peace in our time" strategy, he feels betrayed and humbled by German's invasion of Poland.

After England's declaration of war, Arthur Greenwood, speaking for the Labour Party, expressed his relief that "this intolerable agony of suspense is over. Now we know the worst."

Applause from the House greeted this, and Mr. Greenwood continued: "May the war be swift and short and the peace that follows stand proudly on the shattered ruin of an evil name."

Farley Belvale had hated to leave the hallowed halls of Virginia Military Institute. The whooping and hollering of the graduating class only intensified his sudden loneliness. It was not only the tradition, although Lord knows there was enough of that to go around. Statues of General Robert E. Lee and Stonewall Jackson dominated entrance halls in an atmosphere permeated by echoed strains of Dixie, by the ghostly snapping of a tattered banner, a guidon of red and gray still leading the Lost Cause. The school had become more home to him than the mansion at Kill Devil Hill, despite the rigid discipline. He had grown close to several classmates and knew a spirit of camaraderie that seemed to be missing at the Hill. At least it was missing for him, the kid of the family. His brother, only a year older, was accepted man-to-man even by their father, whenever Colonel Belvale passed through in transit from one duty station to another.

Maybe it was because Owen had gone away to the U.S. Military Academy at West Point. It was always so: the males of each generation dividing, one going to the south, one sent to the north. To keep the family balance, General Crusty Carlisle said, and of course General Preston Belvale agreed, the clan heads making decisions without discussing them with the rest of the family, especially those most affected. That, too, was always so, and would ever be. Damned few traditions ever changed at the Hill.

That made his mother's divorce all the more shocking; again, more so to Owen and, of course, a direct affront to Great-aunt Minerva. She sniffed that she didn't know what this once-respectable family was coming to, what with one divorce after another. She meant the other lone split up, the recent parting of Uncle Keenan and his wife, Nancy. The breakup wasn't a major upset to Farley; he figured his mother deserved any happiness she might find, and if his father didn't supply that . . .

Farley stood on the back veranda of the Hill's great house, tasting the rich purple flavors of the wisteria vine as much as smelling them. They always brought him images of dark wines, of fragile women fluttering their fans beside tall white columns, of gray cigar smoke drifting and ice cubes singing in a crystal pitcher of lemonade; colored servants and mint juleps.

Riding the soft breeze came the not unpleasant scent of horse sweat and stables. No matter where the future might take Farley, that odor would always bring back memories of the Hill and what it stood for. Kids in the family went horseback riding before they could walk well, and could be thankful that they didn't have to learn the bone-breaking art of jousting and the use of shield and lance and spiked mace. The young Belvales-Carlisles of the ancient days in England must have had a rough time growing up while looking forward to their own crusade, their own carrying of the cross to the infidels. Spit-shining a suit of armor must have been a bitch.

He looked beyond the stables, training track and breaking pens to the little roll of higher ground greenly furred with loblolly pine, dogwood and poplar trees and touched by the darker shades of aromatic cedar. On the other side was the burying ground, the grove of honor, where a battalion of white markers were covered down and dressed right, so precisely lined. If he walked there as he sometimes did when he was lonely, a part of him expected to hear the mourning of Taps, faintly bugled and far away. Some of the graves were filled and some were only symbolic reminders, empty but for memories.

Farley wondered if the landed gentry ancestors in the old country kept a memorial garden for family whose armored bones were scattered in the unforgiving deserts throughout Saladin's beseiged kingdom.

So many crusades, so many brave banners fluttering above the heads of war stallions snorting and eager to get on with it. And all in all, nothing had come of the crusades except to bleed both sides and hold down world population. So many had died, and were still dying, in the name of God.

Whoa up, Farley Belvale; that way lies treason to the family or, at the very least, blasphemy. And you were never directly forced into VMI and the family business, unless by osmosis, by the clever shaping of an immature mind.

Straightening, he stared hard at the figure in blue moving beside the main barn. Of course it was Pretty Penny; nobody else flowed with that kind of grace. Lord, she was lovely and walked with a special confidence, that slight arrogance of a beautiful woman who knew she was beautiful and carried it well. She was sleek and she was leggy, and he loved her so much that he couldn't long look her in the eyes, and his throat ached when she was near.

But Pretty Penny didn't love him back and wouldn't if he gave her the opportunity. Lost to him forever, she was married to his cousin Walton Belvale. And Walt was off soldiering in Poland, his image made more glamorous by war and distance. Walt had always been lucky.

She closed on the veranda before he could slide off and hide. Her smile sparkled up at him, and the moist, exotic smell of her overcame the wisteria. Penny was the true southern girl, designed for hoopskirts and slow waltzes over cypress floors hand polished to a glistening shine. But she was also the modern southern girl, headstrong and independent, proud of her individuality. If only she wasn't so beautiful.

"Hi, Farley. Any news on your duty station?"

Her voice walked seductive fingertips up and down his spine.

"Not yet, but I expect travel orders any day now. I still have a week of furlough left. The graduation leave; it'll be a long time before I see this much time off again."

As usual, his eyes fell away from hers and he tried not to fantasize about her, to stop imagining her shining naked in bed. It made him guilty of desecration, as if he had just kicked over an altar. But he wanted her that way, needed her that way, desperately. What would she think, if she knew he was that male rarity, a virgin? Maybe she would be pleased that he had saved himself for her; possibly she would laugh.

Oh God—don't laugh, Penny. She would not; she was never that cruel.

She lay a small, warm hand upon his forearm, and he would have killed to keep it there. She took it back. "I'm a little worried about Walt; I haven't heard from him in weeks, and what with the Nazis overrunning Poland, he could be right in the middle of things."

Farley hoped so; then guilt grabbed him again, and he hoped Walt would make it. What was that about "thou shalt not covet"?

"He'll be all right," he said, and told himself that he wanted to believe it.

CHAPTER 6

AGENCE FRANCE PRESSE—Warsaw, September 4, 1939: Wermacht armor and infantry has surrounded this city. Under a flag of truce the Germans demanded unconditional surrender. Instead of giving up, the population is fortifying the city. Women and children help dig trenches in parks and playgrounds; trolley cars are thrown across intersections; furniture and automobiles barricade narrow streets. The Wermacht has been stopped in its tracks, but around the clock indiscriminate bombing by the Luftwaffe is making a flaming ruin of the city.

Colonel Prasniewski had washed his uniform and used candle wax on his boots. Walt stopped trying to keep up with the man. Nested high in a bombed-out house, they were among the city edge snipers who kept the German scouts pinned down. Walt kept his Schmeisser close at hand, but for long-range shots, he used another Mauser. The colonel had an edge there, also; Walt had never seen such deadly accuracy.

There were plenty of small arms to be had, and many Poles picked them up, for there were no civilians in Warsaw, only bombed-out defenders starving and low on water and medicines. They were out of hope, too, but hanging on grimly.

"Panzers," Walt said. "There—armored car nosing around that pile of rubble; light tanks behind him."

"Wrong order of battle," Prasniewski said, and squeezed the trigger. Its driver head-shot, the armored car wavered across the street to crash into a leaning light standard. The metal standard fell across the car, creasing it in the center.

A man screamed in the wreckage, and beyond the smashed wall, a tank backed out of sight. The colonel kept his rifle lined on the twisted armored vehicle. A soldier struggled from the wreckage, blood streaming his face. When he stood up, Prasniewski shot him.

"Mercy shot," he said. "I would do as much for any animal."

Warsaw, Walt thought, would be a bitch to take.

An hour later the tanks tried again, nosing into the rock-strewn street, their guns firing blindly, raking buildings that had all become sniper nests. Wide-eyed, Walt stared down at men racing from the buildings and waving great twists of burning rags. They ran low and desperate as wolves to throw their torches beneath the rolling tanks. No man made it back to cover, as sweeping machine guns caught them, four men chopped down.

Then with a gout of bright flame and a string of explosions, the first panzer blew up. The second tank had to stop directly over a torch, and tore itself apart as the driver tried to slew it around and take cover.

"A bitch to take," Walt said, and then snugged close to his battered wall as Stukas thundered in very low to chew up the street with their guns. The next run they made was farther along, loosing their bombs and screaming high into the smoky sky.

They had gotten into the habit of sharing one cigarette, and did it now, passing it back and forth while watching the street. Looking ahead where the bombs had fallen, Walt saw another horse down. Always the poor goddamned horses. Poles darted from holes in the ground to cut away its shrunken meat. In minutes, a sickly sun touched ribs and outlined the skeleton. They had left the head intact.

"Shit," Walt said.

The colonel nodded. "One must agree. Does your army still have cavalry?"

Walt found himself telling Prasniewski about Kill Devil Hill, the horses and the family. He even said a few words about Penny, and wondered why. It was something of a confession, he thought—or a last testament.

"No," he said then. "We're going to make it all the way, Colonel. If Warsaw doesn't get relieved by the French or British, hell—we came in by the sewers; we'll go out the same way. The Krauts will be more confused, with their shock troops in the city, and rear echelon soldiers following up."

Prasniewski was silent for long minutes. The bombers came and went, strewing earthquakes, lighting new hells. The colonel said, "Thousands dead and more to die. Have you heard snatches of music at times? That is Warsaw Radio, and every half minute those of us left alive may hear portions of a polonaise. Frederic Chopin's music tells the rest of the world that Warsaw is still in Polish hands."

Walt got hungry sometime later, especially after they ran out of smokes. When they had to search out mud puddles from broken water mains to drink from, he had lost all track of time. Water and ammunition; these were the important things. He ran out of Schmeisser clips somewhere, and beat the machine pistol to death before pulling out of one sniper's position to find another.

The ruins began to blur, and his head throbbed from the constant air raids. Colonel Prasniewski was real, and the goddamned Krauts were real, but not the burning city. The city had always choked him with smoke and brick dust, and the flames danced red all night long. That was good because the firelight showed him another target and another.

When he nodded off, pretty Penny Colvin brought him smiles. When he nodded off again, the crack of the colonel's rifle brought him around again. Walt had to grin through his scratchy, dry lips, because neat and polished Prasniewski was as grubby as everybody else, and the blond mustache drooped into a new fuzzy beard of many colors.

Not as often now that the steel claws closed tighter into

the bloody heart of the city, but at odd moments, they heard wounded loudspeakers sing out the polonaise. Chopin's music floated out across the corpses, and above the hastily dug graves in gardens and parks and paths where families had tried to do right for the thousands of dead.

Pick a target; fire and fall back; search the fallen of both sides for anything of use. Shoot and fall back while return bullets chipped mortar and stones all around them. Find another nest that might offer a good field of fire. Mechanical now, every move slow and studied and one hell of an effort.

The polonaise played no more. One hand gripping the colonel's shoulder, Walt said, "What—what's that other music?"

"A funeral dirge, my friend. I—the officials must have surrendered the city."

Walt came to his feet and leaned his back against a staggered wall. The almost-quiet was unreal, pops of small arms fire, a single tank growling carefully forward. "The sewers," Walt muttered. "Let's get out of—"

And the German plane released its last bomb.

CHAPTER 7

AGENCE FRANCE PRESSE—The Maginot Line, September 4, 1939: Observers here say that defenders now face up to 33 German divisions of the Heeresgruppe C, commanded by General Ritter von Leeb. Some units are being used to garrison the Siegfried Line and others to menace the Belgian and Dutch borders, but the bulk of them are placed directly and helplessly in front of the Maginot Line.

French leaders toast the foresight of earlier military mentors who did not trust the peace of the Prussians following World War I and built this impregnable position. Let *le boche* attack, they say; the defenders are more than ready.

VOLKISCHER BEOBACHTER—Poland, September 6, 1939: Reacting quickly on the principles of lightning war, the Wermacht struck back after the wild Polish assault upon Germany's border outpost. The Wermacht's 3rd and 4th Armies of the Northern Army Group and the 8th and 10th of the Southern Group are advancing on Warsaw. In the blitzkreig General Fedor von Bock's 14th Army captured Krakow and is marching toward the Rumanian frontier. The Polish high command has ordered a general retreat which is rapidly turning into a rout.

It might beat the fatigue of a long road march, but any sensible landser was suspicious of rides offered by panzer grenadiers. The tanks were probably heading into trouble that would call for the use of expendable infantry, always the miserable infantry which had no steel skin to protect them. Besides, the *verdampt* things banged and stank and were easy to fall off. Feldwebel Arno Hindemit hung on to the panzer's deck and turret and hoped this one would not draw artillery fire from the retreating Poles.

Especially not this iron bathtub on clanking metal tracks. It was a Flammpanzer II, without a cannon, and only a pair of flame tubes mounted up front near the single machine gun. The sergeant commanding this tinderbox said it carried enough spare gasoline and diesel fuel to fire eighty two-to-three-second bursts and could reach out thirty-five meters to sizzle and fry some poor, struggling bastard.

There were legitimate tools of war, and some shitty weapons that should remain back with the bloodthirsty civilians who invented them. A powerful flamethrower might well be used to flush out a building or to make an *eierkuchen* of another panzer, a fiery pancake to begin the day. A gush of liquid fire aimed at a soldier was a shitty thing.

The same extra fuel turned the tank into a fat, waddling bomb awaiting only a little kiss of enemy metal to explode. If the Wermacht was equipped with these fire spitters, the French and the English *Tommis* would have them also. Anything to make the life of a cursed infantryman more miserable and much shorter. Only the Poles would be without, because they had believed so firmly in their horse cavalry. No matter; horses on both sides enjoyed taking a vicious kick at an unsuspecting landser.

The panzer bucked over a freshly dug ditch, another desperate and futile attempt to hold off German armor by the disorganized Polish army. Arno said, *"Scheissen!"* and took a fresh grip on the turret. Then the bastardly iron turtle halted suddenly and slid him off with a thump.

"A problem, Sergeant?" Leutnant Witzieli reached a helping hand as the tank engine shut down and the turret cover sprang open like a toilet seat.

"See," Arno said, "the idiot did not look before lifting the lid of his chamber pot. If he didn't throw me off, he would have knocked me off. The engine noise makes all panzer grenadiers stupid if they were not born that way."

He retrieved his machine pistol, shook it hard, and then tenderly blew dirt from the breech of the Schmeisser.

The tank sergeant glared. "*Dummheit?* I am stupid? Not so stupid as to walk when I can ride."

"Twice the idiot: this stinking machine and you are the same."

Witzieli said, "The platoon, Sergeant; until we hear differently, I think they should be positioned as skirmishers along that line of trees. If you think they ought to be dug in—"

"Sir," Arno said, and stepped away to hand-signal the men climbing down from the other tanks. There was something to be said for reserve officers. This schoolmaster-turned-soldier seemed a decent man. He had more or less asked Arno's opinion on the troop disposition; regular officers would not. If they were Prussian, with the holy "von" before their names, they bellowed and popped heels and knew everything about everything. If they were not Prussian, they pretended to be, and what could a lowly enlisted man know.

Enough to keep his lowly ass out of the line of fire. A bullet clanged off the Flammpanzer, and Arno smiled as the commander suddenly dropped back into the bottom of his chamber pot. Arno signaled the *leutnant* to drop down; then he wheeled and sprinted into the trees.

Making himself a part of the shadow and as skinny as possible, Arno flattened against the trunk of a sturdy *eiche*, and blessed the oak for growing there. He peeked around the rough bark to find the sniper. Probably not a sniper, at that; more likely the Pole had found himself isolated when his unit dissolved. And no doubt he was tough, angry and frightened—a bad mixture for his enemies. He could have run away with his troop, but there he was in the corner of a grassy stone fence. A stubborn landser was a model landser, whatever the uniform.

Behind Arno, the Flammpanzer's motor roared into life to rattle the thing across a short patch of open ground and into the thin line of trees. The *dummheit* tanker was brave enough now that he knew that only a lone rifleman was out there.

Brrapp—brrapp—brrapp!

Scheissen! An automatic weapon on the left flank changed things. Bark jumped off the oak, knee high; most of the burst ripped at Arno's bellied-down platoon, just a few inches over their heads. Evidently the gunner had not seen the tank, or he would have held his fire and not exposed his position, so he could get at advancing landsers. Pulling his head in, Arno considered tactics. The lone rifleman could have slipped over the stone fence and been safely down the road. Instead, he offered himself as bait to draw foot soldiers into the machine gun's field of fire. That meant he could not be scared off; it meant that he was ready to die, like those at the machine gun.

For Arno's unblooded platoon it was a rough way to start a war, going up against patriots. Sliding the safety off his Schmeisser, he thought it was also severe upon the patriots. The SS and Gestapo would name them as guerrillas, making it easier to hang them all, instead of separating the wheat from the chaff.

Brrapp—brrapp—brrapp!''

The gun was probably a French Chatellerault, Modèle 24 with a detachable box of twenty-five rounds. No wonder that the gunner was using short bursts. Besides it being good sense not to be seen and draw fire, and not to overheat the barrel of an air-cooled weapon, there remained the changing of magazines. That was a problem for even Germany's MP 40, a submachine gun with a thirty-two-round box. The Schmeisser was efficient, light and accurate; it could be ground into the mud and snow and it rarely jammed, but a man might wish for a longer magazine or some kind of belt feed, as on the crew-served weapons. There would be a bit more weight to carry, but it balanced out in firepower when it was needed most.

Like most professional noncommissioned officers, Arno had been thoroughly briefed on enemy weapons at the Wermacht's training schools. A good idea, that; there would be times when captured enemy arms and ammunition would have to be used. The idea must have sprung from the head of an experienced soldier; it was too simple and workable for army headquarters.

Brrapp—brrapp!—brrapp!

This time Arno's riflemen answered. By the spotty pattern of their shots, he knew they had not found either machine gun or sniper. They were firing to reassure themselves, to be doing something. A landser always felt better firing his weapon or just yelling and making noise that proved he was alive and in charge of his own destiny. Peeping around the tree trunk, Arno watched carefully and picked up a small haze of dust as the gun chattered again. There—one bipod leg planted against a short log for its right flank and beneath an overhang of early fall leaves going to yellow, there was the gun.

Bracing his Schmeisser against the oak, Arno squeezed off four rapid shots head-on at the little circle of blue steel muzzle. Then he walked the 9mm bullets left and right, up and down. Cover the whole target if possible so it doesn't come back at you. There might not be a second chance.

Chung—skee!

The bullet chewed into the oak and screamed off.

Arno hit the ground and rolled. The rifleman; the *verdampt* sniper had been forgotten. Face down, flattened to the earth, Arno waited for an answer from the machine gun. Nothing—it was kaput. He lifted his head to see.

Chung—skee!

Scheissen; he spat bitter bark dust. The bastard had him zeroed in. The Pole must know that his machine-gun crew was finished; it was time for him to run, to save his ass. What could one man with an old rifle do against a German platoon and a tank, with more tanks in the offing? As if in answer, the Flammpanzer's motor kicked over, a threat rumbling in its iron guts.

Damn that; it wasn't right to fry some poor little shit for standing his ground. Of course the Pole had to be silenced; this was war. But there were better ways for a brave man to die.

Arno ducked low and leaned away from the tree. Bent almost double, his Schmiesser thrust before him, he ran hard for the brush where the sniper was holed up.

Zzzpapp!

A bullet whipped so close to his head that it snapped. Arno fired a burst that chewed the bushes to the flank where he had spotted the machine gun. Crashing through the undergrowth, he stumbled over a fallen branch and slammed into the ground. *Nein;* no tree limb tripped him up but an abandoned rifle. The sniper had broken, then; he thrown down his weapon to flee before superior forces. Arno was of two minds about that. He respected a soldier making a determined stand, and equally respected a man's right to keep his skin whole so that he might return to fight another day.

Brrapp!

Hölle was zum teufel! What in the hell—the goddamn gun was alive again. Oh the sly bastard; the sniper threw away his rifle, all right, but only to take over the machine gun.

Only one thing to be done now. Arno could not outrun the next burst, and the Pole knew exactly where he was in the sparse cover. *Scheissen;* Arno had never meant to play the hero or suddenly turn stupid. They were about the same thing.

Machine pistol firing at his hip, Arno ran straight at the gun. Bullets snapped at his jacket; bullets knocked his *stahlhelm* sideways on his head.

There! Shapes and shadows . . . bodies sprawled around the gun . . . a white face staring . . . and Arno blew it apart.

He braced spraddle-legged to stare down upon the first men he had killed. The trouble was, the sniper-gunner was not a man but only a boy no taller than the rifle he had left behind. A bastardly way to fight a war, but sudden death by bullets had to be better than screaming your life away in the torture of fire.

He could not know that. Death came calling in whatever guise, and to truly know was to stand too close.

Arno looked away and saw the *leutnant* trotting a squad along to help. Loading a fresh clip into his weapon, he was surprised that his hands were trembling.

CHAPTER 8

INTERNATIONAL NEWS SERVICE—September 18, 1939, with General Chiang Kai-shek in the Honan region: The leader of the Kuomintang forces said today that the Japanese invasion of his country was "only a skin disease; the bone sickness is Chinese communism."

Looking up from his latest written report, Keenan glanced at the new shoulder tabs Watanabe wore—two white stars set against the red and yellow stripes of all field grade officers; now it was Lieutenant Colonel Watanabe. "Congratulations," Keenan said.

Watanabe's nod was abrupt. "Yes. I had no choice but to order you not to report our casualties at Nomonhan, or the ambush itself. We were moved this far by rail to conceal a defeat and ready ourselves for a victory."

Keenan could slip nothing past Japanese radio operators or message center carriers, but it really didn't make much difference. He wasn't here to write lengthy reports, critical or otherwise; he was in occupied China with the Imperial Japanese Army to observe and remember. What he had to say would mean far more to the old general at Kill Devil Hill in Virginia than to the mummified War Department. He'd like to erase some things he'd seen, but he would forget nothing. Sometimes his kind of near-total recall was a curse. But the old general would approve of what had been learned of *Bushido*, the warrior creed.

"Whatever you say, Colonel. I don't think another Japanese force will be caught the same way again—especially no unit you command." The train trip had taken several days and nights, one blending into the other across a landscape always changing but always the same—primitive, exotic, silently threatening. It brooded along the single gauge track with quick, sharp mountains, flatlands of rice or bamboo and Keenan always felt the dragon was coiled just out of sight.

Watanabe rested his hand upon the black-wrapped hilt of the samurai sword, tilting its scabbard back so that he could sit down. "If I may," he said, surprising Keenan; the ultimate commander asking permission?

The colonel must have sensed his feeling. Watanabe said, "These field quarters, poor as they are, are considered our homes. Courtesy is sacred in a Japanese home. Our islands are small, and our population is large. Close personal contact demands that we be polite to each other."

"That makes sense," Keenan said.

"I do not understand you," Watanabe said. "For me to speak so bluntly is impolite, but here we have little time for courtesy. You are unlike other Americans I have known. You fought well and showed no fear. I would expect an American civilian to help a wounded man, at least one of their own whites, but not a professional officer lowering himself for a dying common soldier—a yellow soldier. You obey orders, also—you, whose countrymen rebel for no logical reason."

"We're not a logical people, Colonel, and as for me—as you said, an army officer. I give orders and accept them, as you do." Partly a lie, that last; Keenan would not follow obviously wrong orders and probably wouldn't accept an outright stupid command without protest. "As for yellow and white—my country is not logical there, either. I have learned to respect the Japanese soldier, whatever his rank."

Outside in the night, he heard troop movement, the soft rattle of equipment and shuffle of hobnail boots, the clink of domed helmets. There was the smoky odor of cook-fires. Watanabe had said something about little time for courtesy. Was the higher command moving this unit back into action with so little rest? He didn't fold his report, but left it flat and open upon the table for anyone to read. Maybe this move was something like getting right back on a horse that had just thrown you, facing the fear before it stuck and beat you.

"There were for us too many tanks," Watanabe said, "led by a General Zhukov. They have withdrawn into Russia, fearing to come deeper into Manchukuo and into a full-scale war. May Zhukov die slowly and his body never return to his native soil; may dogs piss upon his bones. He used us as a test for his armor."

Keenan waited and Watanabe's face smoothed itself. The colonel said, "We move out in two hours—another group of Chinese bandits in the hills above Linsi."

The Japs had already throttled most of China's trade by grabbing major port cities all along the coast—Tsingtao, Shanghai, Foochow, and that unbelievable mess at Nanking. There would never be honor for any Japanese who joined in the bloody, senseless rape of Nanking. Far inland was where they met resistance, some of it stubborn despite primitive Chinese equipment and shortages of ammunition. They held cities, but in the endless countryside the ancient dragons waited.

He said, "What kind of bandits? Communist, Kuomintang or just another free-lance warlord?"

Standing up, Watanabe caressed the hilt of his sword. "A bandit by any other name—we move within the hour, Captain, if you wish to accompany us."

"Of course," Keenan said, and when the man ducked out of the little tent, set aside the report which didn't say anything. Feeling guilty, he began a letter to his wife. He had not even thought of her for weeks.

Dear Nancy—he had never addressed her as dearest, or darling; for too long, their relationship had been almost formal. That was a hell of a thing to say about a marriage, and who was to carry the blame? The cold Carlisle family, of course; Keenan, of course. It wasn't Nancy's fault that she slipped the baby. That happened to the fine thoroughbred mares; more often to the finest; closely bred ones. But she wouldn't have gotten pregnant in the first place if she'd been fitted for a diaphragm. Or if he'd used condoms. In the beginning, they had that much going for them—the tender fierceness of deep sensual needs eagerly met. After the miscarriage, all that changed. Bad enough that he had married just anyone, but a woman gone barren, besides? The families looked away from them; woman existed to bear replacements.

. . . another sally after bandits in the hills. I find myself hoping this time it will be against the communists. As yet, I know nothing concrete about their guerrilla tactics. I do know they have to hit and run, since Chiang Kai-shek and an alliance with smaller warlords gives the Kuomintang far superior forces, but badly armed and trained . . .

Great, he thought, soft and thoughtful words that should bring him closer to Nancy, a field report for wives. Not that she could get a letter to him here; even if she could, it would only be chitchat, the weather, fashions, some girlfriends he didn't know. Never a mention of the family and its ostracism of her, what must be her loneliness. He wondered why she hadn't shaken free of all the Carlisles and the Belvales. It couldn't be just her religion, which didn't actually recognize a Church of England marriage, so there must be something left of those first sweetly giving days. Maybe she was stubbornly determined to make the best of a bad bargain. And he would not ask her for a divorce, for himself or the damned family.

The candle flickered and a shadow snaked across the wooden box for shipping rice he used as a table. He thought a moment before adding . . . I miss you, Nancy. After this assignment, I'd like us to take a furlough to anywhere you'd like. And he signed it with love.

When the regiment moved out, it rattled and bumped by truck to the foot of short, abrupt mountains, arriving at dawn, and Colonel Watanabe's men set up quietly and efficiently. So many replacements, and Keenan couldn't tell recruit from veteran. The sun lifted, hinting blood colors on the mountaintops, casting deeper shadows in the valleys. The air was new, wisped with little green flavors and the smell of water.

Watanabe said, "Through the first valley runs the Lo Hu

River, a shallow stream. Farther along is the village of Shutai, too long a haven for bandits who prey upon their own people as well as attack Japanese outposts. One battalion is circling behind the mountain; one will block here with the artillery, and I will lead the third straight in." Glancing at his watch, he went on: "*Ah so desuka*—our bombers arrive on time."

Looking up, Keenan watched three Sallys veeing in over the mountain, motors rumbling: good morning, Shutai—bandits and civilians alike, grandmothers and little children. He couldn't see the bombs falling, but the rolling thunder of their explosions came quickly back. The Mitsubishi Type 97s were heavy bombers that the Japs often used for strafing runs as well. No Air Corps specialist, Keenan was impressed by the Japanese boast that this utility plane could also be pressed into service as a fighter.

Smoke corkscrewed into the air as the aircraft made their second run over Shutai village and the rattle of their guns became a malignant echo. The lead battalion went in swiftly: regimental point, connecting file spread behind and as soon as the valley was entered, flankers swinging out into position. Watanabe would not be trapped in this dark and narrow gorge without warning.

But the column wasn't fired on until reaching Shutai itself—or what was left of it. A few rifles popped at the trotting Japs then, different sounds, different calibers, Keenan thought. Mud-wall shacks smouldered where bombs had smashed them back into the earth; dust to dust. Not so with the dead, some also smouldering, rag piles and smeared bodies. As Keenan followed Lieutenant Ichiki, his assigned liaison officer, into the outskirts of Shutai, he saw a little girl die. One arm blown off at the shoulder, her clothing blown away, she sat upon rubble without crying, without expression on her dusty face. Then she fell over onto one side.

"Oh, shit," Keenan said.

"*Nandesuka?*" Ichiki asked.

"Nothing," Keenan grunted, and a wink of light from a rifle barrel warned him. He dove for an upended cart of wilted vegetables and tiny dried fish. A bullet split a cabbage inches from his head, and immediate answering fire came from a pair of Nambu machine guns. The pig shed dissolved around the sniper, who toppled face down in the mud, his rifle long and old, so ancient that Keenan couldn't be sure what it was. Desultory fire reached down from hillsides, small arms only, and Keenan saw one Japanese spin and fall. Lieutenant Ichiki walked upright to where the first sniper lay, reached his long sword high above his head and struck with all his strength. The Chinese head leaped from the spouting neck, and as it rolled, Keenan saw silvered hair mixed with the mud and blood.

Even before it had been worked over by the planes, Shutai hadn't been much of a village. A few mud huts, a central building of some sort, tiny shops at roadside, the muddy, shallow stream that fed the rice paddies beyond, little arcs of green stair-stepping up the mountainsides.

Moving with the troops, Keenan carried only the 8mm Nen Shiku Kenju passed to him by Watanabe in camp. It wasn't much better than the freaky pistol he'd carried on the border. Japs weren't much for pistols; this one's safety was on the right, so you had to reach across the weapon to set it. The clip—a bitch to remove if your fingers were sweaty, and again both hands were tied up.

Troops kicked in a door and barked orders to a group of Chinese. They came outside huddled together, old men bent and not looking up, two women, half a dozen small children.

Ichiki ordered them to squat and put their hands atop their heads. Then he called for the interpreter who had been trailing close behind. Keenan looked toward the other end of the valley, where Colonel Watanabe's attack troops were barely in sight. If there had been bandits in Shutai, they were being herded toward the battalion behind the ridge. There they'd run into blistering automatic weapons fire with the backing of mortars.

But they weren't herded; the Chinese came dripping up out of the shallow river itself, muddy leaves clinging to them like scales. For that startled moment they were reptilian things lifting from the primeval ooze. Keenan hit the ground as the shooting started, as the Chinese fired directly into the confused Japanese milling around the ruined huts and the bloody casualties of Shutai. The main body of the town's troops had taken cover in the river and waited in ambush. They were too disciplined for a warlord's ragged mercenaries, so they must be Kuomintang or communist.

Lieutenant Ichiki was chopped down in the first burst of fire, his sword clattering upon the rocks. But he rolled onto his side, blood running over his chin, and shouted to his men guarding the little group of prisoners. Coming to one knee, Keenan waved his arms and yelled, too: "No, damnit! Don't—"

But they all were slammed back against the mud hut by close up rifle fire, and one Jap lunged out to pin an old man with his bayonet. The kids were little flung dolls, and only one had the chance to cry out. The bayonet man crumpled over his victim and other Japs fell as the rest tried to scatter.

A bright light burst inside Keenan's head and he tasted a mouthful of ancient dirt. He watched his fingers crawl along the dirt, slow and clumsy spiders reaching for something he didn't know, for some place he couldn't get to.

Then something hard crashed behind his head and he stopped trying.

CHAPTER 9

INTERNATIONAL NEWS SERVICE—London, England, September 20, 1939: Prime Minister Winston Churchill repeated the speech he made after the miracle of Dunkirk: "The whole fury and might of the enemy must very soon be turned on us. Hitler knows that he will have to break us on this island or lose the war . . . Let us brace ourselves therefore to our duties, and so bear ourselves that, if the British Empire and its Commonwealth last for a thousand years, men will say, " 'This was their finest hour.' "

General Charles (NMI—no middle initial, unless you counted his nickname) Carlisle always liked to approach the heavily wooded hill that deliberately shrouded Sandhurst Keep from visitors until the last moment. The road snaked around and back upon itself until the Keep loomed suddenly over an unsuspecting stranger. Even the initiate were often startled by the gargoyled buttresses and threatening towers. But it was better to come upon the ancient family fortress on foot. That way, its imposing bulk made any man feel his smallness, his insignificance, and was supposed to.

"Granite," Crusty Carlisle said, "stone a million years solid, and logs that were full-grown trees when Christ was a corporal, now so old that they're about petrified. The Keep was raised to stand off anything, meant to last, and by God and the Carlisles, it will."

He strode uphill breathing deeply of mountain air, his

double barrel twelve gauge over one arm. Its double-ought shot was only fired at snags high upon a pine or fallen logs, to keep his eye in and reflexes sharp.

Only damned city fools cut down on boulders and got caught by ricochets, and only mighty hunters blew apart little birds and small animals that couldn't shoot back. And some poachers would hunt in summer, too. If Crusty spotted anybody carrying a gun on this land, the bastard would leave dripping buckshot.

"Fucking psychiatrists may be right for a change," he said to a swift robin that winged across his path, "about so many Nimrods substituting a long gun for a shortness of cock. Last war, the mighty hunters around here beat the draft or joined the navy if they couldn't get in the Coast Guard. Not nearly so much fun walking the woods when the game means to punch holes in your hide, too."

Last war; this war coming so fast that everybody on this side of the big pond would be caught scratching their fat asses and looking the wrong way. And it wasn't that the silly shits hadn't been warned. The Japs had been ripping out China's guts for three years, and what about Hitler, and that blowhard Mussolini?

The Son of Heaven in Tokyo wasn't happy with raping Manchuria; no oil there and his expanding navy needed the oil that Roosevelt was keeping from them. So it would be the Dutch East Indies or any place they could rob. They would never forgive FDR's embargo and try to regain their face lost to the world. Try, hell!

Did the Washington peace bloc actually believe that Heinie bastard with a Groucho Marx mustache over the wrong hole would be satisfied with a few bites of Europe? He meant to swallow the whole world.

Mussolini wouldn't be that much problem. After that fucked-up skirmish in Ethiopia when the spaghetti benders with their big guns and tanks had a tough time whipping naked savages who fought with spears and arrows, Mussolini showed that his mouth had overloaded his ass. When he met modern and well-armed troops, he'd be back stomping grapes or whatever the hell he did for a living before he became *Il Duce*.

"There ain't no ill douche." Crusty grinned, and shifted arms with the shotgun. "Not enough of the right kind, though—or Hitler, Mussolini and the buck-toothed emperor would all have been flushed down the toilet. Early on, we could have pinched their heads off. Now they're full grown and we'll have to stomp mud holes in their asses, providing they don't catch us with a sneak punch that puts us down for good."

Late sun touched his face as he walked on through the perfume of pines and heard the warm wind finger through green needles to shake the brown ones slowly down. Sandhurst Keep reached high above him, and as he did so many times in the past, he put away the image of a moat and drawbridge. It would fit the castle, but not the times. It must have been simple in the ancient times—the strength of a man's arm and the sharpness of his sword.

These days politics came first, and in its slimy trail roared steel dragons and their bastard get, the quick dragons that soared too high for archers. This time, would they also breathe the flaming stink that burned flesh and seared lungs forever? Maybe all armies had learned the horror of poison gas; but there were rumors of a deadlier, more vicious weapon in the works, an odorless, tasteless gas that attacked the nervous system, killing at a touch. Quicker and with little suffering, they said, but you were just as dead.

Crusty looked up at his battlements and took a firmer grip on the small of the shotgun stock. Always, some scientific hotshot, safe in his lab, sat around and figured out one more way to make a doughboy's life miserable. Always the poor fucking infantry.

Right here on this stony land, the civilian infantry of the new republic had met England's best grenadiers and dragoons. The volunteers kicked holy hell out of Johnny Burgoyne's professionals, and downed so many redcoat officers that Crusty's great-great-great-ancestor with a sense of humor named his command post Sandhurst Keep. Sandhurst remained England's training school for officers, its West Point, and over the years the CP was built into a real defense position in case the British hadn't taken their lesson to heart and came back for another.

Come iron tanks, bigger artillery and airplane bombs, until the infantry planted its muddy boots on enemy ground, no war could be won.

Striding through the great oaken gates strapped with iron and across the cobblestone courtyard, Crusty broke the 12 gauge and stuck the shells into his jacket pocket. The disarming was symbolic of the democracies, putting the "war to end all wars" behind them and naively supposing the defeated enemies would do the same, and that allies would remain loyal allies.

He nodded to a yardman and went through a onetime sally port to enter his home through the kitchen. Carefully, he cleaned his boots on the metal scraper sided by bristles; both ends were horseshoes. Sarah was hell on keeping her kitchen floor clean.

He peered through the leaded door panes, knowing damned well that Sarah hadn't stood at the big stove for more than twenty years. He took one more swipe on the scraper and went inside, propping the shotgun in one corner of the mudroom. Heavy jackets and rain gear hung on wooden pegs above the gun and a kerosene lantern waited emergencies atop an oak icebox now used for odds and ends that Sarah would have thrown out. He still missed her.

Peeling out of his jacket, Crusty said, "Refrigerators are efficient, but there's something to be said for chipping a block of ice with a pick, and turning the handle on a freezer."

Round and bustling, the cook came from the pantry flopping white flour from her apron. "General?"

"Just muttering in my beard, Molly." He went for the thirty-cup pot of coffee always kept hot beside the sink.

"You'd look good in a beard, General. More dignified, kind of. Like Abraham Lincoln."

He grunted. "More like an ape inspecting a paint locker; my face hair grows wild in different colors."

"Still and all . . ."

Crusty carried his steaming cup through the long, paneled hall before Molly could trap him in a long discussion. He perked up when he saw Gloria coming out of the smoking room she had converted to an office. He also felt the twinge of guilt that always plagued him for confusing her life. He had numerous granddaughters at military posts scattered around the country, but Gloria had ever been his favorite. The other girls were prettier and one or two were smarter, but none had Gloria's backbone, or her determination to make good on her own.

He wished he hadn't urged her into marriage. He wished he could somehow keep her with him when she was ready to leave.

"Granddad—General Belvale left a message. He has approval for you both to address Congress and you're to call him back right away."

"Thank you, dear. I appreciate—"

But she walked away and he couldn't blame her for not forgiving him just yet. She came by her stubbornness naturally.

To speak before Congress, by God! Maybe—just maybe—he and Preston Belvale could make some of those elected peanuts take a good look at the horizon. He didn't really believe anything could do that, short of Washington being put to the torch again. But somebody had to try. The war clouds were rolling fast and dark.

CHAPTER 10

Crusty Carlisle looked all around the formal sitting room, put his feet up on a coffee table and grunted. "Can you believe those Roosevelt-hating sons of bitches? And the bitches themselves?" He glanced at the doors again. "Speaking of which, where's Minerva?"

"Overseeing the marketing," Belvale said. "She won't sweep in and order you to remove your feet."

"Order, batshit! I just don't want to bite her in the ass and break my teeth."

"Didn't you bring your spare set?" Belvale thumbed his mustache and waited for Crusty to say what was on his mind. They had pulled most of the strings they could reach just for congressional approval to address that august body. The wake-up attempt was a bust; the elected leaders of the country slumbered on, never realizing they would wake suddenly to the worst nightmare of their lives.

"And I always carry an extra pair of balls in case mine get cut off. Told you the peanuts wouldn't listen." Crusty reached for a drink on the silver tray. "I saw a couple of silly shits rolling their eyes and simpering at us ancient mossbacks. I guess it had to be done, no matter how we look in the newspapers."

Belvale tasted his own bourbon, then nipped the end off a Cuban cigar. "So our official try by the book is a matter of record. Now we can start arm-twisting and have the America Firsters siphoned off at the wallets. Reaching some of them will take time."

Grunting again, Crusty emptied his glass. "Which we're damned near out of. Having to go clear around the block to reach Wheeler and Smith and several others—if we can even lay a glove on them. That bunch of America First assholes are so stupid they didn't even read the communist membership flip-flop when Hitler attacked Mother Russia. Suddenly it's a patriotic must to jump on Germany. A couple of weeks ago, the party line was stay out of Europe's war at any cost. Who was that mouthy professor they've got, the guy who runs around making speeches and says that every fourth American boy will get plowed under if we go to war? Fucking peanut. You know, this ain't bad whiskey; good thing he left the bottle."

"Henry knows your tastes."

"And everything else that passes through Kill Devil Hill, and the county itself. If he wasn't so old and decrepit I'd draft him to head a real G-Two." Crusty snorted. "Army intelligence—there's a contradiction in terms for you. When did that shit start—putting suspected queers in the medics and the dumbass eight balls in G-Two?"

"The winning army writes the regulations. Blame Grant's boys." Belvale made a ritual of lighting his cigar, sniffing it first, then rolling it between his fingers, dampening the cylinder with another roll along his lips. Through the first smoke he said, "And if Henry wasn't colored, he might actually get the chance to show what he can do."

"What? Oh, yeah; that color bar will have to change. Can't have the smart ones in labor battalions this time. Look who I'm telling this to—the Massa himself, the Lost Cause plantation owner who never got over freeing the slaves."

"To coin a phrase, batshit! Would you wager that your northern liberals allow the colored to fight as line troops in this war?"

"No bet." Crusty rattled ice in his glass. "And that's a fucking waste of manpower. The old Twenty-fourth Regiment at Fort Benning is as good as any outfit in the army, and black as coal shovels; except for its officers, of course."

Belvale smiled. "Of course the leaders must be white, courtesy of the Yankee army—you're free now, Uncle Tom and Aunt Jemima; just stay out of the officers' clubs and don't ask us about any forty acres and a mule. That's not the army's business, or the army's fault. Go be free somewhere else."

Crusty refilled his glass. "Come off it, Preston. Don't get me started on who saved your precious Kill Devil Hill when all you brave Rebs hauled ass."

Sighing, Belvale said, "Okay. But so much talk about white makes me think of First Sergeant Keg. I wonder if he's still soldiering. I can never remember his real first name."

"Keg White probably can't, either. Got his nickname because he's built like a nail keg, and is just as tough. The stories about that guy continue to grow. How about his: when I blow this whistle, I wants to see a cloud of dust—"

"—and when that dust clears, I wants to see two rows of statues."

Laughing, Crusty added, "And when I say Eyes Right, I wants to hear them eyeballs click! Hell of a sergeant, hell of a man."

Belvale chuckled with his cousin, then sobered quickly. "We reached a few new ears in the Senate and House, and already have friends there. We keep talking sense to the press, keep pushing the politicians and try to place our own people in the War Department. It's all we can do right now. We managed to have observers sent overseas against objections."

"I like arm-twisting better. I'm going back to the Keep and have Gloria go through the records and check favors owed us, put together rosters of them with us and them against us. I'll take it from there."

Belvale drew fragrant smoke from his cigar. Crusty was lucky that Gloria Carlisle-Johnson had brought her baby home after breaking off a marriage she had been pushed into. West Point graduates were not all officers and gentlemen, despite that act of Congress. Some were built-in bastards, and Crusty had found Lt. Cornel Johnson for his granddaughter. It didn't matter now that a most junior officer was so stupid as to maul the blood kin of a major general. Too late, Johnson discovered it was better to resign his new commission and disappear. The other choice was to remain a second lieutenant forever and to tour every crappy outpost in the army, with the word arriving ahead of him.

Gloria was bright, not quite plain, recently turned independent and a sharp accountant. She worked at Sandhurst Keep for pay and was saving her money to go out on her own. Never admitting his mistake aloud, Crusty continued to do all he could to hold her at home, and he needed her for more than keeping his records straight. She could talk him into being diplomatic when his natural style was that of a runaway bulldozer.

"What," Crusty said, "is the word from our observers? My own people still report through your fancy command post."

"No fancier than your war room, just more efficient. Keenan checks in when he can, and his reports are always to the point. The trouble is, the War Department won't believe what he says about the Japanese. Doesn't he drop you a line once in a while?"

Cracking a diminished ice cube in his molars, Crusty splashed a dollop of bourbon into his glass, only an inch. It was his one-for-the-road signal. "Doesn't even write his wife. Gloria says. You'd know better since Kirstin prefers the Hill to the Keep. Choosing Minerva Belvale over me. No accounting for tastes."

Nodding, Belvale silently admitted that his sister-in-law deserved her reputation as a harridan, but the family was stuck with her, and in a way she filled certain needs. "Chad is still with the sitzkreig in France, and Walton anticipates imminent trouble in Poland. Our young Air Corps representatives are enroute to England. If they—"

Crusty took his feet off the coffee table and stood up, tall and younger than his years, a proud gray hawk, a gnarled billy goat. "Flyboys; who needs them? I know, I know— you're damned near batty as Billy Mitchell about air power. Just remember what happened to his insubordinate ass."

Belvale smiled. "When did you ever worry about insubordination?"

"Goose ain't gander." Crusty shrugged. His face turned serious, the lines around his mouth deepening. "We have to keep punching, Preston. Somehow, we have to make all the blind bastards see. There'll be too damned many dead soldiers if we let them keep fucking up."

"It's our job," Belvale said, and held out his hand. "The family destiny has always been to protect and lead."

Boot heels banging on the parquet floor, Crusty stalked to the big double doors and hesitated there. He turned. "May God help us; we need it."

Belvale stared after his counterpart from the north, his blood and his friend. Then he nodded and slowly ground out the stub of his cigar in an ivory bowl. God sometimes heard the prayers of fighting men, of the holy warriors— Joshua and David, Samson and Blackjack Pershing.

Maybe God was listening this time.

CHAPTER 11

ASSOCIATED PRESS—Washington, D.C., September 25, 1939:
Legislators opposed to any sort of Lend-Lease program to
England are quoted as saying that Europe's wars are its
own, and that no American boys will be sacrificed on its
bloody battlefields.

General Preston Belvale hitched slowly across the rotunda
that resembled the dome of Thomas Jefferson's Monticello,
which wasn't all that far away. Kill Devil Hill shone in its
own beauty upon its own rich grass high ground overlook-
ing the Malboro River. But while Monticello was a shrine,
Kill Devil Hill was functional. The upper rotunda was set
up as a war room, its entire interior papered with maps, and
held blackboards and sand tables along the walls, a desk,
lectern and chairs grouped in the center. A teletype, a bank
of telephones and a radio transmitter-receiver waited within
easy reach behind the lectern. From the ballroom below,
only a smooth ceiling and magnificent crystal chandelier
could be seen. Upstairs, the room could be reached only by
passing through the master bedroom and a featureless door
in the bathroom, tiled to match the wall itself.

Propping his blackthorn cane, Belvale sat at his desk and
went through reports, neat folders containing information
from the field. Army intelligence wouldn't have as much,
he thought; if G-2 did, it wouldn't know what to do with
it. Kee-rist, even an old cavalryman knew when it was time

65

to give up horses. But the hidebound peacetime army plodded along, memorizing dusty tactics that were at least one war behind and not really expecting there would be another one. Certainly nobody was preparing for one. That man in the White House was pushing for a war, but not readying his troops or converting industry to military production, and this could become a cardinal sin.

Looking into the China folder, he thought that Keenan Carlisle was doing the best he could under what had to be heavy Japanese censorship. Crisp, succinct reports that detailed little but Japanese progress. But Keenan returned could deliver a detailed lecture on everything he had seen and heard. Perhaps he had more mixed Belvale blood than anyone knew. Kee-rist, at times the general thought that the family lines had been crisscrossed so often that if all the love affairs were known and the truth made readable, it was a book better closed and locked. Whatever those records would show was that the two original families had been made one, made stronger by selection, and by the tragic bloodletting of another, more tragic war. No matter the outside blood added from time to time, the older lines held true and became the keepers of the sword, or swordsmen waiting behind Sandhurst Keep. He rubbed his beat-up knee.

The files on Europe were thicker, the language more bookish and military. Chad Belvale tended to be a little stuffy, but was a good soldier anyhow. He got along well with the staid English and stiff-necked French. Belvale nodded and got up to touch a forefinger to the red pin and then the blue one on the map. In the days of boots and saddles, they would have been his distant eyes, scouting beyond the outposts of danger. Belvale sighed; life was simpler then, sweeter with the perfume of hay and the pleasant tang of horse sweat. Let Crusty Carlisle inhale gas and oil fumes; more effective, but then, so was chlorine gas.

Without the horse, Belvale believed that men would still be in caves. The horse gave of its strength and mobility, only to be gutted on battlefields or put down when it was old, no longer of any use. Maybe it would happen to General Preston Belvale some day. The army had put him out to pasture a long time back, but a man usually had a choice. He could stand in a corner of the field, seeking the warmth of the sun and waiting to die, or he could do what he was still capable of—which was a damned sight better than most of the book soldiers in the War Department. The Belvales had more than duty; they had long been entrusted with a mission.

Classify most of that Washington bunch and they'd be mules or horses' asses. The hell of it was, with armor improving daily, long-range artillery and mines reaching a new sophistication, the horse would still be sacrificed because most of the world's armies were still primitive; horse-drawn cannon for the Wermacht, despite its vaunted dive-bombers, and fancy-pants lancers for the Polish. As for the Russians, they were only a cut in intelligence above a rank horse. And it was only a short time ago that the U.S. cavalry had been phased out at Fort Huachuca, against objections, of course. Keenan reported on the tough Mongolian ponies the Japs used in China, and that the Chinese used anything that could pack a load—mostly their own peasant backs.

Leaning upon his cane, Belvale crossed the room to the stairs, comfortable in his whipcord breeches and worn cavalry boots scarred by long-gone spur straps. Yet, there was something about horse and rider blending, one eager entity really—bugler, sound the charge!—at the dead run, man and horse trusting each other and taking the same gamble. Ah, those army Morgans—all muscle and heart and good sense. It was good that one woman of this family felt the same about them. Often on the sly, Belvale liked to go by the stalls and just caress their sleek hides, have a quiet word with them. He couldn't do that with those damned thoroughbreds; flighty and rank, most of them; brains in their feet.

Downstairs, the grand ballroom of Kill Devil Hill gleamed with polished marble and burnished brass, faceted lights like so many diamonds rainbowed the floors and walls. Subtle spotlighting centered upon the ancient polished cut glass that hung point down within the central chandelier—

some said like the sword of Damocles—that backed the legend of the manor. The staff had done its usual superior job, and exotic odors wafting from the back of the house promised another table the mansion was famed for, almost as much as for its selection of fine whiskies and wines. For Washingtonians an invitation to Kill Devil Hill was a command performance.

For politicians from New York and Pennsylvania, Sandhurst Keep's invites were no less commanding but hardly as pleasing.

This night, Belvale would continue to chip away at bull-dog holders of congressional purse strings, to convince at least another isolationist legislator that the United States couldn't possibly stay out of the war already exploding around the world. Crusty Carlisle was setting things right in his state house before coming here to lend a hand.

Kirstin Belvale crossed the floor to him, a rangy woman whose stride was long, but her legs were made to match. If she wasn't tired or depressed, she always walked as if she were a woman with a destination. He had liked and admired Kirstin, since she first stood the family on its head by bringing in her Morgans rather than going along with the thoroughbred program that had made Kill Devil Hill more than comfortably rich. This year's crop of yearlings would bring millions at auction, especially since most were sired by Derby winners. But Kirstin would rather hang another halter championship ribbon in her tack room, or shelf another trophy for a performance win. Improve the breed, Kirstin said, not just the speed.

"Any word from Chad?" she asked. Kirstin was one of the few women who looked good in jodhpurs and knee-high hunter boots.

"Nothing but official chatter; you know how wordy he gets. He'll probably write you personally when he's settled in France."

"I'd rather he stayed in touch with the boys. They expect it; I don't, anymore."

One son at VMI; the compromise between Belvale and Carlisle. West Point and VMI both turned out top officers. Belvale had always considered Virginia Military Institute a shade better, certainly more gentlemanly and its campus far more beautiful. True, gentlemen warriors had ceased winning wars when the English longbow made armor obsolete at the Battle of Crecy, but a school that had known the boy soldiers who fought with Breckenridge in the Shenandoah, and the teachings of Stonewall Jackson showed a certain style even in defeat. After The War Between the States, perhaps Jackson's posthumous lessons were even stronger.

Belvale said, "You'll be at the party?"

She smiled, a special lighting up of her lean, freckled face, bringing a kind of sunshine glow to green eyes and cropped pale hair. Again he thought his grandson was lucky to have married this woman and produced two sons by her. Chad would be even luckier to keep her. Not one of the family's go-along women, she was about at the end of her picket line, but maybe Chad would be back in time to see it and take hold.

"I invited some horse show people with connections. I'll see to them while Minerva presides over her Tidewater families." Smile fading, she scissored those long legs to the other side of the ballroom and up the winding staircase, passing heavily framed portraits that slanted at left oblique to the second floor. More family paintings continued down the main hall at dress right. Belvale sighed; Kirstin had not yet sat for her portrait, and neither had Nancy Carlisle. Possibly that portended something. He didn't like Keenan's wife so much, but gave her credit for standing fast against the family and refusing to live at the mansion in conflict, especially with Minerva's sniffing.

Minerva Belvale would soon sweep in from the kitchen, all haughtiness and crisp rustlings, supreme widow of the clan and determined to stay that way. So Preston Belvale leaned on his cane and hitched swiftly for a lower corridor that would take him to his room. Minerva was often a pain under the crupper with damned little trying. Working the hallowed halls of military Washington, she'd pushed a reluctant Robert Belvale up through the ranks to a full colonelcy. Belvale closed his door behind him and sighed. His brother's eagles had arrived in time to get him killed at Bellieu Wood. Robert had never been a real combat man, but a whiz at cutting red tape administration. Often that was more important than gunfire.

Maybe loving Minerva had been even more important to Robert, which was enough for Preston to honor his brother's memory through her.

In the bathroom, Belvale showered and thought of what the army needed. Army, hell—air corps and navy as well. The marines would always make do with their major asset, men. But the corps needed expansion, because if—or when—the Japs came slamming across the Pacific, the marines would be few against too damned many.

Out of the shower, he carefully trimmed his little cavalry mustache and rubbed his bum knee with horse liniment before climbing into the tuxedo laid out for him.

There had been a moment in time when he had considered the cross insignias rather than the sabers of the cavalry. That might have turned him into a sanctimonious bastard like Col. Luther C. Farrand. The family's calling was higher than simple religion, a thing holier and perhaps even older; especially a religion corrupted by men like Farrand.

His mirror light winked twice, so he went through the bathroom wall and slipped into the war room of Kill Devil Hill. There he ripped a sheet off the teletype and stared at it for a long moment. Tidily then, he folded and tucked it into his breast pocket. The news was only ten days overdue, so Keenan must have somehow made a friend or found an officer with a little sense of duty left over from emperor worship.

Minerva put out a jeweled hand to stop him when he started out the door that led to the garages. "Preston—where are you going? Our guests will arrive in minutes—"

"Kee-rist, woman," he said, "don't push it. You see to the goddamn guests because I'm going into Fairfax. I have to tell Nancy Carlisle that Keenan is carried missing in action somewhere in China."

CHAPTER 12

INTERNATIONAL NEWS SERVICE—Hong Kong, October 5, 1939: British sources here said today that fighting in the interior has reached a fever pitch between Japanese and Chinese communist forces. General Chiang Kai-shek's Kuomintang armies seem to be standing aside and awaiting final results.

UNITED PRESS—Washington, D.C., October 6, 1939: State Department officials announced today that President Roosevelt's embargoes against Imperial Japan will remain in effect until Japan pulls its troops completely out of China. No pullout, no more oil, FDR commented around a no-nonsense angle of his cigarette holder.

Nancy Carlisle took two steps backward and dropped onto the couch. The news shouldn't hit her this hard; even if the country wasn't at war, there was always a hundred ways for a soldier to die. It often happened on maneuvers or in plane crashes, in tank and vehicle smashups. She sat on her couch and stared at the upturned palms of her hands as if she could see an answer there, but there were only lines crisscrossing and ending nowhere.

"Kee-rist!" General Belvale said. "You're still in love with Keenan."

She made her hands into small fists and looked at him dressed in party finery. "Damnit! Is that against regulations, too? Department of the Army or Kill Devil Hill? I never know which is more official."

He looked over at the sideboard and she told him to pour them both one.

A little guilt nicked her for snarling at him; it was evident he'd left one of the grand affairs at the mansion to drive over and tell her personally. It was just damned difficult to be gracious with any of the family. About the only one she could share things with was Kirstin, and that wasn't often because Kirstin was either busy training her horses or gone with them on the show circuit.

The general handed her a glass of bourbon neat, one ice cube. "Thanks," she said, and added, "I'm sorry. It's just that—oh, damnit; I just got a real letter from him, his field report sort of thing, but this time he said something about our taking a furlough together and signed it with love. With love. He never did that before."

"Here's to Keenan's luck holding," the general said, lifting his glass.

"Or something like," she said, and tossed off her drink. That was becoming easier to do, downing two fingers of bourbon without making a face.

"Nobody is sure he's dead, Nancy; missing is different, and it's primitive country, difficult to get news out. Keenan made some sort of close contact in China or we wouldn't have heard yet, if at all. Getting close to some Jap officer isn't an easy thing, so if there's any other information—"

Nancy got up and went to the whiskey bottle. The general shook his head and she poured herself a big one this time. "I thank you for coming yourself," she said, "but then, you sent him there yourself, didn't you?"

"He wanted the job, and we need his kind of keen observation. It's all closer than you know, girl, closer than anyone thinks. We're trying not to get caught with our pants all the way down." He strode to the sideboard and helped himself. "You married a soldier, which means you also married the army and this family. What would Keenan be like selling insurance or polishing a horse?"

"Alive," she said.

"Walking around, maybe; to be truly alive, a man must reach above himself, above the ordinary."

She flared at him, the whiskey warm in her stomach. "Only because the goddamned family—the glorious family—made him that way. That nursery: no duckies or kittens, just regimental colors and guidons, bugles and sabers. It's not a nursery. It's a battalion command post, centering around a cross, yet—as if there's something holy about murder and suicide."

He touched his mustache and she saw him shift weight from his bad knee. "It's what we must do, Nancy, what makes us what we are and why we're born. I wish you could have seen that early on; I wish I could explain it better. The women are so important to their men, to the family itself."

"They also serve who only sit and wait and pray? I might have been partly content with that, if only—"

"Minerva is such a double-barreled bitch," he said, surprising her as if he had slapped her. "She should have been named Medusa, or at the least, Cassandra. Before I knew what was going on between you, you moved out. Few of us understand Minerva or even want to, but she has her job like everyone else. Minerva was a Lee—Robert E. branch; her family connections are important to this family at times. Besides that, my brother loved her very much. That makes her acceptable—but only to a point.

"I never rejoiced at Keenan's choice of a wife because you weren't military, but by God, I respected you for your backbone."

"I-I'm glad you said—said that." Before she realized it, she was in his arms, her head against his hard chest. No matter how he was dressed, he smelled of uniforms. "Do Carlisle women cry?"

"Hell, yes; Carlisle men, too, but usually when they're off where nobody sees. Ask a Carlisle or Belvale, you do what you damned well want. What I would like you to do—and I'm sure Keenan agrees with me—is to come back to the Hill. Minerva knows how far she can go if I yank on the picket line and you'll be right there when word comes through on Keenan."

"Oh, I can't do that. It's not only Minerva, but—"

"Once more, please let me try to explain my brother's widow. I loved him and Minerva pushed him into the field where he didn't belong. He was killed because of it, because of her. I meant to throw her out, but Robert was a move ahead of me. In paperwork, he always was. His will gave me their love letters. He knew damned well I'd have to make her hostess of the Hill, and the official historian and the Spartan bitch wolf who suckles the young. Forget Minerva, girl; come on home."

Gently, she pushed away from him. "Is there really a chance that Keenan is alive somewhere in China? I'll have to think about coming back, General, think real hard."

Rubbing a hand over his brush cut, he said, "That's all I ask, girl."

With his old-fashioned heel click and the hint of a civilian bow that took the place of his military salute, the general left. Nancy sat a while before filling her glass again. She was getting numb, but not pleasantly so. Had it shown on her face when the old man brought the news? Maybe it was simply a gut reaction and not love for Keenan, missing and soon to be presumed dead. She knew that much about the army.

Keenan dead; no body to bring back to the family grove for the honors, the rifles and three volleys; the flag from the coffin folded triangularly and presented to the widow. If he'd had a son, the boy would hold the flag while the bugler's taps echoed mournfully over the long rows of simple white headstones. In the Civil War, some poet had called a military cemetery "The Bivouac of the Dead."

Jesus Christ, that's how they set up the next generation of soldiers, with pomp and circumstance that made being murdered an honor. Acceptance at the Hill would be nearly impossible because she had not borne them a replacement and never could. Why the hell should she go back, for any reason?

Because she'd be a widow and unable to live on the pittance the grateful army would pay. Skills? She had none, although she was developing one as a drinker. Waitress, salesclerk, she'd sold Keenan a jacket when they met, but she couldn't go back to fifteen dollars a week. She probably couldn't even be a hooker. Too much competition from the V-girls and she was too long out of practice with sex. That had been so good at first, before losing the baby, sex so good there seemed to be nothing in the world to match it, to equal them in their loving.

Minerva said he had merely done his duty as a gentleman by marrying her after she became pregnant. Otherwise, Minerva sniffed, Nancy would never have been invited to the Hill.

Nancy slopped whiskey over her glass. "That's your story, you old bitch. Maybe I never wanted to see the place!"

She held her glass high. "Keenan, you dirty bastard, whether I still love you or not, don't be dead. Damn you, don't be dead."

Nancy sold the furniture to the first bidder from a secondhand store, and threw in the unused layette. The rest of her things went into the "woody," the 1939 Ford station wagon bought last year before Keenan shipped out. She didn't have much to load: her dresses and Keenan's civvies, a few personal mementoes: a handful of pictures and only three saved-back letters from before she married Keenan Carlisle. If Minerva Belvale, starched mistress of the Hill, ever saw those letters, she'd be shocked to her heart, if she had one. They weren't pornographic, exactly, but heated and descriptive in what Keenan had found with her when they were so damned young and excitable with the explorations of each other's bodies.

She was returning to the Hill, but this time, when Minerva got pushy, there'd be an eyeball-to-eyeball confrontation. If the old bitch was too Tidewater Virginia to know the four letter words, she had lessons coming. That should be the quickest way to break off the combat. She looked out the car window at hills that had seen so much real and bloody combat. They had recovered from the agonies and so could she.

Any time of the year, Virginia was beautiful; so many shades of green and the hazy blues that clung to softened mountains. Spring and fall, the colors rioted in blazes of incomparable glory—the Shenandoah Valley, the Blue Ridge Mountains. Even winter seemed awed by the seasons gone before and was seldom black and dreary. Nancy breathed warm air as she drove, tasting late springtime and the hint of richer summer spices to come.

Was Keenan tasting the bitter flavors of his own grave? Would he even have a grave? It might have been premonition that made him sign that last letter with love. At least it meant he had been thinking of her, and damnit, she could have been kinder and not identified him so much with his family. Our family, she thought, turning the Ford gently along a sweeping curve where dogwood trees overhung the road. She meant to give it a good try, just as she meant to cling to the belief that her husband was alive; MIA wasn't the same as KIA, the general said.

CHAPTER 13

ASSOCIATED PRESS—October 7, 1939, on the road with General Chiang Kai-shek, from somewhere in China: The general's forces, in hot pursuit of yet another communist bandit group, are closing on what he calls the "murderers of Shutai," a remote mountain village where a massacre recently took place. More American aid, money and supplies, especially support from the air and additional armor, would prevent repetition of such bloody events, the general said.

He had trouble with his eyes. They would blur in and unfocus, and in between, there was a face. Keenan was pretty sure he was stretched out on his back and that the ground was rocky. The face hung above him like a dirty yellow balloon, flat on one side.

Could it be Colonel Watanbe? If so, how in hell did they get out of the classic ambush set in the village of—of Shutai? Two bloodings in a row for Watanabe's legions, but he could only be faulted for this one, and he'd made his attack perfectly by the book. If he'd committed *seppuku* like his former commanding officer, why was his head floating around up there? The face came suddenly and sharply into focus, the center one of three not Japanese; grimy faces and narrowed eyes watching him, muddied and sleazy uniforms. Oh, shit—Chinese!

He tried to sit up and his stomach gurgled warning. His head threatened to split down the back. He gagged, and hands helped him, lifted him to sit. The center fielder stuck a lighted cigarette between his dry lips and Keenan sucked upon it. Mistake. It was horse shit rolled in a corn shuck. He gagged again and the same guy handed him a small gourd sawed in half to make a cup. Rice whiskey, odorous as if it had been distilled in a gut bucket, but it was strengthening. This time, the cigarette didn't taste as bad; maybe it was registered thoroughbred horse shit wrapped in rice paper.

He swayed. Something had caught him a king-size lick on the back of the head, mortar fragment, bullet swipe, gun butt? It didn't matter. They had his ass and he could only hope the torture would be short before they shot him or hung him to a tree. At least they carried no samurai swords and his head probably wouldn't get lopped off.

"Oh, shit," he mumbled, "as if that matters a good goddamn. Nobody will ever find the body, anyhow." Wouldn't that screw up the family's traditional procession through its own cemetery? Probably not; they'd arrange it anyhow, the black horse with boot toes turned backward in the stirrups, with an empty coffin or an urn supposedly containing heroic ashes.

"American," the middle guy said. "No Japanese." Comic movie accent, *R* changing to *L,* not funny now.

Carefully, Keenan said, "Observer, see Japanese fight, report Washington."

It was the lick on the head he'd taken. Speaking pidgin. "We fought the Russians."

"Chinese, also."

Thank God he hadn't personally fired on this bunch; more thanks if anybody had noticed. But Christ himself testifying wouldn't help; they might ask who He was before they shot Him down.

"My assignment is with the Japanese."

"You fight Kuomintang?" The middle man's eyes were no more readable than his buddies, his uniform no cleaner, thin cheeks showing no extra rations. Yet Keenan couldn't shake the feeling that he was an officer, probably field grade.

"No. I saw them from far away." He raised his hands to mimic field glasses. His stomach dared him again and the officer gave him another drag on the road apple cigarette. "Always in the cities, never in the mountains."

It was the right answer. They all laughed, and that looked good to him, because he was feeling around for any straw. Could anybody float on a single straw?

"Hong," the speaker said, tapping his chest.

Me Tarzan, you Jane—or some white monkey we're about to skin and stuff.

"Carlisle, Keenan Carlisle, captain, United States Army."

Hong made that sharp, indrawn hiss between his teeth, the noise all Orientals came up with when surprised, shocked or delighted. Keenan hoped for the last.

"Officer; good. You know Mao Tse-tung?"

"I've heard of him. Communist leader."

"Mao Tse-tung soon lead all free China; Chairman Mao." Hong rolled another cigarette and offered it. Keenan shook his head and it wobbled painfully upon his loose neck. He closed his eyes, unwilling to show weakness. Hong said something in multitoned Chinese to his side men; eight tones for Cantonese, four for Mandarin? Keenan couldn't remember; he knew one thing for damned-bigod-sure, as they said in Virginia: the U.S. had better build a reservoir of linguists, without delay. That was something that General Belvale had missed, although his interpreters were liable to be rabbinical or evangelistic.

Then Hong said, "You no shoot soldiers. You try stop Japanese dog kill old men, women, young ones. So. You live; now; maybe-so die on road, but live now."

"What road?" When Keenan fought his eyes open again, Hong's flank guards were gone and he realized that he was in a small, dank, but reasonably cool cave. The woman ducked through the narrow rock opening; same uniform—if that's what it could be called—but clean. She carried an aid bag of sorts; her hair was cropped short and shiny. She kneeled behind him and did hurtful things to his head. He swallowed as her fingers probed his skull, and despite himself, a little steam whistle of pain escaped.

Then he held tight, his fingers digging into his thighs and Hong and the woman spoke. Then Hong said, "Chang Yen

Ling speak good. I tell her speak you; she no want, but she soldier also."

In a decided English accent, Yen Ling said, hard voiced, "I have informed Comrade Major Hong that your wound should not be fatal."

"Where did you learn——"

"All foreigners show great surprise that a lowly Chinese woman could possibly absorb anything mental, especially white language or complicated nursing. Would you prefer I speak pidgin? You catchee Hong Kong, Sailor? You catchee clean Chinee girl berry cheap?"

Major Hong spoke sharply to her.

Yen Ling returned to cleansing and bandaging his head. "Basically, you are alive because Leader Mao wishes it. He has tried to make official contact with your government, but has been ignored. Perhaps a personal emissary can make your leaders understand. I doubt that."

Eyes squeezed against the pain, against the weakness in his stomach, Keenan said, "If it's something I can do, I will try. We are a military family known in Washington."

She moved around him upon her knees, a slim, erect woman with flinty eyes. In a different place and time, she might be called beautiful. "Now you say. You are afraid and will promise anything to preserve your precious white skin." With a jerk, she knotted the bandage across his forehead.

Major Hong held out the gourd refilled with smelly rot-gut, and an even smaller bowl of plain, lumped together rice. Keenan drank down the whiskey, and after Yen Ling rose to her feet, said: "Goddamnit! I heard that same white skin bullshit from the Japs. It's too goddamned bad if you were a Hong Kong whore or whatever. Am I afraid? Hell, yes; any soldier not afraid in combat is an idiot. But fear doesn't stop a true soldier from doing his job. As for your bullshit, piss off! You catchee that?"

Her indrawn breath was a hiss of hate, and she stormed out, but Hong laughed; he had understood enough of the exchange.

"No matter, soldier, woman is woman. Eat now, Officer. Japanese or Kuomintang come soon."

Whatever happy Florence Nightingale had done to his head, it felt some better. Maybe it was the booze; whatever, he was able to finger scoop and down the rice. He had a hunch he would need all the strength he could muster. Hong nodded when he got one knee under himself, then the other. One hand against the cave wall, Keenan struggled up and stood there dizzy.

Hong nodded. "Good. Can help, but fight again, no help."

"I understand," Keenan said. "I'll make it."

Or die on the road, but that would beat hanging or a firing squad, or a samurai sword edge. Japs chasing them now or the other Chinese led by the generalissimo. What the hell? Who was minding the store and fighting the Japanese?

His garrison cap had gotten smashed when his head did, and Hong passed him a peasant's conical straw hat, with Keenan's belt and canteen, but no weapon. Moving unsteadily and a little rocky, he went outside to see no more than a platoon of ragged-ass soldiers stringing out over a cut in the mountains. No Shutai village was in sight, so they must have hauled him unconscious for miles, and again he wondered about Watanabe. Nobody could ever like the little bastard, but at least Keenan had been coming close to understanding him and his warrior's code. Now he had to change his focus and concentrate upon these lowest of soldiers, ill equipped and near to starving. They fought damned well—like the Belvale and Carlisle farmer-soldiers before they became aristocrats.

Indian tactics, he thought, as one man cupped his elbow and handed him a stick to help support himself. Major Hong hurried along the line of march, heading for the front of the column. Indian tactics: ambush, hit and run; stand to battle superior numbers only when trapped and desperate. It made sense, and could be damned frustrating to the enemy. Face down as the sun's heat hammered upon the marching men, Keenan was grateful for the straw hat, for the weight of water in his canteen, but as he had done with the Japs, he refused to break water discipline and would not take a swallow until they did. He must earn respect here, too.

He wobbled a time or two and staggered once, dropping

his stick, but there was always the helping hand at his elbow, and the heat did him good. It was dry and dusty, a gritty taste in the mouth and a gummy buildup around his eyes. But it warmed his head and kept clearing it a little more, a little more.

Not like the humid air of Virginia in midsummer, and that tasting of bluegrass, always some flower scent drifting upon soft wind. The horses looked painted against softly rolling hillsides until one lifted his head to look at him, or until the grazing band strolled on to seek a stand-up nap in the shade of live oaks and dogwood, loblolly pines and sweetgum.

"Eyeh!" his helper said, or something like it, and Keenan caught himself. The column had stopped in another narrow defile, seeking cover from the air. This arroyo had a pool of muddy water beneath a crusted boulder. Keenan saw men scooping rags into the green-brown stuff and squeezing them over open mouths. He thought of typhoid and other unpleasant wiggly things. Why didn't Miss Smartass nurse warn them, put a stop to it? Then he realized that this must be a normal situation, and these soldiers were both tough and desperate.

Guilty, he took a long, cooling swallow from his canteen, then offered it to the stooped little farmer type who had been helping him walk. Eyes going wide, the man shook his head, but Keenan gurgled the canteen at him again and smiled. Carefully, the little man accepted the water and took a sip. When he handed it back, he smiled with all six of his teeth and dipped his head in a quick bow.

Christ, the guy must be fifty or sixty years old, scrawny and old and living tightly within his shrunken self to keep pace with the young men. The old man's weapon was slung across his back. It looked like an antique musket, but had a bolt. The man rolled them both cigarettes and squinted up at the sun, measuring the day against his wrinkles. Keenan stared at the gunstock, the rough barrel; the thing had been handmade in some tiny city room, some farmer's hovel, put together to fit whatever ammunition was available, Russian, Japanese or Kuomintang. It would fire, inaccurately, to be sure, but it was a weapon, and stout as the wiry old guy who carried it.

These people meant to fight, and for a moment, Keenan felt inadequate, even with a lifetime's indoctrination behind him. The war here was also holy, though he wondered if any of these men had ever seen an altar. Major Hong's timing had been perfect; by the time a Japanese scout plane flew across their crease in the earth, the mountain held them in a cover of dark shadow from the sun. The plane circled slow and lazy, peeping and prying but finding nothing, and after awhile it flew away.

Nurse Chang Yen Ling kneeled beside him. Saying nothing, she peeled his rag bandage free and smeared burning stuff upon his wound, a grease that stank strongly of camphor. When she tied back the bandage, she didn't jerk the knot. The old man said something to her and she shrugged.

"Father Lim says you share water with him. How democratic."

"Communistic," Keenan said, for the hell of it.

She rose and stalked away, and he could see that her aid kit was almost flat. For some reason, her angry walk brought his wife to mind, almost identical to the way that Nancy had slammed out of the Hill that day, swearing never to return.

He sat with forehead resting upon his bent knees, and when he looked up, the old man had a cooling muddy rag ready for his face. Keenan thanked the man, tone and smile getting his message across. But the rest period was short and they filtered out of the narrow canyon to climb a long and weary slope.

When he got back to Virginia, he would go directly to Nancy and try again, try harder, to explain the family to her, and ask—beg, if he must—to return to the Hill where she would be protected and cared for. It was something he should have done long ago. And if she still wouldn't go? Then it was his duty, secondary perhaps, but obligatory all the same, to be with his wife. Cleaving only unto each other in this case meant within the set parameters of the Carlisle-Belvale family, keepers of the sword, guardians of the Keep. Jesus, at times it got too much for the men of the family. It had to be pure hell on the women. He would compromise and share himself. The family-crossed bloodlines were revered; heraldry charts and lineal graphs going back into dim history, past lance and mace into the conquering era of the efficient short sword and bronze greaves.

So adoption from outside was not approved; who knew what strange and weakening blood could enter the holy throbbing of the family stream? But when the country got pulled into this war—and it would—there would be family orphans.

Nancy would be a good mother, given the opportunity, as she had been a wondrous bride and why the hell hadn't he told her these things before? The old man tugged at his arm and Keenan pressed the heel of one hand to his forehead. He'd been drifting. He looked ahead where the old guy pointed at the crest of the long, steepened slope. The platoon was fanning out into a ragged line of skirmishers, which meant that big trouble lay just over the ridge top.

The old man motioned for him to remain and lie down, and unslung his handmade weapon. Keenan settled his straw hat more firmly upon his head and followed. The old man hesitated, then grinned his few teeth and trotted ahead.

Well, Keenan thought, he still might get the chance to tell Nancy Carlisle what she was entitled to hear from him.

The firefight broke out before he climbed twenty yards and he heard the first high buzz of a bullet. It would be a damned shame if he became a casualty now, perhaps deserved for him but totally unfair to her.

CHAPTER 14

AGENCE FRANCE PRESSE—Yenan, China, October 10, 1939: It is here, the seat of the Red Chinese government, that what is being called "The Long March" ended. The communist leader, Chairman Mao Tse-tung, fleeing from General Chiang Kai-shek's Kuomintang armies in 1934, fought to survive against double pronged attacks by Japanese invaders since 1937, and by their fellow Chinese. Now, say the Reds, they have four fiercely battling armies spread far in the field, and they will run no more.

Keenan Carlisle felt that he had traveled across the world already, on foot, by ox cart and sometimes by downhill wagon. But he'd stopped asking how much farther they had to go. China was limitless and nurse Yen Ling enjoyed being sarcastic about any foreign devil who could not hold his unseemly emotions in check. Impatience, she said, was a failing of the capitalists. Keenan had heard that before, rephrased somewhat by the Japanese.

Capitalists, he retorted, had little need for patience, since they traveled much faster than any primitive barbarian who had not yet used automobiles, trains and airplanes. How long had China had use of the wheel, he asked; when had they discovered fire?

Yen Ling would snap and trot away; the Chinese major would laugh, enjoying the discomfort of a woman better educated and more fluent in English, although technically she was a comrade. She was still only a woman, and even the great revolution would not raise them from the lowly level where time and Confucius had so carefully placed them.

The country had changed and changed again, the snowy mountains, the great grasslands, dry plains, and all the while, this ragged column listening and watching for Jap fighter bombers, for Kuomintang P-40s with the yellow sun on their wings. The fried egg or the flaming asshole wing insignia; both were to be feared and avoided.

There had been no brush with enemy troops of any persuasion for a long time, but the constant road march had taken its toll on Keenan's uniform. He was thankful his shoes had held out, the solid boondockers issued a world and a millennium away at his Governors Island garrison. The rest of him looked Chinese, from the straw coolie hat to his own blouse and shirt patched with whatever rags came handy. His pants were baggy peasant trousers, and the sun had baked him dark. He might pass, if he kept his eyes down and could speak a little Chinese. But translation still had to be left to nurse Yen Ling, and she talked no more than necessary, except for the angry lectures that were growing farther apart.

At the nightly cook-fires, he would sometimes catch her watching him, or thought he did. Firelight reflection could twist and blot, tilt and magnify, and maybe he was looking too hard, seeking depths that had never left the shallows. She always seemed beautiful then, a little tired, her face relaxed when she combed the thick wealth of her midnight hair.

"What the hell am I thinking?" Keenan murmured to the starry sky and night wind that whispered of soft grasses and softnesses beyond. He knew damned well what he thought when he watched Yen Ling's body slide exotically around within her loose clothing. But he still had some good sense left. She would pop a sharp knife through him without thinking twice. Yen Ling probably would have already done it, if not for her orders. It wasn't only capitalists she hated, but all white men. Still, he fantasized.

Hey there, Nancy. He sent the thought winging homeward —hey, I'm not a cold fish. You might have made me like that for a while, but I'm growing out of it. I can look with lust upon this woman and feel no guilt; I can feel this surge in my groin and believe there can be no hurt to it for a woman, no disgrace for a family. Look around you, woman: even this desperate, hungry tribe is a family. We are herd animals, Nancy, like our horses; we need to be together, stay together, share the bad as well as celebrate the good. We have to encircle the young like buffalo and keep our heads down, our horns pointed at the wolves.

Was Nancy still around? Everyone back home probably thought he was dead, and that would be a perfect reason for her to walk. She hated the family enough to grab a quick, uncontested divorce. All right, she had something of cause. Still, to be part of the Belvale-Carlisle clan, to remain with it, you had to be tough inside.

There is much good in our family, Nancy/wife/woman. We guard, we protect. Do you even know the Belvale motto, the words we have lived by for so many years? I didn't force them upon you, but you might have learned on your own, walking through the great hall at Kill Devil Hill. How could you not feel the weight of echoed centuries? How could you not hear the tattered banners whisper of broad sword and lance, of duty that extended beyond armor and uniforms, beyond the scattered tombs of a thousand Belvale-Carlisles and twice that many unmarked graves?

A runner trotted to the head of the column, a squat man dripping sweat that marked his leathery cheeks with small zigzag rivulets. Major Hong trotted back with him, calling for Yen Ling. Now her name always sounded clear to Keenan, even said in the complicated tonal language system. Had they passed close to another group of Red Chinese, a group that had been in a firefight and needed what medical skills she could offer?

"No," she told him, her face more mobile than usual. "Japanese troops have penetrated this far into our land and we must stop them."

"How many—a company, a battalion?"

"Ming Yat Sun says he counted perhaps two thousand men and six tanks."

"Holy shit," Keenan said, "and you're going to stop them with this ragtag bunch of farmers? Hell, how many men do we have—twenty or so?"

"They must be enough."

"And no heavy weapons."

"That too must be endured."

Major Hong said something and went to see to the carts, the ponies and single wagon. Swiftly, they were being pulled off the road into a gulley, to be covered with dry grass and brush, scoops of red-brown dust.

Yen Ling said, "Comrade major says to tell you this is the method of the People's Army, and asks that you observe closely, so that you may take the information back to your masters in Rice Country."

"Let's hope somebody gets back somewhere," Keenan said. They had at last given him a 1903 Springfield and fifteen rounds. He would bet the weapon hadn't been zeroed in and the cartridge cases were green with age. But like the man said, it was a chance to learn something; living long enough to use the knowledge was something else.

"Captain," Yen Ling said, stuffing her first aid kit with rag bandages, willow leaves and bark, and a bottle of fiery native whiskey. "In Hong Kong, I was not a bar girl prostitute, but a cook, a maid and nanny. I had to earn money for school. So my British gentleman employer turned me into his personal whore."

Keenan felt his eyebrows crawl up. A confession from comrade Iron Nurse? More, an explanation, but why now and why to him, one of the despised species?

"I wanted you to know," she murmured, looking not at him, but busily into the contents of her bag. "I know you have been watching me at the fires, and I feel your eyes touch me when I walk past. This cannot be, and when the mission is over, I will explain why not."

"You being raped doesn't mean a damned thing, but I think you're married now," he said, feeding the verdigreed clip of five rounds to the battered Springfield, sliding the bolt home and thumbing up the safety.

"No."

Then she was hurrying up the slope to the right of the road, climbing east. Keenan and the old man who was his bodyguard/friend tugged at his sleeve, then backed off and bowed apology. It turned lonely on the road, so Keenan moved uphill after the troops—the reinforced suicide squad that meant to stop two thousand Japs and six tanks.

He didn't catch up with Yen Ling and the major until an hour later, when his tongue was hanging out and his knees wobbly. The men were spread loosely through ragged brush that barely gave them cover. He had to admire the way they could become one with the earth and rocks. The ridgeline here was choppy, mostly a rotten shale mixed with slate and some dark granite boulders. Bellied down at Hong's wave of the hand, Keenan peered over the edge and saw the enemy column, a dangerous centipede long and fat, raising dust with every footbeat; a great, poisonous centipede protected by powerful small dragons gone ahead.

Only the tail end tank was in sight when Keenan heard the rumble, the earth-moving roar that slid down into the narrow valley. Head turned, he saw an upspin of dust that rose higher and thicker than that lifted by marching troops.

"Be damned," he said, "you pried the mountain down on the Jap tanks."

The getaway tank, safe from the landslide that had buried some of its fellows and knocked others sidewise off the road, swung its turret and blindly raked the ridges with cannon fire. Strung out behind it, Jap infantry squatted while officers stood uncertainly but bravely, according to the code of *Bushido*.

Major Hong fired, and far down at the rear of the column, a man fell. More rifle fire bit down into the Japanese rear. Keenan opened his mouth to ask why the rear of the formation instead of the front, but clamped his teeth. Hell, it made perfect sense. Look how the Japs swung into a defense formation to guard against this attack from behind.

By the time they also laid down a field of fire on the ridges while one company spread out as skirmishers to attack, men at the forward edge of the column began falling. Keenan couldn't hear the Chinese rifles because of the heavy volume of Jap return, but he realized that Major Hong had split his small force and not only inflicted casualties, but confused hell out of the Japanese. They milled around below like pine beetles whose bark cover had been removed.

Keenan set the rear sights of the 03 and lined the fine blade front sight on an officer waving a sword. Hesitating for a split second, he thought: no, that can't be Watanabe. Still, the man was Japanese, and he had in a fashion, begun to understand them, even to admire some of their qualities. But he hated others, and squeezed off a shot. The butt plate slapped his shoulder and reminded him this was the recoil of a Springfield, not a gentle, gas-fed M-1. The officer's sword boomeranged high into the air, spinning around and around as the Jap fell.

Even as the familiar tang of powder smoke touched his lips, Yen Ling said: "Now run with us!" Her voice was sharp but not shaky. As he rolled onto his knees and lifted to follow her, he realized what a veteran she was, wondered how many times she had reenacted this ambush scene. Trotting low, he heard the spiteful whine of Jap 25 calibers too high and tasted excitement, knew the sweat scent left drifting behind a woman running ahead, a strange kind of perfume that he drew deep.

Ducking, twisting along a path through stunted pines, Keenan saw his group catching up with the others. Glad for the chance to catch his breath, he hunkered down beside Yen Ling and stared at what the Chinese were laying out through a clearing and into thinner trees. He had thought that the spare coolie hats, the bundles of rags were the major's quartermaster supplies, pitiful as they might be. Instead, the men were putting together dummies of sticks and hats and spread rags that might look like a group of men under sparse cover, caught suddenly out in the open by—Japanese air!

He had no time to say anything to Yen Ling; the Chinese

were off and double-timing again, downhill this time, taking a slight angle of march that would in time veer them back to the goat path road where their shabby equipment was camouflaged. Hong was one smart son of a bitch, Keenan thought; the Japs had probably already radioed for air strikes, not knowing what they were up against, pissed by the loss of modern tanks to primitive granite boulders rolled down steep mountainsides. Zeroes would buzz in low to search out the opposition, strafe and bomb and pin down until the Imperial infantry could get up the mountain and start killing. The planes would spot the dummies and riddle them, radio to the ground that the Chinese had been fleeing due east. Hong was actually moving out almost due west.

Scooping a pebble from the ground, Keenan tucked it between his lower lip and teeth. Then he concentrated on keeping up with Hong's band, following close behind Yen Ling. Her lithe hips rolled beneath her worn and dusty pants; uncomplaining, she carried her medic bag plus a short carbine that might have come from the Franco-Prussian war. She was Nightingale and the Huntress Diana in one. Just being near her made him shaky.

Before twilight, moving at a slower pace, Keenan heard the Jap air attack far to the rear, sounding like toy planes and cheap firecrackers. The column came out of the rough and onto the road almost exactly on target, only a hundred yards from where the ponies and carts waited. His respect for Major Hong mounted.

They did not move out immediately, and two Zeroes ran the road without spotting them in their gulley. The planes then zoomed and arced away to the east to look for more of the great force that had stopped their army in its tracks, searching while light was left to them.

Hong moved them three hours up the road after dark, and at last into another narrow canyon that smelled wonderfully of water. Hong also had a nose like a desert burro, Keenan thought. He could find the merest trickle of water to sustain his troops.

Of course it was a cold camp, not a flicker of firelight; cold rice rolled in cabbage leaves, generous gulps of cool, sweet water. Keenan didn't sense Yen Ling's nearness until after he had stretched out upon his single, thin quilt. Wide-eyed and staring up, he made out the upper outline of her body blotting out the stars.

"I have come to explain," she whispered, feather light.

"So long as you're here." She didn't quite catch the meaning and asked him to repeat. "For whatever reason," he said, "I'm very glad you're here."

"Thank you. It has been long since any man looked at me as a woman—a woman his equal, not his whore or as a lower status decreed by gods and our ancestors. But I must tell you, Captain, explain as best I can why nothing more can pass between us."

Waiting, Keenan flowed with the murmured cadences of words meant only for him, spoken so quietly that sleeping camp sounds threatened to overcome them. He wanted to reach up for her, to draw her down to him, but was wiser than that.

"Just the word *sex* has always been dirty to Chinese. Kissing, caressing—these things are almost unknown between husband and wife. The bedroom is an embarrassment, and there is never touching in public. I have heard old scholars claim that sex is actually repugnant to them, and if any woman dares show pleasure in the act, she is worse than an animal."

Her voice was edged with tears, and Keenan wondered about the love affair that brought them; surely not the gentleman-rapist in Hong Kong. To help dry them he said, "So why are there so many, many Chinese?"

"Duty," she whispered. "It is especially the husband's duty to make children, and especially sons to continue the family name and please his ancestors." Her voice trembled, the first time he'd heard her do that. "Do you know there are still thousands of women in my country whose feet are crippled from binding, who cannot walk without assistance?"

"Your feet were never bound." Gently he said it: "And neither is your heart, I think; perhaps once it was, but no more."

Leaning back and away from him, her outline blotted out

many stars and the night was darker. "You do not have the soul of a soldier, although I saw you kill a Japanese today, and it is said that you sent many Russians to their ancestors. You have the soul of—of—"

Still quietly, afraid to disturb her, to frighten her away, he said, "Communists still believe in souls, then?"

"Inner spirit, a thing that lives now, not in some opiate and untouchable heaven."

"And the man who bound your heart so tightly?" He heard the indrawn warning hiss of her breath, and caught her hand before she could rise and leave him. "If you don't wish me to touch you, say it, Yen Ling."

She did not take away her hand. It was strong and capable, calloused in little places, but warm, warm. She said, so soft that he scarce could hear: "My—lover was killed by the Kuomintang, and I thought—I believed that I could never—"

"Yen Ling," he whispered, and gently, ever so gently, drew her down beside him on the quilt. Conscious that they were in the open, that she had taken much care to warn him of Chinese mores, Keenan simply held her.

It was not that damned simple. Her slim strength throbbed against the full length of his body, a richly promising feast for the starvation of his own body and soul; inner spirit, if that's what hungered. Tenderly, he kissed her throat just beneath the ear, and moved his lips slowly along the line of her jaw and over her chin to her lips. His hands stroked her hair, her shoulders, lightly and without demand.

Her mouth tasted of—what? A dawn dewdrop from an unfolding bamboo leaf; the faint, faint odor of an orchid's heart, one of those rare, gorgeous orchids that had managed to retain a semblance of perfume. A tremble shook her, and another. She withdrew her lips and breathed tingling into his ear: "You do understand. I desire you within my body; my inner spirit cries out for that, for the tenderness you would bring to me. You have understood that here we cannot have sex and have love. We will reach the province of Guizhou and the town of Zun-yi. There Chairman Mao and his staff await. There also will I await you, in a beautiful garden that was once a mandarin's. You will come to me in the light, in the day so that we may look upon each other and know no shame.''

This time she kissed him, deeper and more strongly than he had kissed her. Then Yen Ling was gone to her own quilt across the camp, across the gulley that smelled of water, and now echoed the breath of a rare orchid.

Heart racing, mouth gone dry, Keenan Carlisle stared up at the stars. This woman would make of him a lover, truly a lover who would know no shame. Yen Ling; Yen Ling. He wanted to mind-shout her name across the bloody land and over the trackless seas to—to—he had trouble remembering his wife's name.

CHAPTER 15

REUTERS NEWS AGENCY—South of Shansi, October 12, 1939:
With the Communist Fourth Front Army: An armed European
was seen here today with a ragged band of guerrilla fighters
that has been ranging nearby mountains for at least a year.
Locals claimed no knowledge of the man, and queries to
higher headquarters about the "white Chinese" were met
with silence.

Luxurious was the only word; he soaked in hot water all
the way up to his scraped-clean chin. The war and the
world were far away and Keenan would have liked to keep
that distance, but had to sigh out of the great wooden tub
and dry on a towel of absorbent flannel. Sr. Off. Jeng Wei
Li waited with clean clothing, a featureless uniform of tan
cotton that buttoned to the throat, and a cap bearing a small
red star. Keenan peeled off the cloth star.

"No offense, sir. We are of different armies."

Jeng Wei Li nodded, a man with the indefinable-age face
of the graying Chinese, smooth and tightened, crinkled eyes,
his mouth marked at the corners. "It is said you were a
good soldier with us, and it is to be wished that our countries may march against our common foe." He spoke a dry
and dusty English, a bookish English perfected God knew
where.

"My country is not at war—yet."

The senior officer—which meant a general of some rank

not named for security reasons—nodded and said, "If you will follow me, please."

The building was old, its wood flaking and cracked, uninsulated. Keenan guessed it had been a schoolhouse; short-legged benches and a few table desks were stacked along a hallway. The main room contained a few stools and a stove with a teakettle, and a beat-up but real desk at the far end, a potbellied stove. But also upon the raised platform where the teacher might sit, waited four men in simple, baggy uniforms; two empty chairs were placed before the desk and a brass tea service upon it.

Sr. Off. Jeng Wei Li bowed to the man in the center, a short man with a double chin and receding hairline. What the hell; Keenan figured when in Rome—and when in China use chopsticks. He bowed, too. The short man smiled.

"Sit," whispered Jeng Wei Li, then, louder: "Chairman Mao, this is the American captain Keenan Carlisle. He traveled and fought with Major Hong's unit. He is brought here at your wish."

Chairman Mao Tse-tung nodded, the smile remaining, making his cheeks rounder. He might appear cherubic, but Keenan watched the eyes, hard, black and deep as unplumbed ocean canyons. The man radiated power. He spoke in clear, unhurried Chinese, looking directly at Keenan rather than at the interpreter. It was effective, more so since Jeng Wei Li spoke directly—not saying, "he says," or "he wants to know," but using Mao's words verbatim, as if they were said one man to another.

"China wishes to be friends with your country," Mao said. "China needs many things America can supply, so that we may drive the invaders from our land. It is to your country's welfare, also. The more Japanese we kill now, the fewer you will have to deal with later."

An officer poured green tea into brass cups, and Keenan was given one. He held it in two hands, smelling the delicate fragrance of its steam. Looking at Mao, he said, "Many powerful men in my country are afraid of communism's stated aim of conquering the world, and watchful of red flags. And they intend to recognize only the Nationalists of

Chiang Kai-shek. The shrewd generalissimo has a strong propaganda force in Washington."

Mao nodded, no smile softening his face now. "Sparked by the beautiful and American educated Soong Mei-ling, Madame Chiang Kai-shek."

Keenan sipped tea. The Chinese communists might meet in a sleazy schoolhouse, and haul war supplies on their backs, but they knew what was going on in the outside world.

He said, "She photographs well, and Chiang's pronouncements make him seem the savior of China, bravely battling the superior forces of Japan."

"Do you believe this?"

"No, sir. I have seen no Kuomintang fighting the Japanese." If he got home, how was he going to make Washington believe this? That would have to be left to General Belvale's persuasive powers. "But I have seen how your troops bleed the Japanese. Very impressive, guerrilla warfare."

"Russia's form of communism is different from the Chinese," Mao said through his interpreter. "Perhaps if your country understood this, the people would be more sympathetic to our cause. The Russians want uprisings in every city, but there the Japanese or Kuomintang garrisons would slaughter our people. Out here we move among the peasants without fear of betrayal. For thousands of years, the poor farmers of China have known nothing but outrage from the warlords and their pillaging soldiers. A uniform of any kind is to be hated and feared. But no longer; we are an army of peasants and the Red Army lives among the people as the fish dwells in the water. The Kuomintang are warlords and pillagers."

On the march here, Keenan had learned something of the early history of Mao and the Reds. The original commander had been Chu Teh, and the political commissar was the visionary and poet Mao Tse-tung. Chu and Mao had captured the peasants' loyalties by ruthlessly attacking the enemies of the common people—the landlords, bureaucrats and tax collectors, murdering some in public displays. Chiang's armies had staged three successive campaigns against "the bandits." The fourth campaign was beginning when the Japanese invaded Manchuria, changing much but not all of Chiang's goals.

Yen Ling, Keenan thought; waiting for him in the garden of a mandarin. How was he to know where and when? And she had warned him of strict Chinese sexual mores. With an effort, he forced her to the back of his mind. "I will bring this word to Washington and tell the leaders there what I have seen for myself."

"These Flying Tigers," Mao said. "A group like that would be of great help to us. As it is, the air is an enemy we cannot fight."

"Mercenaries," Keenan said, "paid for every Japanese plane destroyed, not soldiers but civilians. Chennault is their leader, but not a general."

"But they are tacitly approved by your country, and we do not have the means to pay such mercenaries."

Keenan nodded. "I'll report this, too." He wondered if even the old generals could put together an outlaw air force, but they might try. The problem was how to change the official outlook of stubborn congressmen. It probably couldn't be done, so anything Belvale did would have to be a covert operation. The old general would love that. Bugler— blow the charge! Crusty would snort and say shove it down their throats or up their asses.

"You can be taken to Hong Kong where the British will see to your safety. It is a long march, and dangerous. If you would prefer to be returned to the Japanese at Hankow, we can make you another suitable American uniform."

Keenan didn't hesitate. "The British, sir. If Major Hong leads the way, I'll be honored."

The smile reappeared on Mao's face; the other men smiled, too—especially a tall, thin man with heavy eyebrows. At a nod from Mao, this one came around the table and shook hands with Keenan.

The interpreter said, "This is Sr. Off. Chou En-lai, field commander. He feels you will be a good emissary for China."

"Thank you," Keenan said with a bow, and turned to follow Jeng Wei Li from the meeting room. Belvale and

Crusty and this Chou En-lai had the same look, the eyes of disciples.

Back in his own small room, he thought to ask the man about the garden of a mandarin, but held his tongue in time. Yen Ling would reach him when she wanted to, and although the waiting was difficult, he could sweat it out. Rice with flakes of pork was brought to him, green peas still in their pods and pears. Restless in his communist uniform, he finished eating and paced the room. When the old woman came to collect the bowls, she bowed low and handed him a folded bit of rice paper.

The map was simple and clear, and he held it close. But how was a foreigner to wind through town, even wearing the proper uniform? Yen Ling, glossy midnight hair and her special odor of woman sweat, somewhere in a magic garden where they would come together in the sunlight, unashamed, she said. He put on his cap and stepped out into the street.

Old Father Lim came up, showing his few teeth in a broad grin. "Eyeh," he said, and took Keenan's sleeve. Down narrow, slanting alleys they went, the urine smells strong, the cooking pork odors stronger, sesame oil and charcoal, and many people in each hovel they passed.

The ground rose and the huts fell behind them. There beyond an open place stroked with shoots of greenery, stood the walled house, its pagoda roof of tile, dragon figures peering from the ends of support beams. The gate was thick, dark wood, bound with iron and brass. Father Lim knocked twice upon it, then scurried away. Keenan drew a deep breath and went through the door when it swung back.

Midsummer held no blossoms on the trees, but flowers bloomed at their tended bases, pastel shades complimenting the soft green grass, nodding agreement in a gentle breeze. The great gate closed almost without sound behind him and he did not look around, but forward at the garden's stone centerpiece, a bubbling fountain making small diamonds glitter in the sun.

Yen Ling stood just beyond the fountain, her entire body snugged close by a blue silk dress that reached demurely to the throat after outlining her breasts and belly and thighs, and the slit in its bottom reached to the top of one golden thigh. The sun winked upon her black, black hair and her eyes were warm upon him, and there was only the slightest tremble of her lips.

Unsteadily, feeling that the earth was shifting beneath his feet, Keenan approached her. She murmured, "Yes," and yes again, her voice different than it had been on the march, lower in the pale column of her throat, husky. He had only unbuttoned his blouse when she shifted her hips and whipped the dress over her head.

He had been right about her body, hidden as it had been on the march in her baggy uniform; right and not right enough. Tall and slim, she tapered from sleek curving into smoothness and another sweet shaping. Her breasts were proud, the nipples dark grapes. The V between her long thighs was as glossy, as shining as her hair.

Dropping his clothing, he moved toward her. She lifted her arms and held them out so he could move into their tender circle. Her flesh shocked against his, through his and into places he had not known existed. Sinking with her to the emerald and giving carpet, Keenan felt only this woman and the sun kissing his skin. Her pubic hair was not fluffy, but held a certain wiry cushioning that excited him more.

She made love to him, with him, upon and below him, and as she had promised back by that campfire when first they touched in truth, there was no shame. Keenan was freed of that, released of every emotion that did not have to do with Yen Ling's beauty, with her giving so much that he strove to give, too, holding no part of himself back.

They lay whispering together then, murmuring of love and sunshine. He thanked the departed mandarin who had planted this garden and lifted the high, strong walls that held out the rest of the world. He clung to Yen Ling as he would cling to life itself, knowing the heartbeat of her, the inner throbbing so exotic. He tasted her wherever his lips could reach. She tasted of crushed grass and sunshine, of her special woman sweat.

It was later, when the shadows came slanting over the walls and a cool wind whispered of approaching twilight that she told him she would travel with him to Hong Kong.

He shivered; the march was hundreds of miles and bristling with danger, with samurai swords and Nationalist bayonets.

When he protested, Yen Ling reminded him gently that she was a soldier also, a nurse. He said, "But—you and I, the nights; how can we not be together?"

"A Confucian priest and his followers live and study within this house. If you wish, he will perform a ceremony. Then, on the march we will be permitted."

He hugged her closer. "A marriage; of course."

"It does not have to mean anything. It is not a Christian rite, and when you return to your own country—"

"It will be everything," Keenan said, and never meant anything more. Now all they had to do was try to slip unseen through enemy held territory, or fight their way through if they were discovered. And Hong Kong was so far away.

CHAPTER 16

REUTERS NEWS AGENCY—Crown Colony of Hong Kong, October 20, 1939: Reports from the interior of China point to a buildup of Japanese troops in the three provinces above this city—Hunan, Kiangsu and Fukien. But officials here and in England insist that city defenses are adequate, and that the Japanese are far too busy beating off attacks by Generalissimo Chiang Kai-shek's Nationalist forces to consider moving against Hong Kong.

Keenan stood with Major Hong at the long sweep of the sampan. Rattan sails lowered, it wallowed slowly down yellow mud waters of the shallow Hsiang River. The deck stank with ancient oils and crushed fish scales that had seeped into the wormy wood for too many years; woven reed baskets of salted fish smelled only a little better.

In the bow, old Father Lim repaired nets, his coolie hat hung down his back so his white hair showed. On each side of the bow beneath his knees new eyes had been painted, so that the boat could see where it was going and not run them aground. Behind the old man, at the base of the slender mast, Chang Yen Ling squatted at a clay cook-pot of glowing charcoal. The homey look, Keenan thought, the camouflage of a river peasant family hoping to market their upriver catch at I-ch'ang and Hanyang. Below deck, Hong's veteran band of hard-fighting guerrillas rested out of sight.

Yesterday Yen Ling had told him they would move much

faster by water, drifting almost due south from the interior toward the coast and Hong Kong. She also said Japanese patrol boats ran the much bigger Yangtze River, but had never been seen on this tributary. The main reason was that this was Red Army country, far more dangerous for intruders than the cheesecloth defenses of the Nationalists, and their stay-put city garrisons.

"We may be stopped by Japanese soldiers on the bank and signalled to come ashore, but if so, it should be only a small patrol looking for food, loot and women. There are no reports from the people of any large forces in this area." Then she had given him one of her rare in-public smiles that made his heart turn over. Yen Ling was thoroughly Chinese, and even though a new woman of the revolution, she followed the old teachings about sex and love—at least in public. In private she was beauty and tender fierceness and wonders he could not always name.

If Japs did pull over this simple fishing boat, the surprise they'd get would be the last of their lives. Samurai heaven would receive a new shipment of recruits. Hong's men were well armed and eager to work at what they did best— killing Japanese.

He looked at Yen Ling again, seeing the plain and baggy clothing that masked such a magnificent woman body. He would dress her in the finest silks and satins and furs, present her with jewels such as she had never imagined— diamonds to match the sparkle in her eyes. If ever any woman deserved rubies and pearls, it was Yen Ling.

As the boat eased around a sandbar, and a warm wind caressed the deck, he thought again and decided that she wouldn't like that kind of thing. A simple shaping of cool green jade at her throat would be enough. Nancy had just such a bit of apple green jade, a butterfly, if he remembered correctly. He shook away his wife's dim image. He didn't want to think of Nancy now, and when he might have the time and inclination to concentrate, it would be upon their relationship and what he could do to change it, not upon Nancy herself.

The Hong Kong detail had been days upon this meandering river, and seen no more than a pair of Zeroes that scorned working over such a squalid little boat. From Hanyang, they would either stay aboard or march overland to Changsha, and either way, still be some six hundred miles from Hong Kong. Also at Changsha, they would leave the protective area of Ho Lung and the Second Front Army. All around them would be only Japs and what was left of a Chinese population too beaten down and starved to help much.

But some of those poor farmers would try; despite torture and death looking over their shoulders, they would try. Mao Tse-tung's great strength lay in the stubborn loyalty of the Chinese people, millions and millions of Chinese hoping at last to find a bit of dignity and some kind of life beyond animal labor, tax collectors and warlords.

Just after dark, Hong steered the boat's nose into a soft bank and the soldiers came topside to climb the bank and eat the salted fish and cold rice that Yen Ling had cooked for them. Out of long discipline, the pipes and cigarettes smoked with hidden sparks and the men whispered among themselves as outpost guards were chosen for the night.

Major Hong came back to the deck where Yen Ling had just unrolled the sleeping quilts. Much more polite to her since he learned of the marriage, he waited with courtesy until she blew upon dying coals to prepare him tea in a brass bowl.

Then he spoke softly, but at some length and sipped his tea while Yen Ling translated: "A farm boy has trotted many *li* to bring news and to join this band. His only weapon is a knife used to harvest and bind rice straw, so he bowed low in gratitude and cried without shame when Sergeant Han presented him with a rifle. This night he sleeps with it as with a wife."

Hong said something else, and she nodded. "While their airplanes search across country, and dragon tanks gather for a major assault, the Japanese block every road south as newly arrived divisions patrol the countryside and gunships wait in every river. They blow up many bridges. The Kuomintang do the same, for their interest is more in destroying us than in defeating the foreign rapists of China. But although all Nationalists are running dogs of Chiang

Kai-shek, the Szechwan troops remain in part true Chinese. At this time and this place, that becomes a weakness."

Lighting a cigarette and cupping its glow within his gnarled hand, Major Hong spoke at length again. Then Yen Ling frowned. "We must march to Szechwan, and try to remain undetected during two hundred *li* added to our march."

She explained how bits of intelligence were brought by runners from one village to another, a morsel here, a grain of information added there, until a useful picture emerged.

This intelligence concerned a special bridge hung in a mountain gorge above the torrential Tatu River, a bridge built in 1701 by clever and determined native engineers.

"Chairman Mao and the troops of the Long March used it to escape Chiang Kai-shek. It is possible he remembers the Tatu River Bridge, for his soldiers have removed all planking from the thirteen chains that reach high across the roaring waters far below. Two machine guns wait on the west side."

Keenan said, "How long is the span, the chains?"

"Thirty-two meters."

"Good lord—a hundred feet of slippery chains stretched over a deadly chasm." He stared at Hong. "And if we make it to the Tatu River, you intend to attack across it on those chains."

"To reach Hong Kong while it remains British, this must be done. If we Chinese did not respect age and think upon eternity," Yen Ling said, "this ancient and revered bridge would be destroyed and we would have to fight our way across the river itself."

"Forever," Keenan said, *"eternity;* grand words. Will this be for you and me? When war and duty is done?"

"I know only war, and duty endures more than a single lifetime." Biting her lips, she looked away. Major Hong put down his empty bowl and Yen Ling refilled it from the brass teapot.

"The crossing will be difficult, but it is the only route to the south that remains open to us."

"We can go back," he said, afraid for this woman, who would not be afraid for herself.

"The Chairman has ordered that you be delivered safely

to Hong Kong. Comrade Major Hong says we march overland and cross by the Tatu River Bridge.''

No planking and machine guns dug in on the other side. Did Hong expect the band to tightrope-walk those chains, right into point-blank fire from automatic weapons and no doubt 61mm mortars? The mortar fire did not have to come close to the famous bridge; they'd just eat up everything on this bank, chopping up the little guerrilla band before it even got started.

After the major left the boat Yen Ling spread the sleeping quilts and made pillows from their rolled clothing. The natural perfume of her body remained in the clothing she would cleanse in the river before dawn, the scent of her golden sweat that never failed to reach deep and excite him.

Making tiny splashes in the river as she bathed, Yen Ling did not hurry to the quilts. Keenan wondered if he had caused a hesitation by asking about forever. They had not spoken of the future because with the beginning of each day, there was no promise of sundown. But he was more married to this woman through the ceremonies of China than he had ever felt with his other wife. Who was to say which was legal, and what did that matter out here, where the judge and jury debated through gun muzzles?

If Yen Ling had second thoughts, she didn't express them in bed. The boat rocked gently in the river current, and she rocked him gently in the smooth clasping of her thighs, pillowed his face in the cushioning of her breasts. Each time, she was different; each time, she was soft new miracles, and Keenan knew he wanted this woman forever, if that meant somehow bringing her back to the United States and Sandhurst Keep—and if the entire family didn't like that, they could kiss it, especially Minerva Belvale. If forever came to a bloody end at the Tatu River Bridge, so be it; he had never been happier.

Overland they went, scouts and flankers out, moving slowly and with great care through country of thinning brush and dry open spaces. They went to ground and rolled in dust at the first sound of an airplane, keeping the old leaf camouflage upon their backs and caps. Major Hong's band could disappear into the earth within seconds, becoming lumps of dirt and straggly bush. Keenan couldn't imagine American dogfaces so good at hiding, or even trying to be. The U.S. Army had a hell of a lot to learn, and—he suspected—little time to do it. If he got home, this kind of guerrilla indoctrination would be his first priority.

Three days from the Tatu River, just at twilight, one scout came trotting back to the main body to report a Nationalist roadblock ahead, "Our scouts count ten men and one officer. One machine gun and many grenades. They are not much alert, but sentries sit on high ground, looking each way."

One hand clasped upon her medical kit, Yen Ling lifted her chin at Keenan the way she did when she was being stubborn, and a chill of fear cut through him. He wanted to reach for her, but remembered the traditions in time and she slid away, speaking rapidly with Major Hong.

"No," Keenan said. "Yen Ling is our only medic, and—"

"Only woman," Hong said, and motioned for Father Lim to come up.

Close-up work, Keenan realized, damned dangerous work, and his hands closed so tightly that his fingers hurt. He watched Father Lim get a Nambu pistol, and saw Yen Ling being given only a knife—the long rice knife brought by the band's new recruit.

"What the hell—"

She came quickly to him. "Do not shame yourself; do not shame me, my husband. I am a soldier first and a wife second; you know that. It is also your duty."

"All right, damn it! But be careful, Yen Ling; please be careful." He could piece together the coming action from Major Hong's hand gestures. Other men gathered a big bundle of twigs for Father Lim to carry upon his stooped back, and a small basket appeared, filled with green weeds, which Yen Ling accepted.

They would go right into the roadblock, locals who had stumbled upon the soldiers by accident. Only a grandfather gathering fuel; only a beautiful young woman gathering edible greens. All eyes would be upon Yen Ling, especially the officer's, Keenan thought. Whatever happened in the narrow gulley beside a careless campfire, Hong's guerrillas would come in right behind it to take out the guards and the rest of the Nationalists as silently as possible. Nobody knew how close another group might be.

Touching Hong's shoulder, Keenan then tapped his own chest and held up one finger. He would be first to follow, or there'd be a knockdown fight right here and now. Hong must have read that in his face, because the major nodded. Then he took Keenan's rifle, leaving him only a bayonet. Bobbing his head again, Hong smiled as if he understood Keenan's worries.

Yen Ling and the old man were out of sight before Hong signalled to move on. He was only a step behind Keenan, and Sergeant Han angled off a step behind him as they padded uphill. Keenan was lucky; he heard excited talk below as he bellied down and snaked up on a sentry who had his back turned to watch whatever was happening at the campfire below. Without the whisper of a sound, Keenan came to one knee and choked an arm around the sentry's neck, shutting down hard. Then he rammed the bayonet between the bastard's ribs, reaching for the heart. The man only gurgled, but Keenan jerked out the bayonet and thrust it through the throat. Then he let the body drop and crawled to the edge of the gulley to stare down, his hands sticky with blood and his heart at full gallop.

Good God—Yen Ling stood submissively, her face down, while the officer pawed over her body and his men laughed, those who were not tormenting Father Lim and kicking his bundle of sticks into the fire. Keenan looked hurting away and saw the other sentry across the gulley, kneeling upon his rock crag and grinning. That was the one, he thought; from this side nobody could reach him in time to stop his rifle fire which might warn another body of troops within earshot.

Yen Ling, damnit! That son of a bitch grabbing her breasts and rubbing against her. Then the officer released her and moved away step by slow step until he fell upon his back in the fire, scattering red sparks. She had stuck the farm boy's knife right into his black heart. Two soldiers leaped up and from close in, Father Lim belly-shot them both with the Jap

Nambu. The shots were not loud, muffled by powder burned flesh and the walls of the narrow gorge. The other sentry spun off his high rock, twisting and kicking as arterial blood sprayed from his slashed jugular. Sergeant Han followed after, flinging himself feet first into the gulley, knife dripping.

One man got off a scream and another snatched up his rifle, but never fired it. The guerrillas were all over them, stabbing bayonets and striking hard with rifle butts. It was over in seconds.

Hurrying to her, Keenan forgot Chinese mores and took Yen Ling in his arms. "You're all right? That bastard didn't hurt you?"

"He had not the time," she murmured, and he could tell she was not comfortable being held close in public, so regretfully, he released her. He took a long look at this woman who had only minutes ago plunged seven inches of steel into a man. No change showed upon her face or in her eyes, and he realized that he had a long way to go as a combat man. Chang Yen Ling was given a job and did it. Killing the Nationalist meant no more to her emotionally than dumping charcoal ashes over the side of the old fishing boat they had left behind. She would continue to kill enemies and nurse friends until death caught up with her. But not if he could protect her.

Did he want her any different, even if she could or would change? The question was moot; she had been at war for most of her life. He could hope the years of hardship, hunger and violence would slough from her like old, rough skin when she came into Hong Kong with him, and then on to Kill Devil Hill or the Keep. Keenan hadn't told her of home yet; they'd had so little time.

Mistress of the Hill, Minerva Belvale would react with cold and cutting logic: an Oriental, Keenan? Whatever is the matter with you? Despite his great respect for the old general, he would certainly tell Minerva go to hell. He should have done so for Nancy, but this woman was even more important. There was no mistress at Sandhurst Keep, only whatever wife Crusty chose as hostess of the moment.

CHAPTER 17

INTERNATIONAL NEWS SERVICE—Hong Kong, China, October 23, 1939: The entire country is stirring, according to frightened refugees who pour into this British colony by the thousands every day. Japanese and Nationalist troops are gathering for a major assault while ragged bands of communist outlaws harass both sides.

Shaking himself, Keenan turned from Yen Ling and helped gather weapons, surprised to find that the reported machine gun was the standard U.S. issue 1917 Browning water-cooled 30 caliber. Christ; he'd trained with that weapon—the gunner stuck with fifty-one pounds of steel tripod, but easier to carry balanced than the number two man shifting thirty-seven and a half pounds of gun from shoulder to shoulder. Number three had the water can and a 150 round box of ammo. Anybody else in the heavy weapons squad carried two boxes of ammo and their own shoulder weapons.

"Comrade major wishes to know if you are familiar with this gun," Yen Ling said.

"Totally," Keenan answered. "It's a good weapon. If we reach that damned bridge, I can give good covering fire with it."

The men also gathered food and ammunition from casualties Chiang Kai-shek wouldn't even miss. What the genera-lissimo and the Japanese would miss was this tough band of Mao Tse-tung's fighters that had slipped through a hole in the steel net jointly set in place. The way around to the Tatu bridge lay open, and if they could force that impossible river crossing, Hong Kong might lie within reach. It was still a long way off.

Trotting away from the narrow gorge and the blazing campfire where the Nationalist officer sizzled and cooked, Keenan dropped back to the tail end of the fast moving column so he could hold Yen Ling's hand now and then. The guerrillas took their breaks only at a walk, then went into that ground-eating trot again, before Keenan had time to really catch his second wind, or his third. These men were every bit as rugged as the Japanese, and far more flexible in combat.

The night grew thick around Keenan and Yen Ling and crickets stopped chirping as they passed, only to break into a chorus behind them. There was no stopping to rest, no break for food or water. Only when the first faint streaks of dawn lit the sky did Hong call a halt, and some men collapsed on the earth to hide beneath twisted pines and small clumps of bamboo.

Yen Ling's face was drawn and pale with fatigue, but she had kept up the pace without complaint. Keenan was proud of her. After gulping cold rice seasoned with chipped fish and stringy greens he didn't recognize, he lay beside her to sleep most of the day through.

Hong came to inform Yen Ling as a courtesy to Keenan. She then said, "We are not far from the Tatu bridge. This night we will cross it and break out of the encirclement. Beyond the bridge the Japanese lines are thin. All we must do is attack the bridge and cross upon its chains."

"That's all," Keenan said, and thought that some of them might actually make it. Then he knew the sharp edge of guilt because those who died would be doing it to deliver one American captain to where he could be flown out of China and to a fat cat part of the world not even at war. All because Mao wanted a liaison contact to balance Chiang Kai-shek's, but Keenan might not be able to exert an ounce of influence in Washington.

He had little time with Yen Ling; they moved out at dark and kept moving. It was dry; the night dew did little to lay the dust, and its ancient odors clogged Keenan's nostrils. He tasted his sweat, and after so long in this bleeding land, that sweat's flavor was different. He had lost what—fifteen or twenty pounds? Whatever, he was down to saddle leather and stirrup metal on the thin Chinese diet and constant road marching.

For the first time in weeks, perhaps in months, he wondered what his return to life—if they made it— would do to Nancy and the family compounds. Surely by now he was carried as KIA, privately of course; the army would not like it known among certain legislators that it was losing observers in foreign lands. So if he was mourned, it was within the family, and some would celebrate the return of Lazarus lost. Maybe that included Nancy. She could be gone or remarried by now, and that would solve his problem. Yen Ling; he wanted nothing to stand in the way of Yen Ling going home with him.

Passports; did the British recognize marriage by a Confucian priest? If not, it was time for some weight of the Carlisle-Belvale fortune to come on scene, enough to set up forgeries or pay off officials, to hire or buy a yacht, or a seaplane. Letters of credit could be wired to him. It was amazing, the swath that blank checks could cut through a bureaucracy. So far in his career, he hadn't been forced to use the power of old money, money so heavy that it could break jobs and backs at the same time. Keenan would use whatever he had to, for Yen Ling.

After another night-long forced march that had even Major Hong wobbly at the knees, at dawn they again took cover, this time more pleasantly in a series of little caves holed into soft limestone cliffs. Cool and reasonably clean inside, if you didn't count bat droppings, the caves were perfect hideouts, an out of sight guard at each end of the winding vale. Yen Ling fell asleep before she finished her food, and Keenan laid her down upon a quilt and pillowed her head on her medical kit.

He could smell water and hear the faint sounds of a rushing river; they were close to the Tatu. In the next cave over, a large one that corkscrewed into the mountain, he found Major Hong and the Browning machine gun. Lifting the gun by water jacket and pistol grip, he dropped the pintle into the brass nest of the spidered tripod. Then he flipped the cover and removed the Browning's innards—butt plate, driving spring and rod, bolt handle, bolt and extractor. The parts were in fair shape, needing only a little oil. When he slid out the barrel, he carefully counted the clicks to return for headspace and used a bit of rag and a Mauser ramrod to clear and oil the barrel. He put the Browning back together and with two pulls on the bolt handle, fed the first round of the belt into the chamber at full load.

He looked up at Hong and a half circle of interested men. "Ready," he said. "Good." From one side of the Tatu River cliffs to the other was only a hundred feet, give or take. The gun's battle sights were good for 750 yards before rising above the height of a man; more than they'd need. Flipped up, the leaf sights could be elevated to 2400 yards. This was Keenan's favorite weapon, dependable, accurate and long range. Cared for, it would not overheat and jam, and could lay down one hell of a field of fire.

"This night?" he asked, and Major Hong nodded. Keenan gave the man a short salute and crawled back to the hole in the whitish wall where Father Lim and three other soldiers dozed a short distance from Yen Ling. Sighing, worried about taking a tough objective nobody here had actually seen, Keenan lay down beside his wife—his true wife—placing his body between her and the cave entrance.

He woke to movement, to Yen Ling's soft kiss upon his mouth before she rolled up and away from his embrace. One man had suffered a minor hurt in the gorge fight, and she poulticed his wound with the ancient painkiller, her precious willow bark and leaves, binding the arm with a strip of rag over packed spiderwebs.

Turning back to Keenan, she whispered, "I am to remain on this side of the river, also. We cannot allow you to be hurt, especially when we are so close to success, and I have already objected to Major Hong about permitting you to get into the fight at the gorge."

"He couldn't stop me. You were down there in danger."

Swirling deep and dark, her eyes softened. "Oh, my

husband. You must learn that the movement is more important than all else."

"Not as important as you—movement, your country, my country, the whole damned world. You are more precious than all of it."

A rare tear slid down her cheek, and her fingertips were butterflies upon his face. "Ah—if there were no wars—no rich and no poor; oh, my husband, my husband who can value the simple love of a woman above all else."

"Not just a woman—the incomparable Chang Yen Ling."

He thought he heard a sob catch in her throat as she spun away, as the guerrilla band stirred into action and left its caves. Was he going to have trouble getting her to leave China? He didn't think so; she was worried about the upcoming fight, about his safety. Keenan went to the machine-gun tripod and took it from a small, struggling Chinese.

"I am the gunner," he said, and swung it to his shoulders with a quick, practiced move that settled the front legs across his shoulders and the trail leg down his back. He hadn't forgotten.

Major Hong smiled and moved close enough in the dark so that Keenan could make out his salute. "Let's do it," Keenan said.

Reptile quiet, the advance riflemen bellied along the earth as the voice of the river grew louder, gnashing at boulders and spitting over deep cut banks, cursing its way south. Crouched as best he could under the tripod load, Keenan felt targeted, although the night was black and starless. With the overhead flip of the expert gunner, he landed the tripod upon three legs, and its securely locked cradle didn't move. Swiftly, he worked the leg clamps and folded the tripod so that it could be carried upon one hip. Then he barreled after the end squad, the four riflemen who were to protect the gun's flanks. Ten men, Yen Ling and himself with the gun; that left only twenty to cross the river and take out its guard detachment, its two machine guns and God only knew how many men.

The water roar increased and light, chill spume misted Keenan's face. At least the noise covered movement, but now every signal from Hong had to pass back down the column by hand taps. That kept the men too close together; one burst could cut them all down. Ahead, men fanned out as a firing line at the prone. Keenan discovered a dip in the ground, right at the lip of the deep, echoing gorge. When he felt around and found rocks to pile before the tripod, the Chinese got the idea and built him a half-circle wall that protected the gun and ammunition boxes from almost anything but a mortar shell or well-placed grenade.

There hung the chains like so many sagged boa constrictors, long, slimy and sometimes *tinking!* together in roiled air from the river thundering far below. Leaving their rifles, the first four men slid out upon the chains, knives clenched in their teeth, two with pistols stuck in belts of twisted rope or old leather. Two had grenades saved from the canyon ambush.

It started to rain.

"Son of a bitch," Keenan muttered, then realized that if the rain didn't get heavier and a vicious wind didn't whip up from the river, the weather change was bad and good. Bad because the chains turned more slippery, putting the first four men, and the next just moving out, that much closer to death. But with any luck, the rain would pull some heads deeper into the guard posts across the Tatu River.

Two heavy weapons, Keenan thought, one on each side of the ancient stone supports? Off to the flanks a bit, tucked into the ground behind a few rice bags filled with sand? That's where he would dig in guns. As the third set of guerrillas moved out onto the treacherous chains, Keenan watched one of the first four sway and spit away his knife, watched him struggle for balance, and then topple beneath his chain. Rain slashed down in a winding sheet, and when it lifted, the man was gone. He had not screamed. The poor, loyal son of a bitch refused to scream even as he fell to his death.

How could the Japanese or the Nationalists hope to defeat men like these? An enemy machine gun opened fire, sudden spurts of ball and every fifth round a blazing tracer.

Zeroing in upon the tracer lines, Keenan one-fingered the Browning's curved trigger for a ten-round burst. Not the regulation five shots and break, but quick return fire, and another longer, rolling burst that was right on. Swivelling the gun on its pintle, he didn't wait for the number two Nationalist gun to open fire across the river, but raked the area where he thought it would be. Ten rounds, five; ten rounds, five—and he whipped back to the first gun position, tasting gunpowder, that exciting flavor blowing back into his face from the muzzle. The firing pin clicked on an empty chamber.

Snatching open the cover, he took the belt a laughing guerrilla handed up, fed it into the breech, slammed the lid and pumped the bolt handle twice. He had done some damage with 150 rounds. That number two son of a bitch hadn't fired a shot; he must have caught the guy and the gun just right, sending the bastard to hell in his sleep.

Firing their pistols, Hong and his men scambled onto the far shore, digging free hands into wet rocks as they climbed. Loosening the cradle clamp, Keenan hiked the gun muzzle and worked over the hill behind the bridge supports with overhead fire so close that some guerrillas ducked. One man fell to enemy fire, then another, rolling off the cliff face and into the roaring chasm. Another tipped over on his chain and tried to hang on with both hands. He too fell silently.

"Shit!" Keenan yelled. "Shit, shit!"

Then his soldiers were into the enemy positions, and his flank guards stood up to fire at dimly seen figures trying to escape. Probably some did, Keenan thought, but not enough to matter, only enough to scare hell out of their buddies with the story of the Tatu River Bridge.

Lowering his forehead to his hand curled around the pistol grip of the Browning, Keenan closed his eyes and felt a slight heat from the gun's water jacket drifting back. The gutty Red soldiers died without complaint, fell without making a sound. For him; for what he was supposed to do for their cause. A two-bit captain nobody in the War Department would say good morning to, if not for his family, and now he had to make it work. Somehow, he had to make it work so these men would not have died for nothing.

When Yen Ling slid her arm across his shoulders, he lifted his head. "Where others may see?"

"One comrade comforting another. You are a fine shot with that weapon."

"We lost men."

Her arm tightened. "Fortunate men die for their beliefs; others die for nothing, killed without reason by lesser men."

He stared across the river, at lighted torches and moving men. "They're laying the planks."

Touching his wet cheek now, she said, "So the rest may cross safely."

"To hurry me to Hong Kong."

"Yes; you can make a difference for us. A hundred of those machine guns, a thousand—tanks and food, modern medicines."

Keenan caught her hand and pressed it harder against his cheek. Heavy plank after plank, struggled into position by two men at a time, extended the bridge flooring. Torches danced in the wind, and the rain slacked off. The river continued to rant below.

"You're coming into Hong Kong with me."

Only for a heartbeat did she hesitate. "Yes," she said, "of course."

And three days' march later, she did, slipping past border guards desperately trying to hold back a growing river of refugees.

A British second leftenant blocked Keenan's entry with an outstretched arm and spread fingers. "Sorry, old chap. There's no more room in the city and food supplies are running low, no more entries." He dropped his hand. "Why am I saying all this, anyhow?"

Keenan slipped off his hat. "Because you're a gentleman, and I'm damned glad to see you."

"I'll be damned," the subaltern said, "a white man, and a Yank to boot."

Looking past the man and the closing barricades, Keenan saw with approval that Yen Ling was waiting down the street, making herself not noticeable. He said, "Captain Keenan Carlisle, United States Army. I was on observation duty with the Japanese in Manchuria."

"Be damned again." The officer held out his hand. "Leftenant Kirk, sir. And you're the officer we've been instructed to look out for, keep our ear to the ground, like. You've been gone a long time, sir. If you will come with me to the governor—"

Keenan shook his head. "Just walk me to a good hotel and pay for the room, food, whiskey and cigarettes until I cable home. Oh—and I would appreciate the loan of a uniform and boots. After a bath and shave, then I'll be up to speaking with your governor."

"Of course, Captain; I understand. We shall cable Washington if you wish—imagine! So long in the interior and making it back to the white man's world on your own. We've had flyers and telegrams about you for at least that long. Sir—"

"Just the hotel, Leftenant. I can't stop you from reporting, but I do want to make the contacts myself —my uncle, General Belvale—my"—he forced himself to say it—"my wife. You understand."

"Yes, sir."

It wasn't far to the Pickwick Hotel, and Keenan paused at the glossy entrance, uneasy and out of place in his dirty coolie clothing, his straw sandals nearly worn through and flopping. He glanced over one shoulder and there she was, a new coolie hat hiding her face and hair, medicine kit held to her breasts.

Keenan said, "My loyal batman, houseboy—whatever title he needs. Please see that he isn't bothered."

And at last beyond stares and whispers, past bewilderment and questions that Keenan would not answer, he was keyed into a luxury suite by a white-jacketed bellboy who sneered at what Yen Ling was supposed to be. The kid would faint if he knew how easily she had killed with a blade.

Keenan happily escorted her into the bathroom and left her there as a parade of servants brought food and drink and smokes. And ice, magical, mystical ice for drinks!

Tomorrow, he thought; after touching base with military and civilian officialdom of the colony, he would have dresses brought in for Yen Ling, some of those seductive *cheong-sams* with skirts slit yay high, robes and gowns and anything she might want, everything. Right now, a hot bath with Yen Ling and sometime later, a call to Kill Devil Hill, if overseas lines were working; a cable to the general, teletypes. He shed his shirt and kicked off sandals as he went to the bathroom and opened the door.

The French doors to the balcony were open and she was gone. Yen Ling was gone.

Running to the balcony, he looked down into the street twenty feet below. A crowd twisting and turning upon itself, no individuals. Maybe he could catch her—maybe he could call the British army, Leftenant Kirk, the Hong Kong police.

The sheet of pale rice paper lay upon the sink counter. In carefully inked English it read: I promised to come into the city with you. I did not promise to stay. I cannot, my husband. If you look into your heart, you understand why I cannot.

And then there was the poem, English standing beside artistically brushed Chinese characters; she must have worked on it in secret for days.

> I have lost my proud poplar,
> You your beloved willow.
> They have vanished,
> rising directly into the sky.
> They ask Wu Kang what
> he will offer them;
> Wu Kang presents them
> with good cassia wine.
>
> Lonely Chang Oh spreads
> her wide sleeves,
> dawning eternally for
> these faithful souls.
> Suddenly there is a report
> that on earth a tiger
> has been subdued.
> Buckets of tears flow down.

Keenan stood for a long time, holding the rice paper. Then he put it carefully aside and went into the other room to make his phone calls.

CHAPTER 18

REUTERS NEWS AGENCY—London, April 29, 1940: With their own country's permission, some American volunteer pilots have transferred into the Royal Air Force in order to gain experience flying Hurricanes and Spitfires. They chose the RAF fighters over the relatively slow Hudson bombers furnished on Lend-Lease. Officials on both sides of the Atlantic reiterated that the fliers are strictly volunteers on their own.

They were too easy, perhaps. He was used to pliant women, but the British service lassies offered Gavin Scott no challenge. The Army Territorial Service—army tail service; the Women's Royal Navy, the WRNS—flap it, baby, but forget making a nest; the Women's Auxiliary Air Force—WAAF-WAAFs (barked, of course). Even the Land Army girls, those who tilled the land while the transformed English farmers were off digging in the dirt, not for potatoes, but foxholes. Often big and clumsy, the girls glowed with honest sweat and muscle, and shone with the eagerness of any young trooper, male or female, long deprived of trips to town and ready to breed. The least glamorous of the service women, they were always wetly grateful for the least attention.

And the waiting sweethearts, the good wives; oh yes, the loving wives of the Limeys unlucky enough to be stationed overseas or across the country. Loving wasn't exactly their word; desperation or revenge, maybe, but they could sure tear up a bed. Whoever said English women were cold was stupid. If it took a war to heat them up, then good-oh for wars. This was a cocksman's paradise. For godsakes—good-oh?

Except for one woman, one particular, stubborn, prick-teasing wench who acted as if her precious ass was the last unbroken commandment. Leftenant Stephanie Bartlett, who had been all lined up for a one-night stand in the Piccadilly Hotel until that damned air raid, and until Uncle Chad Carlisle pulled rank and stole her away—the stiff-necked old fart. That was probably the only stiffness she got out of that old bastard. Why would she keep screwing around with him, unless she was queer for old men or had a wise eye out for a chunk of the family money?

She wasn't all that young, and her mileage was beginning to show, but she carried a thing sensuous, a knowing gleam in her eyes, a ripeness of her mouth that would make her worthwhile. And besides being Uncle Chad's mistress, she was some clown's wife. Gavin preferred to screw other men's wives and this one was too much for an obsolete model like Chad Carlisle.

Moving across the Northold tarmac in his wool lined flying suit, Gavin figured it wouldn't be long. Uncle Chad was across the Channel getting his you-all "Yank" ass shot off, and Stevie would need manly comforting. He had a knack for that as well: here, cry on my shoulder, poor girl, and while they were still sobbing, he was between their legs. Sorrow made a woman vulnerable and death called for a reaffirmation of life, a drive to the preliminaries for more birthing.

Spring fog, chill and ghostly, tasting of last night's bombs and the sea, slid across his face as he approached his Spitfire for a quick morning reconnaissance along the coast. Recce, the Limeys called it; baby talk for godsakes, but that's how they were, turning everything cute, joking as if that proved their war was jolly cricket. If this fight came anywhere near being a game for Gavin Scott, it was one he meant to win going away, and fuck anybody's ground rules but his own.

Snugging deeper into his sheepskin collar and the soft

blue scarf given him by—Christine, wasn't it?—he flipped a casual return to the RAF mechanic's popped and palm-showing salute.

"Gassed and ready, Corporal?"

"Yes, sir. Good hunting, sir."

Hunched against the chill, long nose red, the corporal showed buck teeth at Gavin. With his stringy yellow hair, the guy bore a close resemblance to Mortimer Snerd, but he was a good mechanic, obsessive about keeping the Spit in top shape, even lovingly polished. From time to time, Gavin forgot Corporal Jacobs's name, and damned near called him Mortimer.

Gavin grinned back and climbed to the cockpit. He had never brought back the plane holed by bullets or flak and didn't intend to. He was too good for the Jerry pilots he'd run into so far, and no matter that the British kept no standard score for their flyers, one more certified kill would make him an ace in his own air corps when the U.S. officially came into this war. That had to be soon, and then rank would jump so fast it would be unbelievable. How long before it was Colonel Scott, full bird hero and probably the first American ace of the war?

A real worry was the forming of the Eagle Squadron, twelve guys who were publicly designated as individual volunteers, so as not to smudge the Lend-Lease fairytale. Some hotshot colonel was coming in to lead the squadron, and Gavin might be drafted into one flight, just another handcuffed volunteer stuck under American command and no longer treated as anyone special.

Reaching up, Gavin pulled the canopy forward and clicked it into lock position. He toed the pedals with his London handmade flying boots and felt the rudder and flaps respond. Prop spinning and motor roaring, the plane eased onto his takeoff runway. He was glad it was a Spitfire and not the slower and heavier Hurricane. The Spit, darling of British pilots, was a near perfect fighter plane. It could turn tighter and quicker than the vaunted Messerschmitt, and at 370 miles per hour, could outrun old Jerry on the flat. For godsakes—he was beginning to pick up Limey speech patterns.

The Jerries could outclimb the Spitfire with its 1,175 HP Rolls-Royce engine, but Gavin preferred his plane's eight recessed 303 caliber machine guns over the Messerschmitt's two 20mm cannon and pair of 7.9 guns. They definitely outgunned the Stuka dive-bomber that Luftwaffe Commander Goering sometimes pressed into service as escort, even though it was hampered by its fixed landing gear.

Gavin got the wave-off okay from the tower, relayed by Corporal Jacobs, and shoved the throttle forward. Picking up speed, he lifted his eager spirits as the plane left the earth and tucked its feet into its wings. Angled sharply into the air, he headed straight for the coast on his "recce," actually a search and patrol mission. Higher up, the bright sun found him and the fog blanket rolled below the rushing plane like a fluffy gray blanket, only slightly lumpy.

He smelled the engine's heat, the faint scent of oil, and that was good. He felt a twinge of compassion for the ground pounders, the peasant troops who would never know this winged exhilaration, but the emotion passed quickly. Uncle Chad Carlisle and his kind didn't deserve this flight of freedom, no more than they were entitled to the sensual attentions of Stevie Bartlett. Soaring high and prime stuff like Stevie were rightfully reserved—class for class.

Checking the skies around him in all six directions, he found nothing, no swift speck that could be a target or a threat. He knew the silhouettes perfectly, enemy and friend alike, and again he was happy to be riding the Spitfire. True, the Hawker Hurricane's kill ratio was higher, but there were twice as many Hurricane Groups, and they were heavily armored. But their scores were made almost exclusively on Jerry bombers, not nearly so glamorous in the American press, although the British civilians on the ground appreciated dead bombers a lot more.

Over the Channel, the fog opened quick windows in itself and Gavin could make out the choppy waters below. He turned for Dover and picked up the blinks of white chalk cliffs within minutes. He saw the ME 109 come out of England dipping low and heading to sea.

Shoving the stick forward, he dove like a hungry hawk, arrowing down upon the unsuspecting Jerry and clearing his guns with a swift burst that the clown wouldn't hear. In a few more seconds, the pilot would never hear anything again, and Gavin Scott would be an ace.

He didn't know the other Messerschmitt was on him until explosive rounds from its cannons blew out his canopy and fragments of his right wing slammed back and almost tore his head off.

There was only time to realize that the plane skimming the waves had a twin riding shotgun much higher up, and that he'd been sucked into a trap. Then Gavin's Spitfire whirled down and smashed into gray water harder than steel.

CHAPTER 19

REUTERS NEWS AGENCY—London, May 5, 1940: Prime Minister Winston Churchill today repeated his historic "blood, sweat and tears" phrase while thanking U.S. President Franklin D. Roosevelt for the Lend-Lease Act which has helped England to stand firm against the new Hun.

He also mentioned the American volunteers who quietly joined the RAF to assist in the ongoing Battle of Britain. Churchill told his radio audience that throughout the long history of England, "never had so many owed so much to so few," referring to the valiant pilots who defend against the Nazi bombers and their fighter escorts.

Already he had become deft at hiding the left side of his face, angling away with his blue convalescent pajama collar turned up, blocking it with his pillow or cupping one hand from chin to eye socket. In his few less bitter moments Gavin was occasionally grateful that the eye still worked.

He never blew cigarette smoke out anymore, instead releasing it slowly to cloud around his head. And after he broke two mirrors, they stopped putting them above his sink. Moved onto the ward now, he simply made a point of avoiding the damned things. Although he tried, he couldn't avoid the "sisters," the nurses who had fussed over him, greasing his shiny red horror and changing bandages. Every day, he thought of *The Man in the Iron Mask*. Dumas would have known that this mask was worse, because it also locked in a man's soul.

The fucking doctors, those renowned Harley Street surgeons who tweezered and peeled and hurt the hell out of him on morning rounds—he only resented them for being clumsy and stupid and for not shipping him home right away. Famous plastic surgeons in New York, Boston and especially Hollywood would fall over each other for a chance to serve the family. In this two-bit country they'd never heard of the Carlisle-Belvales.

And the sisters, the women who leaned over him clucking and smelling of soap and powder, the solicitous nurses who brought their white throats too close and brushed soft breasts against his arm—he hated the lying bitches. They murmured that he would no doubt become good as new; not to worry, Yank, it's the man inside the face who really counts. Oh, the bitches; as if he couldn't see the shock and revulsion they tried to hide.

For godsakes, he had even run out of American cigarettes and every ward boy—called orderlies here—was too busy to go find an American PX. He had finally bought one, but for now he had to make do with the powdered horse shit in Capstans and Players. The goddamn Limeys couldn't do anything right. Dribbling smoke, he covered his slick, ridged cheek with his cigarette hand and stared out the grimy hospital window at a grimy street below a dirty sky so seldom washed by a reluctant sun.

"Leftenant Scott?" The voice was female, not soft but crisp, definitely English.

"Technically," he said without turning. "Not even more or less, just a hell of a lot less." He must be feeling better; he was being civil instead of telling this one to piss off.

"Colonel Carlisle asked me to—"

Whirling, for a split second he forgot to cover his face. "Godsakes—Stevie! You—I'll be goddamned—Stevie Bartlett."

She looked good, small and erect. She still held that arrogant gleam in her eyes and that dare-you set to her ripe mouth. Trim and tidy in her WAAF uniform, she looked even better than he remembered, drawing a grin from him until he felt no response at the left corner of his mouth. Then he remembered his face, his fucked-up face.

"Dear old Uncle Chad." He turned back to the window. "Where is the old bastard—safe at home with his wife?"

Hearing her footsteps march away, he wanted to go after her, or at least yell what she was at her back. She returned and spun him around, surprisingly strong.

"You're the true bastard. At the very first, Chad told me he was married, and I told him. I have no idea why he should express the slightest interest in your welfare. I shall inform him that you are your perpetual bastardly self."

He smelled her scent through the cheap blue woolens, faintly musky, a touch of flowers and it was too much. "Wait a second, damn it. You don't know me beyond a few minutes in a bar and then a bomb shelter. And this lousy hospital."

Deliberately, he dropped his hand from his ruined face and shoved the raw side at her. Stephanie didn't gasp or look away. He couldn't even find any shock in the depths of her steady eyes.

"You're new to the war, Yank. I've seen worse among my own ack-ack girls after an incendiary bomb hit."

He had been far too long without a woman, and had wanted this one before, wanted her now, if only to let Uncle Chad know who was the ultimate winner.

"Stevie, I need to be with someone like you. I haven't been able to take this"—he clawed fingers to cover his cheek again, showing that he wanted to rip out the scars; that much wasn't all fake—"this ugliness very well. I could wish to be an English soldier, stiff upper lip and all that. If both sides of my mouth worked."

It was working; she didn't walk off. But he sensed better than to milk her pity. Manly was her key, silent, manly suffering. "If the Piccadilly Hotel hasn't taken any bomb hits, I'd like to have a drink there. I haven't been out since I was shot down. Splashed, the RAF says, right?"

Now her eyes wavered and she glanced down, then up again before answering.

"You haven't left hospital? That's not like the brash

Yank who was so impatient to leave the underground and show the Limeys how to fly."

He looked down, too, and held it. "I'm slow growing up, I guess. Would you have a drink with me? I have to go outside sometime."

"All right," she said. "All right, Leftenant."

Breaking down, she was still formal; that would pass. He was doing okay. "Thanks—Leftenant. If you can wait, I'll get a pass and a uniform. I"—just enough hesitation, a touch of trepidation—"Yeah, I think I can make it."

"Of course you can."

Hurrying a shower and shave, he thanked Uncle Chad for this opportunity. It would be a real pleasure to tell the old fart how he had made Gavin a gift of this semiprivate pussy his high rank could no longer protect.

The sister on duty wore three pips and technically out-ranked him, but backed down when he demanded a facial bandage. The hell with her theory that he should face—for godsakes!—the fact that he was badly scarred and therefore rise above his resentment and fear.

He wasn't afraid; he was just, well, pissed at everything and everybody over here, the English and Germans alike, and throw in the "free" fighters clogging London. French escapees, Polish refugees, and all the other odds and ends of Europe who had lost their own countries. After he got back home and had his face fixed by real doctors, he would return and show them all just what a hot pilot he was. That reminded him how he had been cheated out of being the first American ace, and he slung his wet towel across the officers' ward latrine.

Touching her elbow only as a gentlemanly gesture of assistance into and out of the high-topped, lumbering taxi, he kept a respectful distance between them. In the Picca-dilly, his bandage drew no more than casual glances, but he hung his head as if he felt differently. He didn't look up when he slipped the waiter a many-folded five-pound note to make sure the rationed Scotch didn't run out. He didn't have to; the waiter understood money. These damned things were the size of a baby blanket but only meant about twenty bucks in real money. The Bank of England printed them that big so the man on the street wouldn't mistake all that money for a one-pound or ten-shilling note. Tradition? Even the Limeys weren't that dumb.

Money was another key to Stevie or any other woman, to anybody if properly applied. It was why she chose Uncle Chad over him and now he could show her he had it, too. That was one thing not taken away from Gavin Scott—the power of wealth, and he used it well.

Long deprived of a decent meal, she didn't flinch when the black market steaks and even scarcer chocolates were served in a small, intimate dining room. Atop the Scotch, a hoarded bottle of reasonably good Norman champagne made his fictionalized stories about Uncle Chad funnier or more tender for her. Rarely did Gavin talk about himself, but drew her out about her own life and marriage.

She was bonelessly relaxed and almost drunk when the well-paid driver walked away and left the taxi parked in the blackout darkness of a bombed-out block. Lifting her head sleepily from his shoulder, she rubbed her face and he watched her try to steady herself with deep breaths.

No more preliminaries; one hand gripping her shoulder, one hand moving up her skirt into the crude military underwear, he kissed her hard. She tasted of alcohol not yet gone stale, and beneath that, geraniums. Warm and wet, Stevie's tongue did not respond. He clashed his teeth against hers and ripped away straps that held up her thick stockings as he forced her down against the seat. Her head slammed on armrest and the side of the cab.

The bitch; she didn't fight back or scream when he jerked her skirt up over her head. She wasn't knocked out and pretended that she wasn't aroused. The hell with that. The army said throw a flag over their heads and fuck them for Old Glory. If it worked for ugly broads, it worked for wiseass bitches.

She couldn't hold back the quiver that rolled through her body when he packed it roughly into her and he grinned. Grinding the hurt side of his face into her cheek, he clamped down on her breasts with bold hands. He pounded into her then, shaking her limp body and rocking the taxi, rattling its window.

It was over too soon. He had been without a woman for so long it was over too soon. He pulled out as suddenly as he had gone in and sat back to light a cigarette.

She didn't move, but he knew damned well she was faking, that she hadn't really been hurt. It wasn't that he would miss the money she was about to demand for her silence, for not yelling rape and bringing him up on charges. What irritated him was that she would think him so stupid. The taxi driver was bought in advance, back when she had gone to the ladies' room.

He outwaited her, and when Stevie finally sat up, she didn't bother pulling her uniform together. She didn't plead: no more, oh please, no more, or make any demands, either.

She laughed.

The crazy little bitch giggled and the sounds weren't a damned bit funny. Her laughter grew louder, peal after peal of mockery that rang out across the bombed-out block. The cab driver had to hear it and wonder.

"Shut up," he said. "Shut the hell up!"

He slapped her to break the hysteria but she didn't stop.

Even after he kicked open the door and lunged out of the backseat, she continued to laugh at him. Gavin heard her long after he fled through the black night and found the road back to the hospital.

CHAPTER 20

REUTERS NEWS AGENCY—The Hague, Netherlands, May 10, 1940: Queen Wilhelmina said today that she and her government would do their duty following a sneak invasion into neutral Holland by German forces last night. In a three-pronged attack, Nazi troops also struck deep into Belgium and Luxembourg.

Swarms of planes engaged in air fights over Amsterdam before enemy paratroops, some in Dutch uniforms, descended upon strategic points while dive-bombers attacked airfields.

The Netherlands resisted the incursion and promptly opened the dikes to flood the roads with seawater as part of their defense system.

Major Chad Belvale was almost certain that he matched the coolness of his British companions, sweaty palms or no. What he wanted was to get the hell out of the flatlands before the Dutch opened the dikes and flooded the country; they'd do it, although it was already too late. As ranking officer he climbed into the front seat with the driver and Capt. Noel Warner, observer specializing in armor.

The old Bedford one-tonner rattled and bucked over roads already clogging with refugees who had no place to go, but were trying to run nevertheless. Warner said, "Sparks got a clear channel on the radio. It's not only Holland; old Jerry is invading Belgium, also. Damn it; those antiques in the War Office refused to believe this could happen."

The screech began high above the road; the driver yanked on his emergency brake and dove for the roadside ditch. Warner said, "Bloody Stuka! Horrid sound, what?"

The scream gained intensity, a smashing down noise that shook Chad to his bones. Face up in the opposite ditch, he watched the damned plane fill the sky, its nonretractable wheels reaching like talons. The strafing reached down, too—at least four wing guns winking red, chewing blacktop and dirt and whining off at all angles. Aircraft ammunition, Chad's brain registered, one blazing tracer followed by four unseen armor-piercing bullets. Sparks leaped and stones chipped in a wild trail of dust, and then the bomb kicked loose as the Stuka climbed sharply. The ground rocked and the ditch bucked around Chad with the explosion.

"All right!" It was Captain Warner's voice, stretched thin in the shattering echo of the blast. "He missed the truck!"

Spitting dirt, Chad climbed out of the ditch and made for the truck. "Everyone okay?"

"Not until we reach Chelsea again!" A second leftenant laughed.

Chad shook his head and jumped back under the canvas top. The English, at least these young men, made a game of it all. He was glad he was with them, because he found it difficult to feel anything comic about a Stuka bearing down on them with guns blazing. Ranking officer or not, he was learning from this team of young Sandhurst graduates. The British stiff upper lip was more than legend and Chad was glad for it. Warner was the only officer with more than a year or so active duty, and this was first combat all around for anybody, but they all acted like coming under fire was not only expected, but approved.

Warner leaned close to Chad as the driver hurled the blocky old Bedford down the road, whipping up and down the gears with an eagerness that said he meant to make it deep into Belgium before the German army and air force blocked them. Warner said, "If Jerry uses paratroops upon the Albert Canal, they'll be all over. Fort Eben Emael. The Belgians think they can pull their heads into that—ha!

—indestructible turtle shell and the Germans will just go away."

Hanging onto the dashboard and door, Chad could only nod. New as he was to this theater he had agreed with the younger officer corps that the Ardennes forest was not impenetrable, and that by expecting the Nazis to use the same invasion corridor as the Kaiser and a couple of his predecessors was to think Hitler's generals stupid. The swift overrunning of Denmark and Norway proved otherwise, and still no explanation forthcoming as to why the British navy failed to blockade that vital strip of water.

"A new type of warfare," he said, as the truck lurched around a sharp turn and a chorus of protest rose from the back. "Coordination of armor and close air support, plus the use of paratroops backed by motorized infantry throws all our defensive tactics out the window."

Warner grunted and his shoulder bumped Chad on another curve. "Too bloody bad it won't throw out those Colonel Blimps in London. I think we are about to lose all mainland Europe, and damned soon, if the British Army can't hold."

"We have our own Colonel Blimps in Washington," Chad said, "and we're trying to do something about them."

"Immovable objects."

Difficult to move, Chad thought, but with strong pry bars like Generals Belvale and Carlisle, maybe this war could be salvaged without too much loss to the United States. The truck slowed at a bridge jammed with carts and lost people. If that damned Stuka came back now—

A cavalryman pushed through the throng, his horse dripping, its flanks heaving and showing flecks of blood in the froth at its bit. Chad frowned; the fool was killing his mount, and if his mission was that important, that meant the radio system had been knocked out. The Netherlands couldn't hold out more than a few days. Then all of Belgium would fall, and if the French army didn't crawl out of its Maginot Line to fight, it would be outflanked, overrun and trapped. As Captain Warner said, everything now depended upon the British.

The bridge was behind them and the truck was making

good time when the strafing plane caught it. No warning screech this time, just the *rackety-slam!* of bullets ripping through canvas and metal, the roar of the plane's engine an afterthought. The truck slewed and the driver tried to hang onto the wheel, but the Bedford tilted into the ditch and the driver fell out. In back a man moaned and another cursed. Gingerly, Chad untangled himself from the British captain and fought gravity to open the door. He smelled burned oil and turned to reach a helping hand to Warner. The Englishman's hand and wrist were bloody, but he struggled up and over the bullet-gouged door.

Chad broke out his aid bandage and tightened it around Warner's hurt arm.

"The driver's bought it," Warner said, his face pale. "See to the other lads, Major. I'll be right in a moment."

Shaken, Chad went to help the kids, realizing with a shock that's what they were, youngsters barely older than his sons. Scooping up one boy in the fireman's carry, he yelled to the others: "Down the road, and hurry! The truck's about to blow up!"

The driver dead in the ditch, radioman spread over his ruined radio, another limp form being dragged by two wounded leftenants, Captain Warner and the boy Chad carried; casualties all, except Maj. Chad Belvale. He wasn't about to question his luck. Grandfather Belvale's premise was that most battles are won by blind luck, although thorough preparation helped. Great-great-granduncle General Carlisle had a more simple approach: Kick ass before yours gets kicked.

Too close behind them as they staggered along the road, the truck exploded, the heat wave slamming Chad's back, and oily smoke in an inky cloak streaked overhead. Lowering his burden to the ground, Chad turned the boy over. He might have been looking into his older son's face, barely fuzzed, blue eyes wide open and already glazing. Dead, damnit—dead!

"Sorry," Captain Warner muttered, "Leftenant Longhurst is dead, too. Weeks, Merriman—get their identity discs and anything personal from their kits. We must leave them here, you know. Can't be helped."

Weeks limped, thigh cut from ripped metal, not a bullet; Merriman had a shoulder wound. Weeks said, "Where the bloody hell are we?"

Warner held out a red stained map to Chad. "Would you mind? A bit difficult to unfold with one hand."

"I make it just south of Moerdijk."

"Still in Holland, then."

Chad glanced at the leftenants putting personal belongings of the dead into a musette bag. Nobody had a weapon larger than a handgun, the British those clumsy Webley 455s, his own 1911 Colt .45. Rations were lost with the truck, and he saw one other canteen besides his own. Things could get sticky. He oriented himself with the map and looked off across the fields to the west/southwest. "We're lucky, at that. We're thirty or forty miles from where the French lines should be, near the coast."

Merriman, a youngster with a cultivated red mustache, said, "May I suggest we get a move on, sir? If I don't hear tank engines, it's another one of those bloody Messerschmitts that hit the truck. I knew I should have joined the sodding RAF."

Chad cocked his head, listening. He heard the remains of their truck frying and the growling rumble of heavy motors. Armor, all right; so damned much of it that he felt the earth shiver beneath his feet. A tank spearhead pointing where? Directly for Antwerp and Brussels, and it would slice right through to the sea. The vaunted Fort Eben Emael was a hundred miles south, and would be outflanked.

"Let's go," he said. "With any luck, we'll make it out."

Staying close together, leaning upon each other when support was needed, they headed for the coast and the uncertain French lines. Belgian troops in their tinny helmets passed them by, most of them unarmed. But the local soldiers angled north toward Rotterdam, spirits crushed and already done with fighting.

A half hour later, Chad found Lebel rifles in small pyramids, hooked by their stacking swivels, signs of total surrender. There were also a few Modele D'Ordonnance pistols and MAS 1935 autos. Throwing them off into the high grass, Chad passed out the rifles and pocketed the real prizes, a pair of grenades.

They saw the first German tanks and took to the brush to wait until the column thundered by on the narrow road below, its dust cloud rising high and thick. Warner said, "Mark Twos and Threes; light armor really, slow but properly used. Our own tanks are heavier and faster, but the damned War Office insists upon using them like cavalry scouts."

Hungry and tired, stiffening from wounds, Chad's decimated observer group holed up for the night in a brush covered ravine that was little more than a ditch. Often in the night, he would doze off and then waken to hear more enemy tanks cruise by. The last batch was widespread, running much farther apart. Just before dawn, when he shivered in chill dew, a tank stopped so close that he could hear the turret open and the crew climb out talking. He nudged Captain Warner, and the man whispered: "I heard."

"They're starting a fire to heat rations," Chad said. "We need food and water if we go much farther."

"Transportation, too."

"Take the tank?"

"I can drive one; armor expert, remember?"

Passing word to the others, Chad told them to follow to the edge of the road, and they moved off into the tree line. There they set up steel helmets filled with dirt and soaked by gasoline. The soldier's field stove; he'd used the same on a dozen maneuvers back home; the difference between hot and cold rations did much for morale.

He stopped and looked up and down the road; nothing in sight. Chad put one knee on the ground and thumb signalled Warner to take the men on the right. Coveralled in gray-green and wearing those footballish tanker helmets, the men's broad backs were to Chad. He smelled coffee boiling. General, he thought as he two-fisted his .45, it doesn't seem sporting, and inside his head the old man's voice spoke clearly: gentlemen do not win wars.

Chad's shots flung both targets across the cook-fire, and to his right, the captain's Webley went off four times. Still, one German staggered up and reached for a machine pistol before additional muzzle flashes streaked from the trees and bullets knocked him spinning along his tank.

"Sorry," Warner said. "I was never much with a sidearm."

"Spilled the coffee," Chad said, surprised at himself. Then he rolled the dead men from the choked-off fire. "Destroy those rifles; enough Schmeissers here to go around. Oh, yes—let's get the bodies out of sight. Take just the helmets; distinctive outlines."

Merriman had climbed down inside the tank. "Rations here; anyone care for tinned fish?"

Within minutes, Chad was upright in the open turret behind a 6.5 machine gun, and the Mark III's engines had come alive. He took a deep breath of morning air and could swear that he tasted burned flesh. His country wasn't even in this war, and he had killed his first men, executed them, really.

They were still long miles from the coast, and had to roll through German armor to get there. They were not likely to be welcomed by the French at first sight, either. But by God, they had captured their own tank.

As Captain Warren had told him, he tapped both feet lightly on the driver's shoulders: a signal for straight ahead.

"Let's go!" he said.

CHAPTER 21

REUTERS NEWS AGENCY—Dover, England, May 11, 1940: A new word of warfare was coined yesterday and thoroughly understood today. The word is blitzkreig, or "Lightning War." German airborne troops rained down upon the Netherlands and Belgium after armored spearheads crushed resistance and slashed through defenses to disrupt communications and supplies in rear areas.

Chad bluffed it all the way, only his helmeted head showing from the turret, the radio antenna broken and left dangling at Captain Warner's suggestion. No communication, it said, and he had no trouble easing by tank parks, acting as if he knew just where he was going. They had lucked out, not coming into contact with other armor carrying the same unit markings as their Mark III.

Night came, and over the ridges behind, the gun thunder went on, lighting the cloudy sky with fitful lashes. Ahead was quiet, although the tank's compass and dead reckoning told Chad they were not far from the Channel and the French Seventh Army lines.

Tapping Warner's right shoulder with his foot, he had the tank pulled off the road and under the trees in a small apple orchard. Stiffly, he climbed down, cradling the Schmeisser machine pistol. A bare and somehow beautiful piece of killing machinery, it was supposed to have a cyclic rate of fire of nine hundred rounds per minute, but it was impossible to feed clips in that fast.

"Cold camp, gentlemen," he said as the others grunted up out of the tank. "We've gotten this far on pure luck, and tomorrow will see us through."

If the Germans didn't block them; if the French didn't blow them out of the saddle. Getting by those ifs, they still had to swing south and tie in with the British Expeditionary Forces.

They ate German tinned rations and drank sparingly of water. The former crew had left blankets and cigarettes, and even a few bars of liberated Dutch chocolate. Showing no lights, they ducked beneath blankets to drag on cigarettes, and lifted their heads out to expel smoke.

Wounds cleansed and bandaged from German aid kits, they bundled down for the night after Chad volunteered to take first watch. He used the extra gas cans strapped on the rear deck to replenish the fuel tank. It didn't fill; the big motors gulped a lot of gas, but what they had was all they'd get. And so far, riding the treads had beat hiking, plus keeping them under cover. Four desperate men, Chad thought; three of them wounded and the other guessing his way through his first combat command.

He walked around front and leaned against the chill metal, the gun a narrow roof overhead. He could use some wisdom from the old general now. There he'd be in the study, backed up to the log fire in his cavalry breeches and boots, rocking a little upon his heels. What would he say if Chad asked him how to get out of this situation? Almost anything, but most likely: "Do something, boy—even if it's wrong. Just do something."

And General Crusty Carlisle? "Fire full clips."

Kill Devil Hill; Chad had seen mansions in England bigger and richer, but no match for the grace, beauty and strength of the southern home. The northern homestead was strong, not beautiful. He looked up at the gray clouds, searching for a star. He tried to figure the time difference between here and Virginia, but gave up. His wife was probably in the barns, feeding her Morgans and picking up the stalls, chores any stable hand should be doing. Kirstin didn't trust anyone to handle her prize horses, which made the grooms and trainers happy. Different breeds, show horse and running horse people, and maybe that was what had gone wrong between him and Kirstin. Chad never gave a damn about horses, and each time he went off on assignment, his wife stayed behind with her horses.

Shifting the machine pistol in his arms, Chad knew he couldn't lay all blame on her. The second time he shipped out, a newly made captain anxious to prove himself at Fort Benning, she followed a week later and surprised him. Belvale money allowed him to avoid living in Bachelor Officer Quarters on post, which would have been embarrassing, anyhow. His records showed he was married, and he was never so conscious of it as when Kirstin showed up at the apartment he rented in Columbus, Georgia.

It wasn't usual for Chad to tie one on, and more rare for him to rent a hooker for the night. But he never felt comfortable in a normal cathouse, much less a setup like Ma Beechie Howard's cribs across the river in Phenix City, Alabama, where enlisted men and officers passed in the hallways. Suddenly, there was Kirstin in the doorway, looking over his shoulder at the woman on the bed. . . .

Chad straightened up, his finger slipping into the trigger guard of the Schmeisser. A man was walking off the road and right at the tank, little equipment clinks and rattles announcing him as a soldier. *"Hallo, der panzer!"*

"Yah," Chad answered, using up his school German quickly. *"Wer bist du?"*

"Korporal Klassen, drittel infanterie."

Easing farther back into the shadow of the tank, Chad said, *"Kommen zee."* He couldn't fire; if one straggler from the third infantry was on the road, there'd be others. He watched the man scuff across grass under the trees, a tired soldier seeking his own kind, looking for company or lining up proof that he was no deserter. A small man, helmet tilted back and shoulders drooping, a long Gewehr rifle sloped across both shoulders.

Chad took a long stride and smashed the steel butt of the Schmeisser into the man's face. The German went down without a grunt, his helmet falling off to clang against the tank. Drawing a deep, steadying breath, Chad straddled the man and struck down with all his strength, and once again. Tasting salt bile in his throat, he kneeled to listen for breath, to touch a forefinger to the carotid artery. Then, turning his face, he threw up quietly.

When he stood up, Captain Warner murmured at his shoulder, "Nasty business, close up like that. Good-o, Yank; I might have got the wind up and fired. Let me take over now."

"There are probably more stragglers on the road." Chad pulled air deep and thought he tasted apples. No argument about the blood he smelled, so he walked into the dark under a tree and scrubbed the butt of the Schmeisser into the grass.

. . . not real, Kirstin had called him, a hollowness held together by a uniform and Sam Browne belt. I knew that, but I came down here to try. Jesus Christ, Chad—you're not even real in bed. You need a few drinks to even play at sex. . . .

Propping his back against the apple tree, machine pistol across his lap, Chad drifted. So he wasn't one of her huge Morgan stallions, driving that mighty rod so deep into a mare that the horse had trouble staying on her feet, her neck caught by the stud's teeth. The uniform is what we do, what the family is all about, and sometimes the Holy Grail is too heavy. You knew that when you married me. And I'm no stud horse for you to halter and hand breed! He had yelled that at her, both of them forgetting the whore on his bed.

. . . You're right; stallions get stud fees—if they're worth it. If not, they're gelded. . . .

Turning then, her back as straight as if she were riding in the show ring, a slim and always collected woman with depths he had never been able to plumb, Kirstin walked out of the hotel and went home to Kill Devil Hill. He had wanted to scream it at her: maybe you're at fault! So goddamned self-possessed, always in control, like you master those big goddamned horses. You didn't make a sound when the boys were born. Other women sweat and cry and hold out their hands to husbands for security. Not you.

The whore was dressed when he turned around. . . . Not much use going on, huh? She'd pointed at his shriveled penis. Her heavy perfume hung in the room for a long time after she was gone. If she had laughed, he might have tried to kill her.

Somehow in the night, he slept, but so lightly that he heard every sound, every grunt of the men, and snapped full awake when the sounds lifted from the road. Merriman shook him. "Daylight, Major."

He felt his body creak as he stood up to lean against the tree and relieve himself. Would Kirstin think him real if she could have watched him beat a man to death last night? "Captain? Crank her up; we'll chow down on the road."

He saw that someone had dragged the German infantryman out of sight and was grateful for it. He saw something else—the men glancing at him with a new respect. They knew he was real, by God.

The tank rolled about two miles, passing plodding infantry who cursed the dust it raised. Chad guided it due west, turning off onto a country lane marked with other tank treads. Around the shoulder of the last low hill, when wind swept in from the coast bearing the flavors of the sea and the heady scent of safety, Chad saw the two Mark IVs set into a roadblock. Did they know anything about this tank? He didn't see how they could, but he signalled his driver to stop while he took a reading on the situation. It was a definite roadblock, the tanks angled to fire either way, inland or toward the sea. There was very little room between them, and worse—both carried the same ID markings as his own; at last they'd run into the home panzer unit of the crew they'd killed.

Dropping lower into the tank, Chad rattled off the situation, then said, "As I see it, we can fire on the left tank from up close, going full speed and try to ram the other one before they figure out what's happening."

Warner said, "Your play, Major."

Weeks only sighed and settled behind his machine gun.

Merriman said, "I knew I should have joined the bloody RAF. Knock their dicks out, Major."

Chad raised himself and saw both tank commanders staring at him from their turrets, saw one long gun slowly cranking in his direction. "Go!" he yelled, and "Fire!"

The shell slammed in just below the left tank's turret. Splinters of steel arrowed back at them and Merriman got off another shot that almost blew them all up. Foot hard upon Warner's right shoulder, Chad threw his tank desperately at the remaining Mark III. That commander was quick and the flash from his gun muzzle barely passed over. Then Chad's front deck crashed into the other tread cover, and his 76mm blasted, also too high.

The first tank blew up with a mighty roar of gas and ammunition, hurling flame over the locked tanks. Chad knew they had to get the hell out of there, but a machine gun raked his turret. He pulled in his head and remembered the Belgian grenades he'd rescued. A ricochet from the other 6.5 clanged madly around inside and drew a yelp from Merriman.

Right, General, Chad thought—do something even if it's wrong; even if you get killed trying. He stood up as machine gun bullets seared his face and threw the grenade down into the other hatch. Masked by armor, it went off dully and Chad yelled "Get out! Get out! Everything's going to blow!"

Tumbling, dragging at each other, they staggered a few yards, then another few and collapsed as the tangle of armor, gasoline and cannon shells went off, the machine-gun belts popping like subdued firecrackers.

It wasn't easy getting off the ground, and Chad thought for a moment that he had gone deaf. He helped Warner beat sparks from his uniform and Merriman had twisted an ankle. Then he discovered the sliver of metal half into his own wrist. Chad hadn't felt it strike.

"Look away," Warner said, and yanked out the slim piece of metal. This time Chad felt every quiver of pain. Warner asked, "Handkerchief?"

"Only to knot on the front sight of this Schmeisser. That blowup must have caught the attention of the whole French army and somebody's watching us right now."

Proof came in the form of a short burst of fire, perhaps deliberately laid to their left flank. Chad stepped out in front and waved the white rag, but Merriman limped past him, cupped his hands at his mouth and roared what sounded like curses in French and definitely curses in cockney English. The firing from the French lines stopped and someone shouted back.

"Bugger them," Merriman said. "Come on, gentlemen; show these Frogs what we are—damned good examples of His Majesty's army. Uh—the colonies, too."

"I'm proud to be part of His Majesty's observer group," Chad said.

Then they walked and limped and wobbled a bit, heading for the French lines.

CHAPTER 22

AGENCE FRANCE PRESSE—Supreme Headquarters, Army of France, May 20, 1940: General Maxime Weygand complained today that the British army, on its own initiative, retreated 25 miles toward the ports when his troops were moving up from the south where they were to meet their allies.

REUTERS NEWS AGENCY—With the BEF somewhere in France, May 20, 1940: Complaints from French General Maxime Weygand reached this headquarters today. An official source stated that the French army supposedly advancing north has made no headway, and that Weygand's comments show the state of unreality in which he is living; there is tension between the commands.

The only things that marked Chad Belvale as American were his garrison cap, which had somehow survived, and his oak leaves of rank. He was not easy in the short British battle blouse; without the issue suspenders, its bottom wouldn't meet the thick brown pants. The short gaiter-leggings were passable, but the regulation high-top shoe—it carried enough iron to keep a horse shod for rough ground and made that amount of noise—was barely acceptable. His GI .45 was also gone, traded off for the bulky Webley 455, complete with holster and lanyard. Colt ammo was nonexistent, so he also picked up an Enfield rifle. Besides the hat, the rifle brought a lot of puzzled looks from passing Tommies. Shoulder weapons were not traditional for their own brass.

Leftenant Merriman sprawled beside him, tucked and bandaged but refusing to be shipped back to the hospital in England. He had to lean awkwardly on a makeshift cane when he walked, a cane that was actually an aiming stake for heavy mortars. "I can always give Jerry a good whack with it," he said. "Teach him to bugger around with cripples."

They had ridden a supply truck south of Lille, a truck whose bed was a microcosm of what was happening all along the front—a jumble of French, Belgian and British uniform parts, weapons workable and not, ten-in-one rations, all sliding around in confusion.

Chad wasn't surprised when Merriman insisted on staying in France. The boy was tough and driven by something more than duty. Perhaps most wouldn't sense that inner push, but generations of Belvales and Carlisles had grown up with it fixed in the blood and bone, locked into the genes themselves. Keepers of the sword; there were times he wished he had never seen the damned thing.

Merriman said, "It's bollixed up, you know. The BEF is readying to attack toward Arras, where we'll get our arses kicked again. Best we trot for home while we can."

"You had your chance," Chad said, kneeling and peering up often through patches of green leaves. It didn't take long for everyone to scan the skies for Stukas and Messerschmitts, and to keep listening for the peculiar *hum-HUM*, *hum-HUM* motor throb of high-level Junkers bombers.

"Not half, Major. I had a bloody time getting into Sandhurst, and teeth and toenails staying there. Not a sodding gentleman, you know. Effing clots did their damnedest to rid themselves of the cockney who dared their bloody sacred precincts. I had to study harder, jump higher, run faster, and I flipping well did it. Now I'm here to do it again, this time not play acting."

Chad rescued a can of steak and kidney pudding from a tub over the cook-fire, burned his hands and allowed it to cool more. Merriman used the stubby Enfield bayonet to turn the bacon he was cooking. Chad said, "It's like that with my entire family. I think all our swaddling clothes are miniature uniforms. I know that any male who opts not to serve in the military gets about the same reception as an announced homosexual. For three hundred years we've fought Indians, the French, the British twice and our own blood in the Civil War. There's a saying in my country: Texas is good for men and horses, but hell on women. It works as well in Virginia, fitting some of the Belvale-Carlisle women, who sort of get shoved out to the edges of the family aerie, but the others are more like the Spartan mothers, tougher than some of the men."

That surprised Chad, popping out that way. Kirstin was closer to the front of his mind than he realized. Punching holes in the can of rations with his bayonet, he peeled back the top and divided the steak and kidneys with Merriman.

Kirstin would find that hard to believe, him thinking about her almost as often as duty, honor and country. She would not insist that her sons—their sons—return from war carrying their shields or being carried upon them. He blinked into the cook-fire; he hardly knew their boys. Did Kirstin? Both had followed the pattern of military school to West Point and VMI; next would come active duty.

"Bloody hell!" Merriman yelped. "Here come the bastards again!"

The quick and the dead; the lucky and the losers— rolling behind trees for cover not protective enough while hell's banshees screamed down upon them. Dirt leaped in uneven lines across the grass and across the supply truck as the Stukas made their strafing runs and zoomed high to circle before dive-bombing.

"Effing sirens," Merriman said from behind his tree. "They've attached effing fire sirens, as if they need to scare more piss out of us." He braced the Enfield against his tree trunk, sighting and waiting.

Chad did the same from a kneeling position. They'd play hell hitting a plane, even if a bomb didn't dig a mass grave for everybody here, but it dulled the feeling of helplessness, being able to fight back.

When the first Stuka peeled off and shrieked down on

them, a pair of Sten guns rattled from the wounded supply truck and the deeper barking of a Bren backed them. Chad tried to lead the plane according to the book as the earth erupted around him. Then he just worked the bolt and fired blindly at plane two through dust and smoke and that damned screaming siren. He thumbed a new five-round clip into the rifle as plane three came in, the whole world a gigantic roaring in his ears, the taste of gunpowder heavy in his mouth.

A bigger crash shook the ground, and a sheeting of flame burned the leaves off the trees overhead. Chad shielded his face with his arms and backed away. Something had brought down the last German plane, some wild and lucky bit of metal that slammed into the pilot or engine, and the Stuka never pulled out of its last dive.

Fires crackled and stinging smoke floated thick around the area. The new silence was not natural, bringing a deeper ache to the ears than the actual air raid. The Bren gun carrier growled from cover and its gunner swung the weapon's muzzle in a new direction. Someone yelled triumph down the line, and closer by, a man shouted, "Good-o, you Jerry bastard! Fry in hell."

"Have some bacon," Merriman said. "I say we trade off these rifles for Stens. Neat little buggers, eh? Never have to clear a jam; just throw the bloody thing away, since it costs only about nine bob to produce."

Chad looked at bacon and a smear of steak pudding on his mess kit lid. His imagination equated the odor of bacon with human flesh cooking where the plane went in. He chewed on a dry cracker and concentrated on the remarkable little Sten gun: stamped metal and a side feed clip, full automatic. It was nothing special for accuracy, but at short range it didn't have to be. He had heard that the British factories were rushing all-out production, so that every man, woman and child in England could carry one. For all his optimistic speeches, Winston Churchill was no fool; he anticipated a German invasion soon after the Nazis overran the Continent, and overrun the land, they would. Even the tough British Tommy, probably the best defensive fighter in the world, wore the look of impending defeat. The English wouldn't break, but Chad had seen the situation map at HQ late last night.

He knew the impending attack was actually an attempt to break out of a tightening ring of German armor that threatened to cut off any escape by sea. This blitzkreig might well end the war in Europe before it could even be slowed up, before America got pulled in. That would look great to the isolationists back home—for a while. Squeezed between a Nazified Europe, communist Russia and Imperial Japan, the U.S. would be caught between a rock and a hard place, left to go it alone. Chad hadn't yet seen any of the giant aircraft carriers, but he knew they were building, and some were already at sea. The carrier made it possible to hit any nation anywhere; wide seas were no longer barriers, but open ocean pathways.

He wondered what General Belvale was doing about that. The family's strength had always been solidly rooted in ground command, but now it had to look to the sea and the air as well. General Crusty Carlisle might have been a marine, for his attitude of hey, diddle, diddle, right up the middle.

That wouldn't be difficult for the master of Kill Devil Hill; the old man's geneology charts showed the family cousins, great- and grandnephews scattered throughout the armed forces, such armed forces as existed, with such obsolete equipment as existed. Chad had already seen enough German air and armor to scare hell out of him; there was nothing in the States to match them.

Thumbing his red mustache, Merriman showed up with a Sten gun apiece and a canvas bag bulging with extra clips. Chad watched the youngster limp along, propped upon his aiming stake cane. He said, "Are you sure you're up to this?"

"As the tall lady said to the midget? Damned well right. Make a fine rear guard, what? Can't run." Merriman divided the Sten clips as a plodding line of infantry passed, headed for Arras and away from the English Channel. He leaned against a tree trunk scarred by strafing. "But why are you standing fast with us, Major? Observed enough to take it all home, I'd say, and it's not your war—yet."

"Honor of the colonies." Chad grinned. "Run faster, jump higher, right?"

Smiling back, Merriman said, "Right-o, Major. Shall we fall in behind this group of them that don't know any better?"

Even though the column's pace was slow, they had to drop back hour by hour, and Chad pretended not to see the grimaces of pain that crossed Merriman's face. Once they fell out for rations, and twice they were approached by Red Caps, until the military police saw Chad's pieced together uniform and heard his accent.

"Stupid buggers," Merriman grunted, "looking for deserters heading to the front. Why would some laggart be pissing off right on the road and going in the wrong direction?"

By nightfall, they were part of a rough semicircle south and east of Arras, tired men slowly digging in. To the northeast, rumbling flashes streaked the sky, and word came down for cold camp, no fires. The entrenching tools clinked and chukked along the line as Chad and Merriman shared some compo rations washed down with cold tea.

Thinking of the way Kirstin served iced tea on the columned porches of Kill Devil Hill, Chad could almost taste the sprig of mint and touch of lime or lemon. She never smelled like the stables, anyway, and not of perfume, only an Ivory Soap odor, crisp and clean. Not your penultimate southern belle, she didn't like mint juleps, either. He admitted that juleps were highly overrated, and so were horses, and goddamnit—marriage. A deteriorating marriage didn't announce its breakdown honestly or boldly. It was infiltrated by one small thing after another, a penetration of what should have been a sturdy wall of defense; a sniper here, a weak spot in the line over there, all pecking away until the loss of blood was too much to staunch.

There it was again, this odd concentrating upon Kirstin. Was it a harbinger of guilt before death, a foreboding that made him want to make all things right before the panzers came and churned them all into the muddy earth? "Goddamnit!" he muttered. "It wasn't all my fault. She could have helped, allowed me to reach that place she keeps hugged to herself. I never really knew Kirstin, and she didn't even try to understand me."

Merriman passed him a lighted cigarette, one of those dry Capstans, beneath the cover of his battle jacket. "I'd imagine you're married, Major," he said, and laughed.

That's when the first German 88mm squalled in upon the defensive line, followed by a rapid string of sharp, flat explosions. Face pressed into the earth of their too-shallow foxhole, Chad tried to pick out the slam of the guns themselves from the exploding shells. A flat trajectory weapon, the 88 left damned little time between the yank of the lanyard and the wicked whack of the missile.

Mouth close to Merriman's ear, Chad said, "It doesn't sound like battery fire. It's the panzers themselves—bigger than one we captured; Mark IVs at least. There'll be infantry mixed in with them. We can do some damage there."

"Not for bloody long," Merriman said, propped shoulder to shoulder with Chad. "Our lot has a few twenty-five pounders that might back old Jerry off for a time. After they go, there's little to stop the buggers from racing to the Channel."

WHACK! WHACK!

Some great force lifted Chad bodily from his hole and bounced him against the ground. He rolled over and got his eyes focused in time to make out the distinctive outlines of German helmets. He sprayed them with the Sten and felt much better when Merriman's gun joined in; the last shells could easily have turned them both into hamburger, and he was glad the boy was alive.

Machine pistols answered back, and a panzer hurtled through the thin British line until one of the twenty-five pounder guns caught it head-on. The blast knocked Chad down again, numbing him all over. He felt the shadow bulking over him, then focused upon the big German lowering the muzzle of a Schmeisser at him. Chad could barely feel the shape of his Sten, and strained mightily to bring it around and fire.

He knew he wasn't going to make it.

CHAPTER 23

REUTERS NEWS AGENCY—Lille, France, May 20, 1940: British troops failed in an attempt to break out of an encirclement of fast-moving German armor today. French forces around Lille disintegrated under massive pressure from panzers and dive-bombers. A dogged, step-by-step retreat by the British is underway as German tanks launch a pincers movement from Rouen to block escape via the Channel ports.

It was a tree falling, this tremendous weight slamming down upon him, spinning the Sten gun from his hands. It was a mountain slide, a gigantic boulder. Chad Belvale fought for breath, struggled not to die. Whirling through his stunned mind was the idea that he should have felt a series of impacts even if the Schmeisser fired so damned fast. He didn't expect this mighty, individual slam down of tonnage that would crush out his life. But what did anybody know about dying until he got there?

Then he felt the telltale wetness, the hot gushing of blood. So many of the dying soldiers, young and old, called out for their mothers, but Chad could only say Kirstin. Not duty or honor, just Kirstin.

"Tally-ho!" Merriman said, dragging the dead man off him, "or whatever the fucking toffs say."

It wasn't his own blood. He wasn't shot, wasn't hit, and the weight was the big goddamn German falling on him.

"Thought of a carom stroke," Merriman said, reaching

down a hand, "what you Yanks call a bank shot, I think. But Jerry seemed a bit eager, so you simply had to take the bumps. I respectfully suggest that we get the hell out of here, sir. Panzers all over the bleeding place; broke through like we weren't even here, and their sodding infantry trotting with. Except for that bastard. Heavy, was he?"

"We're cut off—behind their lines now?"

Merriman heeled another clip into the left side of his Sten. "No lines, Major; situation fluid, as they say."

Chad got his feet firmly beneath him. "Head for Aire and St. Omer—east/northeast?"

Touching his shoulder, Merriman urged him down again. They squatted low while two tanks and a half-track flak wagon rolled by. Five minutes, ten, and when no infantry appeared, they rose again.

Merriman whispered, "Calais and Dunkirk, I'd say—if we get that far. A bloody long way, Major; makes me wish I'd lived a cleaner life, gone to chapel and such."

"There'll be other cut-off groups and stragglers. We'll hook up with some bunch and fight our way to the Channel."

"I'd feel much better if we would find ourselves another Jerry tank, one that can float. If we do make it to the bleeding coast, then what? I never learned to swim."

Chad felt through the dead German's pack for rations and cigarettes. Robbing the dead? What could the dead use? A prayer, maybe, but Chad had never been one for church. Sitting through the obligatory Sunday sermons at Virginia Military Institute, he had discovered that he could sort of glaze over, more or less sleeping with his eyes open. Now he wished he knew the incantations, not for the German, but for them. He said, "When we reach the water, I'll show you how to dog-paddle—all the way to Dover, if need be. Meanwhile, I think we should move slow and easy, staying off the road until dark."

Later, he was to realize that only saying it was easy; they took cover so many times that Chad lost count, lying unmoving in the brush while armored vehicles and trucks passed. Twice, company-size combat patrols legged by, the troops chattering the way winners will. But since victory had come so easy for them, they were lax; no flankers out, no worry about ambushes.

Behind them, improvised PW camps had been set up, and back still farther, the Gestapo would be casting its spiked net for civilians on their lists. It was the way the Nazis worked: blitzkreig, hard-hitting military stunning an entire nation, and immediately after, the political sweep before any kind of underground resistance could be organized. The Jews, intellectuals of any sort, the leaders—all would vanish. Chad Belvale might feel better if he hadn't studied *Mein Kampf* and the rise of National Socialism, but now he knew what would happen to civilized countries that fell before the twisted cross.

Merriman murmured, "Shall we displace to the rear? Favorite term of Sandhurst instructors, that; never retreat, just displace."

"We have to fire only if fired on," Chad whispered. "They're all over the area, but it looks like the rear echelon hasn't caught up yet. That gives us a gap, a little room to move."

"I must tell you something, Major," Merriman said as they walked beside the road chewed to deep dust by steel treads and hurrying tires, by bicycle troops and horses. "I don't fancy spending the best of my life in some stalag. If it comes pecker to pecker, they'll have to kill me. I'll hold off long as I can to give you time for—"

Moving along quickly, but as silently as he could, Chad said softly, "I haven't learned much Limey yet, but I think that *bugger you* fits all right. If we go down, we go together."

"Right-o." There was a chuckle in Merriman's voice.

The night thickened, and a short convoy rumbled by; everything and everyone moving relentlessly toward the coast. This convoy commander was so sure of himself that his trucks ran with lights on. That caused Chad and Merriman to drift farther off the road where they stumbled over plowed fields. Hours later, they sat to share German rations and water.

"A little rest," Chad said, "but only a little. If I snore off, kick me."

"Wouldn't miss the chance; imagine putting the boot to a bloody major."

Compressed pork, Chad guessed, and black bread squeezed into a hard lump. It beat the standard German canned fish ration. Was that why they had grabbed Norway so fast—for an unending field ration supply? And one time, long ago and far away, Chad Belvale had liked sardines.

Lying back with his head propped in the flat English helmet, deep in the darker shadow of a gnarled apple tree, Chad smelled the night and listened to his heartbeat.

Kirstin; she had never been to France or Spain, and he'd never asked if she wanted to go. The money was always there to travel anywhere and do almost anything, so long as it brought no stain to the family escutcheon. This soldiering family never seemed to think of travel for pleasure, only for duty; observation; intelligence. And ever since that miserable night when she caught him in bed with a hooker, there was no point asking Kirstin anything.

She had her horses, and when she was on the show circuit, traveled with grooms and drivers. Showing several horses called for quick changes of tack and riding habits, for horses to constantly be brushed and polished and cared for. Chad blinked up at the one star he could see in the sky. Did his wife find sympathy and understanding among her own horsey kind? She wasn't sexless; she had been more passionate, surprisingly so, when she was pregnant with their sons. Before pregnancy and after birth, she was only adequate. What could he do, play the old army game and keep her knocked up and barefoot?

Rolling onto his side, Chad remembered the cutting words she'd thrown at him with the hooker listening, how he needed a few drinks in order to perform in bed. As if he were one of her prize Morgans—a touch of the bit, a little leg pressure cueing him to take the proper lead. That wasn't so; whiskey just made him looser, easier in mind and body.

Damn! In retrospect, he would rather his mother had caught him masturbating than Aunt Minerva. Finely tuned lady that she was, his mother would have blanked it out, pretended that it never happened. But at the time, the mere threat of Aunt Minerva telling was enough to keep him on edge and ashamed and completely goddamned miserable. Cold-eyed, thin lips pinched firmly together, she had only to glance his way at table to make him sit up straight and be extra careful about his manners. Most of his young life, he had worried who she had told and how she had told it. His mother, the general?

He had remained frightened for a long time. He didn't have his first woman until after graduation from VMI, and not the girl he wanted, willowy Lisa who had strolled a copycat Flirtation Walk with him. He got drunk with classmates and ended up with a whore.

Merriman nudged him. "Time, Major. I can limp another ten miles before dawn, and listen to the guns off yonder. Our lads are holding out, I should think somewhere near Aire."

"Let's hope they wait for us. From there it's about sixty-five long, wearisome miles to Calais or Dunkirk. If our luck holds out."

The night stretched, pulled at itself until Chad's legs were numb and he had to concentrate upon putting one foot after the other; so damned tired. One or the other of them tripped over stones, and once both of them took a header over a rock wall. The pure guts of Merriman amazed him, hanging in without complaint, using his walking stick and in pain.

"Hedgerows coming up," Merriman said, squinting into the grayness of dawn. "No way around the sodding things, no way through them except openings planned by farmers for a hundred flipping years. Those gaps are right easy to watch. But I could use a cuppa and crumpets about now."

"We have to eat to keep walking. Any farmhouse we pick can be trouble one way or the other. If the people are afraid of the Germans, they'll turn us in. If not, our presence could get them shot. The Gestapo won't be far behind, and the SS is as bad."

Merriman sighed. "We've been at this war a bit longer, Major. There comes the time when you realize it's better them than us. Out here in the daylight, we will certainly bring old Jerry down upon ourselves. The SS won't even think of a stalag; they'll play cricket with our balls for the joy of the game. Besides, I never trusted the Frogs—them and their mighty Maginot Line; them and their million-man Frog army holding arse and doing the old vanishing act."

If was full daylight when they found the little house and its two small barns. To Chad it looked like a playhouse, a dollhouse, its manicured fields divided by hedgerows high and thick enough to stop tanks. It would be a bitch fighting back through this part of the country; openings would have to be blown through the brush tangles and interlocked stones of a thousand years and the enemy could be only yards away and never seen. If any army came back to challenge the victorious Wermacht. If any armies were left to even try it, or want to.

Through the hedge opening and down its grassless path worn smooth by bare feet and wooden *sabot,* they went swiftly to the house. Chad tumbed Merriman around back and poised to kick open the door, his Sten held belly high. Instead, he caught himself in time and knocked.

They were old, timeworn and weathered, the man and his wife. The man, stooped and wearing a stained vest, stared fearfully at Chad and his weapon. The woman was different; chin high and defiant, she braced both hands on her thin hips. *"Oui?"*

Lifting his voice, Chad called to Merriman, and the leftenant came trotting. "I'm sorry," Chad said to the French woman, his gun muzzle moving them back into the room so the door could be closed. "I don't speak French." He balanced the Sten upon his right hip and made feeding motions with his free hand.

"Allemand," the old man whispered. *"Le boche."*

The woman sniffed. *"Mais non, sotte*—fool! *Anglais.* I have *un petite pou Anglais, moi."*

Merriman had a little French, and mixed it in to explain that they needed food and rest until dark. Chad lowered his weapon and shook his head. "You are a constant surprise, Leftenant."

"Jump higher, run faster, right-o?"

The food was milk, buttered heavy bread and sharp cheese. The *vin rouge* was sour and heady. Chad was careful not to drink much of it. The woman saw Merriman's bad leg and washed down the wound, poured a white liquid into it—

which made Merriman gasp—and rewound his leg with clean rags.

"*Calvados,*" Merriman said. "A homemade apple brandy that'll knock your arse sideways. *Merci, madame.*" He glanced at Chad. "What do you think?"

"I trust her, but the old guy—I don't know. He keeps looking at the door."

"Suggest we block both doors with something noisy— pots and pans. I can take first shift; bloody leg burning will keep me awake. Me at this window, you at the other."

The woman protested swiftly in French, but Chad noticed the old man said nothing. Sleep lightly, he thought; a ladder extended to an attic sleeping room and probably another way out at the roof. Such a long way to the coast and the whole German army might be there when they reached it. But they had to try; they certainly had to try.

Chad was next watch, and found it difficult to keep from nodding off. He was bone tired now, and that fatigue would eat right through the marrow in another day. He stood up and leaned against the wall. The woman dozed in a chair, and the old man pretended to. Each time Chad sat again, or squatted, the old man inched closer to the loft ladder, carefully, soundlessly. Chad thought he would give the old bastard another foot or two, to be certain.

But when Chad's head jerked up again, the man scuttled partway up the ladder. Quicker than the lift of Chad's gun muzzle, the woman rose and knocked the bastard off the ladder with the full-armed swing of a frying pan. "*Cochon!*"

Popping awake, Merriman said, "What the bloody hell—"

The woman stood over her victim, raining curses down upon him, threatening with the pan. Merriman grinned. "We were wrong thinking he's her husband; some sort of uncle, nephew—I'm not sure. But her son and grandson are in the French army and he has nobody. Besides which, she says, he is a greedy son of a she-goat who dog shits his bed. *Chein lit;* don't think I've heard that one before. Has a ring to it."

She turned and spoke much slower, adding a word of English now and then. Then she sat and placed one foot solidly upon her relative, pinning him to the floor while a gigantic lump grew purple atop his head.

Merriman said, "My watch, Major. I shouldn't expect any more trouble." Beyond the hedgerows, along the road, more panzers rumbled past, ton after ton of steel and weaponry and exultant Nazi troopers, so far unstoppable. As Chad's eyelids drooped, he thought again how very damned far it was to the coast.

Kirstin, he thought; Kirstin, I should have brought you to Normandy while it was still beautiful. When I had the chance. Maybe I've run out of chances, and will never be able to tell you.

CHAPTER 24

REUTERS NEWS AGENCY—May 21, 1940: At the last defensive positions of the BEF in France, held together at Boulogne, Calais and Dunkirk. Under continuous hammering from the air and the steadily grinding advances of German panzers in a two-pronged attack along the coast of France, British Tommies are resisting. For all practical purposes, the French army has disintegrated and the Belgian army has surrendered.

Chad Belvale hunkered in a shallow foxhole with Leftenant Merriman, unable to tell which of them was the grimiest. Brits were noted for their attention to cleanliness in the field, even to daily shaving, but there had been little time for anything but digging in, fighting until they were in danger of being overrun, and pulling out again to burrow another hole. They were hungry, almost out of cigarettes, and down to a couple of clips apiece for the Stens. The pickup body of confused troops they had attached themselves to were in the same condition.

"It's the bloody armor," Merriman said. "Four flipping days of panzers dashing here and there and shooting up the landscape. General Sir James Gort—despite his bloody toff name—is a fair enough British commander, but damned little Whitehall gave him to fight with."

Merriman still refused to be evacuated, although his wounded leg was no better. Chad took another drag on the Capstan cigarette and passed it to him. If the English had brought over more than two weak armored battalions and much more antiaircraft, there might have been a chance of clinging to a toehold on the Continent. The tanks had struck at the German flank today, backed by a pair of infantry battalions, and had made some progress beyond scaring hell out of panzer commanders that a major counterattack was on the roll.

But the infantry got itself worked over by the Luftwaffe's dive-bombers and was stopped in its tracks. And once the Continent was lost, it would be a military miracle to get it back.

"Maybe we should have visited a while longer with headquarters," Chad said. "But I had a hard time believing that England sent thirteen infantry divisions and only two tank outfits. The French already had plenty of foot soldiers."

Grunting, Merriman said, "Righto—providing the Frogs would fight. Who bloody hell knows what makes the high command so effing stupid? Practice, I'd say. If we had remained around that bunch I'd have effing well told them so. Do you think there's any *vin rouge* left in that farmhouse across the way?"

"I'll go see."

"And I'll cover your arse across the road, Major. After that, protect your own bum. Look out for cellar doors with Jerries under them."

Bent low, Chad scooted across the cobblestone street and slammed his shoulder against the door of the abandoned house. He hoped it was empty, anyhow. Sprawling over a stool, he thumped his hip against a table. It was still light enough to see more than shadows. The people had fled in a hurry, although there was nowhere to hide, no refuge for refugees. The Germans would sweep over them everywhere, and already the Luftwaffe had strafed roads clogged with people and animals running somewhere, anywhere.

Hungry and so tired that he wobbled, Chad searched for food and wine. Orders from the British high command back in London had shown how little was known about the field situation, but General Cort had done his best, even after warning that he had ammunition for only one good fight, and damned little food.

Finding a half-gallon bottle of wine basketed in straw, he held onto it while ripping open a cabinet to discover hard bread and a strong cheese. Cradling his loot along with his weapon, Chad plunged back to the hole to set up housekeeping.

"You're a bloody wonder," Merriman chortled. "We'll be shot with full bellies, anyhow. Now if you'd found a couple of mamselles—"

At nightfall, a probing force of German infantry came easing down the country road and into the deserted village, the scouts moving almost carelessly until the first bursts of British fire hit them. The darkness erupted with quick red-orange flashes and bullets keened off cobblestones, whined at angles from walls and snapped too close to Chad's hole, kicking sparks and chips of rock.

"Caught the bastards this time," Merriman grunted, "but it won't last."

As if in answer, a grenade exploded in the street and its fragments lashed viciously along the road. On the right, a man's scream choked itself off suddenly.

"Potato masher," Merriman said. "With those handles, they can toss the sodding things farther. What does our lot give us? The same old Easter eggs."

"Mortar!" Chad said, and squatted deeper into their hole as the dreaded *shoo-oosh!* hissed down upon them. The blast was followed by another, and another, as the world rocked and heaved and threatened to rip open Chad's eardrums.

In a sudden and warning silence as the covering fire lifted, he raised his head and saw shapes running his way. The Sten muzzle held steady, he fired his last clip and saw men fall.

Beside him, Merriman said, "Respectfully suggest we haul arse out of here, Major."

Leading the way out as Merriman laid down a burst of protective fire, Chad ducked around the corner of a stone wall and waited for his friend. Merriman came hitching along, favoring the bad leg. Side by side they passed beyond the little cluster of empty houses while small arms fire rose to a crescendo behind them. The iron-shod clatter of British boots followed them down the road and into silence off it, for now the survivors were veterans who knew that to keep on living meant finding cover, and quickly. Roads were only guidelines for mortars and artillery, and later, the tanks.

The troops moved slowly, tired and wounded men dragging the specter of defeat with them. Chad had to credit them, though; there was no real panic, only a plodding determination to make it through to the coast and hang on there until something—no one seemed to know what—happened.

Coming across a bullet-riddled German motorcycle and sidecar whose riders had sped too far ahead of their own troops, Chad stripped the bodies of Schmeissers and ammo, and the driver had a Mauserwerke P-38 pistol.

Merriman said, "And only one packet of horse shit cigarettes that didn't get bloodied. Careless bastards."

The retreat to the Channel was steady through the night, and the last firefight had made the Germans cautious about following too closely. Overhead, back and forth, enemy bombers pierced the dark, and Chad was glad for the cover of night. Come daylight, the Stukas and Messerschmitts would come down on the disorganized retreat for a duck shoot.

Was there even a route to the Channel left open? Situation maps at BEF headquarters had shown panzer columns racing along the coast to seal it. If they succeeded in the pincer movement, practically the entire British army would be lost, and the island left defenseless but for a navy unable to stop paratroops. And about that time the German navy would sail out and fight to sink the troop-laden landing barges that would surely be crossing the Channel.

Chad slogged along, making sure to hold pace with Merriman, offering a helping arm when the going turned rougher. Slowly, they fell behind the main body—if the straggling column could be called that—until they became part of the rear guard. British discipline had seen to that much protection, and if the men knew they were a sacrifice to warning, they didn't show it. Chad hoped the dogfaces of the U.S. regular army would be as stubborn and prideful when their time came. It had been a long time between

wars, but their combat blooding was on the way. The isolationists at home would not admit it, but when Hitler, Mussolini and/or the Japs struck at American possessions or at
the country itself, would there be time to build the huge
fighting force that would be needed? It sure as hell wasn't
there now. The First Infantry Division scattered around
New York State, the Second in Texas, bits and pieces at
Fort Benning.

"No fireworks up ahead," Merriman said, "not even
artillery, and I can smell the sea. The thing is, who the
bloody hell among us can swim thirty miles?"

Chad said, "I wonder what stopped the panzers. They
had us by the short hairs, and still do. It doesn't make
sense for them to wait until daylight. The RAF might slow
them after dawn."

"If the RAF can find their own bums with both hands,
much less France." As the march slowed and then stopped,
Merriman went on: "Do you have a family, Major?"

"Military up, down and crossways." Chad pulled his
jacket over his head and lighted two German cigarettes.
Merriman was right; they were rolled horse shit, and of
course that flavor brought the stables to mind, and Kill
Devil Hill; at Sandhurst Keep, it was hunting dogs. Some of
the home images were hazy, not because they were half a
world away, but for the tense screen that combat threw
between him and home, that lifted a steely netting against
civilization. He passed one cigarette to Merriman. "If any
male can't or won't wear a uniform, he's outcast, and the
women must at least pretend to march to the same old
drummer."

Kirstin; she hadn't learned that, and he hadn't helped,
had not given her the time and understanding she needed.
She had compounded her sin by not giving a damn about
thoroughbreds, only Morgans. If he had any time left, he
would divide it with her; if she hadn't filed for divorce by
now or thought him dead. Things here had been too hectic
for contact with the outside world, and if she still loved
him—had ever loved him—Kirstin must be frantic for news.
Or glad the war here would make things easier for her.

"Wife and kiddies?" Merriman asked. Around them tired

men crawled grumbling back to their blistered and bleeding feet. The column inched along on the move again, and the sky over their shoulders threatened an early dawn.

"Two children; maybe no wife by now." There; he'd said it aloud.

Merriman's cigarette smoke drifted close, the spark hidden within his cupped hand. "I had a chance to marry. Nice girl; couldn't talk her into bed without a ring. I held that up against my brilliant career in the army and here I bloody well sit, while some stay-at-home sod is in the feathers with her, or worse yet—some effing pilot or navy rating. Oh, well, up and at them, eh, Major? Don't want to be left too far behind as Jerry bait, do we?"

Bunching up despite angry sergeants trying to curse them into five-yard intervals, the men ahead sought the comfort and anonymity of closeness, no longer individuals, but yielding to the protective herd instinct. No army liked that; one shell could kill too many of the bunched herd. Chad snuffed his cigarette and gave Merriman a hand up. But no army could afford to consider individuals, only the casualties that meant less firepower.

Daylight came swiftly, and with the lightening sky, the approaching thunder of the Luftwaffe. Some of the men began to trot, lumbering along as if safety lay just ahead, if they could only reach it in time. Now Chad could see other uniforms mixed among the English—French, a few Belgian, and even a pair of Hollanders, others that had to be Polish. Not all men owned weapons or helmets, but all had one thing in common—they hadn't waited on the enemy and given up. They still had some vague hope that there was a way out, that their defeat wasn't complete. Desperate for their own reasons, some of them would try to continue the fight. Slogging through a little town already halfway bombed out, its narrow streets filled with rubble and some corpses beginning to swell, Chad held to Merriman. Directly in front spread a wide and curving beach turning black with survivors of the BEF and stragglers both military and civilian. Farther on, the gray waters of the English Channel were choppy and windblown—and empty of miracles.

"No Jerry tanks, anyhow," Merriman panted and went to his knees in the sand.

"Hitler's whole goddamn air force is coming, though," Chad said, and checked the clip of his machine pistol. It would be like throwing rocks at pterodactyls, but firing back always made him feel better.

Surprisingly, Merriman laughed. "You know what, Major? I just decided that infantry warfare is much like screwing. First there's expansion, then penetration, and then withdrawal—if we've any balls left."

The first Stuka screamed down upon the huddled masses on the beach at Dunkirk.

CHAPTER 25

INTERNATIONAL NEWS SERVICE—Washington, D.C., May 25, 1940: Warning that all continents may become involved in a "worldwide war," President Roosevelt asked Congress for an additional billion dollars today. He also asked authority to call the National Guard and Army Reserves to active duty if needed to safeguard neutrality and for the national defense.

Meanwhile, FDR's namesake ocean liner, the *President Roosevelt*, arrived at Galway, Ireland, to bring home more than nine hundred American civilians warned out of the British Isles by the danger of invasion.

Preston Belvale offered the cigar humidor. Crusty Carlisle shook his head and hauled out a sack of the makings. For years, Belvale had thought the roll-your-own stunt was an act, and maybe it started that way, a field grade officer demonstrating that he was just one of the boys. Now it must be habit, or Crusty had always liked Bull Durham or Duke's Mixture. He often alternated the brand he was smoking and never failed to close the sack drawstring with his teeth, cowboylike.

"Kee-rist," Belvale said, "can't you roll them with one hand?"

"Sure, but I spill a lot and the cigarette gets lumpy in the middle. Still better than your damned cigars. You know those fucking Cubans lick the leaves together, slobbering all over the things?"

"Women, mostly."

Crusty snorted. "Cuban women. I have it on good authority that Teddy Roosevelt's boys brought back eight hundred cases of clap, by actual count—two doses caught in passing when men fell off their horses on San Juan Hill."

Belvale smiled and rolled his Havana Special between his fingers. "And I know for a fact that you're inhaling stable sweepings, and probably not even *registered* thoroughbred horse shit."

Touching the flare of a kitchen match to his cigarette, Crusty said, "And I know for a fact that every goddamn Belvale has the Stars and Bars tattooed on his ass—which is the end they usually presented to the Grand Army of the Republic."

Belvale offered the carafe of bourbon, and this time Crusty didn't refuse. Pouring both drinks in silver cups, Belvale said, "Then there's the cliche about Bull Run—all the damn yankees who didn't run are still there."

He sipped whiskey and stopped smiling. He didn't often get to bandy words with the old billy goat, the symbolic rival head of the clan Carlisle, actual and ancient blood brothers to the Belvales. It was happening now because they were both worried about the too-quick collapse of Allied armies in Europe. Today they'd come together and telexed, phoned and dictated letters to every political, financial and military power on their long lists. Then, as was their habit, they relaxed in semifriendly arguments.

"A hell of a note," Belvale said, "family battling family in The War Between the States. It happened everywhere, of course, but it was especially bitter for us."

"Civil War," Crusty banged his whiskey glass. "*Civil War*, goddamnit! You people never learn."

"Sure we do. Yankee cavalry would still be losing their hair to the Comanches if Confederate soldiers hadn't swapped uniforms to fight the Indian Wars."

"Galvanized Yankees; they were called galvanized Yankees, and you know it. Don't hoard that whiskey, Preston."

"Serve yourself; the Hill lost all its house slaves to Yankee scalawags and deserters—before the carpetbaggers, of course." Leaning back in his deep leather chair, Belvale puffed on his cigar, tasting the rich leaf. Long ago, Kill Devil Hill had profitably raised fine tobacco for shipment to England.

"The homeland," he murmured. "How different history might have been if our families hadn't been neighbors in England."

"If they hadn't been screwed by Cromwell's bastards and that peanut Charles II. I always figured the Carlisles and Belvales intermarried to save their respective asses," Crusty said.

"In a way I guess they did. I wish they'd kept better records and written longer diaries. Didn't you ever go through the old books?"

"Just the musty pile of them remaining at the Keep."

Belvale stood up. "I'll bring out our collection. At least they'll be better reading than today's newspapers."

"And the teletypes upstairs. Every time those damned bells ring we lose another country."

Across the room, Belvale reached for the two oldest volumes on the fifth shelf. Taking them down carefully, he ran his hands over the spiderweb cracks across the bindings, once natural leather now so old that it had turned black. The smell of ages rose when he opened the first and passed it across the library table to Crusty, the musty scent of centuries dead but ever held upon the winds of time.

Silently, Crusty took the opened volume and Belvale sat down with the other on his lap, a big book whose hand-inked pages were brittle and faded, the goose feather quills that had written most of them long since gone to dust.

Drinking his red-brown whiskey, floating a cloud of fragrant blue smoke, Belvale settled into his chair. Handling the ancient books of his ancestors always affected him strangely, moving him back in time until he was almost one of them, until he could taste tallow candle smoke and hear fog drip upon a low roof of thatch. . . .

. . . The gamekeeper's hut was all that was left to the surviving Belvales, and across the valley, the last Carlisles were no better off. Part of their castle keep had not been battered and burned, and they lived in its stony circle, amid the fallen walls of the castle plundered by the Roundheads.

In the smoky hut, Sir Erwin Belvale, Earl of Derbyshire, clenched his fist so tightly around the small leather pouch that veins stood out on his forehead. "The whelp—the ungrateful whelp! We stood loyal beside his father and returned from other wars to serve the new king, as Belvales have always done."

He slapped the pouch upon the table. A gold coin gleamed out to lie upon the rough, stained wood. "This is our return for three hundred years of service—a measly purse such as his manservant would toss a beggar. Not a single rod of our lands returned, not a farthing compensation for the fallen buttresses yonder. Turned Dutch, did our Charlie the Second, hiding so long at The Hague, or black Portugese like his whorish wife. There's damned little good to be said of either."

His sister swung the cook-pot from over coals in the fireplace and dipped a wooden spoon to taste. Adding a dab of salt, she moved it back on its iron arms. "Not all potatoes and mutton grease this day," Susan said. "Sir William brought a brace of doves for your supper."

Staring at the shining guinea, Belvale said, "*Your* supper, more likely. I could starve for all of him. Do you always address the old fool by his title? And damned little good titles do either of us now."

"Only a bit older than yourself," Susan said. "And the king gave him naught atall for his services."

"Because he sold his sword to the East Prussians, full knowing that the Swedes had friends in The Hague. You are far too young for the landless gray Lord of Belper."

Susan stirred the pot; meat odors steamed out. "God granted your hired swords did not meet upon the field of battle. Oh, the wars, the ruddy wars. Brother, I am already too gray for the sprouts not harvested by the wars. And Sir William is a good man and gentle man, more the lonely after his wife's death. Oh—all we speak of is death."

He looked up at her, at this girl forced to womanhood too soon, the new lines about her mouth and eyes. "You know I have thought upon the Americas." he said. "A new start in the colonies on this kingly hundred pounds for you and me, so the Belvales may rise again."

"Not me without Sir William," she said, with that set of her chin that defied wars, kings and brothers.

"But—" Belvale stared hard at her. "Has he got your belly swollen? I'll spit the old hound."

"No, but not for lack of trying. I'll marry with him, Erwin—with your blessing or no."

"But the Americas? There, a man's strong arm can yet lift him high, and the bedamned kin of the Portugese bitch will not be owning it all." He reached across the table and caught her forearm, soft beneath the hard callouses upon his hands. "We are all left of a proud family, Susan. The Belvales must go on."

Shaking off his hand she said, "More's the reason for me to wed Sir William and keep the blood."

"Be damned! The brat would not be Belvale, but a Carlisle."

She busied herself at the blackened pot. "Abigail Carlisle is not barren. At twelve years, the poor lad she bore was killed soon after her husband. You will need yourself a strong wife in the New World, Erwin."

"I-God! The wench is long in the tooth and fights the bit as well. She took back her own name after John Pettis went to follow Cromwell. What kind of woman—"

Eyes sparking, she turned on him. "And you would fault her for denying a traitor husband, and a peasant at that? Without lands and entry to the court, you can do no better than Abigail Carlisle, and I say not as well!"

He covered the money pouch with his right hand. "You plotted against me while I went begging in London. I spoke before of the Americas and you, that headstrong widow and her fool brother—"

This time, she spoke more softly. "Not against you, Erwin; we planned to aid you. How long will it be before even this hovel is granted to some Portugese fop? Catherine of Borganza brought our Charlie three hundred thousand pounds for dowry and—and—the colonies of Tangier and Bombay, so he owes the wench! Her kin will have it all back and more."

A few inches of mead remained in a dented metal tankard rescued from the ruins of the castle. Belvale drank them off

and narrowed his eyes at Susan. "It's what comes of allowing women to read and gossip. You'd be the king's advisor,
then?"

"Only lady-in-waiting at your marriage, brother. Your
hundred pounds will buy passage to the New World for all
living Belvales and Carlisles."

The mead was a bit sour, and backed up in his throat. To
leave England forever. It was no dream now, but real and
sharp as a sword blade. He had stood with the Celts against
the rogue Englishmen of Cromwell, and journeyed to fight
with the Swiss. This was only as his ancestors had done in
the Crusades; all knew that, barring a fatal scimitar slash,
they would some day return home.

This time there would be no turning back. At least not
until a true king sat on the throne. That was it; after making
his fortune in the colonies, he could come back to court
when the new and wiser monarch would reign.

"My horse is tired from our long journey from London,"
he said, "so you may ride him only at a walk. Since old
William trapped the brace of doves, he should eat of them,
also."

His sister smiled. "And Abigail?"

He surrendered. "And Mistress Abigail." . . .

. . . "Wake up, Preston. Damn—you're getting too old
for command."

Belvale tapped a long ash from his cigar. "I wasn't really
asleep, just kind of dreaming what it was like with our folks
away back then, before they first came to America."

With one big finger, Crusty shut the ancient book with
care. "Well, after reading this, we know that whatever
caused them to leave home, it was a good thing for you and
me. One thing for sure: they were no fucking peanuts."

A bell rang, and shrilled again, short demanding sounds
from upstairs.

Belvale said, "That could be the clash of a lowered visor,
or a gauntlet flung down in challenge."

Raising one ragged eyebrow Crusty said, "It's those
damned teletype bells and you know it. Go back to sleep.
I'll go see which country we lost."

CHAPTER 26

Compiled from Reuters News Agency, *Manchester Guardian* and *London Times* reports, Dunkirk, France, May 27, 1940: British naval vessels began the task of evacuating BEF troops from this last remaining open port last night. This morning, hundreds of small civilian craft, manned by volunteers who dared Hitler's air force and Nazi U-boats, sailed straight to beaches constantly threatened by the Luftwaffe. There they took aboard every Tommy they could load, many of the wounded handed up from chest-deep water by tired but determined soldiers who went back for more.

Inexplicably, two separate Panzer Corps have halted in place less than ten miles from Dunkirk itself. Although no British artillery is available for defense and few antitank weapons made it to the Channel, the panzers have not plunged ahead to seal the port and kill or capture some 300,000 men. A senior British officer, when asked how long these defenseless beaches would not be overrun, said, "So long as our prayers hold out."

Chad squatted beside Merriman in their shallow hole while the Englishman boiled tea in the top of a dented German mess kit. They were nothing like the U.S. kits, oval pans, but deep enough to cook soups and stews. Where the American belted water canteen sat in a close fitting cup, the German combined cup and pot to lighten the infantryman's load. Merriman had also discovered a cache of standard Jerry cigarettes, the dry *Sonder Mischung,* and traded most off for captured rations.

Chad felt fat on canned liver sausage and beef, and the *Kommiss Brot,* the hard brown bread that would last for months. Even if you had to scrape green off the crust, the inside was edible and filling. He wondered what the U.S. Army was doing about field rations, if anything. When he'd left home, line troops on maneuvers depended upon company kitchens finding and feeding them, then sending them off with dry cheese or bologna sandwiches.

That wouldn't work in combat. Often, it hadn't paid off on maneuvers near Camp Drum, New York; the mess trucks were always getting lost on back roads, and sometimes for days, while soldiers went hungry and cursed the belly robbers.

On this beach where only a few Jerry planes had strafed and bombed, Chad's scooped-out indentation couldn't rightly be called a foxhole. Sand kept sifting in and Merriman grumbled that they couldn't even dig deep enough for a decent grave. But they had a hole where they ate and sipped hot tea and were surprised at an occasional Royal Navy uniform on the beach. Screwed up as things were, those uniforms brought a certain sense of stability, and Chad mentioned it.

"I wouldn't say stable," Merriman said, coughing around a German cigarette. "The buggers probably fell off their ships and got lost." He looked up and grabbed his helmet with both hands." Here comes another one of old Adoph's *fliegers.*"

Huddled in their hole, Chad blessed the sand as an ME-109 screamed down and let go its bomb. Deep and soft, the sand absorbed most of the exploding fragments and nearly all the blast. When the Messerschmitt came back for a strafing run, its bullets didn't skip and ricochet, but just dug in. Even though he was careless and lazy, there must truly be a god for infantrymen, Chad thought. Glancing up, he thumped Merriman's shoulder and said, "A Spitfire—look at that beautiful bastard on Jerry's tail!"

"Another lost soul," Merriman said, but grinned. "Thinks

he's coming into Heathrow airport and tripped his guns accidentally."

Machine guns whacking, the Spitfire stayed behind the ME-109 which began smoking as both planes thundered from sight of the beach.

"Scratch one *flieger*," Chad said, and wondered where the main body of the Luftwaffe was, wondered what could be more important to Hermann Goering than wiping out the army on Dunkirk Beach. Rumor had it that twenty-five thousand men had been evacuated late last night and early this morning, mostly the wounded. The sea had calmed, and that unbelievable ragbag fleet of civilian boats piloted by gutty volunteers was only a fragile and almost unmissable target. A few runs by a goodly flight of planes and the brave fleet would be matchsticks upon the water.

He marked this whole scene in his memory for a some-day report to General Belvale: the Nazi troops were not machine perfect; they could also fumble on the one-yard line.

Something else: the English could be depended upon to hold out beyond common sense, stubborn and tough as they had to be. Even if Hitler at last swallowed the rest of the BEF, he would not find the invasion of England easy. The Limeys were not about to roll over like the rest of Europe. It would take every parachute regiment in the German army to gain a toehold. Chad remembered what Merriman had told him about the Sten machine pistol, that the factories were busily turning out enough of the effective, but cheaply produced, weapons to arm every man, woman and child in England.

And watching the courageous fleet of yachts and fishing boats plowing in close to shore in order to take on load after load of soldiers and hurry them into Dover, Chad knew the civilian population of England would fight. By God, he thought, it made him proud to be wearing a British uniform, even if it was temporary.

Merriman stretched and leaned against the side of their hole, one eye upon the mess gear on the sand. He had guarded their rations at his feet, his Schmeisser a warning to hungry scavengers who had not had the foresight to slow their retreat enough to find food and water. He said, "When will your lot come in, Major? This war has room for Yanks."

"It can't be too much longer. But since some people in Washington think our oceans will protect us as in the last war, Hitler will have to screw up. That means sinking an American passenger ship, or bombing New York harbor. Washington takes a lot of waking up."

Helmet off, Merriman eyed the sky where a pair of Spit-fires cruised, slim English harriers circling to look for trouble, watching out for the squirming bulldog pups far below, flying cover for the bathtub fleet. Chad knew his friend would never admit that; Merriman had the typical attitude of the infantryman, no regard whatsoever for anybody who did not go nose to nose with the enemy under the most miserable conditions.

"No more than Whitehall," Merriman said. "Old Chamberlain with his bloody peace in our time shit. Think anybody stuffed that paper treaty up his ignorant arse? But I do wish you Yanks get here in force before we have to swim to effing Ireland; we'd have to make an assault landing there, you know. Free riders in wartime, the bleeding Irish, kissing up to the Nazi and spaghetti embassies, inviting spies in and making money hand over whiskey glass."

Chad sighed. "Mind if I catch some sleep? You can make a list of Hibernian failings to read me after I wake up."

"You're not Irish descent, Major? I understand half the potato diggers sailed to the colonies with flat bellies and their grubby hands out for charity."

"No, both our major lines are English, and some Norman before that, and probably back to the Picts and Angles." Chad rubbed his eyes. "Wake me when the next Stuka makes a pass."

Merriman grinned. "I won't have to. Just don't begin shooting until both eyes are open."

Chad didn't actually sleep, but drowsed, a newly found animal instinct of survival keeping part of him ever alert to danger. Weeks of that kind of strain and the infantry got to where it could nap braced on its numb feet, even walking on a road march. By then, though, the men weren't much as a fighting unit, unable to move fast and only stumbling through half-heard orders.

Licking his own minor surface wounds, Chad mentally hid out with the old general, helping to plot the movements of observers the U.S. Army and the family would send out, who and where. The why was easy enough, but not Chad's quick acceptance of the European assignment.

Turning restlessly in the little space allowed him in the sand hole, he realized that no excuse was good enough. If he made it across the Channel, the first thing he would do was send a message to Kirstin, a personal note that would surprise the general as he watched the teletype in the war room at Kill Devil Hill, where military communication always came first.

Be there, Kirstin; hang on and wait for me, so I can at least admit to you what a damned fool I was, until I can apologize to you. After that, if you want to leave me, I won't try to stand in your way.

Chad woke later to the smell of the sea and Merriman's tiny cook-fire, to the hot odors of liver sausage. The bath-tub fleet was still bobbing in the water, and farther out, a British destroyer belched heavy smoke as it yawed to port and slowly started down. Shaking his head to clear it, he blinked at the sinking ship; he hadn't even heard the explosion.

To Merriman, he said, "What got her—plane or sub?"

"U-boat would be my guess. *Das kapitan* figured she was enough to use a torpedo on. Jerry is such a rubber bum hole. Two other of His Majesty's ships dashed around in circles, dropping depth charges that damned near sank part of the rescue fleet. They might have chased off the U-boat. Tea time, Major, sir. Too bad we didn't liberate some of that calvados; it goes well with tea."

Taking turns at eating from the German mess pot, passing the hot cup back and forth, Chad couldn't quite clear Kirstin from his mind, but her image faded into the noisy chaos along the beach. Still no appearance by clanking panzers belching hellfire; still no sky gone black with striking eagles of the Luftwaffe; their luck was holding. It continued to hold throughout the lingering summer twilight, and Chad saw that more stragglers were making it into the area, only one or two at a time, and of mixed nationalities. But for every man that the Germans allowed to escape to England, that man would some day cost them. He would have battle experience and be feeding upon the bitterness of losing his country and eaten by worry about his family. He would be eager for revenge.

Chad could foresee separate units made up of Free Poles, French and Belgians, Norwegians and Hollanders, all operating under a Supreme Allied Command, but easier with each other and no language barrier. Some could be parachuted back into their homelands as saboteurs, and possibly, when the Allied Command got straightened out enough to send bombers back over the Continent, shot-down crews would need some people on the ground to help them get back to England and return another time with more bombs.

"I'll try to find some kind of central command," Chad said as Normandy twilight darkened into evening and stars came shining out just as if the world were at peace, and no men would die violently this night. "If we make it out of here, I'll need notes on the big picture, stuff to get back to my family—"

"Not to your army HQ? Fine bloody observer you are."

"That's next, the army. From my grandfather on down, we have more officers on inactive—and that's a misnomer—duty than the U.S. Army has in uniform. But our people are hardheaded and logical; they believe we should stay ready for wars, that the last war is never the last war."

"Bloody heretics," Merriman said. "Wish you'd have spared old clot Chamberlain a few heresies. If you find some sort of HQ, tell the buggers I said that."

Zigzagging carefully through the clumps of restless men and smaller heaps of equipment littering the beach for hundreds of yards, listening to the watery commotion as small boats bobbed in as close as they dared and waders splashed out into the Channel to reach them for the getaway to England, he found an aid station tent covering a pit in the sand. An aid man told him headquarters was dropping its usual clangers farther up the beach.

The tent was bigger and the pit deeper, and still Chad almost fell into it before he made out a flicker of light through a tiny rip. This had to be where the high brass lived its version of immortality; lower ranks believed that light drew enemy fire.

Crowded, thick with cigarette smoke and sweaty officers beneath the light of a Coleman lamp, Dunkirk Beach headquarters seemed every bit as confused as the lowliest two man foxhole. Chad reminded himself that something was being done—that thousands of men were being taken off this beach which should have turned into deadly quicksand by now.

He bumped into a three-pipper in a tattletale clean uniform which said he was fresh from the cliffs of Dover, a British captain who whirled on him. "What the hell, soldier? This is not some Piccadilly bar—"

Suddenly angry, Chad said, "The rank is major, goddamn your rear echelon ass—Major Belvale, United States Army. Get out of my way or get run over."

"S-sir," the Limey murmured, and Chad shouldered him aside to press roughly through the crowd. Now he could see another pit, an old cave, really, that reached back into the land, a better haven for the top commanders and their useless war maps.

"Your pardon," a man said, "I also must report my presence to the generals."

Blinking at the simple suntan uniform made colorful by a cavalry cape heavy with swirlings of gold braid and a high, boxy kepi, Chad said, "Of course, sir." The man could have been a model for Hollywood swashbucklers, and it wasn't only the uniform, but an attitude, an aura. It was evident he was no desk soldier; he had tried to keep clean, but jacket stains, and abrasions on knee-high jack boots that were otherwise black mirrors told he'd fought. The sword he carried said something else—that he'd clung to tradition and damn the German armor.

Chad put out his hand and introduced himself. The man actually clicked his heels, spurs rattling. "Colonel Jerzy Prasniewski, Polish Cavalry, Third Lancers." Heavily accented but precise wording. Remembering news out of Poland of how the blindly brave horseback lancers charged invading panzers, and just kept coming through murderous cannon and machine-gun fire, Chad was happy to shake the colonel's hand.

What they had done was no smarter than the Charge of the Light Brigade against the Turkish guns when "someone had blundered." But it was a thing that General Preston Belvale would understand and quietly salute the raw courage it took. And this man hadn't headed straight out; evidently he'd been a volunteer with other Allied units since his own country fell almost a year ago. Still unwilling to give up, here he was at Dunkirk. "Belvale," the colonel said, "Belvale. A not uncommon American name, yes?"

"Actually, no," Chad said, offering a cigarette.

Another bow as Prasniewski accepted the cigarette, kepi with its brass plate tucked regulation style under one arm. "Then possibly you were aware of Lt. Walton Belvale?"

The name jumped out: "Walt? A kid—ah, a young man twenty years old, twenty-one? I didn't know he was also here as an observer." Damn the old general; Walt was still a kid fresh out of VMI and too young to be thrown into this European mess. Nothing had been said about him when Chad and the general had planned their end of the observer operation. Drawing deeply upon his dry German cigarette, Chad said, "Walton Belvale is my nephew. Was he in Poland with you? Did he get out early?"

Lifting his shaven chin, touching the sharply pointed ends of his blond mustache, the colonel looked directly into Chad's face; his eyes were the same blue as Walt's, Chad thought.

"Still, he is in Poland," Prasniewski said. "A brave officer who died well during the last resistance in Warsaw. When I return to Poland one day, I will show you where he fell and we shall together search for his burying place, yes?"

Chad wanted to scream out a lot of things, to sear the air with every curse he knew, to ask questions. Chewing hard upon his lips, tasting a hint of blood, he said only, "Thank you, Colonel."

Walt was probably the first Belvale killed in this war. He would not be the last.

CHAPTER 27

INTERNATIONAL NEWS SERVICE—Kill Devil Hill, Va., June 1, 1940: Many influential members of Congress and prominent newspaper publishers gathered here today for one of "The Hill's" legendary dinner parties. The Belvale-Carlisle family, well known for their thoroughbred horses, often Kentucky Derby winners and twice holders of the Triple Crown, reach back through the military annals to the settlement of this country. Their racing colors are infantry blue and artillery red, although Maj. Gen. Preston Belvale, Cavalry (Ret.), said he might add touches of cavalry yellow—now also the color for newly created armored divisions.

Kirstin Belvale did her part as junior hostess, as usual. To her were assigned the younger senators and representatives; there were few young publishers anyway. Minerva oversaw the others, moving regally among them and giving them an even higher sense of importance. She was very good at it, Kirstin admitted, the queen with her subjects smiling at the tap of the royal fan or brush of the throne room gown.

Nancy Carlisle wasn't good with crowds and Kirstin had to practically pry her out of her room to attend this second major soiree at the Hill in weeks. The general had been going nonstop since the English evacuation at Dunkirk, if not on a set of phones to Washington and military posts around the country, then at the teletype and radio. He had called Kirstin into the military sanctum sanctorum and softly told her there had been no word on Chad. He explained that communications from England were a total mess, records had been left behind in France and disheartened soldiers were going every which way after offloading from the ragtag, mostly civilian fleet that rescued them.

"We will hear soon," he said, this steely soldier whose tender emotions could break through the defended outer barricades. If only Chad had that quality, she would care more for him, possibly even reach back and love him once more. The general touched her arm, then took her hand. His palms were still calloused from a lifetime in the cavalry and his almost daily riding now. He didn't blink and hide surprise at her horse-tough palms like other men, men she gave only her fingertips to, if she could.

"All right," she had said, "thank you, sir."

Then she had gone to Nancy's room in the east wing, semiglad that she had something else to share with Keenan's returned wife. She didn't love Chad anymore, and had not for a long time, but she didn't hate him either. Mostly she had just felt sorry for him, and that was nothing to base a marriage on. She really didn't have her boys, and if the general was right about how close they were to entering the war, they might also be gone soon, their graduations pushed up. Kirstin would never have them. She hadn't fought back soon enough, or cared soon enough. She had thought of divorce, but there had been no one to look to in the conceivable future. Damnit—she needed more than her horses; she needed love as well.

Nancy came to her across the ballroom floor, a fixed smile upon her face, looking younger than she had a right to. Keenan was still carried as missing in action, and although Kirstin was pretty sure that their wifely emotions ran closely parallel, Nancy looked brighter and happier since she'd come back to the Hill. And she'd shown enough backbone standing up to Minerva that the old bat didn't harass her as she had before.

Nancy said, "I'm glad they've stopped dancing and gone to the tables. I'm so out of practice, and so many of those men, even the old ones—"

"Especially the old ones," Kirstin said. "I don't blame them; that dress looks great on you." She wished she could wear fluffs and frills like those but they only called attention to how tall and lean she was. Kirstin had to stay with simple lines.

Guiding Nancy to the tables, she picked up snatches of conversation ". . . seems to think we'll be fighting within months . . . Don't know about that, Charlie; my constituents are already complaining about the draft . . . The very idea of sending American boys to die in another of Europe's wars is insane, bloodthirsty . . ."

". . . who do the generals think they are? Some of the richest men in the country, that's who, and if you don't want to kiss off the primary . . . Let England fight its own war, I say; what has England ever done for us? . . . Roosevelt and his damned Lend-Lease . . ."

Nancy spooned caviar on her plate and took lobster Newburgh, then dabs of this richness and that. "I'll be hog fat in two more weeks. And I feel kind of guilty. Keenan might be starving somewhere in China, if—if he's not long dead."

Kirstin sat across a patio table from her. "Does it mean that much?" She startled herself; Nancy might care much more for her husband, and that was a hell of a thing to ask, did she really love. She added, "I'm sorry."

Nancy swallowed and stared into Kirstin's eyes. "Don't be. Keenan and I weren't—haven't been on the best of terms since I left the Hill. I don't think my being back would make it any different. Everything was my fault—getting pregnant, then losing the child, then not measuring up to all—all this. And oh, God—that gloomy Keep—"

"Kindred souls," Kirstin said. "I'm really glad you came back. If you'll ride with me, you won't have to worry about getting fat." She wanted to say more, but the men came to join them, men handsome in different ways—the one beside Nancy sleek and dark; she recognized him as a representative from Georgia.

"Texas," said the other man, "and I understand you don't hold much for running horses." His face was sun and wind marked, and his faded blue eyes were the kind that looked off into far distances. He used his slow smile rarely, not at all the politician's obligatory showing of teeth. "Jim Shelby, fooling folks into thinking I'm a sure enough senator," he said.

He had asked about her beforehand, not an unusual maneuver for someone wanting to get close to the generals for one reason or another. But to ask about horses, he had to be a horseman himself, or a phony she would soon trip up.

"Not much," she said, "but the horse can't help it. I don't care much for the people who put weight on a yearling's back, who run him sick or hurt. And if he breaks down running his heart out on the track, the same *sport of kings* owners are back at the stalls working a quick deal with the killers to make him into dog food."

His smile was rueful. "Well, I asked. I run some quarter horses, but mostly mine are working stock and some rodeo—cutting or dry reining, roping, steady horses for steer wrestlers and barrel racers."

It was her turn to smile. She was aware that Nancy and the sleek Georgian were talking more than eating, but this man was interesting. "I'm familiar with rodeos and gymkhanas," she said. "I have a catty little Morgan gelding that shocked six reining horses in Reno—all typey bulldog quarter horses."

When Jim Shelby really cut loose his grin, it made crinkles at the corners of his eyes. "Be damned," he said. "I'd appreciate seeing that one, and any others you want to show off."

"Now?"

"If these fancy clothes don't spook them."

"My Morgans don't spook. I train them myself."

Again his true grin grabbed at her. "I do believe I'd do just what you want, if you had *me* on a longe line."

Kirstin stood up. "We never run out of food here, so if we take advantage of the daylight that's left—" She remembered Nancy and asked was it okay to leave.

Nancy blinked up at her. "Sorry, I wasn't—oh, sure. I mean, Wilson and I are getting along just fine. See you later."

Kirstin seldom walked across the back lawns in a dress, and felt awkward, passing beneath the row of stately magnolias and breathing deeply of the pink and gold honeysuckle hedges trained to connect them. The honeysuckle had never smelled quite as sweet. Jim Shelby was taller than she'd expected, towering over her and swinging along with that slightly rolling gait of the longtime cowboy. She noticed the well-worn boots with semi-riding heels he wore.

By the time he'd gone from stable to stable with her, discussing croup and gaskin and shoulder slope, she had to flick on the lights of her barns. They were still deep in conversation, as only solid horse people could be, she thought, when the uniformed young men strode up.

"Owen," she said, "—Farley; I didn't expect you—"

Looking more like his father, broad and erect in his West Point cadet uniform, Owen said, "Evidently not."

It didn't reach her yet, and she said, "Senator Shelby, this is my son Owen, my son Farley."

Then she saw the tightness in Farley's face, too. The VMI uniform closely resembled West Point's, gray and high collared. Farley was built more along Kirstin's lines, rangy and tall. He only nodded at Jim Shelby and said nothing, did not hold out his hand.

"Boys," she said, "remember that the senator is a guest here. You found me, so you can go back to the house and I'll see you later."

Owen always had the big mouth. He said, "So long as you remember that our father—your husband—is missing in action like Uncle Keenan. Or didn't the War Department get word to you?"

If she'd had a quirt or longe whip in her hand she would have slashed him with it. Pulling in a deep, steadying breath, she said softly: "Get the hell out of here."

Whirling upon their heels, two stiff automatons, they marched back toward the brightly lighted house. Jim Shelby waited a moment and said, "I'm sorry; I didn't know."

"Don't be sorry for them," she said, struggling to keep her voice from shaking with anger. "That's the first time in many years that they've treated me as anything but a convenience. And it is only because Chad is missing as an observer, giving them something even more military to act out." Her resolve broke and she said, "Goddamn Minerva

Belvale! She pumped them full of propaganda every chance she had, and I gave her the chance. Chad is—Chad and I haven't been—together in ages, and missing or not, I'm still not sure I give a damn."

For the first time, he touched her arm. "I'm not sorry for them, but for you. Kids can be burrs under the saddle blanket, but usually the sharp points get rubbed off. You want to go back to the house now?"

She turned off the barn lights and walked silently beside him, the scent of honeysuckle not as heavy about her now, the night not so soft. She stopped an inch short of also damning Chad in her mind, because she saw a flash of his face, whiter than it had been when she walked in on him with that whore; a strange, dead face.

On the wide veranda that encircled Kill Devil Hill she paused. Couples waltzed out here in candle glow, white-jacketed waiters moving among them with trays of champagne glasses. Leaning against the porch railing between a pair of tall columns, she said, "I'm my own woman, Jim. I have been for a long time, perhaps too long."

"I'm glad," he said, and just those words stripped her of twenty lonely years and made her young for one moment, as bright as the fireflies beginning to swarm blinking above the back lawns. Then Kirstin stood up straight and murmured that they should go back inside and give both generals a hand in their maneuvers against congressmen unwilling to believe that the U.S. could be drawn into the war already raging across half the world.

She felt a new and disturbing war starting deep within herself.

CHAPTER 28

REUTERS NEWS AGENCY—the Channel Ports, June 2, 1940: The last of the British Expeditionary Forces reached safety here today. With them came military and officials of other nations overrun by Nazi attacks, men who intend to fight on. His Majesty congratulated the naval and volunteer fleets that saved the BEF from total destruction in history's most daring evacuation.

General Belvale stalked between the teletype and the world map on the west wall of Kill Devil Hill's command post. The stuff was hitting the fan in China and Europe, too. There had been no word on Keenan in months, since that terse note from the Japs, and the War Department carried him as missing in action, although not publicly. Nancy Carlisle knew and had quietly retired within herself for a time. She was coming out of that attitude with some help from Kirstin. Nancy might wait until there was no hope, and she might bow her neck and take off at a gallop. He would have to remind Minerva to let the girl be—as much as Minerva could keep from meddling with anyone's life.

There had been nothing from Chad for weeks, but in a way that was to be expected. The collapse of France and the situation at Dunkirk was chaotic and too fast moving for standard procedures. Chad also could be a casualty, like the kid Walton. Nobody discussed Chad's chances, certainly not Kirstin, although she was militarily as sharp as any man in the family. To her stiff-necked sons, she presented a calm front, an everyday sort of attitude. They must sense the wrongness, but already they were young soldiers and would act out the play scene by scene, by the numbers. He wasn't sure how those two would turn out, book soldiers or fighting men, and the only test would be combat, the time of the quick and the dead.

Grunting, Belvale remembered that Kirstin's days were not prosaic now, that she was no longer going through her horse exercise and training routine as if it were the most important thing in her life. There was that Texas senator. One thing the family could not control, despite Minerva's manipulations, was the love lives of the young. Of course, the Hill's traditions should be respected whenever possible. That made for cohesion, for strength and duty.

Other Belvales, other Carlisles and intermarried relations not officially carrying either name had also shipped out on later tours of duty, to hand-picked listening posts scattered across half the world. But none were yet in local hot spots.

Belvale studied the situation map. The world itself was a gigantic hot spot; each tinderbox just hadn't ignited yet. India, Burma, Africa, the Philippines and the entire South Pacific with its stepping-stone islands that few had ever heard of, or would want to again if the Japs spread out—the flames could spread everywhere, charring all they touched.

Would the continental United States remain untouched? Only if some damned strong and hurry-up preparations got underway sooner than anybody in D.C. wanted to think about. Factory conversions, a sweeping, all-inclusive draft, new arms and modern machines leaping from dusty drawing boards to tested realities. How long to train soldiers, how long to put together a workable, efficient officer corps? And what size army would be enough, how many warships, how to flesh out the fledgling air arms too long neglected?

Thinking on Keenan, on Chad and the Walton boy perhaps sent out too soon, Belvale chose one of the bank of phones and put in some calls.

The knock on the war room door was gentle, feminine. He said, "Yes?" and Kirstin came inside. He said, "Nothing yet, my dear."

"I didn't really expect word." He watched the way she walked, intrigued as always by the proud swinging of her long legs, a stride that did nothing to detract from her womanliness. She'd have been at home in a cavalry garrison at Apache Junction or any other post that demanded tough horse soldiers and strong women.

She said, "I'd like to talk to you, General."

"About the senator. Shall we sit here?" He glanced again at the map, as if some divine light would suddenly flash and regain the lost ground and breathe life into all the lost men. He kept one ear cocked for the teletype.

Kirstin said, "I didn't think we were that obvious."

"Not to everyone; certainly not to Minerva—so far."

Sighing, she bent her head to touch fingertips lightly to her forehead, and he was minded of the way he touched a good horse's neck, communicating a silent approval or silent sympathy.

"You don't mind?" she asked.

"It's not my sector," he said, but softly. "You've never been quite happy with Chad?"

"There are reasons."

"There usually are."

"But I value your opinion," she murmured, eyes still closed and slim fingers still pressing above them. "I value *you*, General."

"Thank you, my dear." He went through the practiced movements of cigar readying, but didn't light it.

"I'm not sure about Jim Shelby," Kirstin said, "about loving him completely, I mean. I think I love him now—or maybe it's the thought of him, a man who laughs when I do and doesn't think he has the most valuable job in the world. I got used to being ignored and my Morgan program not important, just something a flighty woman would do."

Belvale nodded and rolled the cigar in his fingers, felt its veined texture and sniffed the rich fragrance. He was delaying because he didn't have much to say, and Kirstin had a lot.

She drew a breath that she tried to keep from shuddering. "It's a bastardly thing to contemplate, when nobody knows what happened to my husband. It's not like I need him or—even, goddamnit, respect Chad Belvale. But too much of the Hill honor has rubbed off, I guess. And my sons—oh, my spit and polish, brass shined sons—to them I'm already a traitorous bitch. And I haven't done anything yet; not yet."

Lighting the cigar at last, Belvale tasted the luxurious blue smoke. Teddy Roosevelt's best move was that charge up San Juan Hill. Otherwise where would the fine Cuban cigars be? "The senator has asked you to go to Texas?"

She said, "Yes, and I can ship my horses. I might; I don't know. I probably would have divorced Chad by now, if he had been within reach. Since meeting Jim Shelby, that is. It didn't seem worth the bother before."

The teletype clattered and Belvale leaped up, ash scattering from his Havana cigar.

"I'll go," Kirstin said.

"No, wait—"

Braced at the machine, he stared at the first lines the racing keys rapped out, hardly hearing the one-bell signal of least importance. Dunkirk, the need to know what the English had brought out, arms and men; intelligence on the defensive capability of the island, and what the hell was coming over the wire?

"Kirstin," he said, "come over here. This message is for you."

"My God!" Her nails dug into his shoulder and her breath warmed his cheek as she looked down at the swift letter hammers and the slowly turning roll of yellow paper.

. . . Kirstin Belvale . . . In England and well . . . miss you and have learned about myself . . . possibly about you . . . and us . . . love you, Kirstin . . . Chad . . .

Clack, went the machine; *clackety-clack-clack!* Its announcement bell rang three signals and the roll turned for the following message. "Goddamn!" Kirstin said as she whirled away. "Chad always did have a lousy sense of timing."

Belvale heard the outer door slam but now his attention was focused upon the report coming through. General Guderian's Panzer Corps had halted at Gravelines, only ten miles from Dunkirk. General Reinhardt's Panzer Corps had pulled up at the canal line Aire–St. Omer on the other flank of Gravelines. Why the hell didn't they simply close the gap and pinch off every survivor of the BEF? Guderian was a brilliant commander and Reinhardt no dummy; both knew more about the use of armor than anyone else in the world, except maybe for Georgie Patton, and Georgie hadn't been tested in combat. Did the egomaniac himself call the halt to his rampaging panzers, Hitler having another fevered brainstorm?

"Thank God or Der Fuhrer's personal devil for stopping them," Belvale whispered, and focused sharply upon the facts and figures pouring onto the paper. He was happy for Chad; the boy had made it all the way. He envied him his first blooding, for it was true that a man first faced his true self at that moment, that he either vacillated, broke or found a new mettle. Chad had discovered his strength. Possibly he had rearranged himself enough to keep his wife. Belvale would hate to lose her; the Hill would be poor without her.

"Kirstin," he called, and remembered that she had run from the war room. Frowning, he wondered about that, her sudden reversal of moods. Was she disappointed that her husband was alive? Events of worldwide importance were exploding, and individual problems, especially those of military people, were certain to be powder burned and put aside. General Belvale concentrated upon the intelligence information *pop-popping* line after vivid line on the teletype.

CHAPTER 29

MI-5—Downing Street (Top Secret—need to know only): By 2400 hrs, June 2, 1940, 224,000 men of the BEF brought safe away from Dunkirk; 2000 lost in ships sunk en route to England. Approximately 95,000 Allied troops, mainly French, also saved. Desperate effort under fire 2100-2300 hours June 3, 26,000 more French rescued. Three to four thousand rear guard left on beach. Total 338,000 saved. Prime Minister Churchill says WELL DONE.

Nancy Carlisle felt free and excited, released from a kind of bondage, a newness that had grown since her husband was declared missing in action. But she still knew a certain hesitation, as if she wore leg irons nobody else could hear rattle. She sat in the Alexandria Hotel bar and sipped a julep she didn't like. Returning to the Hill because the general had asked, and because she'd in a way wanted to, she had found a real friend in Kirstin. There had always been a goodness between them, but the missing husbands gave them much more in common, a closeness grown to sisterhood Nancy had never known. An only child, she was always a little lonely, always a little forgotten by a mother who had to work damned hard to keep their bodies functioning and had no time left for souls. Nancy could barely remember her father; he left them when she was small.

Lighting an Old Gold, she coughed lightly around it. She didn't much like smoking, either, but she couldn't just sit in this place like a lump, as if she didn't belong. She hadn't been in a hotel since right after she married Keenan Carlisle, although the mansion at Kill Devil Hill felt more like a hotel than a home, when it wasn't being a barracks or command post. And Minerva Belvale was ever the house detective and charge of quarters, officer of the day and night.

The next swallow of mint julep tasted a little better. The hotel bar was slowly filling with cocktail hour people, but no men in uniform. Officers shed their workaday greens and pinks as soon as Retreat sounded, and sooner if they could goldbrick away from their jobs.

"Damn," she whispered into her uptilted glass, "I sound like army for sure, as if I grew up on old Fort Bang-Bang."

Then he slid gracefully onto the adjoining bar stool, and the fragile scent of his after-shave somehow blocked out the harsh odors of beer and whiskey. Every move that Wilson Pailey made was smooth and deft, so that he made other men clumsy, and some women awkward, just being near him. Nancy had gotten beyond that point, but couldn't still the flutter tightening her throat, even after she soaked it down with julep.

Wilson Pailey didn't have to tap the bar top for service; the barman hurried to him for his order. Dark haired, with black lashes women would kill for, he warmed Nancy with a smile that made her stop being nervous. He said, "My secretary called for a reservation. The manager is discreet." For a fraction of a second, his eyes weren't deep chocolate, but obsidian. "He knows to be."

Of course he has done this before, she thought, and in this very hotel. It's close to Washington and the staff is discreet. Wilson was a man of the world, not duty bound, hidebound by family and tradition. That made him exciting, and it had been a long, lonely time since Nancy had been excited. Stimulated might be a better word, or thrilled, or—damn it!—not guilty for Keenan being MIA. That wasn't her fault, she was only minimally to blame for a marriage on the brink.

Keenan and his family; the family and Keenan and the damned army and—"Kill Devil Hill," she said.

His light frown was swiftly gone. "A beautiful estate, a magnificent power base. There has probably never been another family like yours. Not even Lighthorse Harry Lee and Robert E. himself could have put together such an organization under such tightly directed control."

Her second julep wasn't at all gunky and made her lips just a touch numb. "Not really my family. Married in and can't marry out; not just yet." That was the wrong thing to say on her first assignation. "Did they ever tell you the legend of Kill Devil Hill? No? Then Miss Minerva Belvale never got you cornered. Well—"

Two women at a candle lit table stared openly at Wilson; Nancy lifted an eyebrow at them and took a gulp of her drink. "—old Jubal or Hepzibah or some such first of the Belvales in this country started the house. Used to enjoy tippling at the tavern, 'tis said. Until he got himself pursued by a devil, and off darted Squire Belvale for the footbridge because devils can't cross running water."

Pausing, she allowed Wilson to light her new cigarette. "This little heretic devil didn't believe that. Pointy tail over horny points, yonder he came, hoof over cloven hoof. You remember seeing that huge damned sword hanging in the great hall? The squire is supposed to have turned and whacked the devil with it, and the steel was sacred because it had been blessed by George Washington or some such deity. Naturally the satanic little bastard couldn't take that, so he keeled right over, and lo—Kill Devil Hill."

Wilson laughed and covered her hand with long, warm fingers. "I heard a Belvale beat off a British attempt to burn the house when they torched Washington in the War of 1812."

When Nancy nodded, a wisp of hair fell over one eye. "Whupped the Yankees off the lawn, too. I didn't really mean to prattle. It's just—oh, hell; I forgot how to act on a date, and my husband is missing in action and—"

His fingers closed tighter upon her hand. "Having second thoughts?"

She squeezed back. "Getting my first thoughts to dress right and cover down. If—if you're ready, I sure am."

The juleps had something to do with it, but not much. It

had been a long time between men—man, between the only man she ever had and beautiful Wilson Pailey. It was too damned long without being loved.

Oh, Jesus! Loved!

He was perfect and that made the night perfect and the sheets silken, but no smoother than his skin. His mouth tasted of geraniums and honeysuckle and that wasn't at all ridiculous. Gently and expertly, he brought her along slower than she would have liked at first, but so tender and practiced that she squirmed inside her tingling flesh.

It had never been like this. Away back when, she had girl-dreamed it would be, all romance and love and the adoration that lifted her out of herself and into stars where she melted.

"Oh, God," she breathed a sweet century later, "oh, dear God—I thank You." Just enough mystic twilight lingered in the room so that she could see the shadows of his face when he lifted—but without taking himself from her, and Wilson Pailey was smiling.

She didn't ever want to stop smiling back.

CHAPTER 30

AGENCE FRANCE PRESSE—Paris, June 17, 1940: Negotiations are under way to declare Paris an open city, and so protect it from indiscriminate bombing by the German Luftwaffe, if the highly improbable, if not impossible, penetration of Le Boche occurs.

Stunned by the rapid advance of German troops through Poland and the Lowlands, the French high command released a bulletin today stating that the open city request would only be presented if the enemy became frustrated by the solid defenses of the Maginot Line. Then the angered Nazis, frantic in defeat, might very well strike by air at the city's civilian population and at sites of great historical value, with no other purpose than to hurt and destroy.

"The Maginot Line will hold," said a headquarters spokesman. "No Frenchman worthy of the name can doubt that."

Second Lieutenant Farley Belvale, USAR, drew a deep breath and sorted the outside odors—green pine, raw planking and reddish dust, wood smoke and coal smoke. This was the Harmony Church area of Fort Benning, Georgia, sporting newly laid passages through the tall pines, such as the Hourglass and First Division roads. Once there had been a civilian chapel nearby, but Farley didn't remember seeing it. Now there were literally miles of pyramidal tents, all dribbling smoke from split oak firewood on this cold Saturday afternoon. There were wooden mess halls and day

196

rooms whose stoves were fed with soft coal by grimy KPs. A man-made fog hung over the camp.

His first assignment; here he was a platoon leader in a Regular Army outfit, and the troops eyed him as if he were AWOL from a Boy Scout jamboree. He sort of felt like it, unsure and jittery and hard put not to show it. It was better that he'd gone into the 26th Infantry, rather than take his minor command in the 16th, where the family held sway. Here nobody could accuse him of nepotism, of accepting favors from his kinfolk.

"Going into town?"

Second Lieutenant Briscoe grinned from beside his car, a 1937 Plymouth. Farley was surprised that he had wandered down to the company parking lot. Some lot: three cars. One trip to town and Farley could add to the traffic congestion with a glittering new Buick. But it wasn't politic to outshine the old man's vehicle. Captain MacCarthy was very proud of his 1938 Hudson.

"I don't think so," Farley said.

Briscoe rattled the door handle. "Nobody with two bucks in his pocket hangs around here after inspection. Hell, man, we got the whole weekend to be human. Come Monday we can play shavetail lieutenants again."

"Gee—I don't know—"

Opening the car door, Briscoe said, "I got date of rank on you by two months. And since I got here that much earlier it gave me plenty of time to reconnoiter the sight and sounds of Columbus, Georgia, and the far more interesting fleshpots across the river in Phenix City, Alabama. I envy you your first startled exeriences there. Not that it's boring now, but there's only one first time. Look, if you're worried about money—"

"No," Farley said. "It's not that."

What was it, then? Did fresh young officers fret over protecting their reputation, their virginity? Hardly; you didn't even admit it. Everything was different, the entire camp new and raw, the troops challenging and the company commander ever watchful for leadership mistakes.

Was it Pretty Penny Belvale? Could she be the reason he wanted to stay in camp, to remain celibate? If that's what he really wanted, he should have bucked to become a sky pilot, a Holy Joe, a chaplain.

He should have met and married her before his cousin did.

"Okay," he said. "A few beers. Give me a minute to get into my pinks."

Pinks and greens—they were the blouse and slacks dress uniform required of today's officers. If you could afford it, you had them tailored. If you didn't have the money right off, it was better that you saved it or catch every crappy detail on post. Especially in the First Division, the word went, even though high brass took into account being in the field now. But when the outfit got back to permanent garrison, to the spit and polish of the army's showcase regiment . . .

At least the army had dropped the wearing of the traditional Sam Browne belt except on parade or during certain duties. Maybe it, too, would go the way of the ceremonial sword.

Crisp air whipped in through the partly open window of the car. Briscoe said, "Handle's stuck. You sure you haven't been to Ma Beechie's?"

"Haven't been off the post. Trying to get adjusted—first assignment jitters."

Briscoe drove the car deftly through light traffic of downtown Columbus. "Hell, you went four years to a fancy military school. I had a few weeks ROTC at Louisiana State, a schoolboy soldier. You'll be a general while I'm still bucking for first john, or just trying to hang on to these gold bars."

The bridge over the Chatahoochie River was short, but it marked the dividing line between general respectability and life on the wild side. Phenix City had the deserved reputation of being the toughest town in the country and fed off Fort Benning troops. There anything could be had for a price, and trouble-making GIs were fined according to rank and therefore the ability to pay. City politicians and police ruled; opposition often floated the river face down.

"Behold Beechie Howard's joint," Briscoe announced, "better known as Ma Beechie's. Abandon hope all ye who enter here. This entrance is for us high-ranking suckers; the peasant soldiers cavort beyond yon wall. But lo! The whores minister to both sides without prejudice. Two dollars is the standard rate to GIs; a bit more for officers of our exalted rank, but the same hookers."

Farley coughed at the thick swirl of cigarette smoke that almost choked off the smells of sawdust and beer, the clinging attar of dimestore perfume. At the far end of the long main room, crap games and 21-tables were busy with coins and chips.

The bar was long, also, its wood battle scarred and dark. Colorless and cheap, the bootleg whiskey seared Farley's throat; a chaser of cold Jax beer eased the bite. He relaxed to the thumping of hillbilly music. He belonged, damnit. Here soldiers gathered, and he was one with them. He had some more whiskey, more beer. Briscoe kept saying things that made him laugh, and he felt like singing.

She appeared at his elbow, a sleek and leggy girl whose eyes shone with practiced innocence, whose mouth was a scarlet couch set startlingly in the bare cell of a nun. Because she spoke softly and her perfume was light, because she danced lightly against him, he could make believe she was Pretty Penny.

And that stopped him from going on.

CHAPTER 31

Daily Telegraph—London, September 7, 1940: London is being attacked by the largest air fleet the Germans have ever assembled, some 300 high-level bombers and about 600 fighters. The city is ablaze from indiscriminate bombing. In the densely crowded area of the East End, casualties among civilians have reached into the thousands and damage is enormous.

In fetid darkness pierced only by flickering candles, Chad Belvale passed around his pack of Luckies, and thumbed his Zippo for both young officers who sat close to him. "Gentlemen of the family—welcome to London and the war."

Gavin Scott said, "Hell of a place for introductions—away the hell down in a subway." He was close family, his mother a Carlisle, his father a tester of airplanes once too often.

"Underground," the WAAF officer said. "Here they're called undergrounds."

She had a cute Scots burr, and now Chad couldn't see enough of her face by the candle, only the quickness of a smile that said she wasn't really afraid. She was so young, nearer the age of the kids fresh over from the States. Both had been singularly attentive to the first British woman in uniform they'd spoken to, before the sirens went off.

Whamm!

Brick dust sanded loosely down upon them as the bomb went off too close and shook the earth. Two tiles fell from the underground's curved wall to shatter upon the concrete floor. A child cried out and a mother said, "Hush—hush now."

. . . Thump . . . Thump . . . thump . . .

The girl said, "Jerry's getting farther off."

"And here we sit." There was no smile in Lt. Gavin Scott's voice. Chad remembered him as a surly kid who kept to himself unless it was to hang around Minerva Belvale, and the added years hadn't changed him much. How old was Gavin—twenty-five or a little more? Married only to his uniform, they said at home, and a good thing, too. His dark good looks drew women to flutter about him, but he squeezed them dry and threw them away. His father had thrown away Gavin's mother and taken himself off forever.

"Can't run out and throw rocks," Chad said. He drew on his cigarette. Above them and across Shaftesbury Avenue, across the busy action of the Circus, was the Piccadilly Hotel, if it was still standing. When the air raid sirens had gone off, they were all in its bar, seated on those old-fashioned overstuffed couches and chairs. To Chad and evidently the girl, going to the nearest shelter was sensible and automatic. The newly arrived U.S. Army Air Corps officers strolled, to show their disdain for German bombs, but Chad forgave them their stupidity; this was their first air raid.

Whaaammm!

Clapping both hands to his ears, Chad tried to equalize the pressure inside and out. The underground tube rocked and threatened to buckle. The baby cried again and nobody told it to hush.

"Five hundred pounder," the girl said. "Huge bloody things; make terrible craters someone has to fill up."

"Worse when they don't go off," Chad said, conscious now of more than the odors of brick dust and filtering smoke, knowing now the acrid scent of sweating humanity and the sharper stench of fear. A direct hit by one of those big bombs, and the lucky ones in this shelter would die in the explosion; the others would slowly suffocate.

"The disposal squads," the girl said, no doubt being polite and talking to him because the young guys weren't saying much. He'd heard her name in the hotel bar—Stevie? —Stephanie, what? Stephanie Bartlett, that was it. A one-pipper, second leftenant in her blue-gray uniform of the Women's Auxilliary Air Force, the WAAF. Half the women in England wore uniforms of one sort or another, ATS, the WRNS, and Land Army, the military nurses of all branches called sisters.

"Nasty bit of work," she said, drawing upon her cigarette. Its red glow didn't show her remembered eyes to advantage, Chad thought. "Have to go down after the duds, not knowing if they're time-delay; Jerry booby-traps so many." The quick red glow of her cigarette gave a glimpse of her pixie face.

"Spooky," Chad agreed, and listened to bombs falling farther away. The radium dial of his watch showed 2:00 A.M.; they had been below ground for more than three hours already. Would the damned Krauts never finish bombing and go home?

For months, the Luftwaffe had been going after British airfields, trying to knock out the RAF's fighter planes, the Hurricanes and more precious Spitfires. For all that time, Hitler's invasion flotilla built up off Normandy, his Operation Sea Lion not yet launched because his generals and admirals feared the RAF and Royal Navy and sometimes Hitler listened.

If the RAF was wiped out, the Germans could come in with paratroopers, the way they'd done in Belgium and France. They could set up strong points and supply the troopers by air. A stream of small seaborne assaults might follow, few large enough to bring down the whole British fleet, but enough to begin linking up with the paratroops. A handful of soldiers in small boats would infiltrate, repeating a hundred little landings until troop strength built up to attack.

The girl moved closer to Chad; for fatherly protection? Gavin moved aside and crushed out his cigarette, pulled his garrison cap over his eyes and leaned back against the wall, pretending boredom and a need for sleep, Chad thought.

The cap had no grommet and flopped about the ears in the newly acquired air corps style that set them apart more than their silver wings.

"It's the largest raid yet," Stephanie said. "Old Adolf changed his mind about doing in all our airfields, I'd say. Now he's going after the population."

It was a dumb thing to say, but saying something was better than the numb silence of the air raid shelter: "You're a Scot, Leftenant? I haven't been to Scotland yet."

He could smell her now, only a faint spice; heather? "Grenoch—a coastal town. Just come to Britain, Major? It is major? I haven't seen enough Yank ratings to be sure."

"Sort of fresh to England proper, yes. I came across from Dunkirk."

Another bomb shook the underground, but not badly. A stick of bombs thunder-walked across the city going away. Between explosions, Chad heard the faint pops of antiaircraft fire, not enough of it, not nearly enough. The English needed guns and planes and pilots to fly them. They needed many other things, but just now these were most important.

She leaned closer, so that her breath stirred his cheek. Heather; he was sure of it now. Small girl in the hotel bar—no, not small in the general sense, neatly and properly made. He remembered her walking proudly across the hotel lobby, a sureness to the set of her shoulders, walking to the beat of a rhythm nobody else could hear.

"I lost my brother at Dunkirk," she murmured.

"Sorry. I lost a nephew in Warsaw, another Yank observer." The candle near them flickered, and an old man lighted another farther down. Chad saw only the shadows of Stephanie's face, but her breath turned ragged. He said, "Life seems to balance out, though; I found a good friend, a cockney leftenant who stayed with me from Belgium to Dover. We had to report to different places, but I'm supposed to meet him here tomorrow, on leave." He made a small laugh. "Well, not here, but in the hotel."

"For Christ's sake," Gavin said. "All this chitchat. When the hell do we get out of this rat hole? Advance party, my ass. I haven't been near the planes we brought off the ship, and the goddamn Krauts are all over the sky with nobody to stop them."

Drawing a deep breath, Chad said, "Watch your mouth, boy. RAF pilots are dying out there right now, and you don't know a damned thing about combat yet, ground or air. I suggest you learn some patience, or you and those Lockheed Hudsons won't last."

The other cousin or whatever the hell his family connection was, stirred. "Ah, Major—" Lieutenant Wilmot said, "Gavin's just anxious."

Chad ignored the other boy who looked too much like the one killed in Poland. Would he be as good a soldier? Perhaps most good soldiers died, and perhaps that was the family business—dying. "Remember what I said, Lieutenant Scott."

"Okay."

"What?"

"All right—*sir*."

Stephanie's fingers touched the back of Chad's tensed hand, ever so softly, and he relaxed. He hadn't meant to pull rank in public, but memories of the breakdowns in Belgium and France were too fresh, and the U.S. Army's air arm was fast becoming known for its lack of discipline.

She said, "Everyone gets a bit feverish in a bomb shelter. I think Jerry is going home now; look at that grating up there—it's turning light outside."

Feeling for another smoke, Chad found none. His last pack had passed down the line of nervous people. Stephanie touched his arm. "Capstan? Not as good as Yank tobacco, but—"

"Thank you. Anything beats Jerry cigarettes, and these aren't bad."

After the all clear sounded, Stephanie would leave with Gavin Scott, drawn anew by his handsome face, lazy grace and knowing eyes. He was young, but not boyish. He hadn't been a boy since, at age fourteen, he knocked up a stableman's daughter. Chad had often wondered how Minerva Belvale excused that in her favorite, but she had, no doubt blaming the even younger girl.

Long and steady, sirens in London sounded, and people

moved about in the semidarkness of the shelter. Children laughed and some old men rolled tighter in their blankets to sleep where they were.

"Come on, Riley," Gavin said. "Maybe we can get out to Hornchurch Field and have the Hudsons hurried into action."

Wilmot hesitated. "Permission, sir?"

"Go," Chad said, and glanced at Stephanie who stood brushing at her skirt. She would leave with the young and handsome, to find herself in some hotel handy to the airfield. The Hudsons were nowhere near ready to take the air. They'd just been off-loaded and trucked across London, another of President Roosevelt's presents under Lend-Lease. Supposedly capable of playing the full backfield —photography, reconnaissance, bomber and fighter, the American twin-engine planes might not hold up against Messerschmitts and Stukas. They would have to be tested.

As for Gavin, it was obvious that he just wanted to get away from Chad's rank so he could play the visiting adventurer. Riley would get dropped along the way. And later, so would Stephanie Bartlett, like it or not. It was Gavin's way.

Cocking his crushed garrison cap to just the right angle, Gavin said, "Coming, Stevie?"

She tilted her head as if in imitation of his hat move and said, "Thank you, no. Duty, you understand."

"But I thought you said—" Gavin whirled and pushed through the crowd upon the underground's stairway.

"Sir," Riley said and followed his cousin's lead.

Taking Chad's arm, she allowed him to assist her up the stairs. Civilians pushed by them, men and women anxious to discover whether their homes were standing. The air was thick with smoke, with the taste of burning; rubble littered Piccadilly. Firefighters with blackened faces, so tired that they sometimes staggered, hosed down smouldering piles; ambulances out of sight sounded their ululating warnings.

"I'm sorry you have to go on duty," Chad said, letting go her arm as refugees from the bomb shelters rivered around them, bumping lightly. "If you have time, I'll buy you a drink. They didn't get the hotel."

"Plenty of time," she said, walking beside him with

her special grace. "I have until twenty-four hundred on the tenth. It's my first leave and there's little left in Scotland for me now, so I'm spending it in London. Not deserting under fire, as it were."

He stopped in the middle of the street where half a dozen men struggled to lift a blown-over taxi back upon its wheels. "But you said—"

"I lied to Leftenant Scott; a technique he's most familiar with, I should think."

His laughter caused stares from hurrying passersby. "Marvelous! You're so young, and I didn't dare hope you were that perceptive."

"But you did hope?" Gamin face with a smile dancing full lips, blue eyes holding mischief and something else. "Let's have that first drink, Major."

It was the first time he'd thought of Kirstin in days, and that because of the drinks. She had said he had to get drunk to screw, and he'd tracked far back in his mind to fumble out the reasons sex seemed forbidden to him: masturbation and Great-aunt Minerva Belvale. Even now, her name and that act didn't go together in thoughts.

Over the first gin—the hotel's daily Scotch ration had run out before the bombing started—Chad said, "I have to tell you . . . I'm married."

She had this wide grin that made her eyebrows lift and her eyes do a kind of tap dance. "I thought as much."

"Then that means that we—you and I aren't—"

"The bloody hell we aren't. You *do* have a room here and I *did* desert that handsome cad in your favor."

The second gin and tonics arrived and Chad downed his at a gulp. "Why did you, Stephanie?"

She didn't touch her drink and her eyes turned serious, turned darker and direct. Her nose seemed less perky then. "Because you are much the better man. Rather, you are a thoughtful man and he's a selfish boy."

He lighted her Capstan and then his own. Outside, the firemen and volunteer workers must have cleared a path along Shaftesbury Avenue or Regency Street, because the up-and-down beep of ambulances coming and going was almost continuous. Chad was a little guilty for not being out there lifting rocks or something. But that wasn't why he signalled for another gin-and.

Stephanie pushed his hand down. "Does it bother you so much, that you're married? Would it be better if we were both single, or both married?"

"Look—I don't—I haven't seen my wife in a long time, and before that, we weren't—right together. After that mess in France, my first combat, I thought I might—Kirstin and I might—"

Still, she didn't touch her drink, and tapped out her cigarette. "She hasn't seen fighting, hasn't been bombed. Her sentiments ought to be the same, don't you think? This war will change certain sentiments: a man is entitled to sample other women, but a woman daren't. It's not like that now. When I first saw you, I hoped you'd think with me, but if you don't want—"

He swallowed, but dryly. He didn't order another gin. This was his first experience with what he saw as an honest woman. "You're beautiful, and so young—"

"Why, thank you, Grandfather. I'm thirty-two. Would you care to finish my drink?"

"No," he said.

"Good." She stood up, neat and trim in her uniform, the pixie look back upon her face, one eyebrow lifted.

Chad rose and offered his arm. She bobbed in a curtsey of sorts and smiled up at him. Softly he said, "It's a hell of a thing, but I know I'll be glad we spent the night in the shelter."

"Yes, but Jerry won't be back all day, and if he does return—"

Her firm breast pressing against his arm told him that they wouldn't race down to the shelter again, and that was just fine with Chad.

"Tallyho," she said at the lift, and he laughed easily with her, as he had laughed with no other woman.

CHAPTER 32

Associated Press—Boerne, Tex., October 18, 1940: U.S. Senator Jim Shelby (D-Texas) announced today that he was throwing the weight of his office behind a hurry-up rearmament campaign for this country. Senator Shelby quoted a former queen of England: "It is later than we think." He went on to say that America would be drawn into war within a year, and that the country is woefully unprepared, despite the years of war in China and Europe that have given us warning.

Kirstin walked beside the general to the hot walker where she had three horses moving. In boots and cavalry twill breeches, he looked at the Morgans with a practiced eye, and Kirstin saw him smile.

"They stood the trip well, all of them?"

"One stud colt got between the mare and the trailer wall. But he's a squealer, and the driver heard him and pulled over. He walks a little ouchy, but that's all."

She wondered if he saw the ranch as she did, if the quick small hills and the shiny green of live oaks appealed to him. This was not the lushness of Virginia, not the tamed and obedient land, but the start of independent Texas hill country. North of San Antonio the softly rolling mounds hinted of what lay farther north, a land whose wildness and hardship was part of its appeal. Here all was beautiful and good water plentiful, the grass was rich; everything just right for raising horses and the consciousness level of people.

It might have been made more beautiful by who she had become, by who Jim Shelby had always been, by the kind of deep sharing she had never known. She crossed mental fingers. General Belvale said, "Has Chad come home?"

"No. I thought he'd want to hurry, but—as expected, his reports were complete and minutely detailed, and he wanted to stay in London for a while longer, to survey the Luftwaffe's bombing damage. We've sent some airplanes over, and two of the family pilots to contact him. I could order him home, Kirstin, but I'd like to give us a few more weeks, to see if Hitler is serious about invading England. You know what duty means to Chad."

"Oh, hell, yes, duty. By all means, duty. I just wish—once wished—that he would sort out the many kinds of duty and balance their importance. I wrote him after getting that teletype message." Not looking at General Belvale, steadying herself with clean air that held sharp edges of fall, she went on: "I wrote him twice and he answered once. His note was nothing compared to what he said on the teletype, and he didn't really answer my questions. If he has to be ordered home, I don't want him. I'm here with Jim where I mean to stay, but I haven't filed for divorce, not yet."

Walking on toward the stables, the general said, "Please don't. Not for Chad's sake or even yours. This nation needs Jim Shelby in the Senate, and elections are coming up. Any touch of scandal and he will be in trouble. The isolationists are already after his scalp, but that's all right, providing his constituents continue to see him sympathetically as a widower, carrying bravely on, duty before sorrow. Marrying a divorcée who deserted her two children—"

"Oh, for Christ's sake! The boys are hardly children, and if—" she strode to the stalls and peered into one. Bruised hip or no, the little stud was snorty, wanting out. She smelled the good scent of horse sweat and new wood shavings. "I know you're only repeating what will be carried from small minds through big mouths. Besides, Jim hasn't asked to marry me."

"He'd be a fool if he didn't. If he doesn't want you permanently, you can always come home to the Hill."

"Why—thank you, General." She watched him bring out a slim metal cigar case and select a smoke. He wouldn't light it around stable or barn; he was a horseman. She said, "I appreciate the invitation. But Owen and Farley—Minerva—and if Chad knows what I've been doing—"

"He doesn't yet, and you have always stood up to Minerva. That's not hard. The Hill is home for the entire family, not a chosen few. The boys will get over your being with another man; I think Farley already has. He might come see you on his next leave."

A bitter taste joined the last of the Indian summer flavors in her mouth. "If Owen doesn't convince him it's a bad idea."

"Different boys, as far apart as you and Chad." He bit one end of the cigar into a cupped palm and shredded it with his fingers before scattering the minute pieces of tobacco.

Kirstin recognized the move as a simplified version of field-stripping a cigarette butt so that an army post always looked clean; so that enlisted men wouldn't have to pick up that much more when they formed a muttering skirmish line to police the area.

. . . if it moves, salute it; if it lies there, pick it up; if you can't lift it, paint the son of a bitch . . .

She might miss the military flavor of the Hill, the cocky arrogance of soldiers and their special vocabulary. Soldiers and their wives were a breed apart from anything civilian, and proud of it.

Kirstin already did miss the Hill and its people, but only a little. Love chased away loneliness, but if this love died, where would she go to say good bye? She said, "Let's walk over to the stock pond, so you can light that thing. I won't do anything to hurt Jim or his job—so long as he wants the job. I'll try not to hurt Chad, either. I wonder if he *can be* hurt emotionally. When that message came through, it was too late, but I might have tried; he didn't sound like the old Chad."

. . . watch that Belvale bastard, the enlisted men said; he gets his nuts off by gigging doggies . . . if that ain't chicken-shit, then he's sure got henhouse ways . . .

The general flicked a gold Ronson at the cigar and allowed a drag to roll around inside his mouth before releasing a line of pungent blue smoke to cohabit with the sunshine air. "Combat changes men for better or worse. It's the first time a man comes face-to-face with what he truly is. He's a new Chad, but we won't know for a while which way he went, although his reports were exceptional. He should have hurried back to the Hill, returned to you and the boys."

Kirstin didn't say that from afar, he was a much bigger figure to his sons. Up close for any length of time, and they might see him as a little smaller than life. She tucked her hands into her denim jacket pockets. Should have, might have, if; nothing counted except now. Jim mattered; oh, God, yes. But Chad's value had been questionable for a long time. In the shadows of small oaks, again she smelled chill. Frost would soon sneak onto the land during the night and surprise the dawn with crystals. How much protein would the grass lose as it froze? It was something she would ask Jim. She wasn't used to the seasons here, not familiar with anything but Jim Shelby and her horses.

The general blew smoke and paused to thumbnail his mustache. Then he said, "Keenan came home. He cabled me from Hong Kong where Red Chinese troops delivered him. We knew he'd been with a Japanese unit when it was ambushed, and thought we'd lost him."

"Oh, lord! And Nancy wasn't there to greet him when he got back?" Nancy might have been caught in passing, when she stopped in to pick up more clothing, but that would be about the only time. Nancy spent most of her time in Washington and Atlanta, wherever Wilson Pailey went. She was in love and that was beautiful, but she ought to settle things with Keenan. Although she was bright-eyed as a teenager and, she said, happier than she had been with Keenan. Still, her husband would have to be faced.

And Kirstin would have to look into Chad's eyes, when he decided to come home. Look and tell him that she was in love with another man.

"She phones me now and then. I told her that he would

be reporting to the War Department, so if she was in Washington and wanted to meet—''

Walking beside him, heading back to the house, Kirstin thought if the general hadn't gone military, he would have risen high in the State Department, reaching apolitical ambassador status if that's what he wanted. He was a born diplomat, but she knew that duty came first with this man, for cause other than being head of the family. In other times, he would have led Crusadés.

They reached the back porch and as they climbed steps, Kirstin said, ''She didn't want to see him?''

He sat in one of the handmade chairs, rounded oak back and rungs, and a cowhide seat that, if used constantly, would shape itself comforting to a certain bottom. She leaned against the porch rail. Jim's house was big, but not antebellum pretentious; two storey with columns that were only four-by-fours nailed together and painted white. The house was solid and dependable like Jim Shelby himself, unexpected warmth in corners that ought to be chilly—like the story of his marriage. Jim still respected the memory of his dead wife, but he kept her specter thin and misty, so it would not come between him and another love. And if only for that, Kirstin loved him more.

''Keenan wasn't all that anxious to see her,'' Belvale said. ''He stayed drunk for a week, kept our whiskey maker working overtime. The boy was wounded and he mumbled about a thousand-mile hike and bridge chains. He's ground down to muscle and bone, but that wasn't the reason he wasn't more curious about Nancy and why she wasn't home. It's as if he just doesn't care.''

''They weren't getting along, hadn't in years.'' Like Chad and her.

The general opened his cigar case, lifted it to smell deeply, then snapped it shut. ''The way he carries on about China— Communist China, I'd say he's still feverish. I'd also say there's a woman involved. I hope she will be better for him than the congressman is for Nancy.''

Kirstin hesitated, looking off and focusing on a sweetgum tree that was changing into bright fall clothing; just past it, a dogwood was stripping to the skin. Almost from the beginning, she had been a little spooky about Wilson Pailey. He was too pretty, so slick you couldn't get a grip on him. Washington was full of that kind, but Wilson was special that way. Now that the general voiced doubts about the man, Kirstin remembered that he smiled too quickly and his teeth looked sharp. But Nancy thought he was wonder upon wonder, a historical figure to be, an idealist with a genius grasp of geopolitics, and in bed—terrific! Nancy said now she was happy she couldn't conceive; it made sex better all around for them both.

"Pailey is like a pack mule I knew out in Fort Huachuca," the general said. "That sleepy-looking beast would be patient for years, just to get a good shot at killing you. The gentleman from Atlanta is working both sides of the bridle path, kissing up to liberal and conservative alike, testing the wind. That's politics, and Pailey trying to use the family is only turnabout. But where we work for the common good, he's operating for himself, and manipulating Nancy to do it. If he comes solidly to our side, we'll help him. If he stays neutral, that will be all right. If he goes over to the isolationists, we'll unseat him, especially if he's carrying family information to the opposition."

Kirstin folded her arms across her stomach. Poor Nancy. Or maybe not. She was happy, and if Wilson Pailey kept her happy, where was the harm? The family used everything and everyone and not always openly.

She said, "Do you want me to tell her that?"

He seemed surprised. "Not unless you wish to. This was a G-2 briefing of sorts, FYI—For Your Information."

"And to stop talking to me about Chad?"

"Army intelligence could use that kind of intuition—especially in Washington. Chad is family, and so are you." The general carefully field stripped his cigar butt and gave the miniscule bits to the land. "Did I tell you that Crusty Carlisle has come down and taken up residence?"

"Oh, God. That man scares me."

"Scares me at times, but he belongs and we need his head-on thinking." He sighed. "I didn't come here to interfere with you and Jim Shelby, but to protect you both, if I can."

"I understand. I'll do my part." Crossing to his chair, she touched the leather of his cheek with one hand. "Jim will, too; I don't know about Nancy. The women of this family—your family—must be soldiers, also. I just didn't reenlist."

Her sons—would they ever understand? One might, given the chance and time; the other was much like his father, and she had made her choice, the guilt would wear away, and if not, she would carry its cross. Jim was worth it, and goddamnit!—so was she. So was the rest of her life, her life as she meant to live it.

As she followed the general through the back door and across the big country kitchen which always breathed a faint odor of chili, she thought how lightly a contented smile lay upon her lips.

Belvale leaned back in the padded chair of dark leather. He sniffed over the Cuban cigar without lighting it. The medics hinted that he should cut down, only smoke three or four a day, but what the hell did pill rollers know? In the field, a good medic was God's own gift; in garrison they ought to stick with being chancre mechanics and short arm inspectors.

"This is true sipping whiskey, Jim."

"Bottled in the barn and aged in the woods, General. An old fellow in the hill country makes it, an artist in his own time. It's actually funneled into a charred oak keg which is then toted up a tall pine and lashed high there, so the wind can turn it every so often. Stays there at least five years to age so smooth and rich that it shames store-bought whiskey."

"Agreed, but how do we get Congress to live on it?"

"You've met with most of the intransigents?"

Belvale tasted whiskey and his cigar in turn. "Most; I wouldn't talk to bastards that depend on Father Coughlin and his ilk for support. And that woman— she sure as hell will vote against any kind of war, even if the enemy is marching down the street. Margaret Chase Smith of Maine thinks we can talk to those cute little gardener type Japanese and they'll beat their samurai swords into cheap gimcracks."

Pouring more white lightning into glasses, Shelby said, "It's that certain, then? In Washington, the feeling is about fifty-fifty that we can avoid being dragged into the war."

"So we continue to sell the little bastards scrap iron—two hundred million tons over the last five years." Belvale watched Shelby hold his glass of clear liquid to the light and saw the moonshine facets reflect softly, like a gemstone.

Shelby said, "Maggi Smith isn't the only blind legislator; there's Bob Taft. We had a hell of a time getting the military appropriations bill through the House, eight billion dollars to raise troop strength to two million. Nobody is used to talking billions, and along comes Taft gee-hawing. FDR is planning to force us into war, he says."

"Might be right," Belvale said, the whiskey warm in his stomach, good cigar smoke like honey upon his tongue, "but a hit-first strike won't get by Washington, sensible as that is. Jim—all those men won't be worth anything if we can't arm them. The Louisiana Maneuvers are on, the First Divison out of temporary quarters at Fort Benning and the Second Infantry from Fort Bliss, Texas. Regular Army, the best we have, but, goddamnit!—their trucks carry signs saying: *Tank,* and the antitank guns are wooden. We bomb from light planes with flour bags or eggs."

Swallowing his whiskey, Shelby put his glass atop the scarred oak desk. "We may be in and out of the war before we know what hit us."

Belvale shook his head. "Down, maybe; never out. Washington misreads public opinion, which is always a fatal mistake for politicians. The country feels war is coming, and the people are behind President Roosevelt all the way. We've run opinion polls and surveys across the nation, not just spot-checking."

Shelby's smile was lopsided. "The president might have kept us temporarily out of the fight, but only by giving up all honor. And by lifting the oil embargo on Japan, taking Lend-Lease back from the British, little things like that."

Nodding, Belvale finished his drink and stared at the long ash growing upon his cigar. "I just wish he'd push harder. We don't have much time to get set."

Somebody knocked softly at the big sliding doors of the study. "Yes?" Shelby called. "Come on in."

Belvale frowned as Kirstin came stiff-legged into the room. Something had turned her face pale and set her jaw. The hurt colt dead, some other horse to be put down?

Worse.

"Jim," she said, eyes straight ahead, "my husband is here. Chad flew home without telling anybody, and right now he's in the sitting room." She didn't seem to remember that Belvale was in the room.

"Oh, Christ," she said.

Belvale said, "Amen."

CHAPTER 33

UNITED PRESS—Washington, D.C., October 20, 1940: Storm clouds gathered over the nation's capitol today as U.S. Army overseas observers reported to a board of inquiry. Rumors filtering out of the War Department indicated a deep schism between the Old Guard and the Young—some not so Young—Turks over military expenses and defense policies.

Keenan Carlisle stood tall in uniform, still a little shaky inside, a little hung over. Saluting before marching to the long polished table and taking a seat, he put a new briefcase before him, snapped it open and waited. The only references he would really need were in his head, but this board of high-ranking officers would fiddle around with numbers, and he'd be forced to answer in kind, while the main issues went by the wayside. He had to try to make them listen. For centuries, the family always faced this kind of blind deafness. Now it was his turn to communicate if possible.

Already seated to his left, the old general laid out a notepad and pencils, and turned to lift a salt-and-pepper eyebrow at Keenan, to make a quick smile. It was a wonder Belvale was even speaking to him, much less backing him for the War Department report. Keenan sat erect, a throbbing in his temples. He had lost a couple of nights somewhere, and the general had covered for him—"Some Chinese bug, but he'll be all right soon."

"Captain." Thomas Skelton, major general and president

of the board, had a head like a newly mowed lawn. His opening frown was for anybody's hair longer than an inch.

"Sir."

Buck general Benjamin Alexander nodded a wink at the old general before turning a poker face to Keenan; the rest of the board was two full colonels and a coffee-getter light bird.

"This hearing is now open," Skelton said. He didn't glance at the old general, much less acknowledge that he knew him. Skelton's face was a boiled egg with cropped turf clinging to the crown.

Shit, Keenan thought; it's one of the old army feuds between the old general and this bastard. They had crossed swords sometime in the dim past and never forgot or forgave. Sitting erect, hands in his lap, Keenan figured that Belvale had date of rank on his enemy, but the other man controlled this situation.

He leaned toward the general, who whispered, "They pulled a last minute switch on us. Cousin Alex was supposed to chair the board. Don't let Skelton brown you off. He'll harass you."

"If you don't mind, sir, we will proceed." Skelton's voice slid over ice cubes. "This board has read your reports, Captain, and I for one find them incredible."

"Sir?"

Skelton tapped a sheaf of papers. The file cover read: SECRET. "Forty miles a day at road march speed, under full field equipment? Unless those Japs have grown by two or three feet, that's a fairy tale."

"Sir, I was with them all that week; forty miles is correct, sir."

Spreading his small cold smile right and left to his board, "I think you're easily misled, Captain. All that *sake*—"

Keenan hid clenched fists in his lap. "General, I hiked with them all the way. It damned near killed me—and I was in shape, not a garrison trooper."

"They do carry rice whiskey?"

"Ceremonial *sake*, yes, sir."

"And you attended these—ah—ceremonies? I understand

you've been treating some Chinese germs in certain Washington establishments."

"Colonel Watanabe offered me *sake* twice, sir—and what I do off duty—"

Skelton cut him off: "Reflects upon the entire service. When I was with the Fifteenth Infantry in China, we discovered that Jap officers couldn't hold their whiskey. Were your liaison men familiar with the old Fifteenth?"

"Nobody mentioned it, sir."

The frozen smile came and went. "I didn't think so. That outfit knew how to handle Chinks and Japs, too." Skelton riffled slowly through the file and the silence grew. One colonel and the light bird followed Skelton's lead, going over papers already read several times. Beside Keenan, the old general stirred.

"Well, now," Skelton said, looking up. "I see no mention of the inaccuracy of Japanese fire."

Keenen knew the coiling of a spring inside him "Because there is none, sir. They shoot as well as we do, and perhaps better. They're combat seasoned."

"Nonsense!" Skelton flipped the file with a fingernail. "You report the same thing about the Chinese—" This time he fisted the file. "The *communist* Chinese. The *communists,* where you spent far more time than on your official assignment. Reading between the lines on your—ah, combat experiences, you also fired upon your country's friends, the Nationalists."

Blessed be the assholes, Keenan thought, for they have already inherited the earth. The spring inside him shuddered but before it ripped free, his uncle reached over and clamped a hand hard upon his forearm.

Belvale said, "If the president of the board pleases—"

"That depends," Skelton said. "This is an investigation, not a court-martial, and the captain is not entitled to defense counsel."

Standing erect in a conservative civilian suit Belvale said, "General, I request that all lower ranks leave the room."

"Leaving me closeted with a civilian who dabbles in politics? Request denied, *Mister* Belvale; if you wish to present anything this board may be interested in—"

"Okay," Belvale said, "you supercilious son of a bitch, regulations state that a superior will not discipline an inferior rank in the presence of lower grades. But since you want it this way—I don't care how long you carry a hard-on for me. Captain Carlisle's report is of vital interest to the United States Army and concerns the future security of this country. You were a fuck-up in the Fifteenth Infantry and you're a bigger one now. Shut up and listen."

Keenan's coiling spring dissolved in the laughter he fought to hold inside. No one had heard General Belvale use language like that since he retired from the cavalry.

Skelton's boiled egg face looked fried now, red and quivering. "You—what—goddamn it, you can't just—"

"I am back on active duty as of twenty-four hundred yesterday; my third star became effective at the same time. I repeat, shut the hell up and pretend you have a brain." Turning, the general made a slow wink. "Captain Carlisle, please make your oral presentation, in your own words."

"Sir!" Keenan's glance swept over the faces behind the long table, four in a state of shock and Brig. Gen. Benjamin Alexander threatening to pop like a balloon. "As my written report points out, I was with a Japanese unit until I was wounded and captured by Chinese communist troops. In retrospect, I'm glad it happened, for it gave me the opportunity to soldier with the strongest force in China."

And to know Chang Yen Ling . . .

> On earth a tiger
> has been subdued.
> Buckets of tears flow down.

He told the men in this room that smelled of wax and furniture polish and a thousand pompous meetings, told them of the hardy Red troops, the strength of the peasantry that was Mao Tse-tung's secret army. He described his meeting with Mao and the leader's staff that had made the Chinese communists into the toughest, trickiest guerrillas in the world.

He did not tell them of Yen Ling's beauty and warmth; they would not understand the dedication that turned such a woman back into the field to continue fighting. Keenan was just beginning to understand that himself. Taking another deep breath, he spelled out the facts of action in China, pointing out where and why the Nationalists lost ground because Chiang Kai-shek wanted first to root out Mao's forces and take care of the Japanese later.

General Alexander leaned forward. "Mao Tse-tung himself asked you to present his case here?"

"Yes, sir; I believe that he sincerely wants to be our friend and ally. He asks our support and I believe we should give it."

"Communists," Skelton muttered, and subsided.

Alexander said, "Has this request gone any higher?"

General Belvale answered. "We have a White House appointment at sixteen hundred."

Skelton's gasp was audible. Alexander turned his way and said, "Respectfully suggest that this board table the inquiry before it, until word of the commander in chief's decision."

Swallowing, Skelton said, "Suggestion accepted. This board stands adjourned until further notice." He swept out of the room, not looking back, his silent train of tense colonels following.

Alexander held out his hand to Belvale. "You old bastard; you wore civvies deliberately to sucker him in. Still, to chew his ass like that before his entourage—"

And, Keenan thought, he hadn't even mentioned his promotion before.

"He can blow it out his stacking swivel," Belvale said. "I could have brought Crusty Carlisle and turned him loose."

Keenan collected his briefcase and cap, then stood up to officially meet General Alexander. "Coffee shop," Alexander said. "I'll buy. Do you really have a meeting with FDR?"

Belvale laughed. "Hell, no, just with George Marshall. He has a handle on things, and maybe Keenan's report will give him a better grip. But there are so damned many fools—"

The America First Committee, Keenan thought as they walked to the bank of elevators; the castle keep of isolationism, crackpots all. Then there were the anti-Semitic speeches by the air hero Charles Lindbergh. Nobody wanted to think about out-and-out war, and the first peacetime draftees, brought into uniform for a year only, were chalking OHIO on every barracks door: Over the Hill in October.

And the beautiful Chang Yen Ling walked a hundred miles and bandaged wounds, dispensed her supply of pain-killing willow leaves and bark, made poultices with her ancient herbs. Her image stabbed at him like a sharp blade, and numbly, he followed the generals into the coffee shop.

He was out of place among this chrome and glass and luxury. He would be clumsy and disoriented when he finally came face-to-face with his wife. Nancy wouldn't understand his need to hurry back to China, even if he told her about Yen Ling, which he would not.

Sitting at a table and being served fragrant coffee and sugared doughnuts by a colored man in a white jacket, Keenan thought of sharing water with Father Lim, the old man with the homemade rifle. Was he still alive? Oh, God—was Yen Ling?

"That was a hell of a fight at the bridge," Alexander said. "I respect the cold nerve that took, attacking over those bare chains."

"They're dedicated," Keenan said, the rich flavor of coffee on his tongue. Cassia wine tasted better. "They're willing to die."

"I wish they'd called themselves something else," Belvale said around his cigar. "*Communist* leaves a bad echo in this town. Keenan, it's about time you—"

"I'll see her," he said. "Whatever Nancy wants. Just so long as I can make all the speeches and write all the reports and get the hell out of this phony world, get back to reality."

"To China," Belvale said.

"One way or another, General." He noticed that both men were staring at him.

CHAPTER 34

ASSOCIATED PRESS—Washington, D.C., October 25, 1940: Senator Jeanette Rankin today called for an investigation of "warmongering" reports from United States army officers newly returned from overseas observer assignments. She accused the military family at Kill Devil Hill, Virginia, of "inflammatory and misleading" statements designed to draw this nation into the war in Asia. A high-ranking source in the War Department backed up Senator Rankin's statement.

Keenan Carlisle sat across the table from his wife. Better to meet her in this hotel restaurant than at the Hill, where she would be defensive. Aunt Minerva had been at her coldest whenever Nancy's name came up, and it was as if she also blamed Keenan, as she had when he first married.

"Juleps okay?" he asked, and when she nodded, the waiter cat-footed away. Nancy looked fine—uneasy, but sort of glowing. Her new love was doing her good; she had taken off a few pounds and changed hairstyles.

"Well," he said, "I put off meeting you as long as I could. I'm glad you agreed to see me now. I wasn't—ready, before."

"Yes," she murmured, and stared down until the waiter brought her mint julep. After a big swallow, she looked up. "Keenan—I want a divorce."

"All right," he said.

Her eyes widened; a drop of whiskey clung to her full lower lip. "J-just like that—all right?"

"You've never been happy at the Hill, never really adjusted to putting the army first. Recently, I learned about separation and the loneliness of waiting. I don't know how any army wife puts up with it."

After a sip of her julep, Nancy said softly, "You've found someone, too."

"And lost her, but I'm going back to China. The general feels it best that I leave the country before I'm investigated as a communist bedfellow. I'll be gone tomorrow."

"I—I feel strange," she said. "I never hated you, Keenan. I think I'll always love you, in a way. Sitting here talking calmly about divorce and your new love—"

"We haven't mentioned yours. Will he marry you? The general thinks Wilson Pailey is using you politically."

"The general!" She made a face. "He's a nice old coot, but he sees enemies around every corner, while Wilson says we won't go to war at all, that we'll just continue to be the arsenal of democracy."

"Will he marry you?" Keenan repeated.

"It doesn't matter. I—I've never been happier."

"Okay then. Ask the general to run the divorce through the family law firm. Don't be silly about support; be sure you have enough to keep you comfortably." He took the first taste of his drink; it seemed flat.

She reached across the table and touched his hand. "I'm sorry. I—you and I—well, I hope you find your lady again."

He said, "Good luck, Nancy," and meant it.

CHAPTER 35

INTERNATIONAL NEWS SERVICE—Chunking, China, November 16, 1940: Observers here say this city is three-quarters destroyed by Japanese bombs. Air raids, almost continuous for a year, have left many thousands dead and thousands more homeless. Fire bombings devoured the flimsy, crowded shacks of the poor.

Forced to evacuate Nanking and then Hankow, Generalissimo Chiang Kai-shek moved China's capital 500 miles up the Yangtze River to Chungking. The distance, sharp mountain ranges and deep river gorges seemed to offer safety to battered Nationalist troops. Japanese air power negated all natural defenses with murderous efficiency, but the spirit of the Chinese people remains unbroken. As the last bomber flies away, they climb from their holes in the earth and begin the cleanup.

UNITED PRESS—Somewhere in China, December 19, 1940: At least 100 P-40 Tomahawk fighter planes arrived in China recently. Unconfirmed reports place American civilian pilots coming in to strengthen China's fledgling air force. This has long been a project of retired U.S. Army Captain Claire Chennault, confidant of General and Madame Chiang Kai-shek. Named the American Volunteer Group, these civilians—all dressed in odds and ends of U.S. uniforms, are supposedly in training near Loiwing on the Burma border.

It was raining when the C-46 Commando sat down at the end of the muddy runway and fantailed dirty water as it skidded to a long stop. The man beside Keenan unbuckled and pointed. "The damned thing leaks; look at those joint sealings. You have to be a duck to fly these bastards."

Keenan stood and stretched. It had been a tiring flight, but when he climbed down to the soil of China without being trailed by Chiang's intelligence people, he felt rejuvenated.

Little tingles of excitement skipped up his spine, although he told himself that finding Chang Yen Ling was a monumental task. The Nationalists would never stop looking over his shoulder, and when he did discover her whereabouts, getting to her would be yet another story, but at least he was in her part of the world.

This time around, he was with Mao's other enemy—perhaps the more dangerous enemy—the Kuomintang, and had been for months of marking time, of being kept from any action by bowing, smiling bastards under orders to closely watch this foreign devil. Keenan had the feeling that if he had no powerful family behind him, he'd have been lost and forgotten somewhere along the road.

But it had been the only way he could get out of Washington before the baying coyotes closed on him, and as General Belvale said, "Since Chiang is our unofficial under-the-table ally, nobody can squawk."

To which Crusty Carlisle, white hair cropped over a beat-up bulldog face, had added: "The Gitmo—a fucking peanut. Big mistake, kissing his ass. You know his old lady's brother hustled FDR out of a hundred million already? A hundred fucking million dollars!"

General Belvale shook his head. "After you've been away from the Hill a while, I forget that Georgie Patton taught you to talk."

"Patton, my moneymaking ass! Another peanut; silly bastard designs his own uniforms; goddamn wonder he don't drip gold braid all over his pearl handled pistols. Georgie can't hit a pig in the ass with a plank, much less with a fancy sidearm."

The rain stopped suddenly as Keenan walked across the

muddy airstrip, tasting the new sun, feeling the heat beginning to rise from steaming ground. Chiang's people had kept him within city-forts, held him away from battle areas, except for a few long-distance peeps at skirmishes with Japanese. To fill the time, he had studied Mandarin Chinese and dutifully filed bland reports.

Out here, his keepers would still trail him, of course, but he could shake them now and then by mingling with the civilian pilots; didn't all foreign devils look alike? He meant to go on missions, too; the fat headquarters type Chinese would avoid those.

A silent coolie carried Keenan's Val-pac to a stained tent off the rudimentary landing strip, a worn tent squatting in mud beneath the shade of a tree Keenan couldn't name.

Inside, a man rolled over on a canvas cot, sat up and grinned as he held out his hand. "Mel Zachary, welcome to Soggy Bottom. Hey—you're still in uniform—"

"I'm an observer, not a pilot."

"Uncle checking up on us?" Zachary wore smile crinkles around his eyes and mouth, showing that he enjoyed life and laughed a lot.

"Nope; you guys are still classified—more or less; some leaks are coming through news reports." Keenan sat on the other cot and offered cigarettes.

Zachary shook his head. "Can't smoke in the cockpit, so I kicked the habit."

"How's the training?"

Mel Zachary loved to fly; Keenan could tell that by the way his eyes lighted up and how he started into the angled zooms and dives of active hands—a pilot's vividly descriptive language. "The P-40 is old, but no bucket of bolts. Chennault set the tactics for us; we can dive like hell and pull up and away. He said never, never take on a Jap Kate or Zero in a dogfight, since they can fly rings around us that way. What a break—getting a jump on the war and working under a guy like Chennault."

Taking time to clean up and grab a nap, Keenan dreamed of a mandarin's flowered garden and Chang Yen Ling. Nancy never invaded his dreams anymore, but she wrote an occasional newsy note, family information without emotions, duty letters that said nothing of herself and her lover. The divorce papers hadn't caught up, either.

"Hey, Captain!"

Keenan sat up, right hand slapping his side where the .45 normally hung.

Mel Zachary said, "This isn't your first time in China, then? I'd just as soon not wake you up when you're wearing a sidearm. Didn't mean to startle you, but some of the guys are heading into Rangoon, and I thought you might like to go along."

"Why not?"

Not for an extended drunk like the one he'd gone on, fresh back from Hong Kong and the jolting desertion of Chang Yen Ling, but an evening of eased-off boozing where he'd get to know Chennault's pilots. The boss himself could wait until tomorrow. Keenan didn't think there'd be any problems with the man, for Chennault had a reputation as a maverick.

Chief of Staff George Marshall didn't like him or trust him, but Keenan remembered Marshall saying to the old general that Chennault was a tactical genius who probably wouldn't live long enough to gain any kind of respect.

Rangoon was odors and bright clothing on small, neat-bodied women, shiny-eyed women who laughed and danced with the roistering pilots. Rangoon was music and whiskey and anything needed to hold back the war, to fend off the reality of the Japanese who would soon come.

Keenan met two men called Tex, and Johnson, Dewitt, LeBlanc and others whose names would take weeks to remember. They were all technically civilians, volunteers from all branches of service, hotshot pilots who would be returned to their uniforms when America formally entered the war. A platter of spicy food and cold beer made for relaxing. Then Mel and one of the men named Tex cornered the C-46 pilot LeBlanc. "Why the hell not, Cajun? Look— there's all these old bombs just lying around, and the P-40s can't carry them. The Japs are in Hanoi, right?"

"Yes, goddamn—but I say, me—those bombs need racks. I got no racks."

Mel turned to Keenan. "As an honest to God soldier,

Captain, help us convince this mud turtle that bombing the Japs in Hanoi is a good tactic. Jesus—they'll run around like a bunch of pissants, wondering where the hell the Gitmo came up with a bomber."

LeBlanc shook his head. "Goddamn; Chinese bomb, Jap bomb, French, Russian—who the hell knows how touchy, huh? Find me some bomb racks—"

Keenan said, "We can keep the stuff from rolling around."

"Shit," LeBlanc said, "this man just arrives and you fools infect him. *Sacre!* All right—get your bombs. I show you goddamn drunks."

Wind roared in through both open cargo doors, and rough air bounced the load of bombs around, clanking and rolling them, despite men grabbing at steel casings and fins. As Keenan sobered a bit, this surprise raid on the Japs who occupied French Indochina didn't seem like a first-class idea.

Zachary thumped his shoulder as they both hung on to cargo webbing. Mouth close to Keenan's ear, he said, "What the hell—huh, Captain?"

The wind whipped away the words, but Keenan said them anyway: "What the hell!"

Swooping low, the C-46 throttled back and held steady, lined upon the cluster of lights that was Hanoi. The Japs didn't expect bombing and held to no blackout; they would tomorrow night.

"Kick 'em out!" Tex yelled and men pushed bombs with their feet; men lifted the smaller ones and hurled them into the night. Tex almost went out the door when the plane tilted, but Zachary grabbed him.

"Bombs away! Run, you little bastards!"

They flew so low that Keenan could almost feel the concussion from the explosions, and could see the bursts of flame, little red flowers, and big orange flowers. The pilot nosed the C-46 sharply upward, and it protested through every bolt, while boozy, laughing AVG pilots clutched for support.

When it flattened out and headed for Burma, Zachary sat beside Keenan and offered a bottle. Keenan took a long pull. "No AA fire," Zachary chortled. "Caught them flat-footed. Hell, we can come back with gasoline bombs."

"You only surprise them once," Keenan said, leaning back from the roar of warm air through the open door and feeling the vibration of the plane. "I spent a long tour with the Japs. They're plenty tough."

"Good." Mel Zachary laughed. "I'd hate to waste all this combat training on inferior competition."

CHAPTER 36

REUTERS NEWS AGENCY—Somewhere in England, January 7, 1941: New and sorely needed shipments of Lend-Lease supplies and equipment arrived here today. The convoy commander reported attacks by U-boats, but no losses. He credited escort by air out of New York, then the alertness of accompanying Royal Navy destroyers, themselves four-stackers acquired under the American program. RAF fighters and light bombers ranged out from British bases to pick up the convoy and guard it in.

The ship nosed into the twilight of foggy Southampton Bay, still trailing its pudgy barrage balloons with their fatal skirting of dangled steel cables. Chad Belvale watched the gun crews button up as a tug came out to nudge the *Norfolk Belle* into the dock. Five 20mm Oerlikon gun tubs starboard and five port; midships the deadly Chicago Piano squatted, a multibarreled weapon; and the Bofors, twin 40s. The five-inch gun waited aft, and along both rails were the parachute rockets set to burst airborne with their own versions of spiderweb cables.

None of the deck armament was any good unless an enemy sub got caught on the surface, but the layout discouraged dive-bombers, making them peel off higher than accuracy dictated. The Kraut supermen weren't stupid, only in believing they were supermen, smart and lucky so far.

Maybe they'd be lucky enough to make it across the Channel and end the war.

Chill gray fog was a winding shroud as the ship neared the dock, and it tasted of winter and the sea, faintly of fish. The city had taken a beating from the Luftwaffe, especially the dock areas, but somehow the bombers had missed the berth and birthplace of the *Queen Mary*. Limey sailors said she didn't put in here anymore, but into a tight slip at Grenoch, Scotland, where high cliffs and shallow water gave better protection.

Secret word was that the huge, fast liner was being refitted as a troopship and would carry an entire infantry division with all artillery and equipment; eighteen thousand men, guns and rolling stock. What a prize she would be, trapped in the periscope sights of a U-boat. Would she be carrying green American troops?

Turning, he left the deck and went back to the cramped quarters in officer country, the cranny shared with an American major of engineers. In one way, slow as unofficial help happened to be, the U.S. Army was setting up assistance to the English, a sort of advance party for the day when a careless boat commander would torpedo another *Lusitania* and give FDR the excuse he needed to bypass isolationist opposition.

"Feel something like coming home, Chad?" Bob Reasonover stuffed the last of his belongings into the bulging C-2 bag and topped it off with a toilet article kit. "Boy, how I envy you, knowing your way around London and all. I'm depending upon you to fix me up."

"Better than a homecoming," Chad answered, "and the only help you'll need over here is keeping up with all the lonely women."

"Hey, now," Reasonover said, smoothing his pink and green dress uniform.

Homecoming, Chad thought, and Stephanie Bartlett, officer and lady waiting. Her open and honest sex, the coupling that she made fun as well as lusty, had helped him face his wife and her boyfriend in Texas. He hadn't known what to say; what does a guy say when he's introduced to his wife's lover? Keeping up with your homework, Senator? Do you need any tips on satisfying her? I might be able to clue you in on certain positions and foreplay—

Bullshit; if he was that tight with Kirstin, she wouldn't need a lover. And when he looked her full in the face, she didn't drop her eyes, but stared back defiantly. Shelby and the general had absented themselves like gentlemen and given him a chance to speak privately with Kirstin.

I thank you smooth bastards; my wife thanks you, and our sons.

Even after she poured stiff drinks for them both and seated herself in a chair across the room, she kept her chin up and that direct look dared him to fault her.

He said it: "I don't blame you, Kirstin. For a while there, after Dunkirk, when my emotions had been run through a wringer, I thought we might work it out. But when I heard that you had already moved away from the Hill—"

"Who told you? Not the general, and the boys didn't know."

"Colonel Luther Farrand; I think he did it to bring me home right away. Doing his duty for God and promotion."

Kirstin swallowed half her drink and set her mouth so she wouldn't make a face, one of those moves he was familiar with after the years they'd spent together. Even after she went gray, she would always be a handsome woman, and he regretted losing her. But that loss occurred a long time ago. She said, voice only slightly strained by the jolt of strong, clear whiskey, "Chaplain Farrand never did a damned thing that didn't look good on his efficiency report, in the now or for the hereafter. That includes settling trouble in his omnipotent, priestly fashion. Easy enough, since he's usually the instigator. In God's name, of course."

Sipping his whiskey, Chad sat uneasily on the edge of a leather couch. It seemed everything in this damned place was cowhide, horsehide or adobe and Indian woven wool. Everything even smelled different: Texas, chili peppers.

If he could lean close to Kirstin, nuzzle beneath her ear where the tiny curls clung, he thought her scent would not have changed; it would still be a touch horsey, that faint, not unpleasant odor and her soapy clean, fresh from the shower appeal. In all this frontier atmosphere, Kirstin's blondness didn't quite fit; a smoky-eyed Comanche woman with long black hair would be just right. But she was making herself a part of all this, settling in.

He said, "This time I'm glad God's emissary stuck his nose in. He pushed me into coming back. I might not have had the nerve on my own."

She frowned across at him. "A lack of courage was never one of your problems, and the general says you're an exceptional combat soldier."

Finding cigarettes in his shirt pocket, he lighted an Old Gold and offered her one. Kirstin shook her head. He said, "I have been scared most of my life, especially with you—of you."

"Chad—" She put out one hand and pulled it back, lifting her feet and drawing them beneath her haunches in a graceful, fluid motion. Wonderful legs, and she was spreading them for that big bastard. He wasn't afraid of her now; he wanted her.

Because somebody else had her?

Because Stephanie had taught him there was no shame, but only delight? "I'm glad I got the observer job in Europe," he said. "I learned about me."

Bob Reasonover said his name again, "Hey, Chad," and Chad came back to the present, quit playing statue and fastened the straps on his bulging Val-pac. Kirstin was back there in the States and he hadn't even seen his boys, mainly because he didn't want any recriminations. The Point and VMI had swung into intense speeded-up programs, and all leaves were cancelled. He could have visited both schools, but what did he have to say—your mother is shacking up with somebody but she hasn't asked for a divorce? Neither have I, and I don't know why. And don't try to lay blame; maybe it's nobody's fault; maybe it's everybody's, including you two guys.

In minutes he was due to walk down the cold and slick gangway. If Stephanie had her furlough worked out, they would soon be in the land of skirling pipes and Robbie Burns, of Bonnie Prince Charlie and Culloden Field. Stephanie on her home ground would be something else.

By the time this train chuffed into Victoria Station, Chad

would take his unofficial delay en route. He'd go directly to Leftenant Stephanie Bartlett's duty station. If the British in London didn't like that, they could kiss it. He was more or less his own CO, responsible to no one this side of the Atlantic. It was up to his conscience to screw off or not screw off, and any soldier knew there was a time for both.

Returned was the hero, to be more at home here with her than he'd ever been anywhere else, with anyone else. He had missed her. Even in Texas, not really settling anything with his wife, he had missed Stephanie. Accepting the fact that Kirstin was living with another man, little quick images of Stephanie Bartlett flicked through his odd jealousy—her hearty laughter; if she was sitting, she clapped hands and bounced small feet up and down. She liked to laugh, to play like a kid, to flirt and flit. But when she slid beneath the covers, she was all woman. Laughing and tickling and nipping, she was still all woman.

The bitch box's tinny voice ordered officers of all ranks ashore and into the train waiting beyond the dock's wet cobblestones. Chad tugged at his Val-pac, knowing that some English sailor would have to grumble it to the dock, and the thing was heavy. Nylons, Hershey bars, perfume and nail polish; all the cigarettes he could pack, a bottle of bourbon. His previous time in London had shown him civilian shortages to be filled, not for black marketing, but a celebratory spread of luxuries for Stephanie.

"Is that a real train?" Reasonover, his Val-pac at his feet, braced one hand on the ship's rail and pointed with the other. "Migod—the whistle goes *peep-peep!*"

"It will get us to London. I'll check in there, and take off before some Lord of the Home Guard gets ideas about a fast assignment for me. I suggest you do the same; swap your money at Finance and grab a room in the Piccadilly Hotel. I'll meet you there later or leave a message."

Shaking his head, Reasonover wiped at fog congealing upon his face. "You are one hustling dude, Major. I look forward to taking lessons from the master." They walked together for the train.

Chad heard the thing coming. "Shit!" he said and grabbed

Reasonover's arm to run him to the edge of the platform. "Here! Jump down and squat—"

Ka-Whamm!

Jesus Christ. The explosion picked Chad up and slammed him against the wheels of the train. He couldn't see—could not feel—and the only sound he heard was a vast, brain-ripping roar that tore at his skull. Swaying upon his knees, Chad fumbled over his face, staring into crimson-smeared blackness, and cupped hot blood in his palms, blood he could not see.

Blind; oh, Christ, he was blind. Red light swam in the darkness behind his stinging eyes; gory fireflies snapped off and on.

"Bob—Bob?"

Through the buzz in his ears, he heard Reasonover answer. "I-I'm hit, Chad."

A string of other bombs exploded in a row like artillery shells marching. Debris whipped down upon Chad, little chips of mortar and wood splinters. The first blast must have come from a Stuka or Messerschmitt, roaring in low to beat the air raid warnings. The string of eggs had to be laid by a high-level bird and the air raid sirens shrieked belatedly. A thousand lightnings whiplashed from ships in the harbor, bright tracers that crisscrossed the inverted bowl of the sky, and higher up, the deadly flowering of red-orange flak shells.

Chad could see them. He could *see!* Shock—the hammer blow of a near miss explosion had knocked out his sight temporarily. Thank God, temporarily.

"Bob—Bob, how bad is—"

Shit; Major Reasonover sprawled across the tracks, pinned down by the body of an English sailor. The sailor had that flat look of the suddenly dead, just after all life had rushed out. Chad wiped blood from a deep cut on his own forehead and crawled over to roll the sailor flopping off Bob Reasonover. Blood; a lot of blood, and much of it puddling around the stump of Reasonover's left leg.

A cleaver-size chunk of steel had sliced off the man's leg just below the knee, and the artery pumped bright blood. Whipping off his belt, Chad slipped a loop over Reasonover's thigh and pulled it tight. Smoke and the stench of burned things eddied around Chad's head as he pulled himself up, braced against the concrete platform. Farther up the track, two cars of the train flamed red and orange, sending out oily clouds of corkscrewing black smoke.

Men stumbled past, civilians and sailors, and Chad caught at someone's ankle. "Here—need help—man may be dying!"

"Right, mate. George—give us a hand." And as Chad struggled up onto the platform, the man cupped hands to his mouth and called: "Litter bearers—to me, please!"

So goddamned English, Chad thought, finding his hand-kerchief and binding it tightly across his forehead. The men hauling Reasonover off the tracks were in the brown battle dress of the English army, but with no insignia of rank, only the red cross brassard around their left arms.

"Yanks, are you?" the first man asked. "Damned poor introduction to Scotland. Old Jerry comes after the docks now and then. You look about done in; that head wound—"

"I'm okay." The ululating *wheep-wheep!* of the ambulance drew closer. Chad peered down into Reasonover's pale, drained face. "Hang on, Bob—damnit, hang on!"

"He'll be at St. James," the Englishman said.

"Thank you," Chad said. "Good Christ—he just set foot on land."

Gray at the temples, eyes deeply set, the Scotsman said, "Terrible, that. One never gets used to this sort of thing."

Chad pulled up his pants, sagged without a belt. His Val-pac sat unharmed against a steel post; torn open, Reasonover's bag spilled its multicolored guts across the tracks below.

He had to get to London. He had to pound Washington with such sharp reports that somebody would pay attention. If nothing changed, this same thing could happen at Grand Central Station.

CHAPTER 37

REUTERS NEWS AGENCY—London, England, January 18, 1941:
Officials here said today that although the major blows from
the Luftwaffe have been blunted, the nation must stay alert.
Hitler has said he is coming. Air and sea defenses are
foremost in the continuing struggle, but land defenses must
back up these forward lines and construction continues
apace.

Dirty gray water blended with dirty gray sky, and with
swirling fog; at times it was difficult to distinguish between
them. Perfect weather for U-boats, Chad thought, and kept
a sharp eye along the sights of the nose guns of the Hudson
bomber, their 30 caliber belts holding four Armor Piercing
bullets to one tracer. Not heavyweight, but effective close
in.

They had been patrolling the Channel since daylight,
passing over one of Churchill's last-ditch defenses in case
Hitler's Operation Sea Lion came thundering across the
thirty-mile stretch of water the Krauts were calling the
Shite Kanal. All along the southern coast of England, the
best landing beaches, hidden pipelines waited to spew gas
and oil into the water. When the first wave of Kraut barges
approached, a low-flying bomber would flash over the area
and drop incendiaries. An ocean of blazing oil would cook
Krauts in their boats like meat loafs in long pans. There
were other lines of defense—mines and barbed wire and

pillboxes, but the roughest reception awaiting the master race was the ordinary Englishman, old and young, armed with obsolete weapons but backed with an iron determination. Their motto: You Can Always Take One With You.

Chad searched in long swinging circles, starting close to the plane and spreading far out, an increment at a time. If it worked for the infantry, it would work from the air. He thought of Stephanie, of the neat little room they now shared. She had laughed when he first noticed the mournful song of barrage balloon cables in a suddenly risen wind, then she sobered quickly and explained. The English were so used to the low, tremulous wail that they scarcely noticed it.

"I'm sorry, love," she said then. "It's difficult to remember that part of the world is not at war, that some people have never heard the sirens or the bloody dive-bombers. The balloons—yes, before I was in uniform, I used to lie awake listening to them. I thought they were crying in pain and sorrow. If I think about them now, it's to know a dirge."

Going tense, Chad focused upon a feather of white water moving the wrong way against the tide. There it was again—and the telltale black pipe appearing and disappearing in the choppy water.

"Periscope!" he yelled into his microphone. "Left flank—ten o'clock! Port, damnit—port, wherever the hell! Slow this bucket."

Left wing dropped, the Hudson banked slowly, both engines throttling down. The bombing run came first, right on line and low to the water, a pair of hundred pounders arrowing in just ahead of the periscope. Water slashed high behind the plane as the bombs exploded.

"Tallyho!" Chad shouted, looking back and down as the plane peeled off. Black oil geysered into widening circles, and first the bow, then the conning tower of the U-boat lifted out of the sea, rolling and bucking.

The Hudson circled and came back. Chad saw the hatch fly back and men leap out, a few into the sea, but some running for the three-inch gun on deck. Bright tracers reached up at the plane as a Kraut steadied a machine gun on the conning tower. Through a break in the fog, Chad saw why the sub meant to fight, to take a ship down with her. A disabled British mine-layer rocked dead ahead in the water, too close to miss.

Laying the sights in, calculating the lead he had to take, Chad triggered a long burst from his guns and watched the tracers ricochet around the deck gun. Men spilled over the sides before the gun cover came away. He threw a quick burst at the tower gunner and overshot. The tail gunner raked the U-boat from bow to stern, and yelled exultantly into his mike.

"Bring her around!" Chad yelled. "Give me a shot before the bastard goes down."

"They're in the drink," the pilot answered as the sub rolled and filled with water.

Chad's bullets kicked spouts among the swimming Krauts, and he didn't let up until the plane lifted to sweep around the area and drop an orange life raft through the bomb bay doors.

Gentlemen warriors, Chad thought, but he'd had enough of Krauts since France, since the strafing runs the Luftwaffe made on columns of helpless refugees; dead horses with their legs sticking up; dead babies left to bloat in the smoky sun. London burning—human flesh frying like bacon, and the barrage balloon cables mourning the nights away. Then there was the kid lieutenant killed in Poland, Walt Belvale, first of the family to pay the price.

Fuck gentlemen warriors; he was here to observe Krauts— and then kill them.

After they landed, the pilot came up beside Chad. An RAF captain, he was slim and boyish. "You're a ruddy fine gunner, Major. Highest ranking in the RAF, but since you're technically a noncombatant—"

"I'm not supposed to be shooting innocent Kraut submariners. No sweat, Captain—I've seen the Channel patrol and don't have to go back. But I have also seen the bastards murder helpless civilians all over France."

The captain looked uncomfortable as they neared the ready shack. "All respect, sir, but if we lower ourselves to their level—"

"We win the bloody fucking war quicker!" Lt. John J. Merriman leaped from the doorway and caught Chad in a bear hug. "You Yank bastard—where the hell have you been?"

Thumping his friend's back, Chad said, "Caught in a Southampton bombing, and then missed you in London. Are you still unassigned?"

Merriman stepped back and shook his head and thumbed his red mustache. "Secret and all that." He frowned back at the uncertain RAF captain. "We'd best discuss in private. Some of these blokes have no clearance."

Merriman had a staff car, an American Dodge, but no driver. Piling into the front seat, Chad said, "Since when do lowly leftenants rate staff cars?"

Laughing, Merriman wheeled the car off the air base and aimed it at London. "Since effing Red Cross civilians get drunk and carelessly abandon their bloody machinery."

"You stole it?"

"Liberated, Major, sir—liberated, as you did with a Jerry tank. There sat this poor vehicle, and very lonely. I'd say much like this lass who escaped from France and wants to show her appreciation to a brave ally. Motorcars and women are much the same; they go all creaky if not used properly. Need comforting, they do, and a man's strong hand. And when Leftenant Bartlett said you were out playing with the boys in blue, I came to rescue you before they put you on report for being a social climbing infantryman reaching above his proper station."

"They're doing a job," Chad said. "The RAF sure kicked hell out of the bombers."

"Battle of Britain and all that. I'll give them that much, fighting in their own backyard. It's Hitler's backyard we need, and they can bomb that until piss all, but the bloody infantry will have to go in and take it. All due respect, Major—fuck the war; let us go get pleasantly smashed with two beautiful women."

The same pudgy furniture in the Piccadilly Hotel bar, the same layering of cigarette smoke blue and pungent, but Stephanie was never the same. She always had a new facet to show him, another reflection of herself as a woman.

There could be no doubt of her being female—silken gentle, kitten playful, but he felt the stripes of the tiger lay just beneath the surface of her smooth skin. She was a constant fascination to Chad. Sex had never been as good for him; Stephanie could make it a wild, carefree romp or something so deep that at times he was afraid of being carried away by its powerful currents. Then he wondered why he had ever been afraid, and flowed warmly with the pulsing tide.

Merriman's French girl was darkly attractive in a slightly frenzied way that Chad was beginning to recognize as the mark of war upon women here, women who had lost loves or were so fearful of losing them that they closed out any reality but for the moment. If they had to create new life from night music and numbing whiskey and hot-eyed strangers, so be it.

A British sailor climbed onto the piano stool and people drifted to him to sing "Blue Birds Over The White Cliffs of Dover," and "A Nightingale Sang In Berkley Square."

Then the mood lifted with the rollicking barracks ballad from the days of Kipling's India . . .

> There's a troopship just leaving Bombay,
> Bound for old Blighty's shore,
> Heavily laden with time-expired men
> Bound for the land they adore . . .

Sirens screamed; the floor bucked and glasses shattered behind the bar. The walls of the old hotel seemed to sway, to tilt before settling back.

"Mon Dieu!" the French girl chattered. "What is—oh *la!* The bombs—*le Boche!*"

"It's Swallow Street!" somebody yelled. "Children— they're gathering nippers there to ship to the country!"

The crowd surged outside into a leaping of flames and rolling smoke, into gritty clouds of stone dust and the *wheep-wheep!* of ambulances and fire engines.

"There!" Stephanie pointed as she ran. "A child down beside that wall—"

"That thing's about to go!" Chad pushed her back and ran low for the tottering wall. A falling brick struck close to the huddled girl and a ragged chunk of mortar bit into Chad's shoulder as he stooped to reach for her. Catching the thin body of the girl close to his chest, he turned to run her across the street.

Fire licked at them, a searing tongue of scarlet that slammed Chad like the devil's fist, and he tripped over something. Something weighty fell across his legs as he stretched the girl out for someone to take. She was lifted away and a stream of water jolted him, beating back the fire that threatened to take his feet. He pulled at the cracked paving and fought to drag himself forward, but the burning wooden beam held him fast, and the hosing water popped into steam around him.

". . . the wall! The wall's coming down—"

"Bloody fire is too hot . . ."

". . . poor blighter . . ."

There she was, flinging herself atop him and bracing one knee against his shoulder. He felt the beam move and move again as she threw all her weight into her other foot, using his body as a fulcrum and hers as a lever. The wall crashed down, but just as the sizzling bricks rained upon them, Stephanie rolled him free and willing hands snatched at them both, dragged them across Swallow Street.

One ambulance filled with children pulled away; the next rolled up and gaped its back doors for them. Merriman lay unconscious upon a litter with a bloody bandage around his head. His breath was steady and his color good. It would take more than a wayward brick to kill off this man. Trembling as Chad put his arm around her, Stephanie said, "He—he tried to get to you, but was struck down."

"You're some kind of glorious fool," he said, tasting singed hair, tasting ashes and the pure joy of life. His legs began to throb and he realized that his shoes were gone, that his slacks were burned off below the knee. "Are you hurt, Stephanie?"

"A bit skinned and disheveled. Oh, Chad—"

The medics came and helped them into the ambulance, sliding in a blanketed body before closing the doors. "Sorry," the driver said. "Hope you don't mind. We're doing double duty, you know."

He held her close, and she murmured sometimes formless sentences against his chest, and at odd moments as the ambulance zigzagged its way around new rubble, she lifted her mouth for his reassuring kiss.

"Thank you for my life," he said.

Her eyes overflowed. "And—and thank you for l-loving me, Chad Belvale. I never knew—never really knew—"

"Neither did I," he said as the ambulance squeaked to a stop. "I'm asking you to marry me, as soon as I hear from the States that my divorce is final."

Merriman stirred on his litter and Chad touched the man's hand. He didn't take his other arm from around Stephanie.

"Oh, God," she said, "I should have—but I didn't think upon more than a fling. I was lonely and so were you and you have such gentle eyes and, oh, God, Chad. I'm already married—my husband is posted to Singapore."

CHAPTER 38

ASSOCIATED PRESS—Washington, D.C., January 20, 1941:
Lines are being drawn sharply here between political factions
that stand solidly behind the Neutrality Acts voted into law
shortly after the Great War. Others support President Roosevelt's statement that "Peace by fear has no higher or more
enduring qualities than peace by the sword." FDR has pledged
only material resources to Britain, believing that with help,
the English can stand alone against the Nazis.

General Belvale sat beside Crusty Carlisle at the back of
the room, ready to twist the old bastard's arm if he opened
his mouth. Crusty had promised silence, but in his own
words, promises made under duress were about as important as a fart in a whirlwind. Squatted on Belvale's other
flank was the highest ranking chaplain in the army, Col.
Luther Farrand. Belvale didn't know how this one got the
word; probably direct from God. Why Luther was here at
all was another mystery. Maybe every family had to have a
Luther. On the eve of Roosevelt's election to an unprece-
dented third term, the forerunners of this secret meeting
had been held, PLAN DOG. British agents sat in on the
tightly controlled meetings at the White House, Churchill's
personal representatives authorized to make direct decisions.

Now those decisions were being gone over by Admiral
Stark and Chief of Staff Marshall, merely to be rubber-
stamped. Otherwise the room would not be nearly so full of

the curious, but at least no newsman was among them. The story would break only after some of these lawmakers reached phones.

Should the U.S. efforts be directed toward an eventual strong offensive in the Atlantic with England and Canada as allies, while going on the defensive in the Pacific when the Japs made their move? They would move unless FDR lifted the oil embargo and dropped his demand that the emperor's troops get out of China entirely. He had slapped the emperor's face.

"It's a reversal of the original RAINBOW FOUR PLAN," the admiral said, and some legislators looked at each other as if they had known all about that plan, too.

Belvale would not have let so many civilian lawmakers in on this meeting either; there was Jeanette Rankin, peace at any price; Margaret Chase Smith, about the same; Burton K. Wheeler, insistent that no American boys fall on Europe's bloody battlefields. And wearing his usual slick smile, Wilson Pailey of Georgia. Pailey had crashed the meeting on advance information from Nancy Carlisle. Belvale would do something about that, and about Pailey himself.

"I like it," Gen. George Catlett Marshall said. "There's a lot of ocean between the Japanese and us, and if the worst possible scenario comes off, if they get as far as the Philippines, our navy can hold its own until Hitler is defeated. Europe first, then full weight against Japan."

"Concur," the admiral said. "Mussolini is a joke; he will fall of his own weight."

The chief of staff gaveled the meeting closed and swept out, referring all startled questions to the president himself. Col. Luther Farrand started to lead off, caught himself and waited for his generals. The pious, pompous son of a bitch, Belvale thought; do no wrong in the eyes of the army and suck up for promotions. How long since the man had held services or even listened to anybody's troubles? Things might be worse; the son of a bitch might have somehow wound up commanding troops.

In the carpeted hallway, before reaching the chronologically hung portraits of other presidents, Belvale caught up with Representative Pailey dogging the footsteps of Montana's Senator Wheeler. "A minute, boy."

"Ahh—General; I have meetings and a commitment to Mrs. Rankin, so if you don't mind—"

Bullet head thrust forward like an artillery shell about to be loaded, Crusty Carlisle said, "Damned right we mind. We're the only ones who expected you at that meeting and we know how you got wind of it."

"Now look—"

Col. Luther Farrand cleared his throat and Belvale knew the man would slide away. He disliked any trouble he didn't start and control. Murmuring apologies, the colonel eased off down the hallway.

"What Nancy does is her own business," Belvale said, "except when she passes along information, even planted information. This meeting was cut and dried with FDR's direct approval, so none of you could disrupt things. It was actually the fifteenth meeting, to put the official stamp on a plan already agreed on. Too bad you didn't get introduced to the British envoys when they were here. You could have made points with your reluctant patriots group by denouncing them."

Pailey looked down the hall, then up, his face tightening. "Damnit, my constituents have a right to know—"

Crusty horned in: "And they damned well will know what a mealymouthed little shit you are. Kissing Bob Simmons is about to run against you down home, and you might as well pack it in now. Your sneaky ass is finished in this town."

"You can't talk—you can't—my political machine—"

"Already past talking; blocked eight radio stations in Georgia from you, and three newspapers won't take your ads. Didn't know they're family owned, did you? Kissing Bob can spend his campaign contributions any way he wants, all three million."

"Wait," Pailey said, "your daughter-in-law—the publicity—" He shut up.

"Screws you worse than her." Crusty showed his teeth in a savage grin. "The girl's husband is overseas, already a wounded hero, and here comes this sneaky bastard to steal his wife. You'll be lucky if they don't lynch you down in Macon."

Belvale left the man leaning against the wall, and Crusty chuckled along in his wake, making sounds like rusty files rubbing together. Outside the building and returning salutes from military guards newly installed to back up the Secret Service, Belvale said, "He'll run to Rankin and Wheeler, but it won't do him any good, and it might make that pair think they could be in a fight on their home ground, if they want it that way. They mean well, I guess; at least they're sincere, so we back off unless they start acting like that little pimp."

He smiled. "Smart move of FDR's—putting marines out in plain sight at the White House. No more dogs and soldiers keep off the grass."

Crusty grunted. "More uniforms for Walton Belvale's funeral at the Hill today. Honor guard there beats hell out of that bunch at Arlington. Goddamnit, I just wish we had the boy's body. We bury our own on family land."

An olive drab Plymouth staff car waited for them, a buck sergeant driver. Ducking inside, Belvale said, "No point in carrying him MIA any longer since Chad had that report from a Polish officer. After the war, we'll get him a posthumous award and try to find the body."

"Yeah, and we usually do. His girl's already arrived at the Hill, you said? Must be a rare one, still around to pay respect."

"She is," Belvale said, "she surely is. Ah—Sergeant—"

"Donnely, sir."

"Sergeant Donnely; I had a topkick named Donnely at Fort Huachuca, but I guess—"

"My old man, sir. He's still soldiering; two years and a butt to go for his thirty."

"Hell of a first sergeant," Belvale said. "Do you know the way to Kill Devil Hill, Sergeant?"

"Yes, sir."

"Please take us there, and if you don't mind, I'd like you as permanent driver."

"Okay, General—until we get in the war. I run a heavy

weapons platoon, and I'll go back to that—if *you* don't mind.''

Crusty Carlisle laughed, and said, softly for him, "All the good ones didn't get shipped to Valhalla, Preston.''

At the Hill, Belvale went through the front door and into the family room where artillery Maj. Daniel Belvale leaned one elbow against the ivoried mantelpiece, drink in hand. Seated on the gray couch was Adria, Dan's wife and Walton Belvale's mother; her drink sat ice-melted and untouched upon a table beside her. Daughter Joann sat beside her mother, blonde, and teary-eyed.

Belvale leaned to kiss Adria's pale cheek, then raised to shake Dan's hand. "The honor guard is up from Arlington. The chaplain—bugler, firing squad, everything is ready, any time you are.''

"Not Luther," he said, and finished his drink. He was in formal blues, the dress uniform, white shirt and black tie, a Victory Ribbon from the Great War on his left breast above a silver Expert Pistol medal.

"Hell, no; he's not invited. If he shows up anyway, I'll roadblock him.''

From the couch, Adria said, her voice thin and bitter, "Oh, I've been ready for a funeral ever since I married in the family. Don't we all get the Spartan mother indoctrination? Come back carrying your shield, or carried upon it—son. Oh, my God; my Walt won't even be in that hallowed grave in the Grove of Honor at Kill Devil Hill. Oh—my—God.''

"Adria!" Dan's voice was an edged bayonet.

"Mom," Joann said.

Belvale reached for her hand, and drew her up to him, to place her head upon his shoulder. "Shh, now; shh. Walton went down doing what he did well, and where he wanted to be. Your father, the colonel—''

"Yes, damnit," she said into his tunic. "I know how he died—in terrible pain and cursing God for not allowing him to fall in battle. But cancer—and dad was old, and my Walt—so young—''

"Others will live because of him," Belvale said. "Would you like to tidy up, Adria?''

Raising her streaked face she said, "Yes, of course. I'll be only a moment."

Joann said, "I'll come with you, mom."

When they were gone Dan poured himself another drink and offered the bottle to Belvale, who shook his head. The major said, "You have a way with them, General; must come from all that time in the cavalry. Strong hand on the reins and a touch of the spurs?"

"No; gentling a horse or a woman is always the better way. I've seen mares that lost a foal go crazy with the hunt for it and savage anything that stands in their way. Adria is army; she'll soldier through."

Dan gulped his drink, picked up the bourbon bottle and set it down again. "Damnit, General! I hurt just as damned much, and I can't sit around and cry over it. I love—loved—my boy just as much as she did. He was a good kid and a good soldier. If Adria can't understand—at least Joann seems to."

He cut it off when Adria came from the back of the house in her black gown, a sturdy woman with her shoulders squared and chin high. Only by looking closely could Belvale tell she had recently dried her eyes. She took her husband's arm and Belvale followed them onto the back veranda. There he nodded to the waiting guard detachment, and the drummer took up the cadence beat. Beyond the field in the grove of live oaks and poplar trees where generations of Belvales and Carlisles and their blood kin lay beneath simple military stones, many of the family had been waiting. The coffin was symbolic, the grave just deep enough to cover it, and white calla lilies mixed with Cape Jasmine, the last of the season.

Chaplain (Capt.) Charlie Didato was a former Catholic still not trusted too far by the army, but a fervent, believing man who knew the Church of England well. His eulogy was short, simple and moving.

Eight riflemen snapped to port arms. "Ready!" snapped the sergeant. Bolts clashed in unison and blanks were fed into the breeches of the Springfield rifles. "Fire!"

The volley crashed.

"Ready—fire!"

Crash!

And once more a round to end the traditional three volleys. Tangy blue smoke drifted through the eternal live oaks and around the trunks of the poplars. Two noncoms of the guard stepped forward then, to lift the American flag from the coffin and fold it triangular, blue field up, before presenting it to Adria Belvale. The bugler was old line, a man who believed in his art and his army; the mournful notes of taps lingered in the grove and echoed sorrowing over the bowed heads of the attending family.

Adria kept her poise, but when Belvale glanced at Dan, he saw the man's hand upon his wife's forearm, and then a suspicious glint move down his cheek. On Adria's other side stood the incredibly lovely girl wed to Walton, Penny Colvin. She cried openly.

Dan would be a better husband for this moment, and no doubt a better officer, one who had discovered that the weight of command always brought loss and sadness, and it was no military sin to admit it.

CHAPTER 39

The London Observer—January 26, 1941: An American, Maj. Chadwick Belvale, on detached service here as a military observer, plunged into the fiery hell of a German bomb blast last night to rescue a British child of eight from certain death. He saved Felicia Kirkham of Ludgate Hill. Trapped himself by a fallen roof beam that blazed down across him, the major was in turn saved by WAAF Leftenant Stephanie Mary Bartlett. The heroine's husband is First Leftenant Dacey Bartlett, Artillery, garrisoned in the crown colony of Singapore.

He needed to taste the sun and hear the morning. Outside the Hotel Regency the wind couldn't make up its mind. It was wind shouting, a brassy trumpet wind to shake the curtains, then it became a clarinet wind softly fingering the scales. He had not slept worth a damn, nodding off with her tucked close in his arms, the curving of her back warmly fitted to him, only to wake startled and with empty arms. Again and again he had rolled from her, restless and—guilty?

Unknown to Chad, he had probably bedded other wives, and twice that he could remember, women he knew were married, but none that he loved. He loved Stephanie deeper and wilder and as a man rather than a boy; anything he had once felt for Kirstin was submerged in the power of now. Kirstin was getting her divorce but Stephanie was married to a first john stationed across the world in Singapore. No kids, thank God.

Odds were the man would read about his wife and her Yank lover; reporters from English newspapers had gathered at the hospital when they were brought in, lured by the story of an American officer who tried to play hero. The *Daily Telegraph,* the *Observer,* and *Daily Mirror*—and he didn't have the good sense to hide Stephanie away. She'd clung to him, too, and the photographers took dozens of pictures of this brave woman who saved a savior.

How long to Singapore? How long to Kill Devil Hill, which didn't matter, and to the halls of the War Department, which did? Oh sure, it was great public relations for the American army, up to the point where the subjects were both married, but not to each other.

Chad stood upon the narrow balcony and smelled burned London on the capricious morning wind; today it laid a particular ashen bitterness upon his tongue. They were secret here, not noticed when they breakfasted in the hotel restaurant, or when they had the Ploughman's Lunch in the pub across the way. Convalescent leave would soon be up for both of them; Stephanie would return to her antiaircraft gun crews in Brighton. He didn't know where the hell he'd be, since he'd called notice to himself.

Merriman was a true friend; he'd turned stubborn journalists from their trail and kept their trysting place hidden, an expert at outflanking those attempting to follow him. It helped hold them together for a little while longer, although Chad felt a shadow looming off just beyond his line of sight, something dark and threatening. It was almost like waiting for an enemy attack in a foxhole much too shallow. After the first mortar shell, no foxhole was ever deep enough.

Coming up behind him, she slid her arms around his waist and put her body gently against him. Chad breathed her in, the heady scent of her that had made him a devoted acolyte of the church of tumbled sheets. For she also blessed him with a calmness and peace he had not known.

"Good morning, love. We still have this day and this night; I'm sorry you're so restless, but that probably cannot be helped."

He placed his hands over hers, conscious of each inch of

her small body; so much woman in a neat and tidy package; so completely Celtic. He knew what she was going to say.

"I want to ask Dacey for a divorce; I want to be free to bide the rest of my life with you. But I simply cannot. It's not his fault, and we—we were reasonably happy, although it was nothing like this, my bonny man."

"And he's soldiering overseas in a hot spot."

"That, also. Do you really ken how I feel, Chad?" When she was under pressure or excited, Scotland came burred and musical back into her voice. "You would think sour of me if I abandoned Dacey now. A matter of fair play, that."

"Fair play, honor; not cricket? Jesus, woman—would you leave him if he stood right here in London?"

Her arms tightened about him and her hands felt chill. The wind came yelling hoarsely down the street again and he backed into the room, turning to face her. "Would you?"

"I don't think—I cannae be certain, not so long as the bloody war's on. Oh, hinnie—darling, that is. I want you here and now. I want you in the future—if we're to have one atall, warmed snug beneath the thatched roof of a Grenoch cottage while the bannock bakes. I want you forever, and but for the bloody war, we would work all out. Ah, please, please—don't destroy puir us now; let us go as we are. You must love me enough for that, Chad; you must!"

Softly, he kissed her, and her lips were flavored with tears. "I love you enough for anything, Stephanie. Now and for all tomorrows waiting us, I love you." There was much sadness in her, her eyes misty, so he kissed the tip of her nose and said, "I just wanted to see if there was a way to make an honest woman of you."

"Bastard!" She bit his lip.

In temporary quarters at stripped-down Kensington House, Chad received his departure orders the next day, hand delivered by a mechanical British colonel who moved and spoke as if he had been wound up a bit too tightly. He was mustached and erect, blue eyes of marble, and a Red Hat—a provost marshal of Britain's Military Police. When Chad looked down at the sheaf of orders presented to him, he knew why this man had been sent to outrank him and if necessary, have him deposited bodily upon the first available transport, under arrest. The orders were signed by Maj. Gen. Thomas Skelton, the longtime enemy of Preston Belvale.

"Shit," Chad said. Skelton had found a way to get back at Belvale but the son of a bitch had no concept of what he was doing. This needless chickenshit fight was just starting.

"Pardon?"

"Never mind, Colonel. Have I time for a telephone call? While your driver or batman comes to pack my gear?"

The colonel reached for a pocket watch, unsnapped the golden case and studied the face carefully. "Providing the call goes through immediately, yes." Lifting his voice and tilting his waxed mustache toward the open doorway, he called, "Corporal!"

Chad made it to the duty desk with the colonel right behind him. He had the sergeant major there put through an urgent call to Brighton, using the code name of Stephanie's AA gun battery.

"Mrs. Bartlett has been temporarily relieved of her command," the colonel said.

Slamming down the phone, Chad said, "Goddamnit!" He glanced sharply at the blank-faced sergeant major. "Take off, Sergeant; get lost for a minute."

Eyebrows lifted, the man stood to attention and asked the colonel, "Sir?"

"That—is—a—fucking—order!" Chad said. "Unless Colonel Blimp wants an enlisted man to hear the ass chewing that's coming."

The provost's florid face didn't change. "You may leave, Sergeant Major."

Chad whirled on him. "Goddamnit, I try to be a good soldier, without calling on political connections or real rank. I have yet to lower the boom on assholes who try to wipe themselves on me. Because you don't know about my family and the old, heavy money that could buy this entire end of London without making a dent in the interest payments— because you have no idea how many generals and admirals, how many U.S. Senators and Representatives can come down on you and your country like a big fucking blivet, I'll let you back off while you still have your rank. But if you screw around with Leftenant Bartlett in any way—I repeat—any goddamn way, overt or covert or delaying promotion, not only your ruby red ass will be in a sling, but so will your War Ministry, and Churchill will swallow his cigar when some of that Lend-Lease doesn't get here on time, if it gets here at all. Do you read me, Colonel?"

"Ahh." The colonel thumbed his mustache and discovered a folded white kerchief to blot his red cheeks. "Ahh—I shall contact my superiors and deliver your—ahh—communication, Major. I shall wait at the car while you leave a message with the—ahh—lady's battery, if you wish."

He heel-thumped down the bare board hallway and the sergeant major came out of hiding to slide a pad and pencil across the desk. "Jolly good, Major. Oh, my God—Colonel Blimp, was it? I shall see that Leftenant Bartlett gets your message, wherever they've moved her."

Chad fisted his hands because they were shaking. "Thank you, Sergeant."

He turned to leave but stopped when the sergeant said, "Just one more thing, sir?"

"What's that?"

"What is a blivet, sir?"

Chad grinned. "Ten pounds of shit in a five-pound bag."

Dawn had just moved to the west when the taxi brought Chad through the wrought iron and white stone gates of Kill Devil Hill. The driver carried duffel bags across the veranda to set them beside the double doors of stained glass. Chad placed the swollen Val-pac beside them and paid the man for the quick trip from Washington Airport, adding a healthy tip. He'd slept little in the American B-17 on the bumpy journey from Heathrow airport. He was tired, grimy and still angry. He wanted General Skelton's balls on a skewer.

Henry, in his mysterious way that had lasted twenty years or more, appeared to open the door before Chad rang the bell. Slender, gray at the temples, Henry was a picture of decorum, even at this early hour. "Mister Chad—nobody said you were coming."

"Didn't know myself until yesterday. The general home?"

"Having coffee in the kitchen, sir."

"Thanks, Henry. Leave the bags for the yard boys, please."

Chad walked into the marble floored vestibule, and immediately became a part of the whole—the Hill, the family, one with the battle pennants and ancient weapons in the great hall. It was more than returning home, more than just entering a house. It was belonging, unquestioned understanding and the solid feel of duty. It was returning to the blood, and to the sword. Hurrying to the kitchen, Chad saluted the general. Coffee cup in his left hand, straight and ageless in his old robe, Belvale returned the highball and said, "What the hell, boy?"

"Shanghaied," Chad said and crossed to the coffeepot. "Skelton signed the travel orders. I report to Fort Jay as battalion commander."

"Kee-rist; the English service woman incident, but I didn't hear a whisper—"

Pouring coffee, Chad said, "Skelton's brown-nosing somebody in the War Department—civilian, I'd say; assistant secretary or someone like?"

"Has to be a good connection; Skelton's a son of a bitch, but sometimes he isn't quite stupid. He knows I'll stretch his hide on the barn door for this. Let's say he has temporary protection, but I'll line up sights on him sooner or later." Putting down his cup, the general thumbnailed his mustache and said, "Do you want to go right back?"

Chad hesitated. Stephanie had his address at the Hill; if she called him back, he'd go. If not, maybe it would do them both good to take a break. She could decide which meant more to her, a marriage that was pegged to duty and honor, or the rare thing they had discovered. "I could use some troop duty, sir; try to teach what I learned in Europe."

The general's face showed nothing. "The Sixteenth Infantry is at Fort Jay on Governors Island, right in New York harbor. Probably the best duty post in the army. Fine outfit, spit and polish. But here's something for your ears only—we're calling together the entire First Infantry Division, bringing the Eighteenth over from Fort Hamilton, the Twenty-sixth from Fort Totten, and the artillery outfits from posts scattered around the state. One triangular division, one post where it can train the way it should, as a complete fighting unit and learn the ways of the British, learn how the bastardly Krauts operate."

Chad sat at the kitchen table. Two of the cooks came into the kitchen and started a big tray of buttermilk biscuits. There'd be salt cured ham, freshly squeezed orange juice and this morning's milk, yesterday's brown eggs from Rhode Island Red hens. He breathed deeply. There was something to be said for being home.

"I hear there's a lot of building going on at old Camp Devens."

Belvale smiled. "Fort Devens now. Closest reservation of any size and Massachusetts can use the payday money, the civilian jobs that will be created."

"And in return, the politicians will be eternally grateful."

"At least until the end of the war."

Chad looked into his cup. "How's Kirstin?"

"She seems happy. The boys haven't been to see her."

"I'll talk to them."

"West Point rushed its program. You'll get a chance with Second Lieutenant Owen Belvale at Fort Jay; he's a platoon leader in H Company. Farley is still at VMI, but he'll be graduating soon. Some people are paying attention to the signs, to observer reports—even to newspaper stories. I hope we are granted enough time to convince more people."

"And Keenan? He got the business from Skelton, too." Chad decided he wouldn't ask about Keenan's wife. The general had been married most of his life to the same gentle woman, and divorce wasn't common in the family; until now, until so many family ties were coming undone.

"Back in China with the Peanut's forces and the AVG— those aviators are calling themselves Flying Tigers. You know: Claire Chennault's bunch."

Chad blinked. "The Peanut?"

"Chiang Kai-shek; the Gitmo, the Peanut. Crusty's term

and now he's got me using it. I believe he's right. We're spending a lot on Chiang Kai-shek and getting little in return. Tell me, did Gavin and Riley Wilmot check in with you in London?''

They'd been with him in the shelter after he met Stephanie; one a quiet kid, the other Gavin Scott, the lady killer and war lover. "Yes; they're flying Hudsons over the Channel.''

"Call them the advance party; it won't be long before we'll have a real air corps over there, new kinds of fighters and those big B-17s.''

Sighing, Chad stood up. "I'll make it down for breakfast after I shower.''

"That rescue business in London. You're in for the Soldier's Medal.''

"Can you make that two? I'd have been fried meat without Leftenant Bartlett hauling me out.''

The general looked away. "She must be some kind of woman, Chad.''

"That she is, sir. I've been lucky that way.''

He went quietly along the hallway to the winding staircase, feeling his shoulders sag. Maybe he was going about this all wrong; maybe he should let the general whisk him on a return flight to England. What if some bastard Kraut dropped a bomb on her AA battery?

Climbing the stairs, he glanced at the massive crystal chandelier to his left, then his eyes paid quick homage to the row of portraits in uniforms of this war and that war. Had any of them tried to steal a brother officer's wife?

Christ; in the middle of the night, he'd come half awake and wish Dacey Bartlett dead. Then guilt ate at him, and he turned uneasy about the effect of her husband being KIA would have upon Stephanie. She might fault herself, or him, or blame them both, and the guy's specter would always be sharp-edged between them.

Halfway across his bedroom he noticed her sitting on the side of his bed. "Nancy, what—''

"Only Henry knows I'm here, Chad. Please—I have to talk to someone.'' She looked drawn, too thin, and her eyes were red. She wasn't the bubbly, straight-on woman he knew and admired. Crossing to the little bar he said, "Too early for a drink?"

"Maybe too late. Bourbon on the rocks, p-please."

Something else was changed; she had been a white wine drinker. Looking at her, he had to think of Kirstin, of what friends the women had once been. Kirstin and Nancy, putting up a common front against undeserving husbands. Nancy didn't have to tell him that her love affair had gone sour; every line of her face and body said it. Was Kirstin unhappy, too? If so, what was he expected to do about it? People make mistakes; lovers become separated.

Nancy tossed off the drink and he snapped his Zippo to light her Spud menthol. Made sexually alert by Stephanie, he felt strange about sitting beside Nancy on the bed, so he brought a chair across the room and sank onto it. She was still a fine-looking woman, an attractive woman, but even though the fires were banked within her, her sorrow made her somehow compelling, a tearful Madonna.

She said, "I made a damned fool of myself with Wilson Pailey. I wouldn't listen when people said he was using me as an in to the family and to get any information I could give him. The general came down on him for it, and Wilson folded up and said he wouldn't seek office again. He didn't even say that much to me, not even good-bye. He j-just left. I loved him, and he didn't even say good-bye, damn him."

"That's the way," he said, taking her hand small and soft into his. "Get mad and stay mad. It won't hurt so much if you can keep yourself angry."

Eyes bleary, she tightened her grip upon his hand. "If—if he came into the room right now, I couldn't stay angry with him. I don't understand, Chad; we were so right for each other. We fitted. Oh—I don't think I can ever make anyone see what I—"

"I know what you mean, exactly."

Her eyes cleared a little. She didn't release his hand and now he smelled her new perfume, something rich and musky. "Oh, yes; your English woman. Is is like that with her? Was Kirstin so—I'm sorry; I didn't mean to bring up her name."

"That's okay." Why was he so damned conscious of

Nancy's nearness, the defeated softness that made her seem vulnerable? What the hell was he thinking of? Not Stephanie or Kirstin or even Keenan. He couldn't even remember the congressman's name right now. "I'd better shower before breakfast," he said.

"Chad?" Tears diamonded her lashes and her mouth quivered. "Am I so worthless, so used up that no man will want me?"

Leaving the chair, he crossed to her. "Of course not! Nancy, you've always been—you are still so attractive that—"

He kissed her gently, not meaning to kiss her at all, but when his lips touched her soft, quivering mouth, Chad tried to make it light and short and brotherly. It didn't work because Nancy's arms slid around his neck and she lifted to him. Or pulled him down to her. Then it didn't matter which.

Desperate and demanding, her tongue searched his mouth; her teeth clashed with his, and her fingernails dug into his shoulders. Rounded soft and giving, Nancy's breasts strained against his chest. Swiftly, almost violently, he tore away her skirt and underthings; swiftly and with a panting need, she curled her hand around him and guided him to her, hotly within her.

Surging and twisting, thrusting and clutching, he tangled with her legs, her arms, and knew the suctioning of her sweating belly. She kicked away a shoe and a pillow flew off the bed. Twisted sheets trapped Chad's leg and the bed rocked, shuddered and the shaking reached deeply within Chad as she cried out and bit at his throat.

She clung to him as he tried to break from her. She said nothing, but the hot gusting of her breath fanned his cheek. He thought he had no words for her, until he said, "A need—there was a need."

Gently, he pried himself from her and closed the bedroom door before going into the bath to shower. Nobody need know she was here, much less what had just happened. Henry would say nothing, and if Nancy left soon, or even if she decided to stay on at the Hill and slipped off to her own room in another wing, nobody would know. Standing under cold, needled water, Chad tried to sort the emotions churning within him. Who the hell was he, some rampant cocksman proving only that a stiff prick has no conscience? He was in love with Stephanie Bartlett, and still halfway jealous of Kirstin sleeping with the Texas senator. He fretted about screwing a combat officer's wife, yet he laid his cousin's wife. Even if Nancy was Keenan's ex-wife, that didn't excuse him. She was family, and the general would be mightily angered if he found out. Damn; so would Keenan, divorce or no divorce.

Nancy—the poor kid was so distraught, feeling so down and worthless because the great love of her life abandoned her; he had taken advantage of her need to be comforted, to be loved again. Only it wasn't love; it was sex. Chad turned off the shower and toweled himself roughly as if he could scrub away the guilt.

It hadn't been rape, damnit. Nancy wanted it more than he had, needed her kind of reassurance. But it hadn't been honorable, either. Damn; what had he gotten himself into? She might want to follow him to Fort Jay, to make something permanent out of one wild moment. That couldn't be; he couldn't live on post with a captain's former wife. And more, he didn't want to.

Robed in terry cloth, he took a deep breath before going back into the bedroom that smelled of musk and sex.

Nancy was gone. A note lipsticked on the dresser mirror said, "Thanks." He stared at the scarlet word for long moments before smearing it out of existence with his damp bath towel.

CHAPTER 40

INTERNATIONAL NEWS SERVICE—Governors Island, N.Y., February 7, 1941: Polo games for the rest of the year are cancelled as of now, regimental headquarters announced today. Civilians are still invited to the parade ground to watch "New York's Own" troops pass in review, but a change in training plans has suddenly altered athletic schedules here.

"We hope to keep the polo ponies until the emergency is over, rather than ship them back to the artillery," a reliable source said. "A lot of time and money has gone into the training of these horses."

The U.S. government ferry reached Fort Jay in just over ten windswept and chilly minutes. It was an ugly ride, South Ferry docks and the granite towers of Manhattan looming gray and uncaring behind Chad, and Governors Island hunkering ahead. But for the three-storey regimental barracks running the length of the island, Fort Jay sat low and self-effacing. It seemed to be apologizing for the islands floating around it, soggy mounds of interlocked condoms, the tons of rubbers, old and sinking or freshly used, swirled into the bay by the uncounted toilets of New York City.

How many had cleaved only unto one, and how many had survived the passions of adultery? Who the hell cared, after the fact?

Only people with old-fashioned ideas and well-defined rules of right and wrong; perhaps only Stephanie Bartlett.

As the dock neared, Chad said into the wind, "According to some of our fine leaders, the professional soldier has nothing to do but fuck and fight, and ought to be grateful for just room and board; never mind a salary. Jesus—us dogfaces should be so lucky. There's never enough ass or assault to go around."

The MP who directed him to headquarters wore white leather and brass highly polished; beneath the OD blouse with two hash marks on the left sleeve was a spotless and militarily creased suntan shirt. The blue and white checkerboard, the touches of red and gold insignia of the Sixteenth winked from blouse lapels.

Returning the man's snappy salute, Chad said, "You're looking good, soldier."

The corporal sounded surprised. "Thank you, Major."

Chad carried only his briefcase; his Val-pac and personal equipment would wait at the dock until some soldiers on fatigue detail hauled the stuff to his quarters. They would bitch all the way, but that was a solider's privilege, bitching. It was a way of relieving tension, and officers were wise to pretend they heard nothing. When soldiers fell silent for any length of time, that's when they turned as dangerous as a teased cottonmouth.

Col. L.L. Simbeaux was a small and harried man, technically overage for his command, but there was no brigadier's star in the offing. The army's expansion, already underway despite the die-hard isolationists and FDR haters, had no room for bird colonels withering on the vine. Simbeaux would retire and a much younger, newly promoted officer would take his place. Maybe that was good; maybe not.

"Yes, sir," Chad said. "The general got his third star and did much behind-the-scenes work on getting the army what it needs—primarily men."

"And next—armor and weapons," Simbeaux said. He took a short carved pipe from a desk drawer and slowly packed its bowl. The tobacco smelled like apples. "Do you think it'll be all right to drop in on Preston on my way home to New Orleans? I've only been to the Hill twice in—migod! Forty years?''

"Of course, sir; the general always has time for old friends and good soldiers."

"I thank you for that," the colonel said, and lighted his pipe with a wooden kitchen match. "You may not thank me for not trying harder to keep you from the Second Battalion. It's full of General Skelton's cronies—which is why you were shanghaied here, I imagine. They're so well protected that they run their own two-bit version of the army, and it's not good. Discipline is one thing, chickenshit is another. Sorry I couldn't stop it in time, but I can warn you about your assistant, Maj. Clifton Huckbee, until now, battalion CO. You barely have date of rank on him. He's truly one of Skelton's handmaidens."

"Hand—maiden?"

"Could be; he's too slick to get caught. There are good people in the Second, Delvale especially H Company's Butch Crawford, and George Company's CO, Jerry Kurtz. Oh, yes—Lieutenant Belvale is Crawford's exec."

"I'll take care of them, and of myself. I was with the British from the fall of the Maginot Line to Dunkirk, and worse—during the London blitz."

Owen Belvale might be worse than the blitz.

. . . a lady lieutenant cheerful in the bomb shelter, a pixie woman-child who turned down a handsome lady-killer in favor of a graying man and came to mean so much in so little time; Stephanie—damnit!—Stephanie . . .

"So," Chad went on, "I hope to go beyond politics and make tough combat soldiers out of fat garrison troopers. It won't be easy; there's damned little time."

Looking wistful, Colonel Simbeaux drew upon his pipe and murmured that maybe the army would see fit to keep him on duty, if the war came fast enough.

"It's already here," Chad said. "The president just hasn't admitted it to the Congress, and no publicity went out on our losing one hundred and four U.S. sailors escorting English ships out of Murmansk. If I were the colonel, I wouldn't put in my papers unless I were forced. Good luck, sir."

The scent of apples and tobacco followed Chad to the door and beyond. Outside, the odors of the bay pushed them back, and Chad walked erect, purposefully, past the field grade BOQ and then junior bachelor officer quarters. There was the round, Gothic tower of Castle Williams, second only to Fort Leavenworth for general prisoners—those with more than six months sentence to serve—doing hard time. Garrison prisoners were behind the great walls, too. They were the short timers, the men who received special courts-martial for lesser crimes. Daily, they fell out in groups of three to do cleanups and cut grass as young prison chasers stalked nervously behind them.

Do not fire upon an escaping prisoner once he reaches the water, the orders said; double-time the rest of the detail to the guardhouse and report to the sergeant of the guard. And either get your own ass court-martialed or receive the worst chewing of your life.

Goddamnit! Fire on the son of a bitch, you hear me? If you kill him, you get a quick trial and get fined two bucks. For that, they give you a carton of cigarettes. Why do they try you? So the civilians can't; double jeopardy is against the law, even for doggies.

Oh, yeah—and they charge you a dime for the shell you used.

Rumor had it that nobody ever swam the chill and swiftly churning seas to Manhattan or Brooklyn, but that several desperate escapees died in the bay.

"Castle Bill" had a tough, escapeproof reputation to go with its cold walls—unforgiving rock four feet thick, and inside, three tiers of even less forgiving cells. From his research, Chad knew that tier three was a lifelong home to one "Peepsight" Jones, a black soldier who had machine-gunned a squad of his own men at Brownsville, Texas, during the Villa campaign.

Passing Battalion HQ, Chad hesitated before G Company, then moved on to the sally port. Both H and G Companies had back doors that opened into the sally port, itself a lingering echo of medieval days when a small, thick door in the castle wall might be flung wide for a band of desperate mounted knights to sally forth and do quick battle with the enemy in siege around the moat.

Now, through the far end of this sally port, the post flagpole stood above the World War French 75 that signalled the opening and close of each working day. At 5:30 P.M. each day, a bugled assembly would call running troops from barracks to form hasty lines for retreat formation, the boom of the sunset gun and the lowering of the colors.

Thoughtfully, he reversed his field and went on by Howe Company's orderly room, went by George and stopped at Fox. Was he avoiding a meeting with his son? Colonel Simbeaux hadn't mentioned Fox Company's commander as one of the good people; Chad would see about that.

It was cool and shadowy inside the hall as he turned right. The first sergeant's door was open. Chad took a step inside, rapped the door frame smartly and waited a few seconds too long before the sergeant lifted his round, pink and balding head.

First Sergeant Ogden, the oak and brass desk sign announced; he said, "Damnit, the lieutenant ain't seein' nobody today—oh, shit! I mean—" Ogden hit his feet at attention and bellowed: *"Ten-shun!"*

"As you were. Why isn't Lieutenant Mulrooney seeing anyone today, Sergeant? It's not Wednesday afternoon or any other holiday, and all polo practice has been cancelled. Where the hell is Mulrooney?"

"Ahh—Major, sir—the lieutenant said—I mean, Lieutenant Mulrooney went to the battalion commander's meeting—ahh—the other major's meeting, I mean, sir. I guess you're the new battalion commander, since we ain't had no light colonels on the job since Christ was a corporal, sir—TO and E notwithstanding."

"According to the Table of Organization and Equipment, this company should have a captain as CO. Is Mulrooney even a half-ass lieutenant?"

Ogden stiffened. "Ahh, I wouldn't know, sir."

"My moneymaking ass. No more than you'd know that the battalion meeting is at the officers mess over scotch and soda. Loyalty is admirable, Sergeant, but I'm serving notice that every man in this outfit had better watch his own paper asshole. If you see Mulrooney before I catch up with him, or Major Huckbee, both are to remain in their respective offices until I return—even if that should take all month. Do you read me, Sergeant?"

Ogden swallowed. "I read you five by five, sir."

"Loud and clear is admirable, too," Chad said. "So is a certain silence. I'm going to Easy Company now."

"Unannounced; I understand, sir."

"Thank you, Sergeant."

Stephanie Bartlett would have laughed, he thought. She had never seen him throw rank around, except for that one brief moment in the dank London underground when Flyboy Gavin Scott let his mouth get out of control. Chad doubted that she was laughing much now, unless her darling husband was home from Singapore and it was her duty to laugh. She thought so damned much of duty and purpose.

But Leftenant Bartlett commanded her own battery of ack-ack guns that went into action almost nightly. She was on the line, and so was her old man, waiting the Japs. Where was Major Chadwick Belvale, Infantry, a leader for the Queen of Battle? Strolling from one goof-off company to another as if there were no war anywhere in the world, as if no child ever got burned and gutted by a brave dive-bomber pilot. *Seig Heil*, you sons of bitches!

There was a war on, and these military fuckups were about to discover what that meant to them.

But what about Nancy Carlisle? Did she laugh or cry or hurt in silence about the cousin who seduced her, who laid her right there at the Hill? "Thanks," the scrawled lipstick had announced; sarcasm, accusation or actual gratitude? He hadn't geared himself up enough to talk to Keenan's ex-wife. Somehow, that made him even angrier with Stephanie Bartlett; so much for a gentleman by act of Congress; so much for purpose, duty and honor and the family.

Hesitating before the door of Easy Company, the thought slapped him that he'd have to watch himself or he might go over the line again. A competent psychiatrist might think that Major Belvale was out to prove himself with every cooperative female in the country; in the world. One woman had divorced him and another refused to marry him. It made some kind of twisted sense that he should be playing the great lover.

It made better sense to do his job. The Sixteenth Regiment might drag its collective heels about taking on realistic, backbreaking training, but not his battalion. There'd be no more playing around, for himself or his men. They would soon have a war to fight. Then the only difference would be between the quick and the dead. For everyone—to include his own son.

NORTH AMERICAN NEWSPAPER ALLIANCE—Governors Island, N.Y., February 2, 1941: The 16th Infantry Regiment, whose home garrison has been here at Fort Jay for many years, suddenly has a new bugle call. It happened this way:

Pfc Joseph Parelli, 2418 DePuls St., the Bronx, has served with the regimental band for six years, and often is called, as bugler of the guard, to play the army's series of musical calls, from first call at 6:00 A.M. to taps at 11:00 P.M. He is an excellent bugler, but his comrades thought he had overstepped himself when he offered to bet a friend five dollars that he was so close to the commanding officer that he could add extra notes to his bugle calls and get away with it.

"Bet," said the friend, and everyone listened through the day to each call from reveille through chow calls and finally to retreat, played before the flag is lowered as to the colors is sounded.

Parelli had chickened out, they said, nobody messes with To The Colors. The soft, somehow haunting notes of retreat sounded over the drill field and reached the quadrangle where the regiment was drawn up to pay homage to the flag. After the last legitimate note came the addition—unmistakably . . . "East side, west side, all around the town, the kids played Ring around Rosie, London bridge is falling down . . ."

After the dismissed order was given, a stunned silence fell

over the 16th Infantry, even upon those in the know. Within minutes Pfc Parelli was summoned to headquarters and the regimental commander.

"Tough luck," said his friends. "We'll visit you in the guardhouse."

But Parelli was back within minutes, and smiling. "Pay up. The old man liked it. He only said it was too long and to cut the last four bars."

Now after every bugle call, except of course, to the colors, the lilting refrain of . . . "East side, west side, all around the town," . . . is heard. Thus are legends made.

CHAPTER 41

ASSOCIATED PRESS—Kunming, China, February 23, 1941: Ferrying supplies to Generalissimo Chiang Kai-shek is a major problem in this area. Food, ammunition and medicines, as well as all equipment, must be flown 500 miles from the Assam in India across the treacherous Himalaya Mountains to newly scraped airfields here. China Air Transport planes are flown by American pilots, "civilian" volunteers who risk their lives every day to help Chinese battle the Japanese invaders of their country.

Patient elephants, huge and with flapping ears, shuffled steadily in a gray line with fifty-five-gallon drums of gasoline balanced upon their tusks. Sweating soldiers rolled the fuel inside the cargo plane, upending the drums tightly together. Another two-man team rolled by them as they headed back to the door, barrel bumping and the stink of gas fumes thick in the oven-hot air trapped inside the fuselage.

Frenchy LeBlanc squatted native fashion in the shade of the wing, .45 pistol in his hand. Keenan went to join him, grateful to get out of the killing sun for even a moment. Back home, there might be a light dusting of snow kissing the highest Shenandoah peaks. The air would be cool and breathable, tangy with the smoke of burning leaves.

"Why the pistol, Frenchy? Expecting an attack?" It wasn't much cooler in the shade.

The man from Louisiana shrugged. "Just making damned sure no Wog lights a cigarette, me. Bust his rag head."

Wiping his face with a damp kerchief, Keenan said, "You'd blow us up."

"That'd be different. Me, I'd be doing it myself, not some ignorant Wog, no."

"Just as dead." Keenan wished for a smoke himself. It would be a hell of a long trip back without one.

"Uh-uh, Captain. Don't make much never mind *when* a man dies; it's *how* he dies. Me, I'll hate it if some son of a bitch kills me because he don't know no better."

Keenan smiled. "How'd they ever get you over here from—"

"Big Mamou, Louisiana. I'm dusting crops when this recruiting sergeant gets lost. Nobody comes to Big Mamou on purpose. He sees my old Jenny and buys me drinks and *voila!*—the first thing I know—me, I'm in the goddamn army. My cousin Latouche, that coonass got my Jenny plane *and* my girl Celeste."

Remembering the drunken bombing raid on Hanoi, Keenan was glad that Frenchy was a fine pilot who enjoyed flying. Although he navigated by the seat of his pants, he always got his cargo where it was meant to go. That wasn't easy for any pilot, and too many planes were lost crossing the hump.

"Last elephant," Frenchy said. "For sure, they work better than coonass Cajuns. You ready, *mon capitaine*?"

"As I'll ever be."

Lord, five hundred miles from northeastern India back to China, over some of the most inhospitable terrain in the world. Below were the Naga Hills, roamed by a tribe of headhunters, and jungle gorges of three rivers—the Irrawaddy, Salween and Mekong. Then the Santsung Range lifted fifteen thousand feet, and never mind freak weather conditions with winds that hit nearly 250 miles per hour, blinding monsoons and vicious turbulence that could flip a plane as if it were a balsa model.

The C-46 Commando bucked and rattled, plunging suddenly in downdrafts that threatened Keenan Carlisle's stomach. Deep holes in the sky that could drop the plane three thousand feet in less than a minute floated him up against his seat belt, then banged his butt against the metal seat.

This was a trip he wouldn't want to make every day. He just got tired staying on the ground and writing repetitive reports. So long as the Nationalists were leery of him, they wouldn't allow him on any ground patrols—if they ever moved out from their guarded cities. He needed to get out in the countryside.

Yen Ling seemed farther away than ever and sometimes dreamlike, but he refused to give up. She was the reason he had returned to China, and he meant to find her again if it cost him his front seat in hell. The plane bucked again, and the choking smell of gas filled the cockpit.

Frenchy yelled that he was sorry his copilot was sick, and that they'd soon be over the Santsung, the worst of the trip behind them. Frenchy also had a habit of carrying so much vital cargo that the plane crew had to be left behind.

Keenan had known about the missing copilot before they left Kunming, but sickness, injury and death made pilots flying alone not a rare thing. Frenchy was glad for company, and held forth—at the top of his voice—on the superiority of Cajun food over Creole or anything else.

"Hey, man—we so poor, we got no fancy meat for the gumbo, so we throw in whole boiled eggs. You make it to Big Mamou some day, I show you, me. You ever eat alligator gar, man?"

Some pilots made three trips a day, depending upon the weather and how fast their planes could be loaded and off-loaded, but Frenchy LeBlanc tried to hold his flights to two. He was in no hurry to go home where he'd have to stay in proper uniform, him. Here the job mattered, not appearance, and chickenshit didn't bother anybody.

Regretfully, Keenan let go the cherished image of Yen Ling, and watched her fade, trailing the thick wealth of that blue-black hair. In her place came Nancy, sad eyed and by the set of her shoulders, the downturn of her face, lonely. He hoped she would find happiness with her congressman; she was a good person, a warm woman who needed care. Nancy had always been a little unsure of herself, and he tried to remember if that started before or after he brought her home to the Hill. Aunt Minerva and the family could make all but the strongest feel inferior, or at the least, uncertain.

He grinned. They'd play hell making Yen Ling dance if she didn't want to. His grin spread as he pictured bringing Yen Ling to the Hill and watching Aunt Minerva's cold, patrician face struggle for calm when she saw a Chinese woman on his arm, her wedding ring blocking any shocked denial.

"Merde!" Frenchy yelled, and threw the plane into a dive.

Hanging onto the seat arms, pushed hard against his belt, Keenan wondered what the hell. Then he saw a hole pop through the windshield, and had to hold on desperately as Frenchy hurled the C-46 into a turn it was never designed for empty, much less loaded with gasoline drums that could shift and break free at any moment.

The Jap fighter flashed across their path, its fried egg wing markings flashing in the late sun. One tracer in their payload and it was Katy bar the door. They had nothing to fight back with, no 50 caliber guns like the P-40s mounted. Every pilot carried a GI .45 in a shoulder holster, and a few adventurers had scared up some submachine guns. Keenan spared a quick glance at the back of Frenchy's seat and saw the blue gleam of a Thompson 50 round drum. They'd do as well with a slingshot.

This time, when the Zero made its pass, Keenan heard slugs rapping hard against the metal skin of the cockpit and a windshield panel shattered. The goddamn Jap was after live targets, and they could be thankful for that.

Muttering something that Keenan couldn't make out, Frenchy arrowed the plane for the earth, and Keenan's sparse lunch crawled up into his throat. Dark crags and thick jungle loomed below, larger with each pulse-hammering second.

"Grab the gun!" Frenchy yelled. "Shoot the slant-eyed son of a bitch!"

Fighting gravity, Keenan got a grip on the Thompson and wrenched it from its clip holders. The side window was cracked, more air screaming in as the plane leveled out to skim the treetops. The Zero plunged from above and the left flank; Keenan saw the red winking of its guns. He shoved the muzzle of the Thompson through the window crack and held the trigger down. He couldn't tell if he scored on the enemy fighter, but he'd be willing to bet against it.

The C-46 twisted violently and Keenan heard rivets pop. The stench of gasoline was stronger, choking. He let go the Thompson's trigger. Better a Jap bullet than to be fried in an explosion. There was that chance, even with the wind blowing the fumes back of the plane.

"Hey, now! Hey—now!" Still fighting the wheel, Frenchy made a quick point ahead and below. "The son of a bitch went for it!"

The Zero blew up in a gush of bright flame when it plowed the jungle, a gout of fire and smoke swiftly gone behind them as their plane roared over the funeral pyre. Scratch one samurai, Keenan thought, and had a brief memory of the Japanese he had fought beside, Major Watanabe. Did the pilot keep a family sword in the cockpit and believe that ten days from now he would awaken in warrior heaven?

"Greedy bastard, him," Frenchy said, nursing the C-46 higher and barely clearing a pile that clawed rocky talons at them. "Overshot when I throttled back and didn't have room to pull up. Hey, Jap—you worth a five hundred dollar bonus to this happy coonass, yeah. Ain't many transport pilots can claim a kill."

Keenan's breath sighed out and he propped the submachine gun on his lap. He would never make it as a flyer; he had been too long in the infantry, and his reflexes were set to dig in when fired upon, to take cover. There was no cover-up here and no foxhole.

"Ten minutes," Frenchy announced. "Meanwhile, see if you can reach that bottle of Indian type whiskey. Ain't nobody knows what's in it, but I don't care, me. Careful, man—it's got a cob stopper, all them rag heads use. Tastes like the bottom of a gator nest, but it beats a hundred bucks a bottle for goddamn Seagram's, yeah."

Although Frenchy held the plane as low as he could, cold air pouring in threatened to freeze them. Keenan was happy for both the vile whiskey and the oxygen tube, happier for the sheepskin jacket and Sherpa hat that kept him from icing over.

Setting the plane down smoothly upon a recently built and tarred strip, Frenchy rolled it to the far end where grass huts and a lopsided building, which had been patched together from fuselages and wings of wrecked airplanes, stood side by side. The operations office was roofed by a roped down tarp.

Chinese coolies trotted toward the C-46 as its propellers stopped spinning, a long line of lean and work-hunched men in conical hats and twisted cloth G-strings. As Keenan climbed down, still holding the weapon, they were already tugging and hauling at the cargo, as silent and industrious as ants.

As always in China, the laborers were men and women of indeterminate ages, all seeming old unless you knew how to look. Keenan went by the ant column, glancing at women slaving beside the men, the only noticeable difference the baggy blouses they wore out of modesty. Yen Ling had done her share with Major Hong's group of guerrillas, doctoring and fighting without losing femininity. He tried to peer beneath the coolie hats because Yen Ling's face might be there, although he knew better.

He saw the old man up close and whipped around to trot after him, to grab a stringy, muscled arm and spin him protesting out of the line.

"Father Lim!"

The old man shook his head and stooped to retrieve his fallen straw hat. He tried to scuttle away, but Keenan caught him by the twist of cloth. "The hell you aren't Father Lim!"

He was certain of it; this was the old man who had carried a handmade rifle. Keenan remembered every wrinkle in the ancient face, for he had soldiered beside Father Lim for months, sharing water, food and danger.

"No, no," Father Lim insisted. "No Lim." That seemed to be all the English he knew, and his eyes begged Keenan to let go. He nodded quickly, raised a finger to withered lips, and made a hand motion as if following the sun down behind the hills. Keenan let go. The man would contact him after dark.

Several coolies had stopped to watch, and a Nationalist soldier moved toward Keenan, long rifle slung, its bayonet bobbing and winking in the late sun.

Of course Father Lim denied his name; he sweated here deep among enemies and far from communist lines, a spy for Major Hong. Keenan's heart thumped, for Lim would have news of Yen Ling. Maybe the unit was close by, nearer than anyone would believe. The guerrillas could infiltrate anywhere, given time and the opportunity, but so distant from any Mao Tse-dung enclave?

Keenan shivered despite the clinging, humid heat. That could mean a suicide mission, aimed at—what? Destroying the air base? No; the communists realized that the CAT transports and the P-40s operated against the main enemy, the Japanese. Chiang Kai-shek could wait for their attention. What target, then, and why?

"Captain—what's the problem?" A rumpled man in scrubbed-thin suntans without insignia of rank stood by. Keenan knew him for a major on base security when he wasn't flying combat missions in a souped-up P-40.

Making a chuckle that he hoped didn't sound phony, Keenan said, "Nothing; I thought I knew the old guy, but flying with Frenchy can make any ground pounder see things. That, and the Indian booze. Have you heard that he wiped out a Jap Zero?"

Major Harris nodded and walked beside Keenan. The Chinese soldier stopped to fiddle with a cigarette butt. Harris said, "That man is crazy—but in Kunming, that helps."

Keenan glanced at the setting sun. "It helps anywhere in China."

CHAPTER 42

REUTERS NEWS AGENCY—Somewhere in China, March 18, 1941: American Volunteer Group pilots flying outmoded planes against new Japanese Zeros and Bettys, are racking up stunning victories. Stung by repeated casualties and unable to eliminate AVG airfields, the Japanese have threatened to execute any captured American pilots as "guerrillas and criminals."

Smoking a cigarette, Keenan leaned against a heavily damaged P-40 and waited for Father Lim to come to him. He tasted excitement on the night, and a little sharp thrill tightened his belly. Yen Ling; oh, lord—he would get news of Yen Ling. Maybe Father Lim could smuggle him off the base to where she was. He would go to her, if he had to walk clear across China, if he had to repeat Mao Tse-tung's ten thousand *li* march.

Night coolness chilled him more than it should. Suppose Yen Ling was dead? He didn't want to think of that, but a flash picture of her passed through his mind. He saw her again as she allowed the Jap officer to paw her erect body— just before she killed him. His mind showed him her bloody corpse, and his nails dug hard into his palms. Not Yen Ling, lord; not her.

At the thin cry of a night bird, Keenan stirred restlessly and pinched out his cigarette butt to field strip it and scatter flakes of tobacco. Thinner than that bird call, the whisper reached from beneath the fuselage of the plane: "*Ding hao*—okay?"

"Keenan dropped to his knees. When he saw two shadows, he put a hand on his .45. "*Ding hao,* Father Lim, but who is this?"

"Wang, from the Chairman's headquarters." The man's English was near perfect, his voice low and Keenan couldn't see his face in the shadows. "Attached to Major Hong's unit. Since Father Lim speaks little English, he asked that I accompany him."

Hunkered down, Keenan said, "How many more of Major Hong's men are here?" Yen Ling—could she be right here on the base, so damned close?

Wang did not answer. Father Lim put one hand upon Keenan's forearm and said something in Cantonese; Wang interpreted: "He is sorry to have denied his old comrade, but it was his duty, and you will understand."

Patting Lim's withered hand, Keenan said, "Yes—but I don't understand what he's doing here. I would also ask him of another comrade, Nurse Chang Yen Ling."

Lim spoke rapidly and Wang said that the nurse was in good health. Lim was cut short then, and Wang said, "It is better to know no more, Captain."

"Maybe I can help, but if it's a raid against the Americans here, for any reason—"

"No."

"Father Lim, how far away is she? I came back to China to see her, and maybe change her mind. True, nothing could adequately replace Nurse Chang, but a plane load of the newest medicines, privately supplied and landed at any spot of Major Hong's choosing, might make up for her loss. If I could talk to her, just for a minute—"

"That is not possible," Wang said. Keenan was beginning to dislike the sound of his voice. "As for a bride price—Chinese women are free now, under Chairman Mao's enlightenment program."

"Sure," Keenan said. "Damn it, Father Lim, if you can get a message to her, tell her where I am and that I'm looking for her." He glanced at the slim form of the other man in mottled shadow. "If you clowns make it off this air base still breathing, that is. You'd better tell me the plot, Wang. I have this feeling that Americans are in danger. I might have to haul you in and turn you over to intelligence, and I can see your hands. Hold them still.''

Lim sang out another short speech in the eight-tone system of the Cantonese, the biggest language group in China. Mao had made four-tone Mandarin the official language of the communists, but it would take many years for China's thirty-seven dialects to become anything like standardized.

Keenan brought out his .45 and balanced it upon one knee. In a faint wash of moonlight, he could see Wang's hands; they did not move. Wang said, ''Father Lim states that you are a brave comrade in arms who has killed Japanese and Russians. Yet you are here with the Nationalists.''

''As an observer only, as I was with Major Hong, but I am not allowed to go into the country. The Nationalists have also heard of my time with the unit that stormed the bridge chains. I am here with the Americans, not to help Chiang Kai-shek in any way.''

''He is due to arrive soon, the generalissimo?''

''I didn't know he was coming.'' That was it. These wild men were here to kill Chiang Kai-shek. Jesus! Talk about a suicide squad. ''You mean to shoot Chiang Kai-shek?''

''Not unless we are forced. We are to take him to a certain village and keep him there until a compromise is reached.''

Kidnap, then. More difficult than assassination because the work was up close and the hostage had to be kept alive. What compromise did they expect to sweat out of the Peanut, and who was fool enough to trust him? Certainly not Mao.

Then the deal, whatever it might be, had to be with one of Chiang's staff officers. It still might not work, if that officer was ambitious and decided to forget the hostage. What better way to take over an army and most of a nation while blaming the loss of the great general upon his lifetime enemies? World opinion would turn completely against the Reds.

''How will you get him out of here? Without involving Americans, of course.''

"I am a pilot."

"Handy as hell, aren't you? I think Hong's people—including this great old man—are in for a bloodbath. You can't haul troops in a P-40, and those C-46s are ours, too. If you take one by force—*boo hao;* no good."

"There are other methods."

Watching closely, Keenan saw one of the guy's hands move down his thigh like an inchworm. Keenan said, "The ancient and accepted Chinese method, bribery."

The hand continued to edge along. Keenan said, "You cut Father Lim short when I asked about Nurse Chang. Allow him to speak of her now."

Lim answered the man's curt order, talking softly and in a hurry. Wang passed the information along in short and choppy phrases, as if the words left a bitter flavor. Keenan moved the muzzle of his .45 an inch, and the sliding hand stopped moving. The son of a bitch had something within reach in his floppy clothing—a knife or small pistol.

"The woman progresses," Wang said. "She dedicates herself solely to the cause and has no time for foreign devils."

"Or for jealous pilots?" Keenan said it softly.

Wang's hand moved swiftly, but not fast enough. Keenan slapped him sharply beside the head with the .45. Wang fell over without a sound and Keenan leaned over to shake him down. Father Lim sucked air noisily through his teeth in the manner of all Orientals when surprised. Keenan showed him the compact Jap Nambu, a dull gleam in the moonlight.

Lim sat stonelike while Keenan waited for consciousness to seep back into Wang the pilot, Wang the would-be lover of Chang Yen Ling and leader of this insane guerrilla plot to kidnap Chiang Kai-shek. He was also on Mao's headquarters team and probably high ranking in the Red Army.

Keenan was knee-deep in trouble. How would he ever get back to Yen Ling now? How many of Hong's tough soldiers were mixed into the air base work force, and if Chiang did arrive, where would the shooting start? Damn! Keenan had already proved where he stood when his own kind became involved. The problem now was what to do with Wang, and to stop the plot without exposing the troops he'd fought beside, Father Lim and Major Hong's gutty fighters.

Knee-deep, hell; trouble was already at his armpits and rising.

Wang stirred, and a truck raced down the airstrip, slowing at each facing pair of oil drums so men could leap off and light them. Night flight; was the Peanut actually coming to inspect this end of his supply lifeline? Slowly, Wang sat up as the stink of burning oil drifted to the crippled plane that covered them. Tucking the Nambu into his own belt, Keenan showed the man the business end of the Colt .45.

"No yelling, no signal of any kind. I'll kill you."

Easing his head into both hands, Wang swayed upon his knees. Orange light flickering from the oil drums showed part of his hard face. Father Lim still had not moved a muscle. The truck motor roared for the end of the strip, and down the other way, vehicles drove into line so their lights could brighten the landing area.

The cargo plane dropped quickly, its landing lights augmented by spotlights that probed the night ahead. Its props slowed, the C-46 touched ground with a squeal of rubber, and Keenan caught a flash of the stylized white sun insignia, the blue background of China's Nationalists.

Keenan took only a quick glance, then stared back at Wang. Something exploded against the back of his head, and a red-black flower bloomed behind his eyes. The tarred rock just off the landing strip felt cottony against his cheek, and he snuggled to it.

He came to slowly and painfully, his head throbbing and mouth dry because of the gag stuffed in it. He tried to move and managed an inch. He was tied to a ring bolt in a metal floor, and the floor was moving. Cargo plane, and high up; the air was chill and thin. Lim; only Father Lim could have hit him with something from behind.

Half turning, Keenan eyed the yellowish overhead bulb that dimly lighted the cabin. Cord bit into his wrists and ankles and the floor vibrated beneath him. He wasn't alone on the floor; the other guy, long and thin, was cocooned with ropes and his bald head picked up a little light.

The Peanut himself? It sure as hell looked like him.

Wang's crew got away with the kidnap then, and were free in a C-46 some greedy bastard sold them. Angling himself, Keenan peered up at four other men, armed and huddled close together for warmth and comfort. The left motor of the plane coughed, caught itself and hummed on. An air pocket dropped the C-46 a long way, and the Chinese guerrillas muttered among themselves as they clung to webbing at their backs.

When the flight leveled out, one man detached himself from the huddle and walked unsteadily to Keenan. Kneeling, he worked the gag from Keenan's mouth. Father Lim tilted a canteen to give a drink, then wet a rag and applied it to the tender back of Keenan's head. He said something and his hands were gentle, his face sorrowful.

Keenan lay back. "I guess you had a good reason, old man, and I'll never figure how you grabbed the Peanut so easily. But it's still a mess, and everybody's hide will wind up as dart boards."

Lim slipped off a ragged jacket and spread it over Keenan. His wrinkled face was sad as he lurched back to his seat. He wished the old man could speak English; he'd find out something about the kidnap, their destination, and the reason he was being brought along. They could have left him stone cold under that P-40, and it was a wonder they hadn't. Father Lim's doing, he supposed; the old guy wasn't happy about what he'd had to do.

Lord—they had actually grabbed Chiang Kai-shek off one of his own air bases and here they were, spiriting him into communist controlled territory. Even if the generalissimo made it through, how would he save face?

Keenan had a strong urge to scratch his nose. The floor grew colder beneath his shoulders, and his hands were numb. Chiang Kai-shek had not made a sound through his gag, and the guerrillas had even taped his eyes shut. If it got much colder—but the plane nosed downward and the floor tilted. Again the port motor coughed, hacked twice, and Keenan wondered if they'd make it.

Then he thought of where they were—Communist China; he thought of Yen Ling and smiled. The plane sat down hard, bounced and found the airstrip again. It fishtailed down the runway and burned rubber when the pilot used his brakes. They had arrived, wherever it was, and Major Hong would be waiting for his prisoner. So would Yen Ling—Yen Ling!

Even though Father Lim massaged his legs, Keenan had a difficult time walking. He was still dizzy from the wallop on the head, and the high cold had gotten deep into him. But with help, he climbed to the ground and watched them work on the Peanut. There was light everywhere—torch and barrels of burning firewood and a generator's weak bulbs, the headlights of two trucks. The airstrip was still dark.

He saw Major Hong coming, no older, but more worn, stooping a little as he approached the prisoner. Keenan stared behind the man, looking for a slim, graceful figure and didn't find her; he scanned the gathering crowd and didn't see her face. Damn them—had they lied to him about Yen Ling? Was she lying sick in some fly blown shack, or—dead? Damn them for keeping her from him.

"Captain." Hong's voice was flat, tentative, devoid of welcome.

"Major Hong." Keenan fought to keep his legs steady and the heavy smell of wood smoke brought salt into his mouth.

Someone helped Father Lim support and guide Keenan toward a shadow clump of mud shacks; the moon slipped behind a ragged sawtooth mountain. Inside the largest shack was bright with oil lamps, shielded from the night by quilts at windows and door. It was familiar, the table, the plainly uniformed men poised behind it. Keenan thought he recognized the man in the center.

"Ah—Captain Carlisle. Much time has passed."

Keenan was right; this was buck general Jeng Wei Li of Mao's general staff. He had been beside the Chairman when Mao asked that Keenan take a message to Washington. And here he was at an airstrip in the boondocks to see to the captive Chiang Kai-shek. So the audacious plan had come down from the very top. Even so, Keenan still thought the idea was bad, especially if anything happened to the Peanut, no matter the cause.

Wang crossed the room, blue cap in hand, simple blue jacket and high-neck blouse proclaiming him of high rank. From close behind Keenan, Major Hong whispered, "Colonel Wang of intelligence. Bad to strike that one, comrade."

"Yes, General," Keenan said. "I carried the Chairman's message. My superiors did not listen."

Sighing, the general said, "We know, but the Japanese grow bolder, and very soon, your country will be at war with them. Perhaps then your generals will choose an ally more carefully."

"I hope so, sir."

Wang stirred, and in English, General Jeng said, "The operation went well?"

"Perfectly, sir—except for the interference of this foreign devil. The airplane was parked properly, so that when the generalissimo landed, for a moment he was beyond view of the waiting Americans. The bodyguards were tired and expected no attack. We overcame them without a sound and carried Chiang into our airplane. We were almost airborne before the fools realized what had happened."

"No aircraft pursued you?"

Turning his cap in his hands, Wang said, "Two fighter planes found us, but dared not fire. Their fuel ran low and they were forced to turn back before discovering our destination."

"Very good, Colonel. Now, have the generalissimo brought before this board, and we will quickly finish our business."

Wang hesitated and Keenan felt the ice picks of his eyes. "Sir," Wang said, "what of this foreign devil? If it had not been for several men begging for his life, I would have left him in his own blood."

Jeng nodded. "Comrades that have fought hard and traveled long roads together respect each other. His fate is in my hands—my hands alone, Colonel. Now bring in Chiang Kai-shek."

Father Lim and the other guerrilla urged Keenan aside, leading him to a stool against the mud wall. Gratefully, Keenan sank onto it, his knees weak. Head back and touching the wall, he smelled China—memories of food, wisps of urine, animal and human, the echoes of dead and buried oil lamps. What was the smell of hope?

Yen Ling was hope and beauty; Yen Ling was love, but here other gods, ugly gods, were stronger.

Shuffling, face down and bald head gleaming, hands bound behind his back, Chiang Kai-shek was pushed before the table. In his high-necked uniform with the golden sunburst upon his left breast, the old man looked stunned and defeated. He was in the presence of his most hated enemies, and helpless. Slowly, he lifted his face to stare at General Jeng Wei Li.

Keenan caugh his breath. It couldn't be, and yet—oh, lord, what if he was wrong? He'd be suspected of more collaboration with the enemy. But he had seen the Peanut close up more than once, when the man came to plot with Chennault of the AVG, and once he'd come accidently nose-to-nose.

"General Jeng! That man is not Chiang Kai-shek, but a double he often uses!"

For a split second, there was no sound in the hut. Then Colonel Wang hissed like a serpent about to strike, and lunged across the room at Keenan, a knife flashing in his uplifted fist.

CHAPTER 43

INTERNATIONAL NEWS SERVICE—Kunming, China, April 20, 1941:
Generalissimo Chiang Kai-shek is safe in his frontline headquarters, despite a bizarre attempt to kidnap him yesterday.
A strike force of communist guerrillas infiltrated an airfield
the American Volunteer Group flies from and overwhelmed
Nationalist guards. Then they knocked out a man they
thought to be the generalissimo and spirited him off in a
stolen AVG cargo plane. Night pursuit by fighter planes into
the communist interior failed to pinpoint the escape plane's
landing place.

Nationalist intelligence officers immediately announced they
had heard rumors of the kidnap plot and sent in one of the
doubles used by Chiang Kai-shek to avoid assassination.
The generalissimo himself spoke on open radio, condemn-
ing the communists for an outlaw act against a head of
state, and pointing out what he has often said before, that
the Reds are more danger to China than the Japanese
invaders.

Keenan dropped to one knee and got one arm up across his
face in a desperate attempt to block the knife slashing down
at his throat. Too late, too slow; it was a hell of a way to
die.

Wang twisted awkwardly in midair and struck. Only the
tip of the blade nicked Keenan's sleeve and burned across

his forearm. Wang plunged on to land upon his knees and whirl around like a cat.

Father Lim wavered up from the floor where he'd thrown his body across Wang's legs to save Keenan's life.

"Stop!" General Jeng shouted. "This imposter is not Chiang! Colonel—I ordered you to stop!"

Lifting his stool, Keenan stared at Wang crouched with eyes glittering brighter than the steel blade making swift and hungry arcs before him.

"Colonel!"

Wang jumped straight up, the knife extended like a deadly pointer.

The shot exploded like a cannon in the room, and the bullet slammed Wang back into the wall upon a crimson spatter of blood. Into the whirling gunsmoke General Jeng said, "Fool; you were ordered," and holstered his pistol. The Peanut's double curled upon the floor, arms wrapped about his head as he whimpered.

Keenan moved slowly to Father Lim and held out his hand. "Thank you." The old man's calloused palm trembled against his own, and a hint of tears stood in the rheumy eyes.

Jeng said, "Drag that carrion out of here, and take the imitation Chiang, also. Intelligence will question him thoroughly. Now—" he rose and the men beside him did, too. "Now, what are we to do with you, Captain Carlisle? It is unfortunate that you interfered with the raid and made it necessary for you to be brought here. But without you, we might have wasted much time with the imposter, or even gone so far as to claim we had the real Chiang and lost much face."

Keenan said, "Saving face may be the death of China."

"So." Jeng waved his associates from the hut. "You have studied my country?"

"In the field only."

Nodding, Jeng said, "A graduate course of itself. Will you join me for tea, Captain?"

That quickly, the mood changed and the shack cleared; only the bloody smears on the wall and floor showed what had gone on. Keenan didn't say it, but he felt more than saving face was involved in Wang's attack; the other reason was Yen Ling. She wasn't here, but Wang had known where she was. Now who knew? She wasn't a dream, damnit, even though she was the woman that men dreamed of, the princess who walked the night and brought fever to lonely beds.

Keenan's eyes shuttered and memory paraded women across his eyelids, movie queens and strange lovely women passing on the street, all unattainable. Nancy was beautiful in her way—not exotic, but a girlish freshness; Kirstin was beautiful, as a fine blooded mare is beautiful.

But Yen Ling made them all into weak images; skin softer than rose petals and hair of thundered midnight, eyes that reached into the marrow of a man's bones. The hotly clenching depths of her sleek body completed Keenan in a way no other woman could match. The yin and the yang; birth and death.

Opening his eyes, he saw a stooped crone shuffle in with sugarless green tea and some kind of dried weed on a bamboo plate. She did not look up.

"Please to sit," the general said, and Keenan joined him at the table.

"Now—what are we to do with you, Captain?"

Hot and bitter, the tea cleared Keenan's head. "Send me back or attach me to Major Hong again?"

"Ah, yes—the woman."

"In part, yes. The Nationalists know of my time with Major Hong, so I have been kept inactive since returning to China. I am a soldier without a mission, and therefore no soldier at all."

"Nurse Chang is no longer with Hong's unit. She was stationed at headquarters for some time before her present assignment."

Swallowing, Keenan inhaled steam from the tea bowl. "May I learn where she is now?"

The general slurped his tea. "Foreigners never fail to amaze me. Of what importance is one woman, no matter how lovely? There are always other beautiful women happy to attend a man of stature. Upon a sleeping quilt little difference can be told."

Keenan tasted the dried weed; a touch bitter, it wasn't bad. The back of his head still ached from Father Lim's wallop. He said, "If a man is fortunate, he finds that rare woman who fits his hand like a favorite weapon, who fits the grip of his legs like his favorite horse. Even more rare is the woman whose brain is the equal of his own, making the blending complete, and making a man stronger and more complete for it. The yin and yang, General, male and female, neither whole by itself."

"Indeed; my first wife is all those things to me, but my taking other wives was her idea, mostly to ease the house-keeping burden. I don't suppose that Nurse Chang would—" General Jeng smiled. "I suppose not. Foreign devils have a way of infecting us Chinese with modern ideas. Your rare lady is now in Singapore, acting as the Chairman's agent, a listening post."

"Singapore—damn!"

"Yet another jewel in England's imperial crown. Nurse Chang speaks with a British accent and fits in as well as any Oriental can. The Chairman believes that Singapore will fall to the Japanese soon after England enters the war, and wishes to offer support troops to avert such a loss. Our agents there keep us informed."

Taking another bite of the green leaves, Keenan frowned. "I've studied Singapore's defenses. Those huge coast artillery guns—"

"Are permanently emplaced in concrete to cover the sea approaches; they cannot be turned to face the jungle."

"The British believe that jungle to be impassable."

Jeng leaned back in his chair and brought out cigarettes, dark tobacco hand rolled in coarse rice paper. Keenan accepted one with thanks. The general said, "You have marched with the Japanese; do you believe any terrain is impassable to troops driven as much by duty to their god emperor as the flat of a samurai sword?"

"No. If the English can't guard their backs, you're right; Singapore will collapse, and open a rich new area for the Japs to feed upon."

Pungent cigarette smoke eddied around Jeng's head. "You do not wish to go back to the airfield? We intend to return the cargo plane with apologies and denials that communists were involved. We will insist that a maddened warlord set the attack; when we discovered it, naturally we put a stop to such outlawry. We will request that our pilot be sent home."

"Good political move, General. But if I'm to be kept under arrest of quarters, I would rather be in the field. I'll write a letter stating that I am assigning myself as an observer with communist troops."

Word would fly to the Hill and General Belvale, who would understand, if not approve. The Hill seemed farther off day by day, and Yen Ling turned more dreamlike. Keenan clamped his hand hard upon the empty tea bowl. All-out war was hovering over the entire world, a gigantic bloodletting that the United States couldn't avoid. How would it affect him over here? General Belvale would order him home to command American troops.

If the Japanese struck fast and struck hard, just returning home might develop into a major problem. They would control the air and most of the sea. He might conceivably be stationed in the Far East for the duration. And if he still had not found Yen Ling—

Duty, you clown; honor and country and the Hill. These are things more important than man and woman, more important than love, for without the family and the Hill, free men and women might be slaves and love against the law as a democratic weakness.

General Jeng coughed and brought Keenan back to a hut in a country already bloodied by years of war. "Captain, if you truly wish to be with us, we are honored. I am about to send Major Hong on a long and dangerous mission to Malaysia. A narrow neck of land seven hundred kilometers north of Singapore cries out as the perfect natural ambush for a blocking force. When the Japanese come down to penetrate the jungles—and they will come—they will be shocked and confused to find Chinese soldiers facing them. If the British accept our help, we can continue to ferry troops there. It is to our definite advantage that the British remain in Malaysia and Burma."

Keenan nodded. Here sat a man who had no doubt grown

up in a peasant hut, hungry and working hard all his life, a man whose contact with life beyond the borders of China had been negligible, and his education hit-or-miss military. Yet Jeng knew more about geopolitics than most Harvard professors and China experts. Seven hundred kilometers from Singapore and Yen Ling was an interminable jungle haul, but a hell of a lot closer than he was now.

"You will send word to my grandfather? He is—"

"We know of General Belvale. The mission will be difficult and far away, and often with no communication. But he will be kept informed of your whereabouts as we know it."

Keenan said, "Only the Japanese really know anything about jungle warfare so this is a good opportunity for me to learn. My country will need any knowledge I can bring back."

Rising, General Jeng held out his hand. "You are an interesting man, Captain. May we always fight on the same side. I will give Major Hong his orders."

"Sir," Keenan said, and saluted.

Father Lim was first into the shack, grinning hugely as he hurried to wrap his skinny arms around Keenan, showing his few broken teeth. Major Hong no longer stood back, but smiled and nodded, clapping his hands in hearty approval. "Hong's soldiers welcome you back to our ranks."

A gourd of strong cassia wine passed up through the soldiers with tough parts of a duck that had been cooked in ashes. Soldiers packed the little house and spilled over outside to peer through the single window. Seated at the table with his old comrades in arms, Keenan felt the camaraderie that for soldiers made up for cold and hunger and pain.

Leaning close, Hong told him that they were now in the village of Mengshan, fairly deep into Nationalist territory, and that the unit would pull out in small groups to hike overland to the Kiungchow Straits. Crossing there, they would then travel the great island of Hainan to Lingshui Bay, where their boats waited, armed and provisioned.

Boats, Keenan thought, and tried to picture the map in his head. God! They would have to ride fragile seagoing junks past the entire length of Indochina, sailing around a point that was a smaller version of Cape Horn and as dangerous. Then they had to cross open water to Malaya. How far, all told?—eighteen hundred to two thousand kilometers as a shark might swim, through seas that could turn suddenly from merely wild to typhoon insane. They would have to fool Japanese coast watchers and Japanese planes, avoid swift patrol boats.

"Mama said there'd be days like this," Keenan muttered, "but she didn't say they'd come in bunches like goddamn bananas."

"What say?" Hong wanted to know.

"Old American army adage," Keenan answered. "Like being up shit creek with a tennis racquet for a paddle."

"No understand," Major Hong said, having to shout over a group of men singing.

"You will," Keenan promised. "Everybody will."

CHAPTER 44

UNITED PRESS—Ayer, Mass., June 3, 1941: This sleepy little village far off the beaten path is now a beehive of activity as 18,000 U.S. troops have gone into intense training here at Fort Devens. Ayer, its population suddenly more than doubled since the aged World War post was reopened, is coping with this "invasion" as best it can. Olive drab uniforms flood the streets and pack the cafes and bars. The red numeral "1" on the left shoulder proclaims that the wearers are members of the First Infantry Division, the oldest and probably best known army unit.

Fort Devens had a special perfume—raw mud and fresh pine lumber; coal smoke from barracks furnaces. Chad Belvale stared out his window at Second Battalion headquarters and saw much more to be done, more time-consuming labor that could better be used training in the field. This outfit could use all the field work they could get, although the Sixteenth Regiment—indeed, the entire First Division—might be the best trained and most combat ready unit in the army.

It wasn't enough. The training wasn't hairy enough and the men weren't in the hard, sinewy condition that combat called for. During the pullout from France, British soldiers were pushed beyond their limits, and some of them didn't make it. They fell out of retreating columns to await SS execution beside the road, or at the least, to face spending the rest of the war behind the barbed wire of prison camps.

You couldn't train out a tendency for men to panic at their baptism of fire. But loyalty to their friends and to their outfit could overcome that first blind instinct to run, to save their own lives. Chad was glad that so far no draftees had reported to his battalion. He was used to regular army people and their acceptance of rough-and-tumble discipline. He didn't know how handcuff volunteers fresh from easier jobs and loving homes would work out mixing with tough, cynical dogfaces, and he anticipated trouble.

It was a damned shame that United States security was forced to depend upon the Selective Service Act, so recently passed. What happened to patriotism? Shrugging off his irritation and attributing it in part to still no letter from Stephanie, to 2nd Lt. Owen Belvale's know-it-all attitude, and to his executive officer, Maj. Clifton Huckbee. He meant to have Huckbee's ass on toast, but the sly bastard stayed just out of official reach while he constantly and insidiously undercut Chad's programs.

And of all the regiments in this man's army, how in bloody hell did Col. Luther Farrand get assigned to this one? He had too much rank to be the division chaplain, much less anything lower down the pole. But here came the holy son of a bitch in all his divine glory, to help fuck up a good outfit. Was he cunning enough to go hand in glove with Huckbee? The prissy bastard never had much use for Chad, and the feeling was more than mutual. One more roadblock for Chad to overcome, and by God and General Belvale, he sure as hell would break through all of them.

A wet gray wind with no hint of spring washragged his face as he left headquarters. Zipping his field jacket and settling his garrison cap firmly upon his head, he waved off the command car driver and walked.

Chad wore the high-top boondocker shoes of an enlisted man, and used low quarters only on inspections or parades. The whole damned fort was a swamp, except for where the troops had hauled in sand and spread it. In some company areas, squares of grassy sod had been brought in and laid side by side, guarded by Keep Off signs. Some day the scraped off sections of Devens would return to normal dryness and green grass. For now mud or deep sand was an infuriating fact of life.

But as Chad remembered, war zones weren't dry and well-trimmed playing fields. That was something else: his son and most of the other officers acted as if the coming war were some kind of game, to be played by a musty set of outmoded rules as stated in Army Regulations and Officers Mess traditions. Chad had to teach them that there was only one rule in combat: stay alive. A supplementary commandment was kill the bastards.

H Company was loading on the new 39 Dodge half-tons, men wrestling their water-cooled 30s aboard, the antitank section struggling with air-cooled 50 calibers and the mortar platoon fighting cumbersome 81s. For the 30, some squads still used the ridiculous slots in wooden seats with a chain securing the tripod to the truck bed. In an air raid, the gunner was supposed to scramble over and around those seats while trying to get a clear shot at a speeding plane. He'd be damned lucky if he didn't pump a few rounds into the next truck.

At Chad's insistence, division grudgingly allowed him to install tall iron pipes centered just behind the front seats, just the size to lock the gun pintle. It gave the gunner much more freedom of movement, although leaving much to be desired. It was the best Chad could do with temporary gun mounts, and he was grateful for the trucks; General Belvale's attack on Washington? More like Crusty Carlisle. Chad had been expecting the old machine-gun carts that moved as slow as the men dragging them. The Germans were masters of swift movement, the blitzkreig, and American units had better be able to match it. The trench warfare thinking of Washington generals like Skelton was the same as the French and their Maginot Line. Skelton's bunch didn't see the likeness.

"Good morning, sir."

Returning the sharp salute, Chad blinked at the first sergeant he had never seen before: three stripes up, two down and a diamond. Wide shouldered and narrow hipped, the man who stood just outside H Company's orderly room was no youngster, but every soldier should be in such shape. The gray hair was brush cut with white sidewalls—clipped to the skin above the ears, and fist tracks marked a lined face.

"Sergeant—?"

"Donnely, sir; new topkick for H Company; they call me Big Mike, Major."

"What happened to Sergeant Felber?"

"More or less promoted, sir. Warrant officer now, neither fish nor fowl. When I heard of this opening in a line outfit, I naturally applied, sir."

Chad wished that Donnely was in Class A uniform; then he could read the hashmarks for length of service and possibly ribbons for the World War, although Big Mike didn't look all that old. "Wait a minute—Donnely, Donnely; you didn't soldier with my great-uncle, Gen. Preston Belvale?"

"Damned right, sir; damned fine horseman, and a better officer, a better man, never lived. When he called me—oh, shit; begging the major's pardon, sir."

Chad grinned. "I wasn't supposed to know that the general sent me some covert help? Never mind, Sergeant; I'm damned glad to have you."

Donnely's grin was wider. "Was the major coming to visit, or to inspect? There's a field problem today, and the company commander is with the troops, but Lt. Belvale's in the orderly room catching up on paperwork."

"I'll go see him, thanks."

The company clerk was busy at his typewriter or pretending to be. Turn sharp right across the little room for the CO's closed office; knock.

"Yeah—come in."

Hat under his left arm, Chad went in. "Owen; how's it going?"

Snapping to his feet, Owen said, "Just fine, sir. Would you like some coffee?"

"As you were, son; coffee sounds good."

Sitting in the one chair across from the desk, Chad accepted coffee from a silver percolator that cost two or three times what a private drew over the pay table. He told Owen that, and suggested not flaunting the family riches. "People resent you for having money; soldiers will be worse."

Owen poured coffee into china cups. "I never noticed. No chance to spend money at the Academy. Should I trade the Packard for an Austin?"

The coffee cup grated against Chad's teeth. "You should *listen*, damnit! You always have a smartass comeback. Your father may keep taking them; your battalion commander sure as billy hell won't. I thought of shipping you out, say to some underground mess kit repair company where you could retire in twenty years, still a second lieutenant. But you're a pretty good line officer. You'll be better when the bullshit wears off. A second john ought to spend ninety percent of his time listening, and the other ten percent asking questions. Thinking and giving orders come later."

Owen sat behind the desk. "Yes, sir."

Chad couldn't read his son's face; the kid might be faking. He said, "I mean to bear down harder. One thirty-mile hike per week—fifteen out and run a field exercise; fifteen back. One twenty-miler with accent on speed; a pair of nighttime ten-milers, compass check runs and quick defense positions. This outfit needs legs."

Owen put down his cup. "What? G-3 hasn't sent down any kind of word on—"

"G-3 doesn't know it yet, but the colonel will approve."

"Oh, yes, old friend of the family. Is it moral to use family connections, but not the family treasury?"

Leaning forward, Chad said, "What the hell is the matter with you, boy?"

Owen looked down at the desktop, at his fingers tangled there. "I miss everything that used to be—you and mom together, Farley and me; the real family things."

"Have you written your mother or gone to see her?"

"No, sir."

"Why not? I did—went to see her in Texas. If I can make peace—"

Owen shook his head. "I couldn't stand seeing her with that—that guy. You were overseas, missing in action, and she—there she was with another man. She ought to come apologize to you; to Farley and me, too."

Afraid he would crush the cup, Chad put it down on the desk. "Kirstin has nothing to apologize for—not to me, and that much less to you and your brother. *Who* the hell are you?"

"*What* the hell are you? You allow a goddamn civilian to steal your wife and do nothing about it. You didn't try to get her back, but I can't blame you for that. One betrayal calls for another, and—"

Chad stood up. "That's enough! If anybody's at fault, it's me, not your mother. Blame me for not knowing her needs, blame me for things you don't know and can't understand. Blame the goddamn army—anything you want. Then let it go because it's none of your business now. Pay attention to your soldiering."

Swinging out of the office before one of them said too much, Chad stood for a moment in the company street. Kirstin was only on his mind for a second; then Stephanie took her place. Only he knew about Stephanie, and it was better that way, although he longed to talk about her to someone. She was probably with her husband this very minute, Singapore behind him, a casual fling behind her. Goddamn.

He stalked over to G Company and found it almost deserted, the orderly room held down by the company clerk, the kitchen crew readying the midday meal for the Marmite cans which would keep food warm, if not hot. How would the kitchens find and feed their companies under fire? Worse, how would they reach the troops with the Krauts strafing and bombing? An emergency plan had to be worked out for mess sergeants to use, and more stress laid upon finding and feeding the troops. On maneuvers the kitchen truck often didn't catch up for days. It had better not work that way in combat. Men fought better and longer on a full gut because they spent less time scrounging.

He smiled, thinking of Leftenant Merriman and the action they'd seen in France. One hell of a man, John J. Merriman, and Chad hoped he was still all right, still in one cheerfully obscene piece.

And Stephanie at her ack-ack guns? Gutsy, duty bound woman standing fast as the bombs screamed down and the fires roared around her. "Be safe, darling," he whispered. "Please be safe."

F Company had too many men in barracks, men who were supposed to be out in the field. Chad slammed into the orderly room. The company clerk knocked over a stack of papers when he jumped to attention. First Sgt. Ogden was as quick to rise, but without clumsiness.

"Why isn't the company out in the field? Where the hell is Lieutenant Mulrooney?"

"Sir," the sergeant said, "the company's in the field, except for the lieutenant and us—and the men marked quarters from sick call."

"That many?" Chad fisted his hat in one hand. "It looks like half the company's in barracks. Is there some kind of epidemic I don't know about?"

"Sir—the doctor—it's pretty easy for him to mark a man quarters for one day. And the chaplain wanted—"

"Chaplain? Where's Mulrooney?"

Ogden's face quivered and turned redder. Shrugging, he lifted a heavy hand to point at the closed door of the CO's office.

"All right," Chad said. "Now about this chaplain—"

"Bird colonel, sir. Come in here hollering he needs men to landscape his chapel; pulled them right off the trucks, like. Only he ain't come back for them yet."

"Chaplain Farrand?" The bastard was starting early to prove he was a bastard.

"Yes, sir. I never knew chaplains went that high—a full bird colonel."

"You and the clerk go get some coffee."

Ogden jerked a hand at his corporal. "We're gone, sir."

Chad opened the CO's door and closed it behind him when he saw Mulrooney with his arms on the desk top and his head pillowed on his arms. The smell of whiskey was overpowering. Chad stepped around the desk and took a handful of nondescript brown hair; he yanked Mulrooney's head erect. With his other hand, he slapped the man's face hard; back and forth, *slap-slap!* Mulrooney grunted and struggled weakly, pawing at Chad's arms.

"Wha-what's matter—hey, goddamnit!"

Chad let go the hair. "Sit up, Mulrooney! Straighten up, goddamn you!"

"Wha the fuck—"

When Chad slapped him again, Mulrooney swayed and threw a long, slow right fist. Bobbing under it, Chad slammed the man in the belly. Mulrooney fell over on his side and threw up. When he struggled up and wiped his mouth he was pale, and although bloodshot, his eyes were clearer. He struggled to get to his feet and hold onto the desk.

"Half of your company is goofing off in barracks, some of them not even bothering to play sick. And you're drunk on duty, Lieutenant, a court-martial offense."

Swaying, Mulrooney found his chair again. "Wait a minute—wait a goddamn minute—don't give a damn if you're some— some kind of hotshot thinks he's goin' to change—"

Chad didn't slap the clown again, and he didn't throw a punch because he was afraid he couldn't pull it. "Do you want out of the army, Lieutenant?"

"Out—out?" Mulrooney scrabbled in his shirt pocket and found a mangled pack of Camels. He fought one out, dropped the pack and couldn't find a match. "Ten fucking years—goddamn reserve; no promotions 'cause I ain't no ring polisher—but I'm not getting out. Hell, no. Go ahead and gig me for whatever, you—you bastard. You won't get a piece of old Mulrooney's ass."

Coldly, Chad said, "You're a disgrace to the uniform. Worse, you've let a company go sour. I won't gig you, Lieutenant; so Major Huckbee can whitewash the report."

He wheeled from the room and picked up the phone in the orderly room. "Give me the provost marshal."

Mulrooney wobbled from his office to lean against the door frame. "What—what you think—"

Chad spoke into the phone, crisp and concise. Mulrooney staggered forward and Chad put one hand on his chest. "Don't offer me the chance. I'd enjoy stomping a mud hole in your ass and then kicking it dry."

"But you—you called the provost, the MPs—like I'm some kind of criminal or a fucked up enlisted man. Goddamnit —you can't treat an officer like this."

"You wouldn't make a pimple on a good corporal's ass,"

Chad said. "The protect your brother officer, cover up for any officer, those days are gone and pretty soon the whole army will know it. There's a war to fight, and there's no place for losers who get good men killed."

The first sergeant and company clerk stood outside the orderly room and watched the MPs tuck Mulrooney into a jeep and speed away. Chad saw other men peeping through barracks windows.

He said to Sergeant Ogden, "Get all those goldbricks out of the barracks and have them hiked out to the field problem, since they missed the trucks. And if the chaplain wants to know where his landscaping detail is, tell him to call me. Take over, Sergeant—I'll send you another officer."

"Yes, sir," Ogden said. "Oh, hell, yes, sir!"

CHAPTER 45

ASSOCIATED PRESS—Ayer, Mass., August 16, 1941: John D. Rockefeller, Jr., was arrested here today for writing a check.

Now in uniform, Private Rockefeller walked into the local Buick dealer's showroom, pointed out an expensive luxury car and said, "I'll take that one; how much?"

Mr. Robert E. Bridewell, the owner, jokingly priced the car for the twenty-one dollar a month enlisted man. His laugh faded when Private Rockefeller wrote out a check and handed it to him.

Mr. Bridewell called the police.

Private Rockefeller properly identified himself.

The police left.

Smiling, Private Rockefeller drove off in his new car.

Did Mr. Bridewell learn anything from the incident? "Be kind to soldiers," he said. "You never know."

The trucks were spaced well apart, the 30 caliber machine guns ready upon their tube mounts, the gunners behind them nervous, smoking and glancing often to the far right front. That's where the tow plane would come from, the sleeve target floating well behind it.

"It had better be *far* behind the plane," Col. L.L. Simbeaux said. "These men have never fired on an aircraft target before. I'd hate to be that pilot."

The regimental commander looked years younger since his retirement had been postponed. Although he probably wouldn't get to take the outfit overseas, he was making the most of his rejuvenation before being farmed out to a desk job. Chad liked the man.

Simbeaux said, "D Company's guns did very well, and M Company is chafing at the bit."

"If the colonel were a betting man," Chad said, "I would offer three to two on an H Company platoon winning that three-day pass for high score."

Simbeaux smiled. "Done; I'll take thirty dollars from the Belvale treasure chest."

Out of sight, Chad heard the plane motor. "It's a bet, sir." Lifting his voice, he called: "Look alert, men!"

Chuckling, Simbeaux filled his pipe. Then he said, "I don't mind taking advantage of you young troopers. D Company's first platoon scored three hundred seventy-nine hits out of a possible six hundred. Damned good shooting."

"Pretty good," Chad agreed. "The second platoon is up now. Watch the fifth squad, Cpl. Johnny Knowles."

Over the trees came the little Piper, the sleeve target gleaming white. Chad had looked in on the heavy weapons company training as antiaircraft and spoken with Knowles and the platoon sergeant. Now some of the old-time know-how might pay off. In Europe he hadn't seen ground fire down any Kraut planes, but that didn't mean it couldn't be done.

Four guns swung lightly with their wooden ammo boxes attached, four ball and one tracer through 150 rounds in each fabric belt. When the plane passed the firing point, all guns zeroed in on the sleeve, the bright red streaks of tracer reaching for the swiftly moving target. One set was right on, and the rattle of the guns was deafening. The sharp, exciting tang of gunsmoke hung heavy around Chad; he breathed deeply of it and the colonel coughed.

One gun continued to hammer at the flying sleeve after the others had stopped. When it too fell silent, the plane was gone. "Bingo!" Corporal Knowles yelled. "Ate the bastard up!"

Chad grinned; Fifth squad should have chewed up the target; they had sneaked another full belt into the game. No other gun in the platoon—hell, in the regiment!—could fire fast enough to get off three hundred rounds in the time allotted for 150.

Walking toward the celebrating squad to congratulate them, Chad was halted by the colonel's hand on his arm. "Wait up, Belvale! I heard that gun taking off faster than—" Dropping his hand, Simbeaux said, "It takes a real old-timer to know that trick. You used nickels, didn't you—in the recoil group? Damn, and I was going to hustle *you*."

Chad laughed. "Only four, alternating with the fiber disks. Jacked the cyclic rate of fire from five-hundred fifty to about seven-hundred fifty. The coins throw the bolt back about twice as fast since there's no give to them. If we use up a bolt, what the hell; the army has more. It's something the troops have to learn—improvise, work things their way and the hell with regulations. Knowles will pull the coins before anybody thinks to check the gun. The extra belt already got stuffed behind the water can."

"Three day passes for the platoon," Simbeaux said, "for ingenuity if nothing else. Nickels, for God's sake. And I owe you twenty bucks."

"I'll buy you dinner."

Walking beside the colonel to the command car, Chad saw Major Huckbee with E Company's commander. Come to observe, or to look for an opportunity to make trouble? Huckbee had really been shaken by his yes man Mulrooney being thrown into the guardhouse. Frantic calls to Washington availed him nothing because Chad beat him to the punch with a message to the Hill. Mulrooney was being given the chance to resign his commission, and if he refused to take the honorable way out, then there would be a trial he had no chance of winning.

It was rough, ridding the army of a seasoned soldier, one who might have been carried until retirement in peacetime. His kind was often hospitalized for "pneumonia" while he dried out, while other men covered his failings and ran his company. It was no longer peacetime; no more polo and quiet hours in the barracks Wednesday afternoons. Until his blooding in France—and yes, England as well—Chad would have joined the protection society of regular army officers, a group he might have himself needed some day.

Now was altogether different; now was down and dirty and full of blood; now was the enemy whose face these men had not seen. Chad had, and back when he was guiding a captured Kraut tank, realized that only the strong would survive, only the merciless. So farewell, Mulrooney; you'll never get drunk and waste good men.

The command car pulled off the hill where yet another outfit—M Company's heavy weapons—began firing. Chad couldn't detect any stepped-up bursts. The colonel lighted his pipe and the apple smell was recognizable before wind whipped it from the open car. Simbeaux said, "Huckbee giving you a hard time?"

"Trying. I pulled his teeth with Mulrooney, who just might have been his boy. Now he doesn't know which way to slither. I meant it that way, so his cohorts Scruggs and Deas turn uneasy."

"Why don't you give F Company to Lieutenant Belvale?"

"I don't think that's a good idea, sir. He has so little troop experience and would be wide open for Huckbee to stab him in order to get at me."

The open-sided command car—doggies were calling it a "peep" as opposed to the versatile little buggy, the jeep—leaned into a turn and the wind grew colder. Simbeaux said, "I tried to transfer the bastard, but the War Department bucked it back disapproved. But wait until we're alerted for overseas; he'll be long gone to Washington and quick, safe promotions."

The car stopped at regimental headquarters first and Chad saluted the colonel, then rode to his own battalion. Outside H Company a crowd swirled, cooks and mortar men who didn't have to go to the range today. At the fringe of the crowd stood a Plymouth staff car.

"Hey," the command car driver said. "Fight!"

Chad followed slowly; brawls were apt to dissolve at the sight of an officer. Both fighters were bloody but still moving well, circling each other and panting. So long as nobody was getting killed, Chad figured that a good fight cleared the air.

The staff car disgorged another officer, Col. Luther Farrand, red faced and frowning.

"Ten-*hut!*" yelled his driver, a ratty-eyed buck sergeant named—Dunstan? No, Thornton.

Doggies snapped to attention, with the exception of the gladiators, who kept slogging away at each other.

"Stop that!" the colonel shouted. "Do you hear me—stop it, *now!* That's an order!"

One battler stepped back and looked at the chaplain. He was a cook in whites, bloody whites now. The other soldier hauled off a barn door right hand that dropped him in his tracks.

"Arrest that man!" Colonel Farrand ordered, and his beady-eyed driver stepped forward.

"As you were!" Chad moved into the circle. "My battalion, Chaplain, and I give the orders here."

"These—these irresponsible men—"

Chad strode closer. "*Soldiers*, Chaplain, and damn a soldier who won't fight." He stared down the beady-eyed sergeant, who swallowed and backed up.

Over his shoulder he called, "All right, men—break it up!" And as the crowd melted away, he lowered his voice and stood near Farrand. "Training has turned tough and the whole regiment is on edge. Enlisted doesn't mean stupid, and everyone realizes it's a matter of time until we're at war. The men are beginning to wonder if they'll measure up, if their years of service readied them for what's to come."

Farrand's face was still mottled, his jaw set but his eyes starting to slide away. "You give too much credit to enlisted men, Major. Drunkards and fornicators who must be forced to their duties—"

Whispering now, Chad said, "And you're overstepping your authority. You have the rank, but not the command. Stay the hell away from my people, Luther."

Before the man could find an answer, Chad swung off toward his office. Bad blood, he thought; as Kipling wrote, single men in barracks didn't turn to plaster saints. Certain men, like certain boss dogs, would always lift hackles at each other. Maybe a battalion beer party would clear the air and bring on a few brawls that would drain off that bad blood, at least for a while. When this outfit went into combat, every man would depend upon every other man for his life—and for the success of the mission. One was almost as important as the other.

Nodding at Corporal Guist, his clerk, he went into his cubicle and wrote out a personal check, one fat enough to cover all the beer a thousand men could put away next Saturday night, and all the sizzling civilian burgers. No cold cuts a la Sunday menu horsecock, and no shit-on-a-shingle; first class for this experiment. SOS and gallons of icy tomato juice was the perfect day-after-payday breakfast, and the softball players sweating it out in rubbery gas masks was good, too. By afternoon, hangovers were gone and the outfit could soldier. On a Sunday, the men would lick their wounds and recover on their own.

He leaned back in his chair. Lt. John J. Merriman of the Royal Fusiliers would heartily approve, his red mustache quivering. Where was Merriman now? Chad missed the ornery bastard and made a mental note to follow the last unanswered letter with another.

Stephanie; damn it, should he continue writing to her? Lighting a Camel, two packs for a quarter at the PX, he shook his head. As if he had a choice; he might put off writing for a few days, but then his need would pile up, his anger and guilt and whatever the hell else drove him to keep on sandpapering his soul, and he would write. She had answered only twice so far, and only one letter could be called personal.

Had her husband been recalled from Singapore? Duty, Leftenant Bartlett; stiff upper lip and all that. Jesus! Why hadn't he been sweating out the air raid in London's underground with somebody else, damned near any of the neatly uniformed English servicewomen? Life would be considerably simpler.

No Stephanie in it? Who was he kidding?

Chad sat up. "Corporal!"

Guist trotted in and saluted. "Sir."

"Take this to First Sergeant Donnely at H Company. Stay to help him with the arrangements. I'll call the motor pool for a deuce and a half, and have the trip ticket and orders for you to type when you get back. A beer bust, Corporal. Do you think it's a good idea?''

Glancing down at the check he held, Guist widened his eyes and nodded. ''Holy—shit! Holy shit—sir. Whatever the major says. I never saw this much money outside a company payroll. Beer bust, sir? You ain't just woofing, Major.''

After the clerk grinned himself out, Chad drew on another cigarette and exhaled slowly. Colonel Simbeaux would approve of the beer party, and Major Huckbee might see in it his chance to torpedo Chad.

What the hell. Politics were not important, but morale was.

CHAPTER 46

INTERNATIONAL NEWS SERVICE—Kill Devil Hill, Va., October 7, 1941: Legislators gathered here today in an "unofficial" capacity to discuss what one source said was the worsening tension between Japan and the United States.

Sen. Jim Shelby (D-Texas) said that President Roosevelt's oil embargo and the demand that Japan pull all troops out of China has practically guaranteed war with Japan and its Axis allies, Germany and Italy.

"Ridiculous," said Sen. Burton Wheeler (D-Montana). "American boys will never again fight on foreign soil."

Wheeler heads an antiwar, anti-FDR coalition that includes Speaker of the House Billy (Boss) Cawley. This group has successfully trimmed military appropriations bills and takes credit for keeping the United States out of "Europe's bloody wars."

General Belvale smiled as he patted Kirstin's slim, tanned hand and left her to oversee the refreshments coming from stoves and refrigerators. Minerva would normally be in the kitchen, unsettling the cooks and waiters, but her duties as hostess kept her swirling around in the main ballroom, and Belvale was glad that Kirstin had come in with Jim Shelby.

Out on a side porch, he paused for a moment to savor the afternoon, to feast his senses upon the sapphire haze that jeweled the distant ridges. He tasted the excitement of autumn and the spices of wood smoke and magnolia. Also feathering the air was the hint of crisp frosts to come. A mysticism hung over the hills, a softening of any harsh realities.

Fiddler's Green, he thought, that promised final port of liberty for drowned sailors or Valhalla with its 480 gates through which dead soldiers march eight abreast; name it what you would, heaven for a fallen fighting man must be in the Blue Ridge or Great Smoky mountains. If the world held more beautiful places, he hadn't seen them.

The fallen deserved more than a covered-over foxhole or a cheap headstone in a National Cemetery where cheaper little flags—made in Japan—fluttered on Memorial Day. How did the old barracks ditty go?—give him a break, God; he's served his hitch in hell.

Faintly then, from high up on a celebrating ridge of soft green trees, came the throaty belling of a ranging hound that didn't care which hunting season was on. The music and its magic held him for a moment before slipping him back to that time early in his life when he had been sent out into the other world, the unmoneyed, tough world. It was family policy strictly adhered to. Preston Belvale's youthful duty had been to stay and sweat a while with cousins, men who worked the land to live and so, like no others, could truly become one with it.

. . . Never talkative men, they would set a spell on the front porch after supper, their work shirts sweated stiff. They rested in silence, heavy shouldered men, and watched the sun linger down and the moon rise through the loblolly pines. They had no words for the beauty they saw and would scorn anybody who tried to express it.

But every evening that it didn't rain or the mosquitoes whine too thick, they sat and watched the day go home. Then they took turns washing their feet in a chipped basin, calloused feet that had followed a mule all day, turning red dirt, and they went to bed as soon as it got dark . . .

Belvale put his hands upon the porch railing and stared at the forested ridges. He had learned much from the people of the land, not the least being that beauty existed about everywhere a man cared to look. It gleamed in the smoothness of a turning plow or the oiled perfection of a perfectly machined weapon, and echoed in the thump of the retreat gun as the colors came rippling down for the night. Precision might be beauty, and so could courage. There was beauty seen and beauty only to be sensed.

How then, to define the stark ugliness bearing down hard and fast upon this land and its people? Sudden death was never pretty, and made even less so because so much of it could have been denied. Past tense; it was too damned late to hold off the juggernaut; the heavy casualties would have to be accepted. Not approved, just accepted with the accompanying guilt.

Damnit, the guilt wasn't his, and shouldn't weigh down many of the powerful men milling about the ballroom. The farseeing among them had done their best to goad their blinded brethren to action while there was yet time. It wasn't the inevitable entrance in the war; without America in it, Hitler and his cronies would win in a walk, and after he stomped Europe, America would stand alone to be kicked in the balls, no stronger for the postponement, and probably more divided.

What nagged at Belvale was the nation yet being so unprepared. The Carolina maneuvers just past still showed trucks with signs identifying them as tanks. Antitank weapons were still two-by-fours and bicycle wheels and the army joke was: If you haven't got it, improvise, and if you can't improvise, simulate. If you can't fake it, run like hell.

The best thing about the Carolina maneuvers was meeting Chad and Owen, seeing them working together. Chief Umpire General Belvale was able to call his shots and visit where he pleased; RHIP—Rank Hath Its Privileges. Chad looked fit, the thin facial scars he'd picked up in Europe giving him a rakish look. Owen had stabilized some, and seemed efficient in his first command, but the intangible wall still hung in place between them, a bit more than the usual generation gap. It was as if Owen somehow blamed Chad for not holding onto Kirstin, for not fighting harder to keep her. And yet the boy blanked out any mention of his mother, ignoring her very name.

Maj. Clifton Huckbee was another matter. Belvale kept the man's teeth on edge by showing up too often. Huckbee fully expected reprisal, and writhed in anticipation of the axe falling. Although Belvale detested the man and the slimy politics he stood for, fair was fair and Huckbee covered his ass well through the maneuvers.

Capt. Isaac Thornton was another matter, a class A fuckup whose native stupidity deserved mention in his efficiency report. Barring direct interference from God, the dumb bastard would retire still wearing his railroad tracks, an oak leaf only as close as the sundown of eternity. Belvale grinned out at the wondrous ridges that cupped this part of the Shenandoah Valley. That entry in Thornton's file had sent a cold chill through Huckbee's other cronies and would make them better officers, if only for a little while.

Propping one hip and his cane upon the porch rail, Belvale lighted a cigar and reflected upon the Louisiana maneuvers of 1940 and this year's in North Carolina, probably the final mass workout of troops before the real thing. The operation along the Texas border pitted two Regular Army outfits against each other, the Second (Indianhead) out of Fort Bliss and the steady First Division winding up its long stint in the field at Fort Benning, Georgia before going home to New York. The maneuvers shook out both divisions, sharpened them and taught the troops that garrison living wasn't the be-all and end-all.

The operation just past? Basically political. Down from Fort Devens, the First Division did its usual thorough job, losing ground and the make-believe war only because they were supposed to. Their opponents, the weekend warriors of the National Guard, would sulk if their command posts were overrun, and they would complain to their legislators. Everyone knew that the citizen soldier was so much smarter than the misfit regulars who couldn't make it on the outside.

Belvale was impressed with the RA troops, and looked blank when the Guard unit commanders bitched that they were being stolen blind, chow and company equipment vanishing mysteriously. Old-time doggies were nothing if not excellent scroungers; as cheap as Congress was, they had to be.

"General?"

Shaking himself, he breathed deeply of the Hill's special

air and turned to face the pretty woman. "Penny," she said, jogging his memory, "Penny Colvin. I was—"

He remembered her at Lt. Walton Belvale's casketless funeral, the smooth planes of her face set in a mask of acceptance wiser than her years, her dark eyes reaching out for calming answers in the far hills. The V of her rich mouth had trembled, but remained determined not to break.

"Farley asked me to come," she said. "I hope you don't mind. He thought there'd be just a small party, only family and friends—"

The boy's delayed graduation from VMI was bad timing. Wetting down Farley Belvale's new gold bars did call for a family celebration, but his senior year siege of illnesses and playing field injuries had carried him over into makeup time, the school releasing him months behind his classmates. And it threw his special party into conflict with this political gathering.

"Kee-rist," he said. "I haven't even seen the boy yet. I'll apologize to him when we're rid of this bunch. Tell Farley—"

He blinked and really looked at her then, this more than pretty woman, this sleek and graceful woman whose stillness was only a fragile skin. He sensed the hidden movement of strong depths within her slim body. Penny and Farley? About two years had gone by since Walton was listed as KIA in Poland, and Farley was—what?—a year, eighteen months younger than Penny?

Belvale looked into her eyes again, heavily lashed eyes that did not fall away. Then he knew that this woman had been born older than most men, and that Farley was one hell of a lucky boy. Even if he was a passing fancy for pretty Penny Colvin, he had still fallen in a latrine ditch and come out smelling like Evening in Paris. A quick crumb from one woman's table could be richer than a lingering banquet at another's. Kee-rist, with Shaw he mourned that youth should be wasted upon the young.

"Tell Farley that we'll be happy to see you both, and that I'll meet you in the west family room as soon as possible."

Penny's smile was quick and easy, judging and understanding. "All right, General."

Straightening his green uniform blouse and tugging at the officers pink slacks that would never fit as militarily or comfortably as cavalry twill breeches, he flourished his walking stick and started for the ballroom, cigar gone out but tilted aggressively beneath his mustache. He concentrated upon not showing his limp.

Kirstin blocked him on the way, a pale green velvet dress bringing out her coloring wonderfully. Horses did that for a woman, he thought, gave her a proud, erect back and a lithe way of moving, that alert holding of her head. Horses shared their strength.

"That woman—did she come here with my son? Wasn't she Walt's— "

"She did; she was; now she's Farley's girl. Does it matter to you?"

"Not really. But she seems so much more—mature."

"Maybe we're selling Farley short. Whatever, that's a lot of woman."

Kirstin glanced over her shoulder through the ornate French doors of the noisy ballroom. "Can you hold your campaigning a minute?"

"Sure; now it's not so much a campaign as a sly pointing out of something that both camps will remember: misguided obstructionism. So by the next meeting, the isolationists will be only too happy to inundate us with everything we ask for and more. I just wish it hadn't taken so damned long."

Her eyes were serious. "Is war so close?"

"I hope not, but my bet would say yes."

"And poor Keenan is caught somewhere in China."

"He may be better off than the rest of us. Don't you mean poor Nancy?"

Kirstin cupped her elbows with both hands. He thought the weather was too changeable for her to be on the porch without a wrap. Had full summer come blistering to Boerne, Texas?

She said, "Nancy's doing okay; she's looking around for a little business; meanwhile, she's going back to school. Come on, General—you're not all that easy in your mind about Keenan."

Here in the mountains, weather could do an abrupt about-face as thunderheads built up to come howling down the valleys. Texas had gulley washers, he recalled. Was a dark and lightning shift a forerunner of the future?

Gently, he took her upper arm and moved her through the partly swung-back French doors. "A glass of champagne or a snort of bourbon? You ever notice how *snort* and *champagne* just don't go together, but sipping whiskey is just right?"

Was her smile forced? "Because wine isn't made from common Virginia branch water?"

"Something like that; too peasant class for snob Frenchmen." Nodding to this man, slowing to shake hands with that one, howdying a couple of more, Belvale guided her to a reasonably quiet corner. "Bourbon, then. I see Senator Shelby there by the bar."

Kirstin glanced. "Jim's doing his damnedest to be polite to Mrs. Rankin. Lord, if that woman swapped mouths with a rattler the snake would die of poison."

"Not bad." Belvale smiled. "But you could say the same about many of our erstwhile legislators. I heard a kind of snake was named after Congress—the cottonmouth. Or was that flannel mouth?"

Picking up drinks, he turned back toward her, certain now that her smile was weak. Kirstin was worried; not so much for Keenan as for her sons—and Chad? She still carried a soft spot in her heart for Chad.

Toasting her silently over the rim of his glass he said, "You've soldiered long enough to stand up to whatever comes. The family is good at its business; you know that."

"Good won't be enough; perfect won't be enough. Men die in wars."

"Look, Kirstin—so many of the family will be involved: Walt's parents, the kids already flying out of England. It won't be only people you're very close to."

"Don't bypass Jim Shelby. He'll enlist the day war is declared."

"For his kind, that figures. When the country's first shock is over, we won't be desperate for men in his position to stay and fight the good fight for the draft and more money. A potful of congressmen will sign up—or try to—so their constituents will see how patriotic and brave they are. Jim Shelby will be serious, and he'll make a fine, dedicated officer."

Kirstin drank her bourbon and looked into his eyes. "He'll make a fine dedicated husband. I intend to fly out to Reno and mark time for six weeks for the divorce. Nobody will notice that in the uproar over the war. I imagine Jim and I getting married won't be worth any headlines, either." She held her empty glass out to him. "Don't lecture me about duty and country. Don't remind me of the ancient, holy traditions of Kill Devil Hill. I won't be a member of the sacred family much longer."

Belvale said quietly, "You and yours will always be family. There's nothing anybody—not you and not me—can do about that, even if we should want to."

CHAPTER 47

The New York Times—Washington, D.C., November 12, 1941: President Roosevelt called today for Americans "to stay on the job and get things made," warning that America stands at the crossroads. He said that the country faces domination if the people are not prepared to make full sacrifices right now.

Addressing delegates of the International Labor Organization from 35 countries gathered at the East Room of the White House, Mr. Roosevelt said there are still some among us—thank God they are but few—both industrialists and labor leaders, who place personal advantage above the welfare of the nation.

H Company's party roared full blast, pitchers of icy beer lined down the lengths of mess hall tables. As the high-ranking guest, Chad Belvale sat at a small table with the junior officers. Over the rim of his foamy glass, he watched the company commander sneer at the small group of country singers in the far corner, kids from southern states who'd joined the outfit during the Louisiana maneuvers.

Captain Thornton was an asshole, no doubt about that, but Owen Belvale was doing okay as exec and first platoon leader. Second platoon lieutenant was a pimply youngster fresh out of college Reserve Officers Training Corps, Sammy Holcomb. The officer, Lt. Emmet Finn, handled the 50 caliber and the 81mm mortar sections, combined into one platoon.

Sipping the good keg beer, Chad checked through his memory files for identification, a good trick for any officer to practice—remembering men's names. Big Mike Donnely sat near the kitchen door, an unforgettable sergeant; with him was the ex–supply sergeant Felber, the mess sergeant Warner, and—

"Sickening," Captain Thornton said. "I heard more than enough of that hillbilly caterwauling during the maneuvers. And discipline is about to break down at any moment. I don't think officers should be present." He made a sour face. "Unless the colonel insists?"

"No," Chad said, "but nobody else has to leave."

Thornton stood up and looked at Owen Belvale. "This was your idea, Lieutenant. I hold you responsible for any damage."

"Damned good idea," Chad said, refilling his glass from the metal pitcher. "I approved the party, remember."

Lifting an eyebrow, Thornton said, "Of course—sir," and stalked from the mess hall.

The lieutenants glanced at each other. Finn said, "The hell with it," and drained his glass. Owen shrugged and Sammy Holcomb jittered in his chair, but remained at the table.

Cigarette smoke thickened and the din increased. Chad looked through the window at a winter night in Massachusetts, at icicles hanging like spears from the barracks eaves, and at trampled snow. The oufit had done okay against National Guard troops on the Carolina Maneuvers, but screwing around with blanks and contrived field problems didn't mean much. The firing down there had made him jumpy, and the "bombing" of his troops by L-4 grasshoppers dropping bags of flour pissed him off. Nothing had been realistic, nothing to prepare this hall of beer drinkers for real combat.

The snap/whine of Jerry 9mms didn't sound like blanks, and the strafing run of Stukas chilled the soul. He had a vague idea about making training closer to the real thing, but he hadn't worked it out and these troops would never see it anyhow.

He was pretty sure they'd make out all right. Being

regulars, they had the discipline and pride, and the long, tough training they'd undergone lately put them in good physical shape. But there was no way of telling what would happen in their baptism of fire. The debacle of the French army still bothered Chad, that and the powerful blitzkreig tactics of the German army. He looked around the mess hall and focused on the little group of southerners. Barely out of childhood, they were, so young and boisterous, so damned anxious to be soldiers.

Thus it had always been in the South, from Bull Run to Appomattox, the young volunteers, poor boys whose families had never owned a slave; they went to war for the chance of fighting.

"Sing, goddamnit," Chad said, "sing 'Dixie' or 'Birmingham Jail' or 'Mexicali Rose.' "

"Sir?" Lieutenant Finn said.

"Nothing; beer talk." He felt Owen's eyes on him.

Lieutenant Holcomb said, "Oh-oh—there's the first fight. Shall I go break it up?"

"Don't be a damned fool," Owen said, and Chad grinned at his son. The kid was learning fast.

Finn said, "Strategic withdrawal permitted, Colonel?" He took a pitcher of beer with him, and his gnome's smile. "To bed, sir—and sirs."

Big Mike Donnely didn't exactly break up the fight; he collared both men and hauled them from the building. "Fight outside!" he roared, and Chad grinned again.

Another keg of beer and an hour later, half the company was battling the other half out in the street. A few die-hard boozers remained close to the beer supply, but the rest of the men flooded out of the mess hall, either to watch the battles or to enlist in them.

Leaning against the frosty building, Chad put one arm around Owen's shoulders. Blinking hard, he tried to remember the last time he had done that.

Owen said, "Over by the dayroom—Machine Shop is about to tie into Big Mike."

"Machine Shop?"

"Our Polish motor sergeant. It's the closest anybody can

come to pronouncing his real name. I'd better try to stop that before it gets started. Big Mike is too old, and—"

"Wait," Chad said, not really surprising himself. He had been considering leaving Mike behind when the regiment shipped out for combat. The man was old for a line company topkick, unless he remained in garrison. Under fire was something else, where old muscles wouldn't respond and old reflexes couldn't react in time. Line infantry was for the young, the boisterous kids who believed themselves immortal.

Beneath the lights of the company street, Mike had the moves of a man who had climbed into many squared circles, the smooth balance that turned the icy sand beneath his feet into a stretched ring canvas. Machine Shop looked like his name, blocky and hammered iron and all hard angles. Even his hair was scrub brushes and steel wool. He came straight in at Mike, arms hooked wide, and Chad saw there was little real difference in their sizes, but a hell of a difference in their ages.

Mike's jab popped the other guy's head back time and again, and men yelled when the first spurt of blood leaped from Machine Shop's eyebrow. Mike hit him with a vicious right hand and pivoted into a left hook that should have knocked a mule down. Machine Shop shook his head and kept coming.

"This has been building for a long time," Owen said. "The Polack is a damned good mechanic, but a hardhead. He doesn't want anybody telling him anything. That doesn't sit well with the first sergeant."

Machine Shop leaped in and butted Mike in the chest, driving him into the wall of the dayroom. Then he got a big shoulder under Mike's chin and ripped away at the body with both hands, grunting with the power of each blow. Mike hacked behind the head and twisted free.

The body, Chad thought, and it was as if Mike heard him. He hooked a shot under the heart and fired one to the kidney as the guy turned to protect his gut. Machine Shop looped a wild punch that caught Mike over the eye and brought blood. Following through, he angled close to butt Mike in the face and knock him down.

Owen started forward, but Chad caught his arm and said, "Not yet."

"But the old guy'll get killed—"

"Give him his chance."

Men yelled around them, and Chad saw that the other fights had broken up, the combatants gathering to watch this one.

On unsteady legs, Big Mike shuffled around the charging Machine Shop, keeping him off with the jab, a steady hammering that was slowly blinding the man. Puffing, Machine Shop put his head down again and ran at Mike. The first sergeant took a quick step to his left and turned the full weight of his body into a right uppercut. Machine Shop fell as if his legs had been kicked out from under him.

"Son of a bitch!" a soldier yelled, "that cost me five bucks!"

Murmuring apologies, Lieutenant Holcomb moved off into the night. Mike Donnely was the first of several men who kneeled to help Machine Shop.

Owen said, "How did you know?"

"I didn't," Chad said. "It was a test and Big Mike had to pass it. Now that I know he can still tough it out, I'll be damned glad to have him with the battalion when we move out for overseas."

He realized he still held a glass of beer, lifted a toast and drank it off.

"Are you that glad to have *me?*" Half in shadow, Owen's face was serious. "I have the feeling that you've also considered leaving me behind—to keep me out of danger for mom's sake, or maybe just because I'm your son."

Chad leaned close so he could see Owen's eyes. "No," he said, "I wouldn't do that, because you *are* my son."

CHAPTER 48

AGENCE FRANCE PRESSE—The Southern Provinces, China, November 12, 1941: Official sources at Nationalist headquarters insist there are no communist troop movements of any consequence near here. However, rumors are rife that Mao Tse-tung's soldiers are spreading the Red Star's influence beyond the borders of their home country, and the legitimate leaders of China do not deny the possibility.

The strongest of these anonymous reports has communist units penetrating or attempting to enter sections of French IndoChina, Siam, Burma and possibly Malaya.

"If these stories are even marginally true," said a spokesman for Chiang Kai-shek, "they only go to prove what the generalissimo has stated all along, that communism is the true sickness of China, and will infect all Asia unless cured by force of arms."

Keenan Carlisle had shifted persona again. After the long trek and two minor skirmishes, one against the surprised Japanese and one that lost much face for the Nationalists, he was again almost absorbed by his comrades. There were moments when he actually felt Chinese, when he learned to close out fatigue and discomfort and know the meaning of patience as well as the peasant soldiers around him. He did not think so much of the slow, foot slogging months on the road, as of the objective somewhere ahead, the objective certainly to be reached in due time. Modern transportation

323

was in another world, so that a *li* stretched far in the walking, and more so because the march had to be broken off to hide. Sometimes the hiding lasted for dry and hungry days while motorized columns of Japanese troops slowly passed in clouds of gritty dust.

When had ceased to matter as time devoured its own dark tail only to be reborn with the light: day and night, yin and yang. It helped him to absorb a lot of the Cantonese language without fighting its lack of grammar, and without asking why or why not.

Head down, plodding in the harsh sun, his conical straw hat shading his face, he did not know exactly how long the march had been, or how many times they had been forced to take cover and hide from searching Japanese planes or bird-dogging Nationalist troops. Time was a drumroll or a heartbeat, cold or hot, never a single entity.

The other divided thing which was also undivided? Life and death, of course.

They had come upon the Jap patrol as it played vicious little games with farm families in a nameless village that was no more than a few shabby huts folded into leached-out land. When the scouts trotted back over a rise in the earth, Keenan understood some of what they said to Major Hong, the main thrust of the report, anyway.

Two old men hung by their wrists from the arch of the ancient village gate and had been bled many times by shallow bayonet thrusts. One graybeard might still be alive. A small, thin girl lay naked and dead beside the town well. Within the houses, women sobbed and the island monkey men laughed.

"How many Japanese?" Hong asked. "Where are the sentries?"

"Enough," said the younger man, his face twitching, "so each of Hong's soldiers may have one to kill."

Father Lim was the second scout. His ancient, creased face was sad, as if his eyes had seen all hurtful things. "No sentries guard the road or watch from the houses. They feel safe, far from the fighting in the north."

"As skirmishers," Hong ordered. "Surround the houses, but do not fire unless you are forced to. Wait for my shots.

You will go quickly and silently among the men and warn them of this. When I fire, kill them all.''

Keenan unslung his rifle. He didn't have to check his worn 1903 Springfield bolt-action. He knew there was a round of ball ammunition in the chamber and all he had to do was thumb the safety down. Unless the action was hectic, he preferred the 03 with its leaf sight and fine blade front sight to the new and clumsier M-1 Garand. The semi-automatic M-1, not yet issued to all U.S. troops at home, had more firepower but less accuracy, especially at extreme range. He could wish for a good telescopic sight, which might come later.

After years of guerrilla fighting, Hong's men were good; they were as intent as wolves on a hot trail, but silent. Keenan could sense the hunger emanating from them as they flowed swiftly around the village houses, eager for the taste of hot blood.

One man slid to the only window of the first house, rifle at the ready and bayonet fixed. There would be bayoneting, Keenan thought, even after the enemy was shot.

Keenan was only a step behind Major Hong as the man darted through the open door. The shadows inside were light and his eyes adjusted immediately. The jacket of a Japanese junior officer and a pistol belt hung over a grinning sergeant's arm. The officer, his samurai sword balanced across a stool, had his pants dropped. On a straw pallet, he was busy fucking a sobbing girl.

Eyes wide, the sergeant flung away the jacket and pawed desperately at the holstered pistol. Major Hong shot him carefully in the belly, doubling him over a hammer blow of sudden agony.

The officer jerked himself out of the girl and whirled on his knees. Mouth dropped open, he stared at Hong and Keenan, then cut a glance at his sword. Flinching at the steady slamming of gunshots outside, he slowly inched up his pants and yearned at his sword again.

Funny, Keenan thought; even in the face of death, men will try to cover their balls.

"Allow him to reach it," Hong said.

The girl drew herself into a ball. The wounded sergeant's

groans were louder than her crying. Hong took two steps and kicked the man's head against the wall. He picked up the pistol belt.

In English, the Jap said, "You—American, British? These peasant women are of no value, but kept alive I can give important information."

"That so?" Head tilted, Keenan listened to the rattle of gunfire slow and die away to individual pops. Hong's troops would collect many arms and much ammunition; he hoped the Japs had been carrying rations and not feeding off the countryside. Their fish would taste good right now, canned or dried.

"University of Washington," the Jap said, tightening his belt around his narrow waist. He didn't seem to be carrying a hideout gun or a short knife. Keenan kept the muzzle of the 03 steady on the little bastard.

"West Point," Keenan said. "You don't look worth much. My boss here thinks you want to go for your ancestral sword, or maybe your sergeant's rifle against the wall."

The Jap chewed his lip. "The Chinese are animals, but an American officer—an educated man—"

"If you wish to kill him," Major Hong interrupted, "do it slowly, so he can live as long as the turd who watched him rape."

The girl's sobbing almost stopped and she pulled some torn rags about her mauled body, but she still did not look at them, would not raise her face.

Hong said, "She is shamed. If you do not shoot that son of a turtle, I will."

Father Lim shuffled into the house and Keenan understood him to say that all the Japanese soldiers were dead, fifteen of them. But the surviving graybeard had also died. Most of the village women were alive. "There is no radio," he finished, "and they carried no white birds to send messages."

Keenan said, "Major, we both remember one Chinese woman who would take vengeance for herself and her sisters. . . ."

Behind his eyes, blotting out the vicious little son of a bitch kneeled hopefully upon a straw pallet on the floor, he saw Chang Yen Ling standing submissively before a campfire, offering her body as bait. He saw the strutting Jap lieutenant fondling her before she deftly slipped the sharp blade between his ribs. And he remembered the curious flat smile upon her set face as the guns roared around her.

". . . and I ask you if other Chinese women are as strong, if any might use this opportunity to cleanse herself of shame."

Hong showed his teeth in a near smile, then spat swift Cantonese at the girl, too fast for Keenan to follow. She sat up, a smear of blood at one corner of her mouth, either unaware or no longer caring that her bitten breasts were exposed.

"Yes," she murmured, "oh, good officer, yes—yes."

"It is justice," Hong said to Keenan. "I think one of your honorable ancestors must be Chinese."

Then the Jap, realizing that he was about to be turned over to his victim, hissed and lunged for his samurai sword. Keenan shot him through the right knee. The 30 caliber bullet shattered the kneecap and snatched him to one side, away from his weapon. The thunder of the rifle filled the small room and powder smoke swirled thick.

"*Eetai*," the Jap whimpered, "*kami o uyamau! Eetai*—it hurts—*kizu, kizu*—"

"He calls on his god," Hong said. "The same god who watched him rape this girl."

Rolling on the floor, hands clenched around his ruined knee, the Jap didn't notice as Hong retrieved the sword and drove its point into the earthern floor. He looked up as Hong used his rifle butt to drive the blade deep, halfway to the hand guard chrysanthemums. A gasp escaped him when Hong slammed the steel butt plate against the hilt and snapped the blade.

Then he used the rifle to smash the Jap's hands away from his wounded knee, to crush bones in the hands themselves. This time the Jap yelped like a puppy.

Keenan thought of another Imperial Army officer, Colonel Watanabe, who would have died proudly and without a sound. He thought of what he had learned about the warrior code of *Bushido*, and was glad to discover that there were exceptions.

"Woman," Hong said then, "here is a short knife. You and your sisters use it well. I ask that you hide the monkey men's bodies when you are done."

"No!" the Jap said. "No—American, you cannot leave me to be tortured—"

After the girl seated the knife solidly in her shaking hands, after she had lifted her shrill voice to call in the other women, Keenan saw that the sergeant had pumped his life out.

Then he said, "Sure I can," and followed Major Hong from the hut. For now he could speak only for himself, but even though he was a member of a special military family, Keenan didn't consider himself extraordinary. What the enemies of his country would learn to their sorrow, that if pushed hard, the American soldier would peel off his mom and apple pie image like a serpent outgrowing old and useless skin.

That soldier was descended from the hardy frontiersmen who had out-Indianed the Indian to beat the cunning red man at his own game on his home territory. In this war and America's part in it to come, the dogface soldier could be as hard and merciless as any savage on the other side.

He walked quietly beside Major Hong and nodded at Father Lim. The old man had discarded his homemade weapon long ago and proudly carried a Japanese submachine gun. It was longer than it should be, and from all reports, newly issued to the emperor's troops in China. He hadn't seen many of them and wouldn't trade his old 03 for it. With its 30 round box clip, it weighed close to ten pounds and used the feeble 8mm, the muzzle velocity only 1100 feet per second. Ball ammo for the Garand rang up a respectable 2700 feet. But of course, the Shiki Kikananju had a bayonet.

Hong's men had exacted revenge, and many of that bunch left behind them in the village understood about bayonets now. They marched silently, putting flatland and a few rolling hills between them and the village without a name. The sun turned from white to red before Major Hong waved the group off the dirt road.

"Small cover here, and we could have been comfortable by remaining in the village; you wonder about this march."

"A little," Keenan said.

"There is a proverb that begins *Chi fan jian san kou*—At each meal, take three mouthfuls less and afterward walk a hundred steps. It is the recipe for living to ninety-nine years."

"Meaning that if the Japs had other patrols out, or even a few scouts, we did better by getting out of the village quickly, and when the women hide all those bodies, other Japs won't know what the hell or where to search."

Seated beneath the sparse branches of a twisted tree and watching the men scurry about to prepare rice, he thought of Chang Yen Ling. She might have been pinned to that straw pallet while that son of a turtle raped her; she might have been that naked, despoiled little girl lying beside the well.

God, he had to find her again and get her out of this tortured country. He was Occidental once more, hugging his knees and conscious of the thin mist lingering gray through puddles of bloody light left by the setting sun. He became conscious of time, of how little of it was issued to each man by fate, keenly aware of time's ashen taste upon his tongue.

"I don't know about living to be ninety-nine, Major. Would you wish to live so long, to grow so old and feeble?"

Hong passed him a Chinese cigarette and held a lighted twig to the end as Keenan drew in smoke. "I do not know," he said. "Ask me when I am ninety-nine."

Smoking in silence as perimeter guards took their rice bowls and shuffled to listening posts, Keenan said, "Yen Ling. I wish to live beside her for whatever time is given us."

"This may be possible," Hong said, "when we reach the sea."

Keenan clutched the man's arm. "You know something. Damn it, you didn't tell me—"

"It is not certain, my friend. She is to reach us when we near the sea. The fog; smell the salt in the fog. We are close."

Yen Ling and the sea. Keenan breathed deeply of the fog and smiled.

CHAPTER 49

REUTERS NEWS AGENCY—Lingshui Bay, China (via Singapore), December 6, 1941: Reports of a sea battle off the large island of Hainan between Japanese and Chinese have been found to be greatly exaggerated. Coast watchers say sailing junks were probably fired upon by patrol boats, no more than the usual efforts by the Japanese navy to cut off food and supplies reaching the Chinese soldiers.

Meanwhile, Allied troops here are settling in for the winter and all has gone quiet in China. Secure in Singapore's powerful defenses, British businessmen and the dependents of military personnel are planning a traditional Christmas celebration, down to the plum pudding.

She was real. Touching her convinced him of that, and the faintest brushing of her skin was electric. The sparks raced through his blood and into his soul. Chang Yen Ling; she was no less beautiful in her padded clothing, her hair the polished winds of midnight. Keenan found it hard to breathe around the pounding of his heart trapped in his throat.

Appearing out of the cool morning mist like a sea nymph, Yen Ling looked directly at him, and her slow smile was tremulous. He rose from his blanket to touch her, and she drifted away from him, one shaky step, then two.

"Yen Ling—" Why should she be afraid of him? Then he realized that Major Hong and the troops were also staring at her, realized that she was still a Chinese woman, and although married, not allowed to openly display her emotions.

Hong gave orders concerning breakfast to be readied in fire holes dug in the sand so that no lights would show. Patting Keenan's shoulder, he moved away and left Keenan alone with her. He took her firm, capable hand and walked toward a set of rocks he had seen the day before. They were sentinel rocks that leaned against storm-twisted pines and beneath them spread a green and brown carpet of sea ferns. At the rocks, he turned Yen Ling gently to him and kissed her softly, softly. She tasted of the spectral fog; she tasted of unshed tears and banked fires.

"My love," she whispered against his mouth. "Now I am happy."

Drawing her down with him, he sat them upon the ferns. "How did you get here? Who got you out of Singapore? I'm so glad you could come, but this mission is too dangerous for you and—"

She placed her fingertips against his mouth. "General Jeng is a man of compassion, and my duties in Singapore were at an end. He had me brought by sea once he was sure we could do no good with the British. Oh! The English gentlemen are so certain their rich city can never be taken by storm, and they are too stubborn to accept help from Chinese bandits. That is what they call us—bandits, while they kowtow to Chiang Kai-shek, because he smiles and postures as he steals from them and parades his wife for them to lust after."

"Politics and war; must they always come between us?" He tucked her head onto his shoulder so he could stroke her hair. It felt silken. Just out of sight, the sea murmured and soon the sun would arise to dispel the fog wraiths. Snubbed close to shore a pair of fishing junks bobbed on the tide, and just knowing they were waiting bothered him. The long trip across open sea was a gamble, and if they reached the jungles of Malaya, the dangers would double.

Her voice was soft as the mist. "I did not want to leave you in Hong Kong. My heart remained with you, and my poem tried to say—"

Continuing to stroke her hair, he said, ". . . on earth a tiger has been subdued; buckets of tears flow down . . ."

"You understood that it was my duty. Mao needs me; China needs me."

"I need you," Keenan said. "You can't imagine how much."

"But I am first a soldier of the Red Army. You must understand that, my beautiful foreign devil." She paused. "You have spoken at times in my language. We have been apart that long?"

"I study your language to know you better. It brings me closer to you." Keenan didn't feel like a soldier on the verge of an iffy mission. He felt like a lover, a poet. Careful of his pronunciation, he quoted:

> "Mountains;
> From my saddle I urge my charger.
> I turn; what a surprise!
> I am but three feet, three inches
> From heaven."

Half turning, Yen Ling snugged her warm face into his throat, and she smelled of exotic spices, of golden sweat. "Heaven is not promised and we must accept love where we discover it. I am afraid to ask for more, afraid to anger the gods who have given me so much. We came to know each other in the mountains, but now we are far from them, and the sea gods are fierce."

Keenan was conscious of every curve of her body, of the woman warmth held beneath the bulky uniform. He also knew she would make love with him if he pushed her back upon this mossy bed. That would only be if he didn't consider the coming light, if he didn't think of Hong and the troops just out of sight. He wanted her so much that he ached all over, but he wouldn't shame her now. To protect her sensitivities, he would become more Chinese.

"Rice is cooking," he said into the richness of her hair, "and this morning there is fish and cassia wine to begin the day—and the mission. We are to sail on the tide, and you can return on the boat that brought you here. I am forever in General Jeng's debt for your visit, and I will send a letter to be forwarded to my home, a letter that will bring him whatever he asks, particularly if he were to order you to deliver the letter."

"The boat that brought me also waits for Hong's fighters. I go with you to Malaya; that also is the general's order. Medical help will surely be needed."

"Yen Ling—no, damnit! The jungles, the Japanese—"

"I am a soldier, my husband, no less than you. Would you dishonor a comrade?"

Husband; a magic garden where a Confucian priest bound them as close as any ceremony in the world. The mandarin's garden of beauty made more lovely by Yen Ling standing nude and proud among the lesser flowers. He held her close for a long and throbbing moment.

"No less than me," he agreed, "a better soldier than me," and held her hand until they neared the first cook-fire. It was almost as it had been before, this silent sharing between them as they hunkered side by side and ate while the world rubbed its eyes and the sun came sleepy to wipe the mist dry.

Father Lim came to bow deeply before her, and Major Hong saluted her as an equal, startling the replacement soldiers, young farmers new to the unit. Older men, those who had survived the long marches and the bloody fights, approached Chang Yen Ling to welcome her. She had saved some of their lives with her nursing and by her bravery.

Keenan looked to the ocean, where now three small fishing junks rocked up and down, their batwing sails still folded. Three man crews stirred upon the weathered decks, making their own meal. Keenan smelled cooking charcoal and fish oil from the braziers. The ships were worm-eaten and ragged, the guiding eyes painted upon their prows long faded. They didn't look seaworthy, especially since Yen Ling had arrived. Coastal runners they might be, but to cross so wide a sea without modern navigating instruments, to sail through tropic oceans where typhoons lived—

He wanted to throw Yen Ling across his shoulder and take off back up the trail. He wanted to carry her far from the slightest hint of danger, from duty and country and sudden death.

Yen Ling would not go; he knew that, and if duty and country were concepts to be forgotten, what of Kill Devil Hill and Sandhurst Keep and the family? What of the battalion of Belvales and Carlisles fallen across the world because they believed? Keenan clamped his hands hard upon his rice bowl. For the first time in his life, he wished he was no goddamned soldier. He did not, could not, deny his roots; he just wished he was somebody else and somewhere else, and that Yen Ling would be transported with him.

She stood up beside him when Major Hong came to say she was to travel with them on Number One, the headquarters boat. Father Lim, proud of his new rank of sergeant, would command Boat Two, and pockmarked Sergeant Han the third junk. This time, as they waded waist-deep through cold water out to the boats, Keenan held tightly to her hand and balanced her medical kit atop his head with his rifle. Everyone held their weapons and ammo high, and the gray sea was calm, not splashing.

Helping Yen Ling aboard, Keenan didn't have to make a head count of the troops. Divided among the junks were twenty-one men and Yen Ling; add nine sailors and they were thirty-one, a beefed up squad or a decimated platoon. They were overweaponed by captured Jap guns and had extra rations, even a few bottles of imported *sake*, courtesy of the Imperial Army. It was a good start, and they were richer than usual, but it was still not much to spearhead a mission that might be of major importance. Throwing the Japs off stride when they came down the Malay Peninsula could save British asses, and in a roundabout way, protect the wide underbelly of China.

"General Jeng said he would channel in more soldiers when he hears from us, a stream of men to halt the Japanese in their tracks. This boat carries a good radio in its belly. We are becoming a modern army."

He fought the urge to kiss her cheek. She smiled and arranged things in her medicine bags, the standard painkillers of willow leaves, distillation of certain reptiles, the long, sharp needles for acupuncture, a prized small gourd of sulfa powder, strips of cloth washed and washed again, old bandages forever stained but clean to the touch.

The sails went up with a clatter of tarred ropes and bamboo, up the tall masts to a chorus of soft cheers and chanted prayers; Number One junk turned slowly to catch the wind. The sun rose brighter, and Keenan held onto Yen Ling's hand, and to hell with Chinese tradition. She was his wife and could meet him halfway, becoming American as he became Chinese.

The breeze was fresh and salted, the sky benign, cloudless. Keenan watched men mount and lash down the water-cooled 30 caliber in the bow, then saw them yank the bolt handle to half-load. The gunner sat close to the tripod while his helpers covered the gun with faded brown fish netting. Other men went below. From the air, the three junks might not appear suspicious; fishermen from the same village often sailed together.

Yen Ling removed her cap, and allowed the wealth of her glistening hair to cascade down her back. She had grown it long to please him, and he was grateful for its beauty. She knelt beside a charcoal brazier and fanned the smoke, again a decoy, a window dressing to fool any Jap pilot who might fly low enough. But most pilots would dive and strafe, not giving a civilian or military damn, only happy at finding a helpless target, something to work their guns on.

Keenan stared at the gunner in the prow, the man pretending to patch fishing nets. If he was any good, and a Zero or Betty did come in low and slow with guns blazing, the plane could be caught going away, its belly stitched; if enough of a lead was taken. If the first burst missed, you could line up on the Jap when he climbed straight up to come back for another run. Any plane was vulernable then, but especially the Zeros and their *Bushido* brave pilots too tough to require belly armor.

When he got back to the Hill this time, he had a lot more to feed into the general's gluttonous information file. If he got back. Damn—he had to get back, to stand before the great doors of Kill Devil Hill with Chang Yen Ling upon his arm. Smiling, he thought of Aunt Minerva's shock and dismay. Yen Ling could be far more regal, if need be. The dowager empress is dead; long live the Manchu princess.

The junks slid easily through the water, belying the top-heavy looks caused by their high sterns and low bows that lapped the water. Keenan sat comfortably on what would be the poop deck on another ship, because the junk did not rock and pitch much. There was something to be said for design changed but little over a thousand years. The air was fresh and clean, a fine salt spray kissing his lips from time to time. He smiled down at Yen Ling playing her cooking role, the raven flag of her hair sometimes lifted by the wind—beautiful, beautiful.

From the junk riding at port side, Father Lim shouted something through cupped hands, shouted again and turned to point. Slammed free of a line he held, he soared out over the water, an ancient crab to fall awkwardly with a big splash. The leap of water fell behind as the junks sailed on.

"Father Lim!" Keenan cried out, just as a bullet slapped the mast beside his head. It stung him with bamboo splinters and something wet. Horrified, yelling Lim's name in the wake of the junks, Keenan held tight to a rope with one hand and wiped his face with the other.

It came away red with Father Lim's blood. The bullet had torn through Lim and come that close to killing Keenan, too. But where did it come from—and why? Lim—the poor old man, the brave old man who had walked two thousand miles carrying a homemade rifle.

Bullets slashed the bamboo masts and ripped jagged strips from the deck, chewed through the sails. "Yen Ling! Stay down—stay flat on the deck—oh, Jesus!"

He saw the damned thing then, the submarine risen slimy from the sea like some malignant monster. From the open conning tower, a Nambu machine gun raked Number One junk, then passed to Number Two. Short, bandy-legged sailors picked their way over wet duckboards on the forward deck to the three-inch gun, covered by the god-damned machine gunner.

Keenan rolled for his rifle, flipped the safety and came to one knee. Right behind the machine gunner stood a Jap in a blue cap. That one got a second's reprieve while Keenan put a round through the gunner's head. The junk and the sub bobbed and swayed, but Keenan held in close enough to take off the top of the officer's head with an AP bullet. The blue cap spun high, end over end, scattering blood and brains.

Firing broke all around the junks now, and the water-cooled 30 gunner was pretty good. He chipped sparks all along the sub's front deck and knocked the gun crew overboard. The sub lunged forward and Number Three junk with Sergeant Han in command couldn't wheel out of the way. The sub rammed with a great smashing and splintering of wood, a blow that hurled men into the water with the scraps of their boat.

Keenan fired at the conning tower, squeezed off round after round in hope of ricocheting one down into the submarine proper. Squatting out of sight behind the steel wall, another Jap got hold of the Nambu and swung the muzzle slowly back and forth, firing wild and rolling bursts. A fist full of bullets screamed off Yen Ling's brazier and flung burning charcoal along the deck. The Chinese machine gunner nodded twice and fell over the bow. The water jacket of the Browning curled into a dozen shiny metal rips as steam boiled out.

Keenan screamed as loudly, throwing himself down from the stern to land hard on his knees. The sub backed away, its machine gun never slowing up, the flaming asshole painted on its conning tower running water and taunting. Keenan reached Yen Ling. "Oh, God, woman! Are you all right?"

"Ding hao," she said. "Good. The radio?"

"Damn! I don't know. Hong must be with it, giving our position for whatever good that will do. Where did that bastard sub come from? It's backing out of small arms range to bracket us with that deck gun. Oh, damn, damn! Boat Three is sunk and Boat Two is taking water. We have to heel over and pick up survivors."

"It will do no good, my husband."

"Don't quit on me now, woman. Yell for our captain to drop sails long enough for the troops to swim—"

A man in the water shrieked, a terrible, piercing sound.

Staring in horror, Keenan saw the blood bubbles spreading, saw the dark dorsal fin of a shark slice the roiled water, one among many.

Yen Ling's face was pale, her jaw set. Holding desperately to his arm, she repeated, "No good, my husband. The big Japanese gun might be merciful, so that we will not know those teeth."

Keenan couldn't curse and he sure couldn't pray. He held to Yen Ling while his mind raced through and discarded a hundred wild plans. Major Hong came from below just as the first three-inch shell whined over his command boat.

He said, "Our men ashore have our position, and know of the Japanese iron fish. Perhaps it can be tracked to its nest and made to swallow a hook."

The second shell whirred in and exploded atop Boat Two, finishing the job. Another man's scream was cut off short. Keenan clung to Yen Ling and stared at the water. A dead white belly rose to the surface, the long sleek belly of a shark killed by shell fire concussion. He saw another one rolling, struggling to dive. Maybe the goddamn sharks would flee, get the hell out of an area where they were dying by explosive blasts.

Maybe they were in a feeding frenzy where a wounded shark would eat its own spilled guts.

Whamm!

Keenan went to his knees, supporting Yen Ling. Major Hong said into the echo of the explosion, "This boat was turned back for shore at the first gunfire, but land is very far away, even if the sharks are not hungry."

Lifting her head from Keenan's shoulder, Yen Ling said calmly, "I have been honored to serve with you, Major."

He put one hand upon Keenan's shoulder. "And you have been a good comrade, Keenan-*shi;* I have learned that all foreigners are not devils, but men like me."

"Jesus Christ," Keenan said, and not in blasphemy.

"Come on to the far side of the boat. When the next shell hits, we go over the side and grab a piece of wreckage. I still have a pistol; fired under water it'll keep off the damned sharks for a while—maybe long enough for the sub to leave without machine gunning everything in the water. There's a chance, a chance, damnit! We can't quit—"

Blamm-blammmm!

The sun exploded and its blood seared the sky, boiled the sea. It spat flame into Keenan's eyes and down his throat. He beat at the flames with his hands and tried to call for Yen Ling, but nothing would push past the white-hot coals frying his tongue.

The sea was deep and cool, and he sucked at it until his air got away like popcorn and he clawed frantically for the surface. Jagged and slippery, the wood attempted to throw him off, tried to saw away his fingers. He inched upon it, cheek first and then a shoulder, and a slow roll to his belly. The wood sank under his weight but he held on, and the water stopped lapping, did not reach higher than his chin. Sometimes he had to snort it from his nose.

> . . . I have lost my proud poplar,
> You your beloved willow.
> They have vanished,
> Rising directly into the sky.
> They ask Wu Kang what
> He will offer them;
> Wu Kang presents them
> With good cassia wine.

Lifting his head, eyes blurred, Keenan looked all around, searching the ocean carefully. He saw debris and dead sharks wallowed by waves in a rising sea. It took all his strength to hang onto the ribbed section of a junk's scuppers.

"Yen Ling." It was a croak, a frog voice he did not recognize. "Yen Ling!"

He called her name until his throat was too dry. She was not there; nobody was there among the floating bits and pieces of a failed mission.

Oh, God; salt caked his lips and he tasted blood not as

salty. How long had he drifted here? He could not tell. His share of the family luck ran out when that Jap submarine broke the surface. Major Hong was gone; Father Lim; Sergeant Han and all the good men he had soldiered with for so many months.

Chang Yen Ling was gone . . . on earth a tiger subdued as buckets of tears flow down.

Blistered face against the wet planking, Keenan felt his fingers loosen their grip. In reflex, he tightened them, and then wondered why. He didn't really give a damn anymore.

CHAPTER 50

0758 CINCPAC HQ to all forces, 7/12/41: AIR RAID ON PEARL HARBOR. THIS IS NO DRILL.

1150 COM14 CINCPAC. PARACHUTISTS LANDING AT BARBERS POINT.

ASSOCIATED PRESS—Honolulu, HI., December 7, 1941. Japanese planes attacked the U.S. naval base at Pearl Harbor this morning, sinking or damaging warships at anchor. Other flights bombed and strafed army installations at Hickam Field and Schofield Barracks. Fires are reported in Honolulu and any casualty count, military or civilian, is incomplete at this moment.

LT. GEN. PRESTON BELVALE: Kee-rist! Everybody figured they'd hit the Philippines first.

U.S. SENATOR JIM SHELBY: We can say we told you so, but nobody's happy about that.

KIRSTIN BELVALE SHELBY: Who do I pray for first? My men past and present will need prayers.

MAJ. GEN. CHARLES (CRUSTY) CARLISLE: The fucking navy! Caught with their drawers down.

LT. STEPHANIE BARTLETT: Oh, my god.

1ST LT. GAVIN SCOTT: I got my second German kill today.

1ST LT. J.J. MERRIMAN: Tallyho, Chad. Do come back.

NANCY CARLISLE: I feel like a traitor, but I shouldn't.

2D LT. OWEN BELVALE: The old man got this outfit in shape, but we can use more time.

2D LT. FARLEY BELVALE: Penny; Pretty Penny Colvin. I wonder if she'll miss me; I don't want to leave her behind.

LT. COL. CHADWICK BELVALE: It's here and we're not ready, not equipped. We'll hack it because we damned well have to. But where the hell is Keenan?

LOOK FOR BOOK 2 OF

THE
MEN AT ARMS
SERIES
THE FLAMES OF WAR

When war erupts the Belvales and the Carlisles are ready to fight and die. Maj. Gen. Crusty Carlisle takes over in Hawaii to prepare the Army and Marines for the fierce reality of battle, while Lt. Gen. Preston Belvale reports back to Roosevelt on the condition of Pearl Harbor and the potential of mounting a counterattack against the Japanese.

In Burma, Captain Keenan Carlisle faces an extraordinary jungle journey to reach Allied forces at the same time that his cousin, Lt. Col. Chad Belvale, prepares for combat in Europe and North Africa. As for a brawling Marine named Eddie Donnely, he's ready to take on two wars at once: by marrying into the proud, embattled Carlisle-Belvale clan, and by fighting the land and sea battles of the Pacific from Iron Bottom Bay to Midway.